Advance Praise for

The
CRESCENT MOON
TEAROOM

"With a dash of fate and a sprinkle of fortune-telling, Stacy Sivinski has given readers an impossibly endearing tale about three tea-reading witches lured their separate ways. Steeped in magic and sisterhood, *The Crescent Moon Tearoom* will enchant and delight readers with its whimsical charm. Like brewing a favorite tea in a treasured mug, there's something uniquely inviting about this book. It's sure to be a reader favorite!"

—Sarah Penner, *New York Times* bestselling author of
The Lost Apothecary

"Charming, uplifting, and utterly enchanting. The Quigley sisters—what's more magical than witchy triplets?—and their lovely, cozy stories will steal your heart."

—Lana Harper, *New York Times* bestselling author of
The Witches of Thistle Grove series

"Stacy Sivinski's *The Crescent Moon Tearoom* is a decadent tale that wraps you up in its enchanting world like a warm embrace. The magic system is flawlessly executed and the characters are so real that you long to share a cup of tea with them. An exquisitely crafted story about the threads of fate that bind us even when it seems they're pushing us apart and how, as we grow into ourselves, we also grow into our power. I may not be a fortune teller, but I don't need to be able to decipher tea leaves to know that readers will fall deeply in love with this charming novel and all the emotions that come with it."

—Breanne Randall, *New York Times* bestselling author of
The Unfortunate Side Effects of Heartbreak and Magic

"Make your appointment for *The Crescent Moon Tearoom*. It's warm and cozy as a cup of tea on a chilly evening. You won't regret meeting the magical Quigley Sisters."

—Meg Shaffer, *USA Today* bestselling author of
The Wishing Game

"*The Crescent Moon Tearoom* is a truly lovely book—beautifully written and infused with lushly warm, delicious imagery that makes reading it a wonderfully cozy experience. Your tastebuds— along with your imagination—will delight at so many of the descriptions! The three Quigley sisters are each lovable in their own way and the magic of their world is fascinating, weaving through the story like a dream. This is the sort of book you'll want to tuck yourself into and be sure to return to whenever in need of some literary comfort."

—India Holton, international bestselling author of
The Ornithologist's Field Guide to Love

"In this enchanting tale of sisterhood, the Quigleys will have you believing in magic as they navigate the delicate balance between destiny and self-discovery. *The Crescent Moon Tearoom* is a captivating story that brews a spellbinding blend of fate, love, and the power of family. Stacy Sivinski has created three sisters whose wisdom and kindness will be remembered long after the last page is turned. Please serve with a warm cup of your favorite tea."

—Susan Wiggs, bestselling author of
The Lost and Found Bookshop

"Prepare to fall in love with the singular Quigley sisters in this heart-warming tale whose every page will make you feel as though you're basking in the glow of a cozy fire. As lovely and surprising as life itself, *The Crescent Moon Tearoom* will delight and entertain even as it challenges you to reflect on where sisterhood ends and selfhood begins."

—Bianca Marais, international bestselling author of
The Witches of Moonshyne Manor

"Charming, heartwarming, and enchanting, Stacy Sivinski's *The Crescent Moon Tearoom* is a delight! Themes of sisterhood, agency, and fate are brewed together with witchy hijinks and plenty of coziness, all of which create a captivating read. I loved spending time with the Quigley sisters—this book has me under its spell."

—Karma Brown, bestselling author of
What Wild Women Do

"*The Crescent Moon Tearoom* is a wonderfully imaginative and bewitching novel about the bonds of sisterhood and the unpredictability of fate. If you've ever peeked into a teacup, hoping to see your future, you'll enjoy Stacy Sivinski's whimsical story about a family of witches seeking to find their true paths against mysterious odds. This novel shows readers through spellbinding prose and charming characters that we can rely on the power of memories and love to bring us home."

—Celestine Martin, author of *Witchful Thinking*

The
CRESCENT MOON
TEAROOM

~ a novel ~

Stacy Sivinski

ATRIA PAPERBACK

New York • London • Toronto • Sydney • New Delhi

ATRIA
PAPERBACK

An Imprint of Simon & Schuster, LLC
1230 Avenue of the Americas
New York, NY 10020

First Atria Paperback edition October 2024

ATRIA PAPERBACK and colophon are trademarks of Simon & Schuster, LLC

Simon & Schuster: Celebrating 100 Years of Publishing in 2024

For information about special discounts for bulk purchases, please contact Simon & Schuster Special Sales at 1-866-506-1949 or business@simonandschuster.com.

The Simon & Schuster Speakers Bureau can bring authors to your live event. For more information or to book an event, contact the Simon & Schuster Speakers Bureau at 1-866-248-3049 or visit our website at www.simonspeakers.com.

Interior design by Kyoko Watanabe

Manufactured in the United States of America

1 3 5 7 9 10 8 6 4 2

Library of Congress Cataloging-in-Publication Data
Names: Sivinski, Stacy, author.
Title: The Crescent Moon Tearoom : a novel / Stacy Sivinski.
Description: First Atria Paperback edition. | New York : Atria Paperback, 2024.
Identifiers: LCCN 2023054034 (print) | LCCN 2023054035 (ebook) |
ISBN 9781668058398 (paperback) | ISBN 9781668058404 (ebook)
Subjects: LCGFT: Witch fiction. | Novels.
Classification: LCC PS3619.I97 C74 2024 (print) | LCC PS3619.I97 (ebook) |
DDC 813/.6—dc23/eng/20240209
LC record available at https://lccn.loc.gov/2023054034
LC ebook record available at https://lccn.loc.gov/2023054035

ISBN 978-1-6680-5839-8
ISBN 978-1-6680-5840-4 (ebook)

For Sebastián

PROLOGUE

A Broom

Foretells changes to come.

When the taste of cinnamon touched the tip of Anne's tongue, she knew that someone had spoken her name. As soon as she became aware of the spicy sweetness, Anne opened her eyes and glanced around the room like a dowsing rod, searching for the source of the sensation.

But all she saw were her sisters, Beatrix and Violet, sleeping soundly where they had fallen in a state of blissful exhaustion several hours earlier. The three little witches had discovered an enchanted cloak packed in their mother's trunks and filled the evening hours taking turns throwing it across their shoulders and turning themselves into pirates and princesses. They'd only stopped when Violet, who'd insisted on playing the part of a court jester, had collapsed onto a pile of old quilts in the corner of the attic and closed her eyes "for only just a moment."

Looking toward the mountain of calico and gingham fabric, Anne saw that Violet was still wearing the tattered cloak, which looked comically large now that she'd turned back into a young girl.

A soft snore echoed against the rafters, and Anne turned to see Beatrix curled up on a tufted pillow next to a shelf of books. Her hands were still wrapped loosely around the corners of a fairy tale collection that their mother had tucked to the very back of the stack because she didn't want her daughters to think they were destined to grow warts on their noses like the witches who glared at them from the colorful illustrations.

Yawning, Anne started to ease back into the worn curtains that served as her makeshift bed, but the flavor of cinnamon returned, so strong this time that she nearly sneezed.

Something was amiss.

As quietly as she could, Anne rose from her velvet cocoon and tiptoed toward the spiral staircase across the room. Violet and Beatrix didn't appear to sense anything, but that didn't surprise Anne. She was always the first of the three who felt a shiver crawl up her spine just before someone dropped a porcelain cup or heard a popping noise in her ears when a friend whispered a secret that wasn't theirs to share. Violet and Beatrix weren't usually far behind, but the sisters were so often in step when it came to everything else that this slight discrepancy had caused poor Anne quite a bit of concern. She'd only managed to push her fears to the back of her mind when their mother had pulled her aside and given her hands a reassuring squeeze.

"You each have your own special talents," her mother had whispered with a smile as she let Anne lick the spoon that she was using to stir a bowl of Black Forest cake batter.

Now whenever Violet took a second too long to recognize a new sign during their tea-reading lessons or Beatrix stepped over a ladybug that would have given her a dose of luck had she taken the time to wish her a good day, Anne remembered the rich taste of chocolate and her mother's soft words.

Stifling another yawn, Anne extended one of her short, stubby legs out into the darkness, expecting it to land firmly on the ground. But she was on a different flight of stairs now, the ones that would take her from the second floor to the first, and had forgotten that the final step was a bit steeper than the rest.

The house, which had been keeping a watchful eye on Anne since she slipped away from the attic, was ready to catch her when she stumbled. The floor instantly rose to meet her, preventing Anne from falling and hitting her knee against the hard wooden boards. As she straightened herself, she could feel the railing move closer to her hand as well, radiating like a nanny who'd managed to avert disaster at the last moment but was still recovering from the shock of what might have been.

Patting her small hand against the wall, Anne tried her best to reassure the house that she was unharmed. It was protective, and Anne felt a twinge of guilt that she'd frightened the walls so abruptly out of their slumber when she and her sisters had no doubt kept them awake with their playacting upstairs.

Soft fur brushed across Anne's calf then, and she looked down to find a pair of bright green eyes staring up at her. Anne leaned forward to run a hand along the cat's spine, but before she could sink her fingers into Tabitha's inky black coat, she scampered away toward the sliver of light that was peeking around the outline of the door that led to the kitchen.

Anne nearly ran to catch the cat as she trotted closer to the light, but a sudden tingling along her spine told her to pause before the sound of her footsteps could echo down the hall.

"Clara, you don't know what you're asking," a voice said.

The words were strained and somewhat muffled by the door, but it took Anne no more than a heartbeat to recognize who had spoken them.

What was Miss McCulloch doing here so late at night? She normally came to visit their mother in the early afternoon when the two of them could talk for several hours over a pot of tea and several scones bursting with clotted cream and raspberry jam. Though other witches sometimes came to call, Miss McCulloch's visits were the only ones that didn't cause Anne's mother's shoulder blades to pinch together, as if she was bracing herself for a sudden blow.

But since she lived in an entirely different part of the city, Miss McCulloch always left well before dusk. She never stayed as late as this, not even when she and Anne's mother were so caught up in conversation that they became oblivious to the chimes of the grandfather clock.

"But I do, Katherine," Anne's mother replied, her tone firm. "I need to learn more about how it works."

"You know I can't share any details," Miss McCulloch insisted, clearly confused. "It wouldn't be responsible. That type of magic can be dangerous in the hands of someone who doesn't know how to weave it properly."

"I understand," Anne's mother said, a note of defeat texturing her voice.

"Clara, won't you tell me what's been troubling you?" Miss McCulloch begged. "You've been acting strangely for weeks."

"I'm afraid I've already said too much," Anne's mother replied. "The signs I've been trying to untangle are so complex that even one misstep might push everything on the wrong path. I have to be careful," she sighed. "For their sake."

Anne's eyebrows knit together in confusion. She'd never heard her mother sound so serious about a premonition. What had she uncovered at the bottom of a teacup to inspire such a reaction?

"You're speaking in riddles, Clara," Miss McCulloch groaned.

Anne heard the creaking of a chair and could picture the older woman leaning back in wonder and frustration.

"I won't be able to rest until I know they'll be together again," Anne's mother said. "That they'll have a choice."

"What do you think is going to drive them apart?" Miss McCulloch asked. "Can't you tell me?"

"I can only say that—" Anne's mother began, but before she could continue, the cat whined and thrust her paw toward the kitchen door, pushing it open and casting the bright light on Anne.

"It seems that we have a visitor," Anne's mother murmured, the hard expression on her face instantly softening at the sight of her daughter's white nightgown floating like a ghost in the shadows.

"Yes," Miss McCulloch said, rubbing a palm against her temple as if in pain. "It would seem so."

"Come here, sweetheart," Anne's mother said, opening her arms wide in invitation.

Anne took two hesitant steps forward and then ran the rest of the way, throwing herself into her mother's lap and burying her face into the crook of her neck. The earthy smell of marigolds that always clung to Clara's skin tickled her daughter's nose, and the familiar scent caused Anne's lips to curve into a smile.

"What are you doing up?" her mother asked as she ran a hand through Anne's unruly auburn curls. "Your father told me that you three fell asleep in the attic."

"I tasted cinnamon," Anne answered simply.

"Ah," she replied with a nod. "That explains it then."

"Her magic's developing rather quickly," Miss McCulloch commented, and when Anne turned her head a bit to the left, she saw that her mother's friend was staring at her with open curiosity.

"Yes," her mother replied. "I know."

Anne wanted to ask why her mother looked so scared, but she held back, unsure of how to phrase her question and fearing the answer.

"Katherine, would you mind bringing me that biscuit tin over there?"

Anne felt her mother gesture toward the shelf above the stove, where all sorts of colorful metal boxes and milky glass jars stuffed with dried flowers rested outside the reach of the sisters' eager hands.

"This one?" Anne heard Miss McCulloch ask.

"Not quite. I want the white one with the orange lilies printed across the sides."

Miss McCulloch murmured a noise of understanding, and before long Anne heard the clink of a metal lid popping open and smelled a floral, hazy fragrance float toward her little nose.

"What's that?" Anne asked as she turned around to see what sweet treat her mother had uncovered.

"A biscuit," Anne's mother replied as she reached into the tin and pulled out a piece of shortbread with a flower embossed across the top. "But it's special."

"What does it do?" Anne asked curiously, her gaze fixed on the treat.

"It makes you forget," her mother answered honestly. She always told her daughters the truth, especially when it came to enchantments.

"Everything?" Anne asked.

"No," her mother explained. "Just a sliver of time. Only a few fleeting minutes, really."

"And what does it taste like?" Anne asked.

"Sugar and sweet dreams," her mother replied. "Do you still want a bite?"

Ever the careful child, Anne took her time to decide. She wasn't like Violet, who often answered without giving herself a second to think, or Beatrix, who lingered so long over a choice that the initial opportunity often passed her by entirely. No, Anne somehow always knew just how long to wait before acting.

And she soon decided that she didn't want to remember what

she'd heard while standing on the other side of the kitchen door. Her mother, ever confident and assured, had been frightened, and that made Anne feel so uneasy that biting into the biscuit seemed like a blessing.

After making her choice, Anne nodded and then eagerly slipped the biscuit into her mouth. It crumbled between her teeth, and in an instant she tasted just what it felt like to slip into a long and peaceful slumber.

"Will she really forget?" Anne heard Miss McCulloch ask as her eyes started to close.

"She'll remember," her mother said as she pulled Anne closer to her chest and kissed the top of her head. "When the time is right."

CHAPTER 1

Lines

*Suggest that you will soon go on a journey;
straight lines indicate movement toward
happiness while wavy lines foreshadow difficulty.*

The Quigley witches were pitied for all the reasons that they believed themselves to be exceptional. The humans who neighbored their shop thought that as women who had to work for their livelihoods, they were a sorry lot deserving of consideration, if not respect. To the other witches who roamed the streets of the city, the Quigleys were an anomaly as well, and that was certainly saying something, seeing as most of their kind thought dancing naked around a fire under the light of a full moon was the height of cultural refinement.

Not only had their mother, a talented witch of the Chicago coven, decided to marry a human—an almost laughably ordinary tailor whose greatest claim to fame was his ability to tie a double Windsor knot to sheer perfection—but she had made the unforgivable choice of settling her household outside the magical district and into the rooms above her husband's shop, which was just a hair's breadth away from State Street. The Quigley sisters were thus fated to a reputation of unconventionality among their mother's people before they were even the barest twinkle in their father's eye.

Even stranger still to both the humans and the witches was the fact that the sisters had decided to continue living in the home above their father's tailoring business and use the shop below for their own purposes after the tragic deaths of their parents, though each group had different reasons for their confusion, of course.

The humans were still puzzled that three girls of marriageable age and striking looks didn't immediately sell the house and attach themselves to the first men who happened to take notice of them.

No, indeed, the Quigley sisters had done just the opposite and transformed the once Spartan-looking shop into a tearoom that catered to the ladies who were now beginning to flood the ever-growing department stores taking root downtown. What had once been a quiet, traditional neighborhood of industrious Chicago businessmen was transforming as a new breed of women began to wander about in search of the Crescent Moon Tearoom on their way home after a day of shopping at Schlesinger & Mayer or Marshall Field's, their colorful skirts and wide sleeves demanding space along the sidewalks and in the streetcars.

The witches were equally dissatisfied with the sisters' decision to open the shop. Not because they had a problem with women running their own businesses. No, the difficulty with the sisters rested in the fact that they had not situated the Crescent Moon in a closer and more convenient location. Now the witches had to traipse all the way to the Loop and act "normal" as they waited to be served, unless it was the last Thursday evening of the month, of course, when the shop was reserved for the exclusive use of the city's more magically inclined.

But come they did, even if it meant having to keep their tools of the craft hidden beneath large hats and corsets. This was because the Crescent Moon was not an ordinary teahouse and the sisters could give their customers something much more unusual than a fragrant pot of Earl Grey and platter of pristinely cut cucumber sandwiches: they offered a glimpse into the future.

"A summer wedding, did you say, my dear?" an older woman asked Violet, extending herself over the table to peer into the cup that she had just flipped onto her saucer and spun around three times. She was leaning in so closely that her spectacles, which had been creeping farther down her nose, were about to slip off entirely and fall right into the cup.

"I said no such thing, as you well know, Mrs. Hildegrand," Violet said with a smile as she tried to keep the tea leaves out of her customer's eager grasp.

"Oh, Mary, and you so wanted to see Albert married while the rose garden was in full bloom," one of Mrs. Hildegrand's companions moaned. She had brought two this time, both well-dressed, with wide eyes and eager expressions that hinted they would soon become regulars themselves.

They'd visited on just the right day to receive a proper introduction to the Crescent Moon. Spring was the house's favorite season, and in celebration of the buttercups finally peeling open their yellow petals, it had buffed a fresh coat of beeswax into the floorboards and cracked open the windows to let in a crisp breeze that brushed the lace curtains against vases brimming over with peonies of the softest pink. Now the whole front parlor smelled of sunshine and new beginnings, encouraging more than one customer to ask that their names be jotted down in the reservation book on their way out the door.

"What I see is that your son will fall in love this winter," Violet continued, tilting the cup to get a new perspective of the leaves that had settled along the bottom. She resisted the urge to pace around the table as she deciphered the messages depicted in the remnants of Mrs. Hildegrand's tea. Sitting still had never been an easy task for Violet, whose thoughts only seemed to come together when she was moving. But the sisters' customers rarely appreciated having to crane their necks as Violet made circles around them, and so, not for the first time, she forced herself to remain still. Instead, she settled for tapping her foot as she attempted to focus on the leaves over the sound of her customer's voice, which was becoming more insistent by the second.

"And if he finds a girl then there will surely be a summer wedding! I see no use in a long engagement. He's almost thirty, for goodness' sake!" Mrs. Hildegrand cried, then after meeting Violet's gaze remembered that the woman telling her fortune was no debutante herself. "Not that *you* should concern yourself, Miss Quigley. You don't look a day over twenty, and that's all that matters in the end, I suppose. You still have some time to catch a husband—if you're quick about it, of course."

Violet wanted to tell Mrs. Hildegrand that she had no intentions of catching a marital prospect of any sort. Not when she needed to help keep the shop running like a well-oiled machine.

That thought suddenly made Violet recall that she'd left a bowl full to the brim with cake batter sitting on the kitchen table. She'd mixed in a sprinkle of cinnamon, generous spoonfuls of amber honey, and a few whispered incantations meant to soothe any worries that the Crescent Moon's guests carried into the shop. But Violet had become so distracted in the front parlor that she'd forgotten to give the batter a final stir and pour it into the pan that was waiting beside the oven. And if the scant crumbs that littered Mrs. Hildegrand's plate were any indication, their customers were going to be asking for second helpings soon.

Her heart racing now, Violet glanced up and was surprised to see her sister Beatrix waving frantically at her from the kitchen door. One of Mrs. Hildegrand's companions spotted her as well, and a look of shock immediately spread across her pinched features.

"Don't be wary, Mrs. Tittler," Violet sighed as she rose from her chair and brushed a strand of hair from her eyes. "My sisters and I are triplets."

"Oh, dear me," Mrs. Tittler replied with a sigh of relief. "For a moment, I thought you'd managed to duplicate yourself."

"No, that's not where my gifts lie," Violet said before turning back to Mrs. Hildegrand. "Albert will most definitely meet a woman this winter, but only if you give him room to spread his wings. The girl will not be of your station—"

Mrs. Hildegrand looked like she was going to choke on the bite of citrus scone that she'd just swallowed.

"But, I'll tell you quite frankly, if you manage to push them apart, your son will never marry anyone else. He's going to lose his heart completely and will refuse to have another . . . or continue the family business."

That last bit of information made the old woman's eyes widen to a shocking degree, and her two companions leaned forward, their hands firmly wrapped around not-so-discreet vials of smelling salts, ready to unveil them if needed.

"Best listen to her, Mary," one of her friends whispered solemnly.

"If you'll excuse me, ladies," Violet said as she rose from the table and rushed to the kitchen, leaving the three women to strategize among themselves.

◆

Just before Violet hurried to the kitchen, Anne had been trying to decide if the symbol at the bottom of her customer's cup looked more like a bat or a sparrow when she suddenly felt as though someone was drumming the tips of their fingers across the middle of her back, a warning that something unusual was about to happen. No sooner had she registered this sensation than the sound of cast iron crashing against the floorboards rattled from the direction of the kitchen.

"Pardon me, Mrs. Brooks," Anne apologized as she gently placed the porcelain cup on its saucer and rose from her chair. "I'll return in just a moment."

Taking care to avoid stumbling over the colorful skirt hems that pooled beside her customers' chairs and across the aisles between the tables, Anne made her way through the room, pausing only once to look down at the delicate gold watch that she kept pinned to her chest from morning to night. Her sisters often complained that it made her look like a schoolmarm, but time was easy to lose track of in a place as busy as the Crescent Moon, and so Anne thought it best to keep a clock close to her chest, where the clicking of the gears might blend in with the beating of her own heart.

The kitchen was in a state of comfortably controlled chaos when she walked through the door. Peggy and Franny—the girls they had hired to help prepare the tea and refreshments and wait on their customers—were pulling the last of the day's baked treats out of the oven and boiling hot water for the final rush of customers.

Stuffed to the brim with dried herbs and teapots of every conceivable shape, size, and pattern, the kitchen was a kaleidoscope of colors and aromas. When Clara Quigley had moved in on the first warm spring day of 1873, the house had sensed her magic and started to awake. Every building has its own personality, and this one was eager to please but rather strong-willed when it came to matters of decoration. Made of brick, it was one of the few structures to have survived the Great Fire, and with the memory of the tragedy still as fresh as its new coats of paint, the house was more determined than ever to be beautiful.

After the sisters decided to open their own tearoom nearly two years ago, it had taken all of Anne's efforts to convince the house, which was partial to towering ceilings and large, open windows, to maintain its original size. But it could not be persuaded to leave the kitchen untouched, and as a result, the room was slightly larger than it should have been, though still cozy enough to trap all the delicious scents that beckoned from the oven and stovetop.

Anne took a moment to breathe in the smell of honey cake and freshly risen raisin bread before turning to her sisters.

Violet, who could normally be found darting between the parlor and the kitchen to check on something or other, was pacing in front of the hearth, anxious but unable to sit still on one of the stools that littered the room. In one hand she gripped a large wooden spoon that she was in the habit of hitting against her palm in moments of particular concern. About every third step, she pushed out her lower lip and shot a strong puff of air in the direction of her nose, hoping to push aside the longer strands of a rather uneven fringe. Violet had burned the locks that framed her face a few weeks ago when she prodded the fire in the stove a bit too roughly. She was glad that her hair was growing out, but it had gotten to the point where she was always having to brush it away from her eyes, which was unfortunate considering her hands were covered in biscuit batter most of the time.

Beatrix, the third part of their matching set, sat unmoving at the oak table, staring at a small piece of paper with fixed attention through a pair of round wire spectacles. Years of reading had made her nearsighted, and though she rarely wore them when working in the front of the shop, her glasses could nearly always be found dangling from a chain around her neck.

Walking closer, Anne couldn't help but be reminded that the three of them were mirror images of one another—a fury of red hair that balanced out their extraordinarily fair skin and sharp facial features. The only way to tell them apart was their eyes, which were different colors. Anne's were a light blue, Beatrix's a deep brown, and Violet's a striking shade of purple that had earned her name. Their temperaments, on the other hand, were not what you would call identical, and that, along with their eyes, was what allowed the shop's hired help and the most devoted of their regular customers to keep track of who was who.

"Are you two all right?" Anne asked as she glanced down at her watch to mark the time. "We still have several tables' worth of customers waiting to have their fortunes read. What are you both doing in the kitchen?"

"We're here because the shop is about to erupt into complete disarray!" Violet cried, her arms flailing wildly about her tense body, sending some of the batter that was still stuck to the wooden spoon flying across the floor and straight onto the sleeve of Anne's crisp white blouse.

At that, Franny and Peggy gave each other a knowing glance and quickly slipped out of the kitchen and into the front room. They could withstand the odd magical happenings that often took place in the shop but like most people—human or not—balked at the idea of getting in the middle of a familial dispute, especially one that involved three witches.

"Oh dear, have we run out of flour again? I thought you'd started ordering an extra supply each week after the last incident, Bee," Anne sighed, knowing that Violet was particularly anxious when it came to the state of their pantry.

"If only that were the problem," Beatrix whispered as she

pressed the piece of paper she'd been reading on top of the table, her voice so quiet that Anne had to lean in to hear her.

Anne straightened at the sound of her sister's distress. Beatrix was painfully shy, and she often was at a loss for what to say while reading the fortunes of clients who were too quick to criticize the taste of the tea or her interpretation of their leaves. On more than one occasion, Anne or Violet had gently asked Beatrix to take care of something or other in the back room while they stepped in to decipher the signs that rested at the bottom of a particularly difficult customer's cup. But her habit of speaking too softly for others to hear hardly ever emerged when she was alone with her sisters or when the three of them were doing a reading together.

"What's wrong?" Anne asked as she walked toward Beatrix and placed her hands on either one of her shoulders, giving them a reassuring squeeze.

"Violet moved some of the tins last night," Beatrix began to explain as she nervously thumbed the corners of the paper. "And I didn't realize before it was too late."

Anne didn't bother asking Violet what she'd been doing rearranging their kitchen when she was supposed to be in bed. Ever since they were children, Violet had either slept like the dead or stayed awake long after the moon was high in the night sky. And she often exerted her extra energy moving things around the pantry or linen closets, which sent everyone else into a state of confusion for at least a week because her system of organization was about as obvious as a trunk of trinkets that'd been shaken about on a transatlantic crossing.

"I made sure to leave a note this time," Violet interjected as she pointed her spoon toward the piece of paper in Beatrix's hand. Her sharp movement sent another glob of batter flying across the room, this one nearly hitting Beatrix in the spectacles.

"It must have fallen on the floor," Beatrix said. "I'm so sorry."

"What's happened?" Anne asked again, her hands fluttering about her sister's shoulders. She hated the tension that she found there, knowing that whatever Beatrix had done, she was undoubtedly working herself into knots.

"She's given the Murray cousins a pot of truth-telling tea," Violet sighed. "The two of them will be tearing each other's hair out any moment now."

Anne resisted the urge to groan, knowing that it wouldn't help the situation. The Quigleys used truth-telling tea whenever a customer needed to find the right path but wasn't being honest enough with themselves to make the best choice. When served to the wrong table, however, it could cause long-festering feuds and hidden slights to simmer to the surface.

And though Rose and Liza Murray had a standing reservation to share a plate of scones on the first of every month, their decision to see each other had more to do with figuring out who had been left the most in their uncle's will than any sense of friendship.

Needless to say, they weren't the type who should be sipping on truth-telling tea.

"Have they already started drinking it?" Anne asked quickly, the gears turning in her head.

"No," Beatrix answered. "Peggy brought the pot to the table, and I smelled that something was off when Rose lifted the lid to plop in a few sugar cubes, even though I told her that she should wait until she poured it into her own cup. The tea's still steeping, so I came in here to see what might have happened."

"I don't suppose we can just tell them we've mixed up the orders and give them a new pot?" Violet suggested.

"No," Anne replied. "You know how truth-telling tea works. Once you get a whiff of the scent, it starts to take effect. All their subconscious thoughts are already working their way to the surface."

"Not that they have very far to go, I gather," Violet sighed.

"They need to be honest with one another, or the urge to tell the truth won't wear off," Anne said. "And then they'll leave the shop like this, which wouldn't be fair."

"For them or anyone else," Violet added.

"What are we to do, then?" Beatrix asked. "When I go back to the table, they'll expect me to pour the tea."

Anne lifted her hands from Beatrix's shoulders and walked toward the metal bins and jars that rested above the stove. As the collection of dried herbs, tea leaves, biscuits, and spices had grown over the years, so had the shelves, thanks to the dutiful efforts of the house.

"What are you thinking?" Violet asked as she hovered behind her sister, trying to guess where her outstretched hand would land.

"If we give them something similar but not quite as stark, that might be enough to satisfy the urge to be honest without causing any damage," Anne murmured as she reached up to grasp a jar full of small, uniform seeds.

"Fennel tea," Beatrix whispered with a note of understanding.

"Yes," Anne said. "After a sip or two of this, they'll want to flatter one another, but the praise will be genuine."

"I see," Violet said. "They'll tell the truth, but it will be much sweeter this way."

"That's the hope," Anne agreed with a nod as she pulled a clean teapot off the counter with a similar pattern to the one she'd seen on the Murrays' table and poured hot water over several spoonfuls of fennel seeds. "So, the only thing left to do is figure out the best way to make the swap."

"What we need is a distraction," Beatrix said as her eyes drifted over toward Violet.

The Quigleys knew that out of the three of them, Violet was the one who could be most depended on to cause a sensation.

"Leave it to me," Violet insisted, her wide grin causing two devilish dimples to form on either side of her cheeks.

"Perfect," Anne said as she lifted the pot and took a moment to breathe in the faint smell of licorice before dropping in several cubes of sugar. The Murray cousins liked their tea so sweet that they wouldn't even notice the difference in scent.

"I'll keep the two of them talking until Violet makes her move," Beatrix said as she rose from the chair, her shoulders a bit straighter now that she knew her sisters were going to help her out of this mess.

Grasping the warm teapot in her hands, Anne followed Beatrix and Violet to the door and waited until she knew that the time was right.

She listened attentively at the threshold, and just as she heard the steady chatter of their customers suddenly ebb, Anne pushed into the room.

Casting a quick glance around the parlor, she saw that everyone was staring at a table of middle-aged women sitting in the corner next to the small fireplace, all gathered around a teacup that Violet was holding like a precious relic. They were packed so tightly around her that Anne was reminded of a flock of hens who'd caught sight of their feed bag.

"A house, you say!" one of the ladies was yelling as if she'd just spotted a gold ring on the sidewalk. "That means a business opportunity!"

Anne recognized the woman and instantly understood what all the fuss was about. When it came to getting advice at the Crescent Moon, Mrs. Richards' sole focus was unearthing any tidbits that could be passed on to her stockbroker. And she certainly wasn't the only one in the shop that afternoon interested in keeping her eyes open for a sign that the market was about to shift.

"My husband told me this morning that the stock in grain

might fall today," another customer chimed in from the opposite side of the parlor.

Her comment was the spark that set off a powder keg of excitement, and in a matter of seconds every woman in the shop was engulfed in a vigorous debate about whether to grab her cloak and sell her stock or stay and enjoy her remaining sips of Earl Grey.

Rose and Liza Murray were not immune to the chaos, and once Anne saw that their faces were turned toward Violet and her brood, she glided across the room, grabbed the truth-telling tea with one hand, and set down the fresh pot with the other.

Beatrix cast a grateful smile in her direction moments before the cousins turned their attention back to the table and asked if the tea was ready to be poured.

By the time Anne returned to the kitchen door, the Crescent Moon had settled back into its normal, even rhythm, just as Anne knew it always would.

Though, if she'd taken just a moment longer to breathe in the scent of beeswax and chamomile or listen to the steady chatter that filled the room, Anne might have noticed that the sensation of fingers tapping against her back was still there, subtly warning her that something unexpected was still waiting close to the rim of her own fortune.

CHAPTER 2

An Anchor

Symbolizes rest, stability, and safe havens.

As always, convincing the ladies to leave the shop at closing time was a nearly impossible task. Many of their customers had just settled their sore feet, and the lingering taste of Violet's honey cake kept them asking for second and then third servings. It didn't help that the streets of Chicago still held a spring chill that wouldn't fade until well into the summer months. The Crescent Moon was warm from the flock of clients who had nestled in for the afternoon, and the thought of walking through the front door and needing to tuck deeper into shawls and coat collars was almost too much to bear.

But go they must, and Anne was determined that they do so on time so that the sisters could close the shop and prepare for the morning to come.

When the vibrant array of cloaks had disappeared from the pegs near the door, the house let out a shudder and then stretched, managing to elongate the chestnut wainscoting and sage-painted walls without knocking down a single picture frame, of which there were many.

Anne was tempted to sink into the oasis of the front parlor as well, where a fire still licked at the grate and the scents of vanilla and lavender perfumed the air, just like the aroma that emerges from a freshly opened tea tin. The house, which had eagerly absorbed all the satisfied murmurs and happy chatter that had echoed against its walls throughout the day, was purring with the pleasure of a job well-done. Anne could practically feel the floorboards vibrating against the bottoms of her boots as the house infused the front parlor with its own kind of magic, one that beckoned you to forget the worries that awaited you outside its doors and linger in a sanctuary of silk and saffron.

Wondering what it would feel like to ease herself into one of the worn velvet chairs that circled the hearth and do just that, Anne almost took a step toward the welcoming fire, but the steady clicking of her clock reminded her that the best of dreams need a dash of practicality to be stitched into something real. And so, she smiled and turned to the task of tending to the remains of a prosperous afternoon.

Though the Quigleys had initially been hesitant about how the humans would react when they turned the corner on State Street and found themselves facing a fortune-telling shop, to their great surprise, the women of Chicago had flocked to the Crescent Moon in droves. All it had taken was for a handful of high-class customers to wander in when their doors first opened and the walls of the front parlor had been bursting at the seams ever since.

It had even gotten to the point where they were starting to have to take reservations weeks in advance to ensure that customers weren't waiting out on the street to get a table.

Anne had been beyond pleased with their good luck, of course, but the stacks of empty cups and stained linen napkins at the end of the day were a tangible reminder of how much hard work was necessary to keep the business alive. By the time they locked the shop for the night, the sisters' voices were hoarse from interpreting the signs nestled among the tea leaves, and their feet ached as if they'd walked down the entirety of Michigan Avenue.

When the bell on the front door chimed as their last customer left the shop, Beatrix had fled to the back room, where she immersed herself in the letters and accounts that helped keep the Crescent Moon running. She was quickly followed by Violet, who locked herself away in the kitchen to check on the doughs that needed to rest before being twisted and twirled into buns and pastries the next morning. That left Anne to clear away the tables and load the dishware onto trays that she'd wheel into the kitchen and leave the house to clean. The sisters had tried to wash everything themselves when they first opened the shop, but there had been too many broken handles and chipped rims for the house's comfort, and since then it refused to let them so much as fill the sink with sudsy water.

As Anne lifted saucers and tea-splattered spoons off the white tablecloths, she found herself peeking into the cups once more and reading the signs that waited to be scrubbed from the bottom. There was something she found comforting about spotting anchors and clovers where others might see only chaos. And while she took her time weaving together the remnants of her clients' hopes and fears, Anne felt the quick pace of her breathing slow and the tension she usually carried in her chest ease.

This evening tradition reminded Anne of when she'd help her father gather up the scraps of wool and tweed that had slipped to the floorboards while he tucked in the pleats of his clients' coats and hemmed up their trousers. And the sound of the delicate porcelain cups clinking against one another as she pushed the wooden cart to the kitchen called forth memories of the tea-reading lessons that her mother led at their kitchen table every evening after the dinner dishes had been cleared away.

These little pleasures brought Anne back to times when the house echoed with the laughter of two more voices, and she savored them for as long as she could before the rattling floorboards insisted that she pick up her pace.

"Violet?" Anne called when she finally wheeled the wooden cart toward the kitchen door. Sometimes, her sister was so focused on her own thoughts that she'd drop whatever she was holding if Anne rolled the dishes into the room and began to speak without warning.

When she didn't receive a reply, Anne wandered into the kitchen anyway and found Violet standing on the threshold of the back door, which opened into an inviting garden that, by all logical standards, shouldn't be there. To appease the house, their mother had let it grow an oasis of flowers, vines, and herbs when she first arrived, pointedly ignoring the fact that the thin backlot had quadrupled in size and was always, no matter the season, overflowing with black-eyed Susans, roses, lavender, and whatever else happened to strike the house's fancy. At the moment, the peonies that filled the vases in the front room were multiplying in such profusion that the neighbors were beginning to wonder where the sweet floral aroma that saturated the entire block was coming from. The scent spilled into the kitchen and mingled with the fragrance of fresh soap and cinnamon buns left to rise in the candlelight, lending the space an atmosphere that tempted Anne to ease the stiffness in her shoulders and enjoy a cup of chamomile tea.

"Are you ready to go upstairs?" Anne asked.

Though she'd spoken in a tone just above a whisper, Violet still gave a start, turning her head so quickly that Anne worried she might hit her temple against the doorframe. She was often like that, lost in a daydream of her own weaving and reluctant to return to reality.

"Of course," Violet said as she blew a breath toward her singed fringe and closed the door to the garden. "I've saved us some honey cake and have a pot of tea waiting."

"Wonderful," Anne sighed with delight, relishing the thought of tasting the cake's warm flavors and taking her first sip of piping hot tea after propping her feet up for the evening. "I'll go collect Bee."

Violet nodded in agreement, trying to reorient herself toward the tasks at hand and allowing her sister to serve as a compass that pointed her spinning thoughts in the proper direction, as she always did.

Walking back into the hall and around the corner that led to a small study behind the staircase, Anne found Beatrix hunched over neat stacks of receipts and checklists. Even from the doorway, she could see that her sister's hands were covered with ink smudges that never seemed to wash off properly.

"Bee . . . !" Anne called out after knocking softly on the doorframe.

Her sister's head slowly shifted upward, and she took her time leaning back from the desk, as if her body were physically attached to the polished oak surface.

"Are we heading upstairs already?" Beatrix asked, her spectacles having slipped to the very tip of her nose. "I've completely lost track of time."

As Anne stepped forward, she noticed that Beatrix had been writing in a tattered notebook. Its original purpose had been to keep track of the amount of flour and sugar they ordered from the market, but instead of facts and figures, the pages were now filled to the very edge with Beatrix's careful cursive.

"Still working on a story?" Anne asked gently.

After their father passed away from a wasting disease over two years ago and their mother had followed too quickly behind him, Beatrix found herself jotting down lines on scrap pieces of paper.

At first, the act of writing had simply been a way to express what seemed simple enough on the surface: that she grieved for her parents and the life they had all shared together in the shop. Whenever she tried to sort out the emotions knotted within her over a cup of tea with her sisters, the words that came out of her mouth didn't seem to describe even the barest essence of her inner world. Saying, "I miss them," and, "Will this pain ever fade?" felt like biting into a bitter chocolate casting that was hollow at its center.

For some reason, the aching weight that crept up on her in the oddest moments became easier to confront when it was crafted from pen and ink, and she'd managed to make it through the first year of mourning by scratching half-unfinished notes to her mother into the margins of their account books or along the backs of envelopes. But as the months passed by, the lines had grown into sentences, sentences into paragraphs, and paragraphs into pages. Beatrix found herself writing short stories about characters who were able to convey her desires and deepest fears in ways that she couldn't dream of articulating out loud. It had helped her, somehow, to know that the most profound parts of herself couldn't be captured through anything she said. They could only be experienced when stretched out on the page, where her scattered thoughts fell into unexpected patterns and wove something that finally made sense.

"I suppose I'll keep working on it upstairs," Beatrix said with a faint smile as she rose from her chair.

Looping a hand through the crook of Beatrix's arm, Anne nodded in agreement, but she didn't ask whether her sister might let her peek at the tale she was spinning.

Beatrix hadn't invited her sisters to so much as glance at her work, and though Anne would be lying if she said that didn't bother her in the least, she understood. Her sister was slow to take risks, and opening her written world for others to see was going to be a process. But Anne knew they had time and, as always, was willing to wait for Beatrix to realize that she had something worth expressing.

"I could use a slice of cake myself," Anne said as she returned Beatrix's smile and they moved into the hallway, where Violet was waiting at the foot of the steps, the spout of the teapot spilling over as her foot tapped relentlessly against the boards.

The Quigleys could already feel the tight muscles in their necks and lower backs soften at the thought of the sight that would greet them upstairs.

Though the first floor was a pleasant balance between comfort and order, the state of the family parlor at the top of the steps edged a dash closer to chaos. A virtual explosion of the sisters' interests, it teemed with piles of books that Beatrix was eternally adding to, baskets overflowing with oddly shaped bundles of knitting left half-abandoned by Violet's busy hands, and crumpled papers, which contained Anne's discarded ideas for menu specials and different types of tea enchantments. Anne knew the house had already kindled a crackling fire and that the windows would be shut tight against the evening winds that whipped westward from Lake Michigan and threatened to sink straight into their bones.

Walking up to the parlor with a tray full of teacups and leftover treats had become their evening ritual. Ever since they opened the shop, the sisters had found themselves nestling into the soft comfort of the room after long days of filling their customers' stomachs and soothing their concerns about the future.

The sisters' business may have been built on platters of delicate cakes and pots filled to the brim with sugary tea, but the news that they delivered to their clients was not always so sweet. And as much as they would have liked to shed light on only the joys yet to come, an important part of their craft was making the sorrows of life more palatable. The Quigleys were eager to help their customers navigate the emotions that came with confronting what most would rather leave in the shadows, but days where symbols of ravens and hammers outnumbered hearts and horseshoes often left the sisters' souls sore.

These tensions gradually faded away, though, as they walked through the parlor's threshold, and by the time they'd settled into their respective spots—Anne in the worn armchair with a patchwork quilt and Violet and Beatrix on opposite ends of the lumpy green velvet settee—it was as if the day's troubles had already been forgotten. Sometimes, they'd look up from whatever they'd decided to occupy themselves with, whether it be a notebook or a piece of sewing, and talk about an unusual customer or a particularly scandalous rumor that they'd overheard. But more commonly, it was their habit to relax into the quiet ease of one another's company and the sound of the logs crackling in the hearth.

When the Quigleys pushed open the door to the parlor on that particular evening, the sight of an unexpected visitor nestled in a basket of books and quilting scraps stopped them in their tracks before throwing them into a state of excitement.

"Tabitha!" Violet cried out, running toward the small black cat.

At the feel of Violet's hand caressing her shiny coat, the cat opened a disinterested eye and then went back to sleep, her purrs so loud that they echoed through the room.

"I thought she was gone for good this time," Beatrix said, her brow furrowing as she sank onto the settee, resisting the impulse to push her feet out of the shoes that had tortured her the entire day and lean forward to rub away the pain crippling her toes.

Like all the other facets of their lives, Tabitha was far from ordinary. For one, she'd been passed down from one generation of Quigleys to the next for so long that stories about her origin had taken on the texture of an ancient legend. For another, she had the ability to slip through time, disappearing at the most random moments and returning just as suddenly, her fur smelling of things that, though not exactly unpleasant, were often difficult for the sisters to place. Despite the fact that their cat traveled through decades—perhaps even centuries, though no one could be sure of this but Tabitha, of course—they suspected that she remained in the same place, if her familiar relationship with the house was any indication. Like old friends, the cat and the house played tricks on each other unceasingly, with Tabitha tearing down a drape that the house had just managed to settle on after months of minor alterations and the house hiding some of her favorite toys atop shelves that were impossible to reach, even for a cat.

But for now, the two were content to merely rest, to the relief of the sisters, who, like one of Violet's balls of tightly wound yarn, were in need of loosening.

"She's been gone for nearly two weeks," Violet said as she brushed her face against Tabitha's coat. "And smells of strong coffee and pine. I wonder where she went this time."

"I believe you mean *when* she went," Beatrix clarified as she lifted a book from the end table and began to flip through its pages, comforted by the feel of paper slipping across her fingertips.

Giving Tabitha a final pat, Violet moved toward the other end of the settee and threw herself so aggressively into the cushions that Beatrix nearly lost hold of her book.

The two of them quickly fell into an animated debate about whether one of their clients should accept a marriage proposal, their voices growing more impassioned as they traded playful remarks and discussed the signs they'd seen nestled among silver-tipped green tea leaves and jasmine flowers.

Anne shook her head in amusement while she poured herself a cup of tea and bit into her first slice of honey cake laced with delicate layers of brown sugar buttercream. Her toes curled in contentment as Violet and Beatrix became firmer in their stances, and she wondered how life could be any more satisfying than it already was in that moment.

"What do you think, Anne?" Beatrix finally asked. "Should Katie marry Mr. Baxter?"

"I'm afraid I don't have a strong opinion on the matter," Anne replied, taking another bite of her cake. "I think that if the leaves show they will marry, it's already set in stone."

Beatrix and Violet nodded in agreement, their debate coming to an easy close.

There didn't seem to be much point in arguing about Miss Katie Meyer's future if everything was written clear as day for the sisters to read at the bottom of her cup. As seers, the Quigleys had long ago accepted that questioning what they saw in the remnants of their customers' tea was about as useful as trying to wash cherry jelly out of a silk blouse.

Every witch had their own unique gift. Some could talk to animals, while others found that their talents rested in stirring up love potions or calling upon the dead. Anne, Beatrix, and Violet, like all the Quigleys before them, possessed the ability to see into the future, and they did so with a surprising degree of precision that wasn't always typical in their sort of witches.

Clara Quigley had developed a reputation that proved to be the sisters' legacy. She'd managed to decipher the signs before she could even toddle across the floor, and by the time she was able to finally talk, the city had already marked her to join the Council of Witches as the next Diviner. Along with three other witches with different talents, she was destined to ensure that their coven was kept safe and secret, no small feat considering most of their sort rebelled against subtlety.

Of course, what everyone expected hadn't come to pass. Clara had met their father, a human, and in leaving their coven to live with him she'd forfeited her place on the Council. The position would have come with prestige and power, but she'd never regretted her choice, even though she knew that her greatest love would also grow into her deepest tragedy.

Seers might peek into everyone else's future, but they couldn't make sense of their own. No matter how long they gazed into their dregs, no signs ever emerged. It wasn't clear why that was exactly, but everyone assumed it had something to do with maintaining balance. The Quigley sisters couldn't even decipher one another's futures, as their lives were too entangled to get a firm reading.

Birthdays were the exception to the rule. On that very special occasion, a seer got the chance to peek ever so slightly beyond the present and into their own unknown.

These annual revelations never painted a clear picture of a critical event, however. It was not the same as when the Quigleys looked at the bottoms of their clients' cups, where the signs were distinct and crafted a story that the sisters could neatly knit together. No, these yearly revelations were merely a sweet taste of what rested ahead, the barest echo of their future. They were the feel of a soft caress on their arms or waists. Or a nervous tingling that tickled their toes and then shot right up through their spines. Or the delightful flavor of aged bourbon burning the backs of their throats. In essence, these glimpses were little sensations attached to everyday moments destined to take place in the years and decades to come that would somehow prove to be meaningful.

Their mother always told them that on the eve of her fifteenth birthday she'd taken one glance at the bottom of her cup of English breakfast tea and known what she was destined for. A heart entangled in a cross could only mean one thing, after all: a love that ran deep but would end in suffering and sacrifice. Their father would be everything she could ever dream of, but he would die young, and she along with him. For when a witch found their true match, they tended to be physically affected by any sudden or dramatic break in that bond, especially when it came to loving humans, who tended to be more fragile. But even with her knowing what was in store, finding her soul mate hadn't been something that Clara Quigley ever came to regret either.

Given her own experience, Clara had encouraged her daughters to savor their birthday revelations, no matter how minor they might seem in the present.

The Quigley sisters always celebrated their birthday when the first snow of the season coated the street in front of the shop. Their mother had never told them the exact date of their birth, only that by the time the world outside the bedroom window looked like the top of a finely powdered cake she and their father were holding three beautiful baby girls.

And unusual things always occurred when the snowflakes hit the pavement and began to stick for the first time every year. The Quigleys were looking forward to the next time they'd feel the fresh snow against their cheeks and get a glimpse of what Fate had in store for them.

In the meantime, however, they'd have to content themselves with reading everyone else's fortunes. And because they did so with the skill and care that everyone had expected of them given their mother's talents, the shop had proven to be a roaring success.

As Violet propped her throbbing ankles up on the settee and pulled a piece of paper from her pocket, she couldn't help but think they could use a few less customers, in fact.

"What's that?" Beatrix asked curiously as she moved to get a closer look at what her sister was holding.

"It's an advertisement that I found on my way back from the market yesterday," Violet explained as she turned the colorful illustration toward her sisters. "A circus is coming to town."

"A circus?" Beatrix asked. "You can't be serious. The winds will blow them clear over the lake into Michigan."

"I assume that they've nailed everything to the ground, Bee," Violet replied with a laugh. "Can't we go?"

Visions of lion tamers and jugglers danced across Anne's mind, making her feel like a child again. But they had the shop to consider, of course, and they were tired enough as it was to think of adding an evening's excursion to their calendar, which was already straining under the weight of their other commitments.

"Perhaps," Anne said hopefully, not wanting to sound too much like a governess. "It could be rather exciting."

But Violet didn't seem to be listening, and Anne suspected that she was already daydreaming about what she might encounter under the twinkling lights of a red-striped tent. Beatrix's attention had also drifted, and she was scribbling with great care in her notebook, unaware of what was going on around her.

That was fine with Anne, who leaned deeper into the wingback chair and let the house tuck her quilt a bit higher around her shoulders. She was perfectly content being here with her sisters and listening to the sounds of Beatrix's pen and Violet's tapping foot blend into the crackles of the fireplace.

After all, there was no sense in worrying about their future when they didn't have any sense of what waited for them there.

CHAPTER 3

A Letter

Indicates that news is imminent.

The moments before the sisters opened the shop carried their own sort of magic.

After the crisp linen tablecloths had been draped over the tables and the cups and saucers arranged just so next to delicate silver spoons and napkins embroidered with miniature moon phases along the edges, the house, for one second of the day, became still. Although it enjoyed rattling the windows and adding an inch or so to the countertops just in time to catch something that Violet was about to drop to the floor, the walls of the Crescent Moon couldn't help but pause and breathe in the beauty of the parlor.

That morning was no exception. As Anne slipped the last peony into a cracked teacup on a shelf near the coatrack and placed her hand on the brass lock to open their shop to the world, she waited and took in the calm anticipation of the scene alongside the house.

But all moments, no matter how satisfying, must move forward into the next.

Anne turned the lock, pulled open the door, and was instantly met by a flurry of elaborate feathered hats and colorful bustle skirts.

"Miss Quigley, I know that I'm usually seated at the table next to the fireplace, but today I must ask to have a chair near the window."

"Miss Quigley, this might be a trifle inconvenient, but my niece has decided to join me this afternoon. Would it be possible to add a place at our table for her?"

"Miss Quigley, do you have any of those rose and elderflower biscuits left from my last visit? I've been dreaming of how they tasted all week!"

Anne met these requests with good humor and a smile, ushering the crowd into the shop and guiding everyone to their proper places. As she continued to greet the first flush of customers, Anne spotted the bright white cotton of Peggy's and Franny's aprons out of the corner of her eye and knew that they were already flitting from one table to the next, greeting their guests and discussing the tea specials of the day.

"It's quite busy in here this afternoon!" a familiar voice called from behind Anne's shoulder just as she took in a breath that carried with it the scent of frankincense and sage. "Not that I'm at all surprised, of course."

A bit of weight that Anne hadn't realized she'd been carrying lifted when she turned and saw their mother's oldest friend standing near the front door. Katherine McCulloch had been in the Quigley sisters' lives long before Clara had heard the tinkling laughter of three little girls echoing from her future on one of her birthdays. And as they had grown older, their mother's friend had become their own, so much so that she'd insisted they set the name Miss McCulloch among the other relics of their childhood and call her Katherine. Though her hair had started to whiten at the temples and her footsteps were now accompanied by the soft tap of a cane, Katherine's smile and the way her eyes crinkled at the corners whenever she was genuinely pleased hadn't changed an inkling since the sisters were young girls.

Though Katherine's craft was casting curses, hexes, and blessings, she radiated a sense of safety that had offered a solid foundation for the sisters to grasp onto in the weeks following their parents' deaths. She'd been a regular guest at the Crescent Moon since the first day the sisters had turned the Open sign to face the street, though in recent months a seasonal demand for the tricks of her trade had kept her from visiting the shop. Her enchantments took some time to settle, and the witches of Chicago wanted to ensure certain requests were met well in advance of the flurry of social events that would take place toward the end of the year.

"I didn't know that you were stopping by today," Anne said with delight as she reached forward and placed her palm on the lace-covered hand that Katherine was using to hold her cane. "You should have sent word this morning and I would have made sure that we saved your regular seat."

Katherine preferred to sit in a worn velvet chair at the very back of the room. Anyone seated there didn't have the best view and had to place their tea on a walnut end table, which was charmingly crafted but could only fit a small porcelain pot along with a cup and saucer and absolutely nothing else. But a portrait of the sisters' mother hung just to the right of the chair, and Katherine liked to be able to glance up at it as she took sips of the tea that reminded her the most of her friend: a strong Darjeeling blend softened by a generous dash of vanilla essence.

"Think nothing of it," Katherine said as she patted the top of Anne's hand. "I'm going to an appointment at the other end of

State Street and only wanted to pop in for a moment on my way. Though I can see you're already preoccupied for the afternoon. Where are your sisters?"

Anne glanced about the room but didn't see Violet's or Beatrix's red hair among the crowd. She sighed inwardly, thinking that they must still be tucked away in the study and kitchen, so wrapped up in their pastry dough and paperwork that they'd forgotten the time. Normally, Anne didn't mind retrieving her sisters, but for whatever reason, that afternoon the idea of having to push them back on course made her eyebrows pinch together just a fraction.

Suddenly, Katherine's hand stiffened, pressing Anne's fingers together in an uncomfortable grip.

When Anne glanced down, she saw that Katherine was staring into her face with a stricken expression.

"Katherine?" Anne asked, concerned that her friend was feeling unwell. "Is something the matter?"

Instead of responding, the older woman leaned an inch or two closer to Anne, staring intently into her eyes.

A prickling sensation formed at the base of Anne's skull and slowly trickled down to her toes, and she resisted the urge to shudder. She'd never experienced it herself before, but it was common knowledge that when a hex witch turned their inner eye to look upon your soul it felt like pins and needles.

Then suddenly the sound of porcelain crashing to the floorboards and a flurry of apologies echoed through the shop, breaking Katherine out of her trance.

She blinked exactly once and then shook her head, as if clearing away a foggy thought.

"Katherine?" Anne asked again, her stomach sinking as she noticed that her friend's skin had taken on an ashy hue.

"It can't be . . . ," Katherine murmured to herself as her mouth tightened into a firm line.

"What can't be?" Anne asked. "What's happened?"

Katherine gazed up at Anne, looking so unsure and hesitant that she almost seemed unrecognizable.

"I need to go," Katherine finally said.

"Go?" Anne asked, desperate for the barest inkling of a hint as to what had caused Katherine to react so strongly. "But why?"

"May I call on you this evening?" Katherine replied in a rush, already pulling her scarf tighter around her neck and reaching a hand toward the handle on the front door. "After the shop's closed for the day?"

"Of course," Anne answered, more confused than ever. "But can't you tell me what's troubling you?"

"No, dear," Katherine said simply as she opened the door and began to step into the chilly spring afternoon. "I'm afraid that wouldn't be for the best."

As Anne moved closer to the window and watched Katherine shuffle down the sidewalk, she couldn't help but feel that something profound had just taken place.

If only she had the faintest idea of what it was.

◆

At the same moment Katherine passed through the threshold and onto the street, Beatrix was standing at the back of the shop, her hand grasped around the handle that would usher her into the flurry of the front parlor.

As she adjusted her spectacles and attempted to slow down the rapid beating of her heart, the house threw open the thin stained-glass window above the door that led to the garden and wafted the scent of lavender in Beatrix's direction, hoping the fragrance would bring her some comfort.

She'd been like this ever since the first day they'd opened the shop, so nervous about having to talk to their customers for hours on end that her words were already tangling into knots on her tongue. Her sisters thought that Beatrix had greatly improved over the past two years, but she wasn't so certain.

It didn't help that this particular afternoon was more nerve-wracking than most, though the reason for her worry had more to do with what might be sitting in the mailbox mounted on the front of the house than their customers' desire to make conversation.

Today marked exactly three months since she'd sent a short story to a publishing house for consideration. It had taken her quite some time to work up the confidence to write the address for Donohoe & Company on an envelope and bring it to a post office several blocks away from the shop, where she had the luxury of pacing up and down the sidewalk without the risk of being spotted by her sisters.

During the month following that momentous day, Beatrix had let herself slip into the occasional fantasy of what it would feel like to flip through the stack of bills and correspondence and find a letter addressed to her and her alone. She imagined the suspense of peeling open the envelope and the eventual thrill of seeing the words "We're pleased to say . . ." at the very top of the page. And then, when Beatrix had become fully immersed in her daydream, she thought about how she would surprise Violet and Anne with the news. Sometimes, she pictured herself running into the kitchen, shaking the torn envelope triumphantly above her head, but that never seemed quite in character. So, her mind would shift the scene to the family parlor, where she announced her success just when her sisters were settling in for the day and they could celebrate with a bottle of champagne that the house only unearthed on very special occasions.

And then, when Beatrix could finally be certain that her work was worth reading, she'd share her story with them.

But when the fourth week slipped into the fifth and then sixth, Beatrix's thoughts started to turn in a different direction. Instead of imagining herself opening an envelope thick with praise, she'd see a thin page with a simple denial etched across the front, her dreams dashed with only a handful of haphazardly arranged words. And she'd started to doubt that her writing would ever take on a life outside the confines of her battered notebook.

Drawing in one last lavender-laced breath, Beatrix hunched forward and gently pushed open the door with the fleeting hope that no one would notice her as she stepped into the front parlor.

As Beatrix had expected, the room was so full of chiffon and chatter that she could hardly hear herself think. Trying her best to avoid being caught by a customer, she took slow and deliberate steps toward the front door, which, thankfully, wasn't blocked by anyone hanging up her cloak or waiting to be seated.

Beatrix wanted to linger there for a few more seconds, but her presence in the shop wouldn't go unnoticed for much longer, so she opened the door and pushed her hand into the cast-iron mailbox that was bolted just beside the pristine Open sign that Anne had carefully painted when they first opened the Crescent Moon.

Her hands were clammy now despite the sharp wind that was blowing down the street, and they shook a bit as she counted the number of envelopes that were waiting to be sorted through.

As she turned each one over, the fluttering sense of expectation that had been building in her chest gradually dissipated. They'd received several bills from the local grocers and a few pieces of correspondence from familiar names, but not a single one of them had *Donohoe & Company* scrawled across the top left corner.

When Beatrix finally reached the bottom of the stack, she paused for a moment. Though the second-to-last envelope looked ordinary enough from the back, when her fingers brushed against the sides to turn it upward she felt a strange sense of foreboding sink into her shoulders, as if she were reading tarot and had flipped a card upward to see the three of swords, a beacon of sorrow to come.

Unsure of what to make of this odd sensation, Beatrix remained still, her knees shaking against her linen petticoats.

But, eventually, she did work up the courage to turn the envelope over, and when she saw what was written across the front she nearly dropped the entire stack of mail onto the dirty cobblestones.

Three of swords indeed.

✦

While Beatrix was considering the envelope she'd just uncovered, the house was trying to pull Violet's focus back to the task at hand. Her fingers were tucked in a bowl filled to the brim with sweet bread dough, and as the smell of cloves saturated her senses, her thoughts had wandered out of the Crescent Moon and toward the candy-striped tent on the front of the flyer that she'd left buried under her knitting in the family parlor.

The scent reminded her of the circus because she'd found the advertisement while leaning over to smell the brightly colored mountains of nutmeg and star anise at the market's spice stall. One moment, she'd been breathing in the array of fragrances, and the next, she'd felt a piece of paper tickling her chin. The wind had blown the flyer straight into her chest, as if it was bothered by the fact that she hadn't paid enough attention to see the others stapled against the neighboring billboards and decided to take matters into its own hands.

One glance at the ferocious-looking lions and flying acrobats was all it took to draw Violet's thoughts to the attic, where she knew a miniature carousel had gathered dust or, perhaps, been lost entirely. Her mother had brought it home for them as a surprise one evening, and they'd all taken delight in watching as the white horses galloped off the circular track and floated about the room, whinnying and nickering to a fast and cheerful tune. Even their father, who still had a great deal to learn about magic, had been fascinated.

At first, Violet had smiled at the memory of his rich laughter entwining with her mother's chuckles, but then something cold and steely settled over her heart. She always felt that way now whenever these tokens of the past crept up unexpectedly: nostalgic and then guarded, as if she was trying to protect herself from the bitterness that threatened to well to the surface.

But, as always, Violet had managed to tuck these feelings away and allow her mind to race ahead to the next string of thoughts, wondering where they might take her. In this case, it was toward the circus, and she'd instantly started making plans to see if the performances beneath the tent were as spectacular as the flyer claimed.

The clattering of pots and pans snapped Violet's attention away from cinnamon and circuses and toward the smell of burnt pastry.

"Medusa's curls!" she cried, remembering that Peggy had asked her to keep an eye on a tray of strawberry tarts that were baking in the oven.

Rushing to the iron beast, she threw open the door and was met by a cloud of smoke that blew straight into her eyes, causing them to water.

Staring down at the tray, Violet saw a dozen blackened pastries, burned to an absolute crisp.

"Violet!" Anne's voice echoed through the kitchen, followed by the sound of the door slamming shut.

"It was an accident!" Violet cried as she whirled around to face her sister.

But, to her surprise, Anne didn't seem to be aware of the rivulets of smoke that were billowing from the oven. No, her gaze was fixed on a letter that she was holding with the care of a falconer trying to maintain a gentle grip on a particularly anxious bird.

"What's that?" Violet asked, stepping forward to try to get a better look.

"A calling card," Anne murmured in a whisper as she turned the front of the envelope in Violet's direction.

The surface was entirely blank except for a wax seal so red that it looked like someone had bled onto the page. And at its center was the impressed shape of a balance, perfectly even on either side.

Violet took one look at it and dropped the metal tray to the floorboards with a harsh clank.

"For Hecate's sake," she whispered.

"I just found it in the mailbox," Beatrix whispered as she slipped into the kitchen and closed the door quietly behind her, not wanting to alert the customers in the front parlor to their brewing troubles.

"That can't be from . . . ," Violet began, finding herself unable to say the words without shivering.

"It is," Anne replied, her expression firm. "The Council has decided to send us a calling card."

The witches of Chicago understood that the existence of the Council was necessary to maintaining order and balance in a world where magic still needed to be kept secret, but they also knew that this type of work sometimes required difficult choices to be made. And it didn't help that the four members of the Council preferred to remain in the shadows of society, pulling seemingly invisible strings in the background to ensure that none of the intricate knots in the web of destiny came loose. It was a habit among their folk to say, "The Council must have passed through," when a bundle of hemlock had vanished into thin air or a train that normally rattled up to the tracks on time was delayed. They preferred to interfere in subtle and meticulous ways that, when accounted for all together, caused a lasting impact, like steady drops of water that eventually wore away at stone.

In the Quigley household, the Council's doings had taken on an even darker hue. Though Clara had tried to shield her daughters from the worst of it, her fellow witches hadn't taken too kindly to her decision to refuse the position of Diviner, viewing her choice as a betrayal. And whenever Katherine had mentioned the Council at the kitchen table, the sisters had watched their mother's face harden, as if she'd just stepped on a bundle of iron jacks.

When the sisters first opened the Crescent Moon, they feared that the Council would appear at their door, displeased that a fortune-telling shop was blooming right in the middle of State Street. But as the months had slipped into years, they came to believe that their shop hadn't upset the balance in the city and they'd be left well enough alone.

But when confronted with the image pressed into the envelope's seal, the Quigleys realized that they might have not gone unnoticed after all.

"What's inside?" Violet asked as she and Beatrix gravitated to either side of Anne.

Beatrix looked like she wanted to ask the same question but was having difficulty finding her words. Instead, she wrung her hands around her apron strings and suffered in silence.

Knowing there was only one way to find out, Anne peeled

open the seal and pulled out the stiff white card that rested inside. When Anne held it closer, she smelled black lead and beeswax, the same scents that saturated the cupboard where the house kept all its cleaning supplies.

"It says half past six," Anne replied in disbelief.

"That's it?" Violet asked as she reached forward and pulled the card from Anne's grasp. "There doesn't seem to be anything on the back."

"I think that's quite enough, isn't it?" Anne said with a sigh.

"What do you mean?" Violet asked.

"The Council is coming to pay a call," Anne explained. "Tonight."

As soon as Anne finished her sentence, the card lit up in a burst of flames and disintegrated into ash, the cinders dropping slowly to the floor.

"Tonight?" Violet gasped in disbelief. "With so little warning? That doesn't give us any time to prepare."

"I think that's the point," Anne said, a list of tasks that had to be completed between now and then already starting to unfold in her mind.

They'd need to close the shop at least half an hour early, of course. The thought of trying to push their customers out the door before their regular time was almost as frightening as the prospect of confronting the Council. The women who slipped into the shop toward the end of the afternoon were the ones who wanted to melt into the seat cushions and enjoy a good dose of gossip alongside their oolong tea while they recovered from a long day. Needless to say, they found every little excuse to stay beyond closing time, and getting them to leave early was going to be like trying to push a cat who'd been sleeping by a warm hearth out into the rain.

"What do you think they want?" Beatrix finally managed to

ask, pulling Anne's attention away from her own thoughts and back to her sisters.

She noticed that Beatrix's hands were shaking and Violet's foot was now tapping against the floorboards in an unsteady tempo.

Wrapping both her arms around her sisters' shoulders, Anne took in a deep breath and pulled them in close.

"I'm not sure," Anne said. "But what I do know is that we three are going to be just fine. Because when you put three Quigley witches together, you create a force to be reckoned with."

Violet laughed and held up the singed oven mittens that she still wore over her hands.

"Quite a force we make indeed," she said. "When we can't even manage to keep our tarts from burning and run the front room at the same time."

At that, Beatrix started to chuckle as well, and Anne felt some of the tension ease from the room.

"Let's just focus on getting through the afternoon, and then we'll face whatever comes," Anne whispered just loud enough for Beatrix and Violet to hear as she gave them one last squeeze.

"Miss Anne, Miss Anne!" Peggy suddenly called as she poked her head into the kitchen. "Mrs. Hildegrand just walked in and insists on getting a reading from you as soon as possible. She wants to know when the best time is going to be to give Albert her grandmother's sapphire engagement ring. And her friend is asking if there is another reader who can give her some advice about her financial portfolio while Mrs. Hildegrand is getting her fortune told, so we need Miss Violet or Miss Beatrix as well."

"We'd better get back in there," Violet sighed as she pulled off her oven mittens. "Before they start tearing the shop apart searching for us."

"It seems we have a lot to do before closing time," Anne murmured as she laced her arms around her sisters and led them toward the front room, grateful, not for the first time, that the shop would distract them from their worries.

But, as each sister would find, there was just enough time for their thoughts to wander back to the pieces of ash and burnt paper that were still scattered across the kitchen floorboards.

CHAPTER 4

Clouds

*Signal that serious trouble is on
the horizon.*

The ladies of the Crescent Moon certainly did not appreciate the early closure, as the Quigley sisters had foretold.

When it came time to make the final rounds and whisper gentle reminders that the shop would be shutting its doors at half past five, the remaining customers practically dug the heels of their boots into the carpet and begged for just one last raspberry petit four coated in white chocolate.

By the time Anne had persuaded the last pair of customers to rise from their table and begin slipping into their cloaks, it was already quarter to six, leaving them precious little time to prepare for their appointment with the Council.

"How do you think they'll make their entrance?" Violet asked as she frantically piled saucers and spoons onto the wooden cart. The house nearly trembled at the sight of the delicate porcelain being thrown about this way and began to resign itself to the fact that the china cabinet would mourn a casualty or two later that night.

"Well, I don't expect that they'll knock on the front door," Beatrix replied while she flipped through their reservation book to ensure that no one had scribbled in their name when the sisters weren't looking.

The members of the Council of Witches weren't ones to wait out in the cold, and from what the sisters had heard, they didn't need something as mundane as a key to enter someone's home. It was much more likely that they'd show up unannounced and in a way that even the Quigley sisters couldn't predict.

"I think it would be best to make a pot of tea and wait upstairs," Anne suggested as she threw down a soiled napkin in defeat.

They'd sent Peggy and Franny home an hour ago with the intention of avoiding the merest possibility of them crossing paths with the Council, so there was no hope of clearing out the front parlor before half past six and what little time they had left was best spent trying to gather their frayed nerves.

The sisters wandered into the kitchen and hurriedly filled one of their most decorative teapots with water that was still warm from the stove, infusing the room with the scent of Orange Pekoe leaves. As Anne placed the pot on a tray and began to walk toward the foot of the steps, Beatrix grabbed seven matching cups while Violet piled their remaining petit fours on a plate.

The Quigleys doubted the Council would take any of the refreshments they offered, but they were comforted by the smell of steeping tea, and the habit had become so ingrained that the gesture was really more for their own sake than that of their unwanted guests.

The usual comfort that kindled in the sisters' chests as they ascended the steps and neared the family parlor didn't appear that evening. Instead, a lingering sense of unease hovered around them like gnats as they opened the door at the top of the stairs and saw their worried expressions reflected in the towering mirror that hung just above the mantle.

"What kind of magic do you think they have?" Beatrix whispered as they arranged the tea and treats on the table and nervously assumed their usual seats.

"I haven't a clue," Anne replied, feeling disconcerted by just how little the sisters knew. The witches who came into the shop enjoyed gossip, but even they kept their lips sealed about anything that had to do with the Council.

"Katherine would know," Violet said, reminding Anne of the promise that she'd made to their friend before the day had been turned completely inside out.

"Katherine!" Anne groaned as she rubbed a palm against her temple. "She's supposed to visit us this evening."

"Now?" Beatrix asked, looking about as if she expected the older woman to crawl out of the woodwork.

"No, no," Anne said quickly. "She asked to come after the shop had closed for the day, and she knows that we normally need an hour or so to get everything back in order. So, we have a bit of time."

"If we're still here after the Council is through with us, that is," Beatrix sighed.

"Of course we'll still be here!" Anne insisted. "They aren't murderers, after all."

"That you know of," Violet scoffed. "I've heard stories that would make a broomstick curl."

It was on the tip of Anne's tongue to ask her sister to not be so dramatic, but the instant she parted her lips to speak, the sound of a grandfather clock striking the half hour filled the house, drawing them away from Violet's morose comment and toward a new set of worries.

As soon as the echo of the final chime faded away, the mirror that sat above the mantle began to shift ever so slightly. It still reflected the parlor, but the sisters' images grew dim, and the shadows that were left behind shifted unnaturally, like acid freshly poured and bubbling. And by the time the haze settled, the Quigleys were facing three entirely different witches.

"Good evening," an older witch wrapped in layers of shawls that had seen better days said from the spot where Anne sat on the other side of the mirror, her voice thick with smoke and secrets.

"Good evening," the Quigleys repeated in unison, unsure of how to proceed. Given the nature of the Council's entrance, it seemed absurd to offer them the tea and petit fours that they carried upstairs, and this left the sisters feeling rather lost.

The older witch seemed amused by their discomfort, however, and smiled silently for a moment longer, watching them through her pair of wrinkled and mischievous eyes. Reaching toward the pot of Orange Pekoe and an empty cup that appeared in the mirror's reflection, she poured herself some tea and inhaled the rich scent, clearly pleased. Anne, curious, turned toward the table and saw that the pot was still in the place they'd left it but noticed steam rising from the spout, as if someone had just set it back on the table after helping themselves on the other side of the mirror.

A broad-shouldered man with an unruly beard and eyes that could cut steel scowled from the spot where Violet's reflection should have been, clearly displeased with the witch's playfulness.

"Let's get on with it, Hester," he growled, the sound of his rough voice sending icy chills down the sisters' spines. It reminded them of full moons and dark forests. "We don't have all night."

Hester chuckled, but the final member of the Council who sat in Beatrix's spot on the other side of the mirror merely stared straight ahead with a blank expression, as if he was looking through the sisters and into another dimension. This, of course, was not entirely out of the realm of possibilities. His eyes were such a light shade of gray that they were almost transparent, and the sisters suspected that he might be able to see things that they couldn't.

"Patience, Nathanial," Hester cooed. "We're about to ask a favor, after all."

At that, the Quigleys shuddered. A favor from the Council was a frightening request, indeed, with many strings attached that could quickly transform into chains.

Hester caught the glint of terror that briefly crossed the face of each Quigley sister, and her smile widened.

"Don't look so worried, my dears," she said, her words a cross between a hum and a cackle. "We're certain at least one of you will be up to the job we have in mind."

These hollow reassurances did nothing to slow Anne's or Beatrix's rapidly beating heart or the quick *thump, thump, thump* of Violet's foot, which was threatening to dig a hole straight through the floor.

"There are three elderly witches who have failed to complete their Tasks," Nathanial said, his stern voice laced with disgust.

"Medusa's curls," Violet cursed under her breath, which granted her stern looks from Anne and Beatrix.

Every witch had a reason for their existence. That could be something as grand as leading a revolution or finding a long-awaited cure to some horrendous disease. But it could also be as simple as returning a lost purse or providing a kind word to someone in great need of encouragement. Regardless of its apparent importance, no Task was in any way trivial, as it set a sequence of actions in motion that were vital to pushing everyone's destiny in the proper direction.

Though it wasn't uncommon for witches to recognize their

Task later in life—the Quigleys themselves had yet to identify theirs—it was practically unheard of for someone to reach old age without having completed this errand, let alone figured out what exactly they were meant to do.

"How is that possible?" Violet asked bluntly, so shocked that she forgot to fear breaking proper decorum.

"They've mistaken them," Nathanial explained with a shake of his head.

This was even more unbelievable. When a witch finally came to a realization about their Task, an all-consuming sensation racked their body. The sisters' mother had once told them that it was like a pitcher of warm oil being poured on the crown of your head and sinking into your very veins, bringing with it a feeling of surreal contentment. It was distinct and, as the Quigleys had believed until only seconds ago, unmistakable.

"You know what will happen if this issue isn't resolved before they pass over," Hester continued. She wasn't asking a question, but rather emphasizing the ominous fate in store should the witches fail to discover their Tasks.

For if a witch died without having met their destiny, they were doomed to linger as a spirit for all eternity. Not to mention that the delicate web of Fate became slightly unraveled, which typically resulted in minor natural disasters and other odd happenstances. Needless to say, it was in everyone's best interest to ensure that no Task was left unattended. And because the Council's core reason for existence was maintaining order and avoiding undue attention, they wouldn't rest until every witch's Task was complete.

"How would you like us to help?" Anne asked.

Out of the corner of her eye, she saw the silent witch's hand flash toward the tea tray and grab a petit four, which he proceeded to swallow in a single bite, seemingly uninterested in the conversation taking place around him.

"Isn't it obvious?" Hester asked as she poured herself another serving of tea. In her distraction, Anne hadn't kept track of how many times she'd refilled her cup already. "You'll need to help them discover their Tasks. Look into their pasts to see what's been missed and toward the future, where their errand awaits them."

"We're honored that you've approached us with this favor," Anne continued, watching Beatrix's face scrunch into a grimace, as if she'd just swallowed a spoonful of vinegar. "But isn't this a duty better suited to the city's Diviner?"

The Council always included a witch whose specialty was divination. They were, without exception, the most skilled in their craft and carried a great deal of power, both socially and magically. Though the Quigleys hadn't met the current Diviner, they were positive that none of the witches facing them now were masters of that particular craft, and the glaring absence puzzled them.

"She's away from Chicago at the moment," Hester said in a clipped tone. "And so, we require your services. Immediately."

"Immediately?" Beatrix asked, wondering if more guests were going to start filing into what was starting to feel like a very crowded parlor.

"Nearly," Hester continued. "You must start as soon as possible. These witches are very near their end, and every instant is precious. I don't think some of them will see through the year."

It was spring now, and the thought of having to discover someone's Task by the time Chicago's sidewalks were coated with snow made the sisters feel like ice had just been dropped down the backs of their blouses.

"How many witches need our assistance?" Anne asked.

"Three," Nathanial answered, holding up his fingers for emphasis.

"Three?" Violet gasped, horrified.

One witch might have been acceptable, but helping three avoid eternal unrest was impossible if they were all only a hair's breadth away from passing on.

And the Quigleys had no experience whatsoever advising witches who were trying to discover their Tasks. It was not a topic of conversation that typically arose in the tearoom, and they doubted whether they were in fact the best choice when it came to helping these witches find the right path.

"Expect the first soon," Hester said as she took her final sip of tea and set the cup delicately on the table. Their meeting was clearly coming to a close. "We'll be checking in now and again to be sure that things are progressing accordingly."

"There is the final matter," Nathanial added, his gaze sharpening.

"Oh yes," Hester replied, as if eager to be reminded. "If you fail to identify the Tasks of these three witches, I'm afraid we must close your shop."

The room became so cold that clouds formed when the sisters gasped.

"Close the shop?" Anne finally managed to ask. "But why?"

"Consider it a test of your abilities," Hester said. "Witches who share secrets about the future must tread carefully. People take your advice to heart and often make important decisions based on what you read in the leaves. And since we can't have seers who aren't equipped handing out suggestions as if they were pieces of toffee, we have a responsibility to curtail your influence if you prove to be too weak to rise to the challenge."

Anne wanted to question their judgement and demand more answers, but one glance at their stern expressions was all she needed to know that the words waiting on the tip of her tongue were useless. They wanted the Tasks of these witches completed, and if the Quigleys failed, the doors of the Crescent Moon would be permanently closed. She wasn't sure how they would go about it (forbidding the witches in the city from giving them business, releasing a plague of rats into the pantry, and encouraging the humans to build a new street right through their front parlor were all definite possibilities), but if the Council members decided to destroy the shop, there was no doubt in the Quigleys' minds that it would happen and in the most emotionally painful way possible.

The only thing that Anne, Beatrix, and Violet could do to save themselves now was find a way to help these wayward witches avoid their own unfortunate fates.

"Succeed or perish," the third witch, who had been silent for the entire conversation, murmured, his voice taking on the texture of scratched glass.

"Precisely, Isaac," Hester said, that unnerving smile stretching across her face once more.

Before this ominous declaration had finished echoing across the room, the only reflections that the Quigleys could see in the mirror were their own.

Their meeting with the Council had reached an end.

"Well," Violet said, pausing to take in a deep, shaky breath. "We're doomed."

Anne reached for the tea to pour herself a cup and gather her nerves.

But as she tipped the spout downward, she found that the pot was entirely empty.

CHAPTER 5

A Leafless Tree

Suggests some sort of family conflict.

"I hardly think this is the end of the world," Anne reassured her sisters as they settled around the kitchen table, each with a strong cup of Earl Grey tea in hand.

After the Council had faded from the mirror's reflection, they'd all taken a few moments to collect themselves.

Anne had drifted toward the kitchen to make them all more tea. Beatrix had pulled out a clean sheet of paper to write down every word the Council had uttered, and Violet had abandoned her seat to pace up and down the hallway, which only made her more anxious and did nothing to calm the poor house. All of the gas lights from the first floor through the third were flickering unceasingly now, and a curiously acidic smell was rising from the basement cellar.

Tabitha, who'd been trying to nap under the proving drawer, had abandoned them without hesitation as soon as they entered the room, slinking out of the kitchen and toward one of her favorite burrows in the attic.

But now the Quigleys were all back together and ready to discuss their next course of action. Though Violet seemed like she was going to spring from her chair at any moment and Beatrix had such a tight grasp on her delicate saucer that the broom and dustpan inched a bit closer, ready to sweep up any porcelain that might fall to the floor.

"No, only the prelude to our own personal apocalypse," Beatrix sighed as she released her cup and pulled at the chain of her spectacles.

"Now who's being dramatic?" Anne muttered.

"I don't think she's overreacting in the least, Anne!" Violet exclaimed, giving in to her greater instincts and leaping from her chair to prowl about the room. "Helping three witches figure out their Tasks is no small feat."

This, at least, was something that Anne could agree with. The trouble with unveiling someone's Task was that it involved considering the past, present, and future all at once. Untangling the Tasks of three individual witches was going to be difficult, indeed, and in order to prevent everything from getting knotted, the sisters would need to focus.

"We don't have a choice," Anne replied. "Not with the shop at stake."

The Quigleys became quiet, each struck by the thought of losing the Crescent Moon. Without the shop, it was unlikely they'd be able to make a living. The house was theirs, of course, but their parents had only left them enough of a nest egg to fill a swallow's burrow. They'd put it all toward the shop, and though their clientele had certainly grown, the sisters hadn't saved enough to see them through the foreseeable future if the front door was abruptly nailed shut. And then what would they do?

These worries were interrupted, however, by the sound of a soft knock on the back door.

"Katherine," the Quigleys said in unison before they turned around and saw a cloaked figure who smelled of sage and frankincense step into the kitchen.

To their dismay, their friend looked a bit older than her age that night. She leaned more heavily on her cane and hunched forward to support a velvet bundle that was thrown over one shoulder. It didn't help matters that her lips, normally turned upward in a cheerful grin, were pinched together.

"Won't you take a seat?" Anne asked as she rose and touched one of Katherine's arms to lead her toward the kitchen table.

"And have a cup of tea?" Beatrix inquired.

"Or a biscuit?" Violet echoed.

Katherine sank into the chair that Anne pulled out for her but waved away their offers of refreshment.

This was an ominous sign indeed.

"I must tell you three something of great importance," Katherine finally said, her voice as hard as granite. "I'm afraid it is a very serious matter."

"Is this about what happened earlier today?" Anne asked, hoping to shed some light on Katherine's odd reaction.

Katherine nodded and replied with a sigh. "When I looked at you this afternoon, Anne, I saw a spell reflected in your eyes. You are cursed."

For the second time that evening, the Quigleys were struck into silence.

"Cursed?" Violet finally managed to say. "How is that possible? Wouldn't we have noticed it before?"

"I believe that it's a settling curse," Katherine explained. "One that is cast on a child. The spell lays dormant until some kind of inciting incident sets everything into motion. This one must have been crafted by a very talented witch, because I had no sense of it until this afternoon when I looked at you, Anne, and saw the shimmer reflected in the back of your eyes. It's very faint now, like shining a light at a cat in the darkness, but it's there. And growing stronger by the day, I suspect."

"I don't understand," Anne said, her words becoming rough. "Why would someone have cursed me when I was just a girl?"

At that, Katherine's face hardened even more, and she took a moment to rub her temple before continuing.

"But that's the trouble," Katherine said. "It's not just you."

The sisters' gazes flickered to one another as they began to put the pieces of this bleak picture together themselves.

"You're *all* cursed. I can see it in the windows to your souls," Katherine said as she gestured toward their eyes. "And if I'm guessing correctly, as I normally do, I don't think you have much time before it takes full effect."

"How much time?" Beatrix asked as she tugged at the chain hanging from her spectacles.

"Settling curses typically come to fruition on an occasion that's meaningful to the affected individual," Katherine replied. "Since this spell was cast when you were just children, the witch performing the enchantment would have to pick a day that they knew would be important to you throughout your whole lives. A day when your magic opens up just enough to let something else in."

"Our birthday," Anne murmured, her heart beating so rapidly in her chest that she worried it would loosen the clasp on her watch.

"Yes, that's when I believe the curse will build to its full strength," Katherine agreed.

"But that only leaves us until the end of autumn!" Violet cried.

"Can you sense what the curse will do to us?" Anne asked, her mind jumping to all the horrid possibilities.

"I'm afraid I have my suspicions about that as well," Katherine answered with a sigh as she tugged open the velvet bag and pulled out a small wooden box.

A marigold was carved on the top and painted with bright yellow and orange brushstrokes. As soon as Katherine set the box on the table and an earthy floral scent seeped through the cracks and into the kitchen, the Quigley sisters realized they had seen it before. It looked so foreign now that it wasn't sitting on their mother's dressing table surrounded by satin ribbons and delicate glass vials of perfume that smelled of summer flowers.

"When you were very young, your mother began asking me questions about my magic. She wanted to know about curses," Katherine began. To the sisters' ears, it sounded like the first line of a fairy tale from one of the books that were gathering dust in the attic. "In the beginning, it was just a comment or two, and I thought she was merely curious. Witches are often that way when it comes to their friends' crafts. But soon, I could tell that her interest was rooted in something more serious. And I began to sense that she was afraid."

"Why was she frightened?" Anne asked, moving to grip each of her sisters' hands in her own.

"I tried to persuade her to tell me," Katherine continued. "As her questions became more detailed and I could see that something was weighing heavily on her mind, I begged her to share the burden so that I could help. But all she ever revealed was that she needed to make sure you three would be together. That you would have a choice."

"She was worried that we would be separated?" Beatrix asked, trying her best to keep her voice steady, though she was shaking with fear.

"When your mother abandoned the coven to be with your father, she left quite a few disgruntled witches behind," Katherine replied. "Many were envious of her talents to begin with and then resentful that she decided to cast them aside. They believed that with her seated on the Council as Diviner, the city would be a safer place for our sort. And then she had you all at once. The first set of Fates that they had seen in generations."

Fates were three seers who were sisters born at the same time, and witches believed that they carried a special kind of ability to reach into the future. Their mother had been careful not to mention anything about it when they were younger, but Anne, Violet, and Beatrix had caught their customers whispering the term on more than one occasion.

"I began to suspect that your mother was worried someone had woven a curse to separate you three, either as an act of vengeance against her for leaving or to ensure that her power did not become too great." Katherine paused to collect herself before moving forward. "But then Clara's questions stopped abruptly, and the dark circles under her eyes faded away. She seemed so free of worry, just like in the days when she first met your father, and I assumed that she had accepted there was nothing to be concerned about. Now, I see that I was mistaken."

"So you believe the curse is trying to pull us apart before our next birthday?" Anne asked.

"I do," Katherine replied. Then she rested her head between her hands and held it there, as if the weight of what she'd shared was too heavy to bear.

"Well, that explains the visit from the Council, doesn't it?" Violet said as she smacked her hands across the table and began to pace back and forth along the floorboards.

"What visit from the Council?" Katherine asked, her head snapping up so rapidly that Anne and Beatrix nearly jumped.

"They were just here," Anne explained. "They've told us that we must help three witches identify their Tasks before they pass on. And if we fail, they'll close the shop."

"Oh dear," Katherine said, her face growing paler. "It seems that the curse is surfacing with a vengeance. I've only known of the most experienced of seers being able to uncover someone's Task. And after a great deal of time and effort. This is a strange request indeed."

"What's to be done?" Anne asked. "How can we stop the curse from taking effect?"

Katherine averted her gaze, and Anne's heart sank.

"Is it impossible?" Anne whispered.

"Not impossible," Katherine said. "But I won't tell you that it's going to be simple. Curses are complex and temperamental, and to be completely honest, there is very little that I can do to help you when it's had so long to settle into your souls. You are the only ones who can figure out how to untangle it."

"So, there's a chance?" Beatrix whispered.

"Yes, child," Katherine said as she reached forward and placed a palm over Beatrix's trembling hand. "There is always a chance. And if you three have even a drop of your mother's determination, I know we have reason to hope."

"What needs to be done?" Anne asked as she straightened in her seat, steeling herself for the challenge ahead.

"It's not like checking off a list," Katherine warned them. "This type of magic doesn't follow a clear set of steps like when you make a potion or ask a broom to fly. It's about assessing your instincts and deciphering which are your own and which might be tethered to the curse. One of the most important things you can do, though, is try to resist the curse and find out why it was put there in the first place."

With that, Katherine lifted the lid of the marigold box and carefully withdrew a leather-bound journal.

"This was your mother's diary," Katherine said as she pushed the book toward the sisters.

Beatrix was the first to lean forward and touch the worn surface. As soon as she did, a flood of memories that had nothing to do with magic caused tears to pool in the corners of her eyes. Eager to start feasting on the words between the covers, Beatrix flipped open the book and looked at the first page.

"It's blank," Violet said, her tone heavy with surprise and disappointment.

"No," Beatrix murmured as she ran a finger along the page and felt the barest pulse. "It's enchanted."

"Very good," Katherine said with a nod. "Your mother must have purchased the pages from a very skilled word witch. The sentences are hidden beneath the surface, and you'll need to coax them out."

Word witches specialized in writing, and though they focused their talents on stringing words of their own together, they didn't mind occasionally helping others put pen to paper as well, especially when someone needed to keep what they had written from prying eyes.

"That sounds like just the job for you," Anne said as she turned to give Beatrix a faint smile.

"After your father died and your mother knew she didn't have much time left, she brought the diary to me and said to give it to you when I thought the time was right," Katherine explained. "It was the only other instance she mentioned her desire to keep you together. Now I realize that she might have saved something in here to help guide you. If you can decipher the writing, you may be able to learn more about who cast the curse."

"Is it possible there's anything else like this left in the house?" Violet asked. "Could she have hidden any other clues?"

The house, startled that it had so suddenly been shoved into the center of their conversation, swished the curtains in the kitchen closed. The sisters knew that their home would help them if it could, but it had the habit of keeping certain objects tucked between bedroom walls and forgetting that it had moved them there to begin with. If their mother had left them any other clues, it would be some time before the house remembered.

"It's certainly not an impossibility," Katherine replied.

"Then that's my chore," Violet said as she clapped her hands together.

The house shuddered at the prospect of Violet tearing through its neatly stacked linen closet and taking a hammer to its freshly polished floorboards.

"And what does that leave me?" Anne asked as she turned toward Katherine, eager to hear that there was something more tangible they could do to keep the curse at bay.

"Keep the shop open," Katherine answered. "If the Council is threatening to close the Crescent Moon, I suspect that losing it could be the catalyst for you three to separate. So, you'll need to do your best to discover the Tasks of the witches that they send your way."

Anne nodded, happy that the shop might prove to be the key to seeing them through another challenge, as it had when the loss of their parents was still fresh and unfamiliar. Lost in thought, she picked up her empty teacup out of habit and let her eyes flicker to the bottom, where the dregs of her Earl Grey awaited.

And when Anne's gaze finally focused, she felt the blood drain from her face.

"Everything is going to be just fine, my dear!" Katherine said as she patted Anne's hand. "I will do what I can. You might not have access to the coven's social networks, but I certainly do. And I'm going to do everything I can to get a sense of the larger picture here."

"We can't express how much we appreciate that, Katherine," Anne finally said as she set down her teacup and slowly shifted her gaze from the dregs.

"It's the least I can do after all the joy your mother brought me," Katherine said as she rose from the table. "Please send word if you uncover anything, and I'll be sure to do the same."

The sisters followed Katherine to the back door, embracing her as they said their goodbyes.

"Remember!" Katherine called out as she stepped over the threshold. "Reflect on your instincts."

The sisters watched as their guest made her way along the path of moonflowers that the garden had sprouted to guide her back to the street before turning to one another.

"This has been quite an eventful evening," Anne sighed as she shut the door and heard the lock click into place.

"Do you really think we can do it?" Beatrix whispered as she wrapped her arms around her sisters' waists and pulled them closer. "Can we break the curse in time?"

"We don't have any other choice," Violet murmured. "We can't be torn apart."

For a moment, the three sisters stood with their foreheads pressed together, just as they used to do when they were children and the shadows in the attic seemed to take on a fearsome life of their own.

Then they heard the grandfather clock chime, and they knew it was time to leave that moment behind and embrace the next.

"I think I'm going to rest upstairs," Anne said, unable to face the dirty dishes stacked in the front room. They'd need to be handled early in the morning, but for now, everything could stay where it was.

"If that suits you best," Violet replied as she moved toward the door that opened next to the stairs. "I'm planning to dig through the attic to see what I can find up there."

The house drew in a breath at that, causing all the curtains on the windows to pull inward.

"And I'll start looking through this," Beatrix added as she ran a finger down the diary's spine. She was eager to see what secrets she could find nestled in those yellowed pages.

"Don't overtire yourselves. Remember we have a long way to go," Anne warned as she grabbed her empty teacup from the table. If her sisters had been paying closer attention, they might have noticed the way she held the cup so that the leaves were shielded from view.

Violet and Beatrix nodded in agreement, but Anne knew she'd likely find them sleeping across an old stack of bed linen in the attic or atop the desk in the study when the sun rose the next morning.

But she decided not to say any more about it and gave them each a kiss on the cheek.

And with that, the sisters said their good nights as they went their separate ways for the evening, their voices echoing through the house like the fading notes of a lullaby.

CHAPTER 6

A Closed Book

Hints that a secret is being kept from you,
or you are keeping secrets.

Whenever Beatrix shut the door to the study, she experienced a sense of relief. The room wasn't much larger than the pantry, and it was stacked so high with books and records that Beatrix couldn't stretch her arms backward without hitting a pile of papers. But it was the only space in the house that was truly her own. She was tongue-tied in the front parlor and a disaster in the kitchen, but at her desk with a pen in hand, Beatrix could be herself.

Gazing down at her mother's diary, though, she didn't feel quite so alone. It was like having a living, breathing person sitting across from her, waiting patiently for a conversation to begin.

The trouble, as it so often happened with Beatrix, was that she hesitated.

Here, at this very desk, her mother's words were waiting to be uncovered. It was the gift she'd been silently wishing for—a chance to talk with her once more, to reach across the bars of death and touch her spirit. But as Beatrix's fingers grazed the corners of the cover, she wasn't sure if she was ready.

What if her mother's diary ripped open the wounds that Beatrix was still stitching back together with her own words?

Releasing a shaky sigh, Beatrix reached into the pocket of her apron and pulled out a folded envelope. Though the Council's calling card had certainly been the most shocking piece of news, it wasn't the only surprise waiting in the mailbox that day.

Beatrix had already opened the envelope and read the pages that waited inside, but she wanted to look at them again and assure herself that what she recalled was in fact a memory rather than one of her fantasies. After unfolding the paper and pressing it flat against the desk, Beatrix allowed her gaze to soak in the letters that had been pressed onto the page with a typewriter:

```
Dear Miss Beatrix Quigley,

We have had the opportunity to read your story
and are pleased to say that we would like to
publish it as soon as possible. At your earliest
convenience, would you write back and let us
know when you might be able to come to the office?
We believe that your writing is going to capture
the attention of our readers and would like to
discuss future possibilities.

Sincerely,
Mr. James Stuart
Executive Editor—Donohoe & Company Publishing
```

Here, at last, was a sign that her work might be worth reading. The sheer satisfaction of it set her heart racing, and the house tried its best to expand the room to give her more space to breathe, though the position of it made the task difficult.

But as the initial wave of exhilaration started to ebb, Beatrix shifted back to the hard truths of her situation. What business did she have going to see a publisher about a short story when she and her sisters had just discovered they were cursed? Yes, they had several months left before the effects fully set in, but what right did she have to dream about seeing her writing in print when she faced the possibility of being separated from Anne and Violet? Her cheeks flushed with guilt at the mere thought of feeling joyful when sorrow loomed so clearly on the horizon.

No, as Beatrix almost always determined, it was best to wait and take the matter as slowly as possible. And when she managed to help her sisters break the curse, she'd reconsider the matter of publishing her writing. Of course, it was unlikely that Donohoe & Company would be forgiving and agree to reconsider printing her piece, not after she'd taken so long to get in contact again. But perhaps that was for the best. After all, wasn't it more thrilling to linger in the possibilities and avoid having to trim daydreams into something that better fit the frame of reality?

And so, Beatrix carefully folded the letter in half and tucked it back in her apron pocket, along with any intention of ever stepping through the threshold of the publishing house.

As soon as her hand left the envelope, though, the diary on the desk shifted, causing Beatrix to jump and hit the back of her head against a box overflowing with receipts. It was a small movement that inched the book just a bit closer to Beatrix's outstretched hand, but it was enough to give her quite the start.

Carefully, Beatrix reached toward the cover and flipped it open. Once again, she was confronted with a blank page, but after a few moments of concentration, she could see something dancing beneath, like goldfish shimmering just under the surface of a moonlit pond. Catching this hint of magic gave Beatrix just the dash of curiosity she needed to continue.

She'd learned early on that books and paperwork didn't react well to force. They needed to be coaxed to reveal their secrets, and so she began chanting to the diary, mostly conversational words and compliments, but there was a spell or two laced in here and there as well.

For enchanted objects, like people, prefer to take their poison with a dash of sugar.

Beatrix's patience was soon rewarded, and as she persuaded the words to reveal themselves, they climbed onto the page, becoming clearer and clearer as the rhythm of her speech steadied and a single paragraph took shape:

> Today, the house surprised us all and opened a room on the first floor that has been locked for five years now. I believe it used to be a space for the housekeeper to go and make sure that the budgets were balanced, but when the girls were born, the door suddenly sealed up. I suppose the house got a glance at the children and decided it needed to keep at least one place to itself. But this afternoon, Beatrix decided to test the knob, and then it clicked open. I don't have plans for the new room, but I suspect that the house has its own ideas in mind. And to think that Beatrix was the one to discover it! She may be the most quiet of my three, but there's a wealth of wonder beneath those brown eyes. And I believe that's the most beautiful part of her yet to be shared.

Beatrix stilled as a tear fell from her cheek and onto the page. When the water hit the paper, the words swirled and then disappeared into the drop, as if someone had pulled the stopper of a drain. Frantically, she flipped through the diary to see if the sentences had slipped onto any of the other pages, but they were all blank.

Leaning back on her chair, Beatrix relished what she had managed to uncover and the feeling of her mother's pride. One of Beatrix's greatest regrets was that she hadn't started writing until after her parents had passed. As a child, she'd spent countless hours curled up in the corner with a book, and though it felt like absorbing the stories of others was helping her build toward something important, Beatrix hadn't figured out what that was, exactly, until they were gone. And now her parents would never know that Beatrix had finally found that she had something to say.

Her hand dipped into her pocket again, pulling out the envelope and unfolding it next to the blank diary.

Her mother wouldn't want her to wait. Of that, she was certain.

Without a trace of hesitation, Beatrix pulled out a fresh piece of stationery and began to pen a letter, one that was addressed to Donohoe & Company.

✦

Two floors above, Violet was pushing back the loose strands of her hair while she tossed around lost treasures in the attic. The house had tried to lure her back to the kitchen by lighting a fire in the hearth and infusing the hallways with the scent of caramel corn, but all its efforts were for naught.

When Anne was rattled, she was able to find peace by pouring piping hot tea and talking with her sisters. By the end of the conversation, whatever had been twisting her into knots was unraveled, and she was able to move forward. Beatrix couldn't convey what was troubling her through speech, but after a few hours of scribbling in that notebook, her shoulders always seemed to relax, and some of the grief faded from her eyes.

But Violet was a creature of action, and she'd never managed to find a way to work through her feelings that didn't involve burning the edges of a pie or breaking half the cups in the pantry. The walls seemed to close in on Violet if she lingered for too long in a single room, and though the house was doing its best to accommodate her by adding an extra inch or two of space here and there when neither Anne nor Beatrix was looking, it never seemed big enough to contain her.

"Medusa's curls!" Violet cursed when she tried to tug a pile of velvet curtains from the mountain of curiosities stacked to the rafters and sent the whole jumble tumbling to the floor. Most people would have begun at the top and worked their way down, but Violet was more inclined to reach right into the mess of things and see where the pieces fell.

Stepping back to avoid the worst of the wreckage, Violet's boot caught against the leg of an infant's cradle and sent her crashing to the ground. She laid there for a moment, wondering if any part of her was seriously injured, before turning her head to the left and spotting a flash of red and white stripes from within the depths of an upturned trunk.

Pushing aside porcelain dolls and picture books, Violet finally unearthed what rested beneath the worn remnants of her childhood: the carousel that had enchanted them that magical evening so long ago. Funny that she had remembered it for the first time in years only to find it so unexpectedly.

Unable to help herself, Violet turned the gear in the back and waited for the horses to gallop around the rafters as they had before. But they stayed fixed to their gilded posts, unmoving.

It seemed that the toy had lost its magic.

Violet tossed the carousel roughly on top of the upturned trunk and cast spell after spell, trying to get the horses to fly and recapture what it had felt like to hear her parents' laughter entangling in a duet. The sound of it had faded from her memory, and she so desperately needed it back.

Finally, Violet gave up and knocked the toy off the trunk, the chimes and bells within tinkling a rusty tune when it hit the floorboards.

Not for the first time, Violet realized that she was angry. So, so angry and frustrated with her mother for knowing how everything would end and choosing the path of sorrow anyway. Clara had cherished the thought that loving their father would be as easy as breathing in a fresh burst of spring air after a long winter, but she had known that choosing him would mean her death and that she'd be leaving behind three daughters to pick up the pieces on their own.

Their parents' love story always took on an idealistic hue when Anne or Beatrix reminisced about the past, but it wasn't the same for Violet. She couldn't quite accept that love always overshadowed sorrow, and it kept her from relishing the rare instances when she did remember the scent of her mother's perfume or what it felt like to hold her hand as she sung them to sleep.

Suddenly, a cheerful melody intruded on Violet's thoughts, shifting her attention toward the dormer window that looked out onto the garden.

It was the same tune that had once spilled from the carousel, but it wasn't coming from the toy.

Curious, Violet rose and stepped to the window, pushing the pane open to poke her head into the night air. The song was stronger now, its notes as crisp and clear as the midnight breeze brushing against her cheek. And in the music, she heard the strangest underscore, a murmuring noise that didn't quite fit with the harmony.

Taking in a deep breath, Violet caught the scent of warm apples and sawdust.

And then she remembered the circus. Again, images of lion tamers and ribbon dancers filled her mind, pushing out the dark hues of her bitterness and replacing them with flashes of vibrant color. The tent was only a walk away from the shop, and it was so late in the night now that Violet wouldn't be missed.

But how could she consider going to see a show at a time like this?

Snapping her focus back to the mess of memories that still needed to be sorted through in the attic, Violet sighed and closed the window with a click. She didn't intend to go looking for distractions beyond the Crescent Moon when she managed to find so many already without even stepping over the threshold.

But later that night, after Violet had worked herself into a state of blissful exhaustion and fallen asleep on a long-forgotten mattress in the corner of the attic, her dreams were laced with the scent of sawdust and the same steady melody.

✦

Back in the family parlor, Anne was staring down at her now-empty cup, tilting it this way and that to get a new perspective on the dregs that were nestled at the bottom.

She'd managed to carry it upstairs without attracting the attention of either Violet or Beatrix. Though that wasn't surprising considering how quickly they'd been lost in their own thoughts. For once, Anne was grateful that her sisters always managed to slip into distraction.

"Oh dear," Anne sighed as she glanced down at the leaves, which were now cold and starting to dry around the edges.

When Anne had looked at the bottom of her cup during Katherine's visit, she'd found something that made her eyes widen in surprise. For the very first time in her life, she had caught a glimpse of her own fortune.

And in the hours since, she'd settled into her chair in the parlor and tried to interpret the signs that had emerged from her tea.

A rabbit and an owl.

The first bespoke of a change for the better while its neighbor warned against embarking on a new venture.

What a jumble of juxtapositions. Near but far. Temporary yet enduring. These were the suggestions that emerged from her leaves as she swirled what little liquid rested at the bottom and saw them transform into new shapes.

Not for the first time that evening, Anne wished that her mother were there to help her understand what was happening. When she was a child, Anne believed that there wasn't a single problem that couldn't be solved by simply waltzing into the kitchen and asking her mother for an answer. And when she'd passed, Anne had done her best to serve that same role for her sisters, who never listened as carefully as she did during their lessons and still needed to be reminded that dream tea could only be brewed under the light of a blue moon or what it meant when a heart was crossed by a hare. Though Anne thought she had filled her mother's shoes well enough in this respect, there were moments that her confidence wavered.

As she looked down at the bottom of her cup and tried to make sense of the signs that rested there, Anne felt like she was nothing more than a pale copy of Clara Quigley.

She was sitting on the edge of her seat now, ready to rise from the chair and tell her sisters the news. But she never got around to lifting herself from the cushions, and her eyes remained fixed on the shapes that marked the white porcelain.

When her sisters learned that Anne could read her own fortune, they would believe their fate was set in stone. A seer looking into her future was an impossibility reserved only for birthdays, and so they wouldn't be able to help but view Anne's newfound ability as a sign that the curse was growing in power. Something important had clearly been knocked off-kilter.

She'd always been the most stable one of the three. When they were younger, Anne's mother had often told her, "Violet has her head in the clouds, and Beatrix's nose is in a book. But your feet are always planted firmly on the ground." After the deaths of their parents, Anne had found her mother's words echoing in her thoughts more and more. Like the cogs in her watch, she knew that all three of them were essential to the shop. But as the years had worn on, Anne felt like she was the one tasked with remembering to wind the gears to keep everything running smoothly.

Her sisters needed balance and security, not more problems that threatened to pull them apart.

As Anne's gaze shifted from the cup to the fireplace, she couldn't help but acknowledge that there was something else lurking beneath her concern for Violet and Beatrix . . . curiosity.

When they'd sat at the kitchen table as children hovering over cups of leaves as their mother taught them how to make sense of scepters and sparrows, Anne was always the first to piece together the signs. It had come as naturally to her as finding the shape of a hippo in the clouds, and at first she'd relished shouting out the answers before her sisters had a chance to work through their own puzzles. But when she'd realized that Violet and Beatrix might never catch up, Anne had purposefully taken longer to answer, pulling back her own abilities so that they could be in step with one another yet again.

And she'd been more than happy to do it . . . then.

A wave of guilt washed over Anne as she remembered what her first thought had been when she'd seen her fortune earlier that evening.

Finally.

Somewhere underneath layers of responsibility and love for

her sisters, she'd hidden the desire to kindle the power that had so excited her during their divination lessons as children. But it had been there all along, this thirst to keep pushing herself beyond a boundary and see just how far she could go.

And the thirst was growing stronger, just like the curse.

Shaking now, Anne turned back to her cup and shifted the handle here and there in the hopes of discovering a new truth tucked somewhere at the bottom.

"I'm going to fix this," she whispered to herself.

Though it hesitated a moment, the house soon clicked the lock on the door. No one would glimpse Anne as she leaned into the forbidden.

The sound echoed through the parlor like the caw of a raven harkening change that lurked just beyond the shadows of sunset.

CHAPTER 7

A Saw

*Warns that you should expect trouble
from strangers.*

"But should I consider his proposal?" Anne's customer asked
later that week, her hushed question barely perceptible
above the voices of the other women in the shop. Marshall Field's
was having a semiannual sale that afternoon, so the ladies were
surrounded by the goods they'd managed to pilfer from the department store. The shop was full of tissue paper and the sound
of vigorous debates about who had struck the best bargain.

The enchantment that Anne had laced into the special tea for
the day also helped stir the conversations that were growing between their customers. It was a white peony blend that loosened
the lips of strangers, and Anne noticed that the clients who'd
decided to order it were now leaning toward neighboring tables
with warm smiles on their faces.

Glancing about, Anne couldn't help but think that the woman
sitting across from her looked like a pigeon in a cage of macaws.
Mrs. Stephenson was a middle-aged widow whose gray blouses

and skirts were as unchanging as a bishop's frock. Recently, she'd focused most of her readings on trying to sort through her feelings about a man, to the shock of the Quigleys, who—though they knew everyone hid certain parts of their lives, even from themselves—were shocked that the wispy, temperance-touting Mrs. Stephenson had perhaps found herself a match.

"You know I'm not in the business of telling customers what they should do," Anne replied. "And I imagine that a woman of your experience has the right to make these kinds of decisions based purely on her own personal desires."

"Oh, I wish you hadn't used that word," Mrs. Stephenson whispered as a scarlet blush started to stain her thin, pale face.

"What word?" Anne asked, confused.

"'Desire,'" Mrs. Stephenson hissed, becoming redder than the strawberries that garnished the top of her pastry.

"Mr. Stephenson has been gone for a rather long time now, hasn't he?" Anne asked.

Mrs. Stephenson nodded but refused to meet her eyes.

"And I'm sure he wouldn't mind you seeking out companionship, especially with your own children now grown and on their own," Anne suggested.

"Oh, is there a way you can ask him about it?" Mrs. Stephenson inquired, perking up a bit at the thought of reaching beyond the veil for her dead husband's counsel.

"No, unfortunately, communing with the spirits is not our line of work," Anne said firmly.

Calling on those who had passed on was a complicated craft. Only the witches who practiced death magic could commune with the spirts, the poor souls unable to move into the afterlife. Since humans didn't have Tasks, they ended up caught in this in-between space more frequently, unable to feel the closure that they needed to know with certainty that their time had been well spent. And witches who practiced death magic were some of the wealthiest among their coven as they were always in high demand among the humans, who were willing to keep quiet about the occasional floating candle or rattling piece of furniture if it meant they had a chance to speak to their loved ones again.

But even witches with death magic couldn't talk to those who'd fully crossed over, which was why the Quigleys had never called on their services. The sisters' parents had so much time to accept their fates that it was a certainty they'd moved on.

"But you can recommend someone who could help in that respect?" Mrs. Stephenson pressed.

"I don't believe that would be for the best," Anne sighed. "The choice to marry again isn't Mr. Stephenson's in the end. It's yours and yours alone."

Mrs. Stephenson seemed to ponder this for a moment and then said, "But the ladies at my club would find it absurd. He's almost ten years younger than me!"

"Yes, but I see that he truly feels for you and wants to live the rest of his days by your side," Anne said, lifting the tea leaves and running her fingertip just above the fortuitous signs that she'd found resting there. "If it is love and companionship that you want, Mrs. Stephenson, he is most certainly your match."

At that, a nearly imperceptible grin began to tug at the side of Mrs. Stephenson's cheek, and Anne knew which way the winds of Fate were going to blow for her.

"I'll consider it," Mrs. Stephenson said stiffly, all business again.

She rose from the chair, and Anne followed her to the front door.

"Oh, the sweet aroma of young love," Violet sighed happily into Anne's ear as they watched Mrs. Stephenson step into the cool April breeze, which the house did its very best to keep from drifting into the shop.

"Mrs. Stephenson is no spring chicken, Vi," Anne chuckled.

"It still counts as young love if she's never felt this way about anyone before. When it comes to the language of romance, our Mrs. Stephenson is still on her first primer," Violet argued. "And it's high time she finds herself some affection, since that's what she wants. Why, when she came into the shop a few months ago and started asking about her Mr. Mortemore, I saw a horse galloping along the rim of her cup."

"Vi! Don't tell me you told her what *that* means. Her heart might have given out!" Anne exclaimed, thinking about how a woman of Mrs. Stephenson's sensibilities would react while listening to Violet explain such a sensual symbol.

"Of course I did. You can't think that I would pass up an opportunity like that," Violet replied. "And, I'll have you know, Mrs. Stephenson's heart did not give out. Quite the opposite, in fact. I thought our iced scones were going to melt by the time she was done listening to my predictions. Why do you think she's stuck with him for this long, hmm?"

"I suppose everyone deserves to have some amusement," Anne agreed, though her words were laced with skepticism.

She was grateful to have a moment of lightheartedness after the last few days. Since the Council's visit and Katherine's revelation, the sisters had been trying to return to their normal rhythm while taking stock of what to do next. But they felt stalled, waiting for the Council to make their next move while trying to decipher their mother's diary, dig through the attic, and keep the shop running.

The bells on the door chimed, and Violet's eyes filled with dread.

"Medusa's curls," she cursed under her breath just as Anne turned around and saw the witch on the Council who'd been tangled in layers of tattered shawls walk through the door. Anne shivered at the memory of the icy tingles that had crept down her spine as she watched her from the other side of the mirror. Now that they were standing in the same room, Anne couldn't help but notice that Hester was much taller than she had first expected, and the feeling that the witch was looking down on them from above was unnerving.

"Good afternoon," Hester said as her eyes flitted across the parlor. "I see that business is treating you well today."

She reminded Violet of a vulture who had just landed on a branch and was surveying the brush beneath for its next prey.

"Take care of the customers while I speak with her," Anne whispered to her sister as she gave her a quick push, hoping that the witch wouldn't cause a scene. They'd needed to use their day lily biscuits only once to get a human to forget something they'd seen, and Anne didn't want to break open the tin a second time.

"There wasn't a need to send your sister away," Hester cooed after Violet had returned to her table and Anne moved closer to the door, where they were less likely to be overheard. "I've only stopped in for a moment."

"How can I help you?" Anne asked, straightening her spine so that she felt as tall as possible.

"By uncovering the Task of the first witch," Hester replied with a grin. "Who will be stopping by at exactly five o'clock."

"Five o'clock?" Anne gasped.

The shop wasn't supposed to close until six. Even if they shoved all their customers out onto the street right that instant, the Quigleys would only have an hour to prepare all the divination tools they needed. Once again, the Council had placed them in a seemingly impossible situation.

"Is that going to be a problem?" Hester asked, clearly pleased at Anne's discomfort.

"Not at all," Anne replied stiffly. "We will manage."

"Very well," Hester said, her tone suggesting that she'd been hoping for a different response. "If we can be of any service, please don't hesitate to let us know."

Anne doubted that she or her sisters would be reaching out anytime soon.

"Of course," she replied instead, boldly opening the shop's door for the witch.

"You are the most stubborn of the three, aren't you?" Hester said as she slipped onto the street, so softly that Anne wasn't certain she was meant to hear her.

But before Anne could think to ask her what she meant, the witch had already turned a corner and disappeared from sight.

✦

"But that's too soon!" Violet cried when Anne told her the news a few moments later in the kitchen. "We can't possibly get them all to leave in time."

Anne had managed to pull her sisters aside and ask Franny and Peggy to tend to the customers, though they wouldn't have long before people started asking where the Quigleys had slipped off to.

"We don't have a choice," Anne sighed, pressing a hand to her temple, where a fierce headache had grown since she'd greeted Hester at the door.

Shaken, the sisters went about the task of closing the shop, and after plenty of persuasion, their very last customer was scurrying onto the street, her arms heavy with boxes of Violet's strawberry shortbread.

"Leave the parlor for Franny and Peggy to clear," Anne said with urgency as she walked toward the very back of the front room, where the walls were covered in thick velvet curtains the color of forest moss. "We need to get things ready for our visitor. The witch could arrive at any moment."

Pulling back the heavy fabric, Anne revealed an ornately carved door with hundreds of symbols etched along its surface. Violet and Beatrix joined her, and they all whispered a quick greeting, which caused the runes to glow and the door to creak open of its own accord.

The sisters walked through the threshold, taking a moment to check that the house hadn't made any changes since the last time they'd been there.

Circular in shape, the room was lined completely with shelves that stretched from the floorboards to the slightly uneven ceiling. They were teeming with books, decks of cards, runes, feathers, vials filled with a variety of substances (some of which were crawling within their glass prisons), bundles of dried flowers, several bags of salt, and, to the sisters' surprise, Tabitha, who was sleeping on the table in the center of the divination room next to an ornate crystal ball.

"How in Hecate's name did Tabitha get in here?" Anne asked as she stepped toward the table and inspected the creature, who hadn't batted an eye at the sound of their arrival.

"That will likely remain one of life's great mysteries," Beatrix sighed as she gently nudged Tabitha awake and off the table. The cat gave Beatrix's dangling spectacles a halfhearted swat but eventually relented and sauntered out of the room, turning around at the door to cast a disapproving gaze in the sisters' direction before slipping away.

Anne sighed and got to work setting things up for their first witch. They didn't know what form of divination would be required, so all their equipment needed to be readily on hand.

Normally, the sisters had a sense of what kind of craft was necessary for a given customer. Tea reading was obviously their specialty, but they were trained in the other arts as well. And each individual case required a certain method. Just as a bitter oolong was the perfect blend for one customer but distasteful to another, so were the different types of divination practices that the sisters could utilize. It was all about finding the best fit for a certain situation.

"Let's start with the basics and move outward from there," Anne suggested as she reached for a set of tarot cards. "Tea first, and then the cards. Hopefully, we won't need to do anything beyond that."

As she and Beatrix finished moving the crystal ball from the table to the shelf, Violet, who had quickly found an excuse to escape the cramped room, reappeared, pushing a cart of hot tea and biscuits. Somewhere on her path from the kitchen, she'd acquired a purple ribbon that had fallen from a customer's package and tied it around her head in an attempt to restrain her fringe. If they ended up trying to read the witch's fortune in the coals, she didn't want to risk getting singed again. Though a few of the shorter strands were already starting to make their way out of captivity.

"Please tell me that you had a chance to make a batch of soothsaying shortbread," Anne said. Aside from being delicious, the recipe was designed to help those who consumed the buttery treats become more connected to their subconscious.

"Yes, though it was difficult to keep them away from Peggy," Violet replied. "Has anyone knocked yet?"

Just as these words left her lips, they heard the shop's bells chime.

By the time they reached the doorway, an elderly gentleman had already let himself into the front parlor, where he stood with his hat in hand looking around as if wondering whether or not he was in the right place. He was a gangly fellow, so thin that one blast of Chicago's winds would certainly knock him over, with wispy white hair clinging to the sides of his head by the grace of the Goddess. A pair of spectacles were perched on the very tip of his nose and magnified his eyes, which were full of uncertainty.

"Welcome," Anne said, stepping forward to greet their guest. "You must be the witch that the Council has sent to us."

Startled, the man took a step back and nearly lost his balance.

"Yes," he finally said after taking a moment to survey the sisters. "They have sent me."

He looked none too happy about it either, but the Quigleys suspected that anyone so close to passing on without completing their Task wouldn't exactly radiate enthusiasm, so they brushed his reaction aside.

"If you'll let me take your coat," Anne said as she approached the man and helped him out of the long garment that seemed to weigh down his slight frame.

Most witches wore an enchanted coat or cloak when walking the streets of the city. It helped mask their magic while they were moving among humans, who weren't always the most observant but sometimes sensed that something was just a dash . . . off. Anne wouldn't be able to tell what kind of powers their guest had been gifted with until after he'd slipped out of the thick woolen garment.

Once free of the coat, their guest's powers shone bright, and the sisters froze.

This witch specialized in death magic.

It was absolutely shocking that he'd failed to identify his Task, not when witches of his sort witnessed firsthand the consequences of failing to cross into the afterlife.

"Please, come this way," Beatrix finally whispered as she extended her hand toward the back room, where candlelight beckoned through the partially opened door.

Silently, the witch followed the sisters, his pace slow and, if the sisters didn't know any better, rather reluctant.

"If you could take a seat here," Anne said, gesturing toward one of the four chairs around the table. "Please excuse us for not knowing your name. The Council hasn't given us much information, to keep us from making any premature assumptions, I'm sure."

As the witch took his seat, the earthy aroma of chrysanthemums filled the room. It wasn't a sweet odor, but Anne recognized it instantly, thinking it was an odd choice of cologne for the reserved and serious individual who sat before them.

"Oh, yes. I'm sure that's the reason," Violet muttered under her breath, which granted her a swift poke in the back from Beatrix.

"I'm willing to supply whatever details are necessary," the witch said after a moment's hesitation. He took off his spectacles and nervously began cleaning them with a handkerchief. "My name is Crowley. Capricious Crowley, though I beg of you not to use my given name."

The sisters wondered if that was because he didn't like it or he would prefer they not get too familiar with one another.

"First things first, can we offer you a cup of tea?" Anne asked, already moving her hand toward the pot perched on the cart.

"Oh, no," Mr. Crowley said. "I don't like tea."

An awkward pause saturated the room, and the sisters tried and failed to keep themselves from turning toward one another with horrified expressions.

"But, Mr. Crowley," Anne finally said. "We are tea readers."

"Yes," the witch said, fiddling with a gold signet ring on his left hand while his gaze flitted about the room, avoiding the Quigleys' desperate faces. "I did worry about that when I saw the sign outside."

"Are you sure it isn't a particular blend of tea that you find distasteful?" Beatrix asked, skeptical that someone could rule out tea as a general category altogether.

"No, I am quite certain," Mr. Crowley replied.

"Well, tea isn't our only option, thankfully," Anne said diplomatically, trying to keep the session on track.

Mr. Crowley didn't seem reassured by that statement, however.

"I'd hate to put you through the trouble," he said, his eyes wandering toward the door.

"It's no trouble at all," Anne insisted, confused by the man's attitude but determined to plow forward nonetheless. "Before we settle on the best method of divination, let's get a few particulars out of the way."

"When did you approach the Council about your difficulty?" Beatrix asked, trying to get a sense of when the witch had realized he hadn't completed his Task.

"I wasn't the one who reached out to them," Mr. Crowley replied, huffing in annoyance. "It was my family. They suspected what was happening to me and thought it would be a good idea to alert the proper channels."

"And when did *you* realize what was happening?" Violet asked, leaning forward, which made the witch inch back until he was as far away as he possibly could be without moving his chair.

"Oh, I suppose when the ravens started to flock around the house. They are persistent animals, and it took a very long time to get them to leave," Mr. Crowley replied.

The sisters exchanged what they hoped were subtle looks of concern.

Ravens meant that the witch was very close to his Time. He was likely already getting visits from the Reaper, even. He wouldn't see the end of the year, leaving him precious little time to identify his Task, let alone complete it. The thought made the sisters' toes clench with worry.

"Would you like a piece of shortbread, Mr. Crowley?" Violet asked, practically waving the plate of biscuits beneath their guest's nose.

"Thank you," he answered primly, turning his face away. "But I must decline. My family has me on a very strict diet now that they believe I'm going to waste away as a ghost for all eternity."

"Understandable, I suppose," Violet said with open disappointment as she bit into a biscuit of her own.

"Now, before we begin," Anne said, hoping to start the session in earnest. Obviously, there wasn't a moment to waste in Mr. Crowley's case. "Could you tell us anything about your situation that might be useful? What did you believe your Task was before the signs started to reveal themselves? Do you have any clue about what it could be?"

Mr. Crowley was quiet for a minute but eventually said with a dash of hesitation, "I believed my Task was to take over my father's business. And I did so successfully, or so I thought."

"Don't worry, Mr. Crowley," Anne assured him. "We'll do our absolute best to help you discover your true Task."

Their guest did not look pleased by Anne's declaration and hunched a bit deeper into himself, as if hoping the movement might allow him to disappear from the situation altogether. And after several hours of trying to get a sense of Mr. Crowley's future in the spreads of several decks of cards, through the smell of dried rose petals, and even among the ether of their great-grandmother's crystal ball, Anne, Beatrix, and Violet began to feel the same way. None of the signs were coming together to create a cohesive narrative, leaving the sisters with a scattered set of impressions that were impossible to connect. It felt like trying to make a clear picture from puzzle pieces that they'd poured from different boxes.

"I appreciate all the help that you three are offering, but I'm afraid it's getting close to my next appointment," Mr. Crowley said in the same polite yet firm tone one might use with a department store clerk who was taking more time than necessary to wrap a package.

"This is very peculiar, Mr. Crowley," Anne said with feeling, thinking about what the Council was going to say once they learned that this first meeting hadn't been a success. "Finding an appropriate method of divination for a client normally takes minutes, not hours. But I'm still certain that we'll be able to discover your Task. We will devote ourselves to the cause, I assure you."

Mr. Crowley merely nodded and began to rise from his seat, obviously in a hurry to leave the shop.

"We'll be sending along some treats to your home tomorrow afternoon," Violet said as she helped the witch into his coat. "You must take them as prescribed in order for our next session to be successful. They should encourage you to become more familiar with your subconscious thoughts. A few odd dreams might make an appearance after you eat them, and you should keep a journal of any fantasy or visceral images that arise as you sleep."

"Yes, erm, I shall try," Mr. Crowley said doubtfully. "As I said, my family has me on a strict diet."

Before the sisters could impress upon him the importance of following their directions, the witch had slipped out the door and was hastily walking down the street, as if trying to get as much distance between him and the shop as possible.

"How odd," Violet commented as they watched him through the open door. "You might think that he doesn't want to figure out what his Task is."

"Nonsense, Vi," Anne scoffed. "Why would someone want to doom themselves in that way? No, he's clearly nervous about the whole affair."

"And it's a point of pride among witches who deal in death

magic to be prepared. I'm sure this is an embarrassing predicament for him and his family," Beatrix added. "We must try to be sensitive."

"I am being sensitive," Violet said pointedly as she closed the door. "As sensitive as one can be when they've been on their feet all day, anyway."

"It is getting late, isn't it?" Beatrix sighed as she fiddled with the chain of her spectacles.

Tomorrow was the only day of the week that the doors of the Crescent Moon remained closed, but that didn't mean Beatrix had no plans.

"It's a bit too late to rest in the parlor, I suppose," Anne said sadly as she glanced down at her clock and started listing all the tasks that she'd need to complete the next morning. Though she preferred to let her sisters and the house rest on the days when they didn't have to tend to customers, someone still needed to take care of the bits and pieces of the business that had been shoved to the side all week.

Since she wanted to keep a roof over their heads, Anne was more than willing to take on the extra trouble, especially if it helped them resist the curse. But she couldn't go without sleep, and so, as much as Anne wanted to warm her feet next to the fire and let the rhythm of her sisters' voices lull her away from the worries of the day, she knew there wasn't time for simple pleasures that evening.

Violet's bones ached as well, though she suspected her body wouldn't let her rest for very long if she went to bed.

"Do you think the Council will be angry that we weren't able to discover Mr. Crowley's Task tonight?" Beatrix asked as they shifted toward the stairs.

"I don't expect they'll be pleased," Anne answered honestly. "But uncovering a witch's Task isn't easy. I doubt even the city's

Diviner could piece it together in one session, so they shouldn't be too surprised."

"Next time will be better," Beatrix said with a nod, wanting to end a day full of disappointments on a hopeful note.

"I'm sure of it," Violet added, leaning forward to give her sisters a final embrace.

As the Quigleys said their good nights and wandered up the steps to their beds, they managed to leave some of their troubles on the first floor and weave together rosier thoughts for the future.

But though they could blind themselves to a growing sense of unease, the house was not as easily tricked. It felt their discontent and knew that the source of it was different for each sister. Letting out a shaky sigh that rattled the shutters, the house tucked itself in for the evening and sank into unsettled dreams about what the days ahead might hold.

CHAPTER 8

A Heart

*Appears just before an instant and
thrilling connection.*

It wasn't Violet's feet that were leading the way, but her ears.
That cheerful circus tune had been whispering to her all
week, lacing her dreams with the scent of caramel apples, pop-
corn, and sawdust.

Each night, she expected to fall asleep the instant her head hit
the pillow. Since learning about the curse, Violet had spent every
moment of her evening hours digging through piles of mementos
and stacks of family heirlooms. Moving around iron bedposts and
oak trunks was strenuous business, and by the time she washed
the dust and grime from her hands and face, her muscles were so
sore that drifting into a steady slumber seemed inevitable.

But that song was stuck in her thoughts, swirling round and
round like the toy carousel that Violet had so carelessly shoved
to the floor.

The night after their disastrous encounter with Mr. Crowley
was even worse since Violet didn't have any time at all to work

herself into a physical state of exhaustion in the attic. Now her mind and body were wound tighter than a top, and a midnight walk was the only remedy.

At first, she'd followed her familiar route toward the market, where the stalls would be tucked up tight for the night. But the farther she walked, the more Violet began to drift toward the lake, her footsteps falling to the tune of the rhythm that'd been dancing through her thoughts for days. Even the streetlamps seemed to flicker in harmony with the silent but deeply felt song.

And when she finally turned the corner that would bring her in full view of the docks, Violet was startled by the sight that winked back at her from the darkness.

Strings upon strings of red and white paper lanterns encircled a circus tent, where a good-sized crowd of spectators mingled among the outdoor stalls and engulfed the ticket booth, eager to save their spots for the show that would soon be taking place inside. Under the full moon, the circus took on a fantastical appearance, shimmering against the night sky like a nocturnal mirage.

"What's this all about?" Violet heard a bystander ask as she stepped onto the circus grounds.

"It's the midnight show, my good lady!" a loud, jovial man dressed in a colorful patchwork suit replied, his voice so inflected that the words nearly came out as a song. He was very round and wore a tall, battered top hat but exuded confidence, as if he had a secret that would change all the world for the better. In his hand he carried a roll of tickets like a lasso, ready to ensnare anyone who dared wander too close.

"Will it start soon?" Violet asked, stepping toward the man.

"Yes, indeed!" he replied, his fingers already ripping a ticket from the roll. "Everything begins at the stroke of twelve, and that's only a few minutes away. Better get in there now and grab a seat."

Violet told herself that it would be best to turn around and walk back home right that instant. She couldn't spend the rest of the night watching a circus show, not when she should be shifting through the attic.

But she found herself reaching for her purse, nonetheless.

"Oh dear," Violet sighed, realizing that she hadn't bothered to bring her bag. And she didn't have a single coin tucked in the pockets of her dress.

"What it is?" the ticket master asked, his bushy eyebrows pushing together in an expression of concern.

"I haven't any money with me," Violet explained. "I was only expecting to step out for a moment."

The ticket master nodded and started to walk away, but he seemed to catch sight of someone over Violet's shoulder and quickly retraced his steps.

She turned her head to see who might be standing behind her, but all Violet caught was the coattails of a man with dark curls who quickly disappeared around the corner of the tent.

The ticket master glanced around to make sure no one was standing too close to hear them and then leaned forward to whisper, "Go on and take it. You can pay me back next time you come."

"I couldn't," Violet said on impulse. "I don't know that I'll be coming back at all."

"Something tells me you will," the ticket master said with certainty and a wink. "Now go on before anyone sees us."

It was on the tip of Violet's tongue to refuse again, but her hand shot out almost of its own accord and grasped the strip of red paper before the words could leave her mouth.

"Thank you," she said instead with a grin, which the ticket master returned with a smile of his own and a tip of his top hat.

"Be sure to get a good seat," he insisted before turning on his heels and walking up to the nearest group of people who were wandering closer to the lights, like moths drawn to a flame.

Pulling aside the tent flap, which had been left hanging rather than being pulled up to show off what lay inside, Violet stepped through the red and white fabric and walked straight into a lucid dream.

Towering candelabras encircled the ring and radiated out into the stands, casting the tent in flickering shadows. Violet could only catch glimpses of the other spectators, but she could tell by the warmth of their bodies and the hushed but ever-present chatter that the seats were very nearly full. The light of the flames occasionally caught against their eyes, which were turned toward the ring, fixed on a pair of contortionists who were performing a slow dance with sparklers that cast odd shapes against the back of Violet's eyelids whenever she blinked.

She watched as their bodies twisted into impossible positions, the sparks of light causing their figures to emerge from the darkness at the most striking moments, emphasizing the odd but somehow elegant angles of their torsos.

Until suddenly the sparklers and the candelabras flickered out, all of them extinguished at the same moment by invisible hands.

The crowd murmured in anticipation, and Violet stumbled toward an empty seat in the front row. For a few moments, the tent was veiled in darkness and filled with only the sound of the bemused spectators, but then that now-familiar tune unfolded, starting as soft as a whisper and then shifting into another kind of melody, one that reminded Violet of lazy summer afternoons that slipped effortlessly into twilight.

And then, something opened at the very top of the tent, allowing a perfect circle of moonlight to shine through the darkness. It landed on a man dangling from a trapeze that was drifting ever so slowly toward the ground. Though he wasn't swaying upside down, the performer's peaceful expression reminded her of the

Hanged Man in the tarot, a figure who was waiting for the next chapter to begin, suspended patiently in between. His strands of glossy black hair and the spangles of his onyx-tinted costume caught the moon's rays, giving him the appearance of being covered in midnight raindrops.

Violet's skin felt warm as she took in the sight of him hovering in the air. He was as mesmerizing as a meteor shower, and as she continued to stare, the man's eyes drifted down and seemed to meet hers. Though Violet told herself that it was impossible for him to see her in the shadows, the way his mouth tucked upward into a playful grin made her feel like he was looking at her and her alone.

But before she could shift deeper into the darkness, the man lounged gracefully across the bar and began to murmur a song that wove into the tune that had already been playing, the sound drawing her even closer.

His voice was low and raspy, as if he were singing while sitting at the edge of a window, where he expected to remain alone and undisturbed, but the hushed quality of his delivery made the audience lean forward, eager to capture every word.

> *"Where do dreams fade into sunshine?*
> *When do moonbeams give way to day?*
> *Even when my eyes are open,*
> *My thoughts always stray*
> *Back to bookmarked places*
> *That stay tucked within my mind.*
> *I live my life in sleeping hours*
> *Where night and day entwine."*

When the man's feet touched the sawdust and he whispered the final word of his song, dozens of chandeliers suspended across the tent suddenly came to life, revealing an entire cast of performers who were standing still, as if frozen in place during a particularly fantastical moment of their acts.

Violet felt as if her own heart were pausing, trying to match the sudden shift in time that was playing out before her eyes.

But then, the music changed again, ever so subtly picking up in pace, and one by one, the circus troupe came alive, statues breaking free from their bronze and plaster chains.

A juggler stretched his legs like a rusted wind-up soldier and began tossing his props in the air. The crowd gasped when the edges of his clubs burst into flames and he continued his act, as if the fire were fifty feet from his face rather than a hair's breadth.

When the very last of the clubs had come alive with light, a group of performers who'd been dangling from ribbons slid down the copper silk streams, as if waltzing with the fabric. The bottom edges of their tethers soon caught fire, and they ran up the ribbons and leapt onto new ones that appeared just as they were about to reach the ceiling.

As soon as their hands grasped the waiting silk, a flock of ballet dancers dressed in clouds of gold tulle shook themselves awake and began to fly across the ring. When they made a full lap, the chandeliers flashed, and the rest of the performers stretched out of their stillness and started to show off their own talents.

The tent was a patchwork quilt of sparkles, song, and imaginative wanderings of the type that Violet normally only witnessed in her deepest dreams. Her eyes were restless, flitting from the lion tamer to the acrobats to the puppeteer and back and back and back, not wanting to miss a single moment.

But she found her gaze always returning to the man with the mischievous smile, who was now flying across the top of the tent through crackling rings of fire with the ease of a child swaying gently on a swing.

Though his act was not as ostentatious as the illusionist who was transforming frogs into night flowers or the twirler whose batons were drawing fiery spirals against the shadows, there was a quiet, controlled grace about his movements that kept Violet from glancing away for longer than a few moments.

The music began to fade ever so slightly, opening enough space for a single soft voice to be heard amidst the snapping sparklers and crackling flames.

"We now invite the audience to join us in the ring!" the smallest of the ballet dancers called, her announcement echoing through the tent like a wind chime.

The crowd rustled, clearly tempted to stand and wander closer to the creatures who had so captivated them but fearful of the fire that could quickly catch the hems of their coattails and petticoats.

As if in response to the nervous sensation that was sweeping through the crowd, the flames dancing from the edges of the props vanished and reappeared in the candelabras nestled along the edges of the ring. The performers were now moving in a sea of shadows, the dark shapes of their bodies revealed in patches as the fire flickered atop the candles.

"Don't be shy, ladies and gentlemen," the dancer said, though Violet could no longer see where she and her flock of ballerinas were in the flames and moonlight.

Emboldened by the shadows and the air of secrecy that they cast across the tent, the spectators began to rise from their seats and drift toward the ring. They didn't rush, as eager children might, but instead moved with the slow and slightly unsteady pace of sleepwalkers in the midst of a particularly soothing vision.

Violet found herself doing the same, lifting herself from the wooden bench and being pulled toward the center of the tent.

Unsure of where to go but determined to be a part of the chaotic beauty, she wandered about, stopping here and there whenever she caught sight of a dancer twirling through a moonbeam or felt the fur of an animal's coat brush against the back of her hand.

And somewhere between the juggler and the flock of ballerinas, Violet had the sudden urge to look up.

When she lifted her face toward the top of the tent, she saw that she was standing directly under the trapeze artist with the playful grin and laughing eyes, who was in mid-swing, his bar so low to the ground that she thought he was going to crash right into her.

Raising her arms to ward off the blow, Violet felt a pair of strong hands wrap around her outstretched wrists and found herself being lifted straight from the sawdust. The force of the movement pushed the purple ribbon from her head, along with several pins, and she felt the heavy weight of her hair whip across her shoulders and down her back.

She screamed, but her cry was lost among the music and the appreciative claps of the crowd below. Her fingers dug deeper into the man's arms, searching for some kind of purchase amidst a swirl of terror, and scraped against the fabric of his costume. As she pressed her face into the side of his forearm, her nose filled with the scent of fireside smoke and brisk evening air.

But suddenly she was sitting upright again, the bar now steady beneath her and rising ever so slowly toward the top of the tent, as if someone in the rafters was pulling it upward. And when she lifted her chin, Violet found herself staring once again into a pair of laughing dark brown eyes.

"What were you thinking?" Violet hissed as she clung to the

rope and leaned away from her handsome companion, hoping to put some distance between them. She refused to act as if they'd stumbled into each other at a ball and were making polite introductions. By now, her momentary fear had given way to a desire to gain control over the odd situation she'd stumbled into. "I could be killed dangling up here!"

Surprisingly, the mischievous-looking stranger wasn't taken aback by Violet's outburst. In fact, he seemed quite pleased by it, his grin widening even further.

"My name is Emil," he said, their faces so close that Violet couldn't help but notice the way his smile softened his face. "Won't you tell me yours?"

"Why did you pull me up here?" Violet asked again, ignoring his question and the amused glint that caused his eyes to twinkle.

"You wanted to fly," Emil said matter-of-factly, as if the answer was obvious.

"Excuse me?" Violet asked, flustered and confused.

"I watched you," Emil said. "Your feet never stay put on the ground."

The fact that Emil had been observing her so intently should have made Violet feel embarrassed, but instead, she was shocked to find that it pleased her. And this realization only served to fuel her frustration.

"That doesn't mean I want to be dangling so far above it," Violet spat, her breath stopping for a moment when she dared to look down at the figures below. Her grip tightened on the rope at the sight of it.

"But you do!" Emil cried. "I'm the same. We can't find any rest down there, where everything is so still. Our peace comes from being able to move freely."

With that, he threw his feet up, causing the bar to start swaying back and forth, as if they were sitting beside each other on a porch swing instead of suspended dangerously high above the crowd.

The movement took Violet by surprise, and on impulse, she clung to Emil and tucked her face against his chest. She'd never been this close to anyone but her sisters, and yet a curious and unmistakable sense of familiarity had taken hold of her as soon as her cheek brushed the curve of his neck and she felt his hand press against her lower back, trying to steady her as the bar swayed. The sensation of touching his warm skin sent a wave of heat from the base of her spine all the way down to the tips of her toes, causing them to curl in her boots.

Shocked by her response, Violet pushed Emil away as much as she dared. She still clung to his forearm, and his free hand was wrapped firmly around her waist, but there were a few inches between their torsos now, which gave Violet just enough distance to take in a deep breath.

"You see," Emil said as he continued to swing the bar back and forth. "We're the same."

Violet looked down at her own feet and realized that she'd started to subconsciously sway her legs in harmony with his, as if she weren't terrified at the thought of crashing to the ground.

Angry that her body seemed to be growing comfortable dangling at the top of the tent beside a charming stranger, Violet tried her best to hold her feet still, rejecting her ever-present desire to move. But they still twitched, unwilling to stay in one place.

"Let me down," Violet demanded.

"If that's what you want," Emil said with a shrug, lifting a finger toward someone in the shadows.

The bar started to sink to the ground, the movement steady but fast enough that Violet found herself pulling so close to Emil that she could feel his laughter against the side of her face.

"Won't you tell me your name?" Emil asked as they descended into the crowd of skipping ballerinas and sparklers. Violet felt his hands tighten ever so slightly around the smooth curve of her waist, like he didn't plan to let her go until she told him.

But as soon as their feet touched the sawdust, he released his hold, giving Violet the space that she needed to lift herself from the bar and step onto the ground once more.

"I certainly will not," Violet replied as she wiped her palms against the sides of her dress, as if the movement would help her brush away the tingling sensation that ran over her skin whenever he spoke. "You had no business pulling that trick, and I won't reward you for it."

"Then I'll have to come up with something to call you myself," Emil said as he playfully leaned forward on the bar so that their lips were suddenly separated by no more than a whisper.

"I don't think that's necessary considering we won't be seeing one another again," Violet huffed, but she didn't move, refusing to be the one who backed away first.

At that, Emil chuckled, the heat of his breath dancing against Violet's lashes. Again, the smell of fireside smoke seeped into her senses, and Violet could feel blood rushing to her cheeks.

"What?" Violet asked, frustrated by his obvious amusement.

"You'll be back," Emil replied, his tone as strong and certain as Violet's when she was reading someone's fortune.

"You can't know that," Violet murmured.

"But I do," Emil said, his eyes twinkling with delight.

They remained like that for a few moments more, locked in a silent battle of wills that, for once, Violet wasn't entirely sure she wanted to win.

Somewhere behind Violet's shoulder, a pair of cymbals smashed together, bringing her back to reality with a start.

Not bothering to say goodbye, Violet grabbed a handful of her skirts and ran toward the tent flap as quickly as her boots could carry her, weaving through the maze of ribbons and waltzing couples. She didn't even turn around to see if he was still watching her, and her stride kept that quick, even pace until she crossed over the threshold of the Crescent Moon.

The house moaned at the sudden intrusion, shaking the curtains on the windows and pulling them tighter as a child does when their parent tells them it's time to greet the day. But it was too tired to take much notice of Violet, whom it was accustomed to seeing out and about at odd hours of the night.

As quietly as she was able, Violet climbed the stairs, shook off her cloak, and slipped between the sheets of her bed, closing her eyes tight and willing her body to sleep.

And it finally did, her muscles relaxing and allowing her to drift into a deep slumber.

But in those moments between wakefulness and dreams, Violet still felt the heat of Emil's hands on her waist and tasted the scent of cinders.

CHAPTER 9

A Hat

Signals success.

*J*ust as the first rays of sunlight began to brush against the windowpanes the following morning, Beatrix tiptoed downstairs, trying her best to avoid the squeakiest of floorboards. She knew which spots on the staircase were creaky, but the house was changeable and, perhaps more concerning, prone to being playful whenever one of the Quigleys tried to walk through the halls undetected. Like a young terrier, it enjoyed nipping at their heels first thing in the morning, hoping to grab hold of their attention after hours of sleepy silence.

Luckily for Beatrix, the house was preoccupied with unfolding some tulip blooms in the garden and decided to let her pass by unbothered. It was still rattled by the sense of uneasiness that had slipped from the sisters' conversation and into the floorboards the evening before, but the bright yellow and orange petals were cooperating so well that it preferred to embrace distraction for a little while longer.

Though the sisters were early risers (Beatrix by natural inclination, Anne by necessity, and Violet by sheer persuasion), it was still well before the time they normally opened their eyes on the only day of the week the Crescent Moon remained closed.

But this was not an ordinary morning, and Beatrix had a special errand to attend to before her sisters woke up.

Putting a gloved hand in her pocket, Beatrix made sure that her letter from the publisher was still there. Only two days after sending her response, she'd received another message in the mail from Mr. Stuart confirming the date and time of their meeting.

Over the past week, she'd nearly changed her mind so many times that the wastebasket in the study was overflowing with crumbled pieces of stationery marked with her apologies. But every time she picked up her pen and began to write: *It is with my deepest regret that I must cancel . . .* , her mother's diary would shake, pulling her attention away from the sense of anxiety that was welling in her chest and toward some sort of story that brought a smile to her face.

As Beatrix draped a cloak around her shoulders and stepped out into the cold morning air, she tried to focus on remembering the words she'd seen rise to the surface of the page. Though the diary never revealed more than a paragraph at a time and preferred to skip around rather than share the narrative in a linear order, it captured the texture of her mother's voice perfectly. And slowly, Beatrix was starting to remember what it was like when Clara was there to wrap her in a warm embrace and tell her not to always fear the worst.

She could practically feel her mother's arms around her shoulders as she stepped off the streetcar and found herself standing in front of a commanding brick building with the name Donohoe & Company etched above its doors.

What seemed like hundreds of glass windows peered down at her, whether it be in judgement or invitation Beatrix wasn't entirely sure. They made her feel small and inconsequential, and a knot of fear gripped her right in the stomach.

But the words that had emerged from the diary—*there's a wealth of wonder beneath those brown eyes*—gave Beatrix just enough courage to pull the heavy wooden door forward and slip inside.

Taking in a deep breath, she gazed around the lobby, which was full of desks but empty of people aside from a lone figure sitting toward the back of the room.

As she stepped closer, Beatrix couldn't help but notice that the young man was thin framed and tired, from either working through the night or arriving much too early. His hair was slightly longer than was fashionable, and the severely bent angle of his neck suggested he was in the habit of arching over his writing desk for hours on end.

When Beatrix first started walking toward him, he had been staring at a stack of papers with deliberate focus, but once he heard her footsteps, his eyes snapped up and filled with surprise.

"Hello," he said, his voice friendly even though it was rough from lack of sleep. "Can I help you?"

"I'm here to see Mr. Stuart," Beatrix replied softly, cursing herself for whispering when she needed to make a good impression. As she cast her gaze down toward the desk, she noticed a small plaque buried beneath overturned books and piles of pages that read: *Editorial Assistant*.

"Miss Quigley?" he asked, his eyes widening a fraction.

"Yes," Beatrix replied as she wrung her fingers together in agitation.

"Wonderful!" he exclaimed, pushing himself away from the desk in such a rush that he sent his pile of papers flying to the floor. "I can't tell you how eager I've—I mean we—have been to meet you in person."

Startled by this sudden exclamation, especially from someone who had looked so exhausted only moments before, Beatrix took a step back.

"Oh," she finally managed to say. "I hope I'm not too early."

The assistant followed her gaze around the empty room.

"Not at all," he said quickly, obviously trying to reassure her. "Mr. Stuart always prefers to speak with his most important authors before the others get here, when it's quiet and he can focus."

That certainly gave Beatrix pause. Had there been some kind of mistake? Surely, the publisher didn't consider *her* a writer of any importance, not when he'd only read just one of her short stories.

"Give me a moment, and I'll let Mr. Stuart know you've arrived," the man said before shuffling down a hallway.

Beatrix could hear his pace quicken once he was out of sight. This was odd indeed.

"She's here?!" a voice boomed from down the hall. "Why didn't you tell me?"

Beatrix braced herself as she heard a door slam shut and footsteps pattering closer and closer.

Finally, a stout man emerged from the hallway with the assistant following close behind. Beatrix could only assume that the person barreling toward her was Mr. Stuart, the executive editor. He'd taken off his jacket, which gave the impression that the day had already become too busy for him to endure an added layer of clothing. He also wore a pair of small spectacles that somehow made his face look even rounder, and his brows scrunched toward the lenses, as if trying to hold them in place.

"Miss Quigley!" he cried in his thundering voice as he walked straight up to Beatrix and grabbed her hand in a firm grip, shaking it so wildly that she worried the movement would cause her own spectacles to slip from her nose.

"I can't tell you how excited we are to meet you in person," Mr.

Stuart said as he continued to shake her hand. "Please, come right this way, right this way."

The three shuffled toward one of the private offices down the hallway in a swirl of boisterous greetings and compliments.

Finally, Beatrix found herself sitting across from Mr. Stuart, who had to push several stacks of papers aside so that they could speak to each other over his desk.

"Miss Quigley, I must tell you that I'm normally very reserved when it comes to vetting new authors," Mr. Stuart began. "Poor Jennings can tell you how many submissions we turn away every year. He's the one that reads through the work first, and let me tell you, most of it ends up in the rubbish pile."

The assistant gave Beatrix a shy smile, and she was surprised to find herself wanting to return his grin. But before her lips could so much as twitch, Mr. Stuart's voice snapped her attention back to him.

"Donohoe & Company has been in business for quite some time now," Mr. Stuart continued. "We have offices on both sides of the country and a London branch. Our expectations are extraordinarily high, and we accept only the best of the best."

The words were rushing out of Mr. Stuart's mouth so quickly that Beatrix had difficulty keeping up or predicting where this conversation would lead.

"But from the moment my eyes glanced over the first page of your story . . ."

Here Mr. Stuart paused, to either take a sorely needed breath or allow himself an instant to revel in the memory.

"I couldn't put it down! In all my years, I've never had that kind of reaction. Interested—oh, yes, I've been interested. Engaged to the point of needing to read something quickly to discover the end, even. But with your story, I couldn't find it in myself to put it down—quite literally! Poor Jennings can tell you that I sat in this chair the entirety of the afternoon, rereading it and enjoying every single word. All at the expense of my other appointments for the day, which has never happened in all my years here!"

"That's very kind of you to say, Mr. Stuart," Beatrix said, a bit taken aback by the editor's enthusiasm. Was she not supposed to suffer at the mercy of ruthless publishers? Where was the crippling sense of rejection and failure that she had been certain would come from her initial attempts at submission? It was as if she had overslept and was merely walking through a fantasy of her highest hopes and expectations.

But confusion and disbelief were soon overshadowed by excitement, and she found herself gripping her hands together to keep them from clapping.

"And you haven't even given us a novel yet," Mr. Stuart continued.

At that, Beatrix froze.

"A novel?" she asked, stunned.

"Of course!" Mr. Stuart cried. "Your work is riveting, and I expect our readers will swallow it whole when we print it in one of our monthly journals. But what the people want nowadays is novels! And once they've gotten a taste of your writing, they'll expect nothing less. Tell me, do you have an idea for a book?"

"Well," Beatrix replied, her mind instantly filling with all the intricate plotlines she'd fleshed out in her notebook. "Yes, I suppose I do."

"Then I want it!" Mr. Stuart exclaimed as he slapped a palm against his desk, causing Beatrix to jump. "And I'm willing to pay you handsomely."

When he told Beatrix the exact sum he had in mind, her mouth dropped open.

"You're willing to pay me all that? For a book?" she asked, her voice barely above a whisper.

"That's just the advance," Mr. Stuart said. "Once you deliver the manuscript, we can start talking about royalties. But I know a good thing when I see it, Miss Quigley, and I refuse to let another publisher catch you."

"That's very kind of you to say, Mr. Stuart," Beatrix murmured, still too taken aback to say much more.

As Mr. Stuart continued to rattle on about timelines and publicity, Beatrix's thoughts wandered back to her notebook. There was a seed of a plot there that she'd found herself flipping back to recently, and she wondered if it might be worth letting her characters grow beyond the restrictions of a short story.

"The end of September would give us the best chance at launching it," Mr. Stuart said, drawing Beatrix's attention back to the present.

"Pardon?" Beatrix asked, unsure of what he was referring to.

"The deadline for your draft," Mr. Stuart replied. "I'd like to have the whole kit and caboodle by then. As you finish the chapters, drop them by the office so that Jennings and I can keep track of your progress."

"September?" Beatrix gasped, alarmed by the thought of needing to write an entire book within that time.

"Is that a problem?" Mr. Stuart asked, his bushy eyebrows knitting together in concern.

"No, no," Beatrix replied, worried that her hesitation might cause Mr. Stuart to reconsider his offer. "I can do it."

"Wonderful!" Mr. Stuart said as he clapped his hands together, sprang up from his chair, and began to herd Beatrix and Jennings toward the door. "I can't wait to see the first chapters. Now, you just sit down and focus on getting this book out. The world's waiting for it, after all!"

With that, he slammed the door shut, leaving Beatrix alone in the hallway with Jennings and her whirling thoughts.

"Don't mind him too much," Jennings said after giving Beatrix a moment to catch her breath. "Mr. Stuart's a bit of a bulldog, but no one gets the job done quite like him."

"Does he really like my work?" Beatrix asked as they walked back to the lobby, which was beginning to fill as more workers started slipping in for the business day.

"He adores it, and so do I," Jennings replied. "Your work, well, it's like nothing we've ever seen before."

"You've read my story?" Beatrix asked, her eyes widening in surprise.

"I'm the one who showed it to Mr. Stuart to begin with," Jennings explained.

Not knowing what else to say, Beatrix merely nodded, a bit bewildered by the knowledge that people were beginning to read and share her work.

"Please don't hesitate to let me know if I can be of any assistance," Jennings said as he opened the front door for Beatrix and reached his hand out to clasp her own in a gentle goodbye.

"Thank you, Mr. Jennings," Beatrix said. "I appreciate your support."

"It's very easy to give," Jennings replied. "You really do have something special to share."

Flustered by these compliments, Beatrix felt a blush spreading across her cheekbones.

"Enjoy your morning," she managed to say before turning quickly away and stepping onto the sidewalk.

While Beatrix walked down the block, she lectured herself for acting so foolishly. Professional authors didn't turn the color of a ripe strawberry whenever someone praised their work, after all. But as she continued down the road and toward the cable car station that would take her back to the Crescent Moon, she stopped second-guessing everything she'd said at Donohoe & Company and started thinking about something else entirely: the first lines of a novel.

CHAPTER 10

Stairs

*Indicate that you could be moving
closer to a goal.*

When Anne woke up to the sound of metal cannisters rattling in the milkman's wagon, she had a clear vision of her day. The morning would be spent helping the house shine their set of silver spoons, which always required a bit of an extra touch because the tiny moon phases carved along their handles sometimes caught the polish. After that, she'd write out the specials for the week on paper trimmed with daffodils and hyacinths. And then, if she managed to fix the mess that Violet had made of the tins on the shelves and take note of what was running low in the pantry, she'd be able to spend the rest of her afternoon on the chore that she always saved for last because it was the most enjoyable: experimenting with new enchanted tea blends.

Though Violet and Beatrix helped prepare the magical blends when they first opened the shop, Anne had gradually taken over that task. Beatrix was always too precise, no matter the fact that the tone of the day might demand a slight variation. Her fear of making a mistake kept her from wavering in the slightest from the recipe she'd been given. Violet, on the other hand, was volatile whenever she was charged with this duty, tossing in whatever incantation came to mind without any steady magic to weave everything together. But with Anne, the blends were perfectly balanced between strength and surprise. The customers always felt more attuned to themselves and the delights of the shop whenever she mixed the tea, and so that responsibility grew to be hers and hers alone.

Today, she wanted to create a blend that would cause the person drinking it to remember their fondest memory of spring. And if she managed to complete everything on her list and check in with Violet and Beatrix about their progress with the search of the attic and deciphering their mother's diary, Anne could give herself the luxury of an hour or two of enchantment.

The thought of her sisters made Anne's shoulders tighten. Since their disastrous visit with Mr. Crowley, Anne had grown more determined in her belief that the only way to fight the curse was to resist it.

If the crashing sounds that echoed from the attic every night were any indication, Violet was doing her best to search through the house for any additional clues. But no new secrets had emerged from beneath the boards that she was starting to pry open, and Anne seriously doubted any ever would. Though the house occasionally misplaced objects of importance, Clara Quigley certainly never had. That was why she had entrusted the marigold box to Katherine, and Anne, who believed that she out of all of them had known her mother best, was convinced that there was nothing else of use to be found. Still, Violet's treasure hunt was keeping her busy, and Anne was grateful that her energy was being spent in an area of the house that was far, far away from the shop on the first floor.

Beatrix, on the other hand, seemed to be making progress with their mother's diary. When the sisters tucked into their parlor on the second floor after the Crescent Moon shut its doors for the day, she told them about the brief snippets of the past she'd been able to lure to the surface of the pages. Anne and Violet enjoyed hearing about how their mother recounted episodes from their childhood, but they had the sense that something important was lost in Beatrix's retellings. The words, which never appeared when the three were together, always vanished before Beatrix could show them to her sisters. As much hope as Anne had initially held in the diary, hearing Beatrix talk about it felt like finding an old photograph in the back of the wardrobe. It was a pleasant enough distraction from the task of folding the linens and deciding what needed mending but ultimately didn't contribute toward getting everything in order.

The best course of action now was ensuring that they succeeded in pleasing the Council and kept the shop open. Anne had faith that would be enough to push the curse into submission and allow them to stay together.

She just needed to find a way to sway the odds a dash more in their favor, and that meant adding an item to her list of tasks for the day.

Stepping lightly down the hall, Anne gently pushed open the door to Violet's room and saw her sister's wild curls peeking out from the covers. Reassured that she'd remain asleep for at least an hour or two yet, Anne then wandered down the steps and put an ear to the door of the study, where she could hear a pen scratching against paper. Beatrix was obviously already deep into her own business for the day, and she wouldn't be roused until the smell of their mid-afternoon meal started seeping into the hallway and her stomach started to growl.

Content that her sisters were preoccupied, Anne walked into

the front parlor, pulled back the heavy curtain, and slipped into the divination room.

Once again, Tabitha was stretched across the table, snoring softly as Anne went about the task of lighting candles and running her hands over the shelves, stopping every step or two to run her finger over the leather spine of a book or peer into a glass jar.

Since the night she spotted the signs swirling at the bottom of her cup, Anne's abilities had continued to grow. One afternoon, she'd caught sight of Violet's fortune in the flour that she'd left on the countertop, the white clumps forming what looked to be some kind of musical score. And whenever Anne flipped through their accounting books and happened upon one of Beatrix's inky fingerprints, she was overpowered by the same pungent odor that seeped from the city's paper factories.

She'd been holding back from trying to catch a glimpse of her own future, however. The thought of finally peering beyond her present reality made Anne hesitate. Seers weren't supposed to read their own fortunes, and there must have been a reason for that. Taking that step felt like breaking a rule.

But Anne always knew when to push aside her worries and act, and this case was no exception. They'd failed to even figure out what means of divination to use when working with Mr. Crowley. If she didn't take advantage of every tool at their disposal, the sisters wouldn't have any hope of uncovering his Task and saving the shop.

And if Anne was being honest with herself, she wanted to know just this once what it felt like to be irresponsible.

When Anne stood in front of the crystal ball, she stopped and pulled a candle closer so that shadows danced across its smooth surface. Releasing a deep breath, she closed her eyes and started to rid her mind of needless clutter. It took quite a bit of time to push aside thoughts of menus and flour sacks, but when she finally managed to do it, Anne opened her eyes and studied the crystal ball.

After a moment or two, the shapes that swirled around the center of the sphere began to solidify, merging together to create a distinct impression. Anne knew that she must be looking into the near future, somewhere closer to minutes than months or years, because the picture taking shape was sharp around its edges.

Anne saw herself gazing into the crystal ball, but her perspective was that of someone peering at her from the doorway. Resisting the urge to turn around and reassure herself that she was alone in the room, Anne kept her eyes locked on the crystal ball. And then she watched as the miniature version of herself turned away and reached for a metal cannister that was sitting on a shelf to the right. Squinting, Anne leaned forward to see what the tin looked like, but she was only able to make out tiny splashes of orange and yellow before the vision faded entirely.

Once she was certain that the image in the crystal ball wasn't coming back, Anne took a step toward the wall of cannisters, jars, and herb bundles. Her gaze flitted across the shelves, taking in all the different possibilities, but she stopped at the sight of a metal tin with tiny marigolds painted across the sides. Anne lifted the tin to her nose and caught the barest scent of dried earth and sunshine. But she didn't open the lid, sensing somehow that the time wasn't quite right.

A faint smile worked its way into the corners of Anne's mouth as she returned the cannister to its place on the shelf, gave Tabitha one last stroke across her back, and blew out the candles in the room.

They may have a curse to contend with, but Anne had a strong suspicion that the odds had just turned in the Quigleys' favor.

CHAPTER 11

A Candle

Foretells new insight or revelations.

As the days slipped into weeks and the bite of spring's chill began to soften, the Quigleys found themselves wondering if the Council was still watching them at all. They hadn't seen Mr. Crowley since that first disastrous meeting, and though they always kept their eye on the door for another visit from Hester, life at the Crescent Moon seemed to slip back into its normal rhythm.

Anne took it as a sign that they were managing to keep the curse at bay and thanked her lucky stars that nothing seemed to be changing. Her step lightened as she walked about the shop tending to their customers, and whenever they crossed paths in the kitchen or hallway Beatrix and Violet would comment on their sister's newfound playfulness.

On a particularly busy day in late spring, the sisters faced a rush of customers who were ensnared by the bright pink geraniums that winked at them from every window of the street front, giving the impression that the house was batting its eyelashes.

For hours, Anne, Beatrix, and Violet hurried from table to table, foreseeing lost treasures, healing hearts, new partnerships, and unexpected travels. Talk of daggers, dragons, and foxes caused customers to gasp and grit their teeth, while elephants, fish, and greyhounds set them laughing and toying playfully with the edges of their cloth napkins.

It wasn't long, though, before the last customer had taken her final sip and said good evening, giving the house permission to exhale a deep breath that swished the tablecloths and rattled the picture frames ever so slightly.

"Thank Hecate everyone's gone!" Violet exclaimed as she threw herself onto the nearest open seat and ran a hand through her fringe. "I thought they'd never leave."

Anne and Beatrix were about to echo their agreement when a voice emerged from the back corner of the shop.

"I'm sorry to say that isn't the case."

Startled, the sisters turned toward a wingback chair that faced the hearth.

It was on the tip of Anne's tongue to say that the shop was closed for the evening, but then the figure sitting in the chair rose, revealing their unexpected guest.

A willowy woman with a headful of gray hair barely contained by a loose chignon stood before them. She wore a simple white dress that they couldn't help but notice was stained with dirt on the sleeves and hem, as if she'd merely taken a break from her gardening to grab a glass of water from the house. When she took a step closer and shook out her skirts, the sisters caught the rich scent of rosemary and thyme and instantly felt the stiff muscles in their necks relax.

It seemed that they had just been greeted by a garden witch, someone whose magic was rooted in what they could coax from the soil.

"My name is Fiona Pickwix," the witch said, stretching her hand out in greeting. "I believe the Council may have told you to expect me."

The sisters froze as they realized that she was one of the witches who still needed to identify their Task.

"I'm afraid they didn't give us any notice," Anne apologized as she took Fiona's hand in her own. She felt calluses there and knew that they'd been earned through decades of gripping a trowel. "But we're still very pleased to welcome you to the Crescent Moon."

"You can't know how reassuring it is to be here," Fiona said as she smiled at the sisters with a genuine expression of appreciation. The Quigleys released a silent sigh of relief as they came to terms with the fact that Fiona, unlike Mr. Crowley, was eager to figure out her Task and more than willing to cooperate.

"Come," Anne said. "Let's get settled and see what this is all about."

They wandered toward the divination room, where the house had quickly lit the candles and filled a pot with steeping hot water. The house normally didn't tend to tea, preferring to leave that chore to the Quigleys, but it knew everyone already felt off-kilter and that a few sips would help smooth the transition from one type of work to the next.

As soon as Anne pushed open the door, the floral scent of sweet rose tea tickled their senses, urging them to roll the knots out of their aching shoulders as they took their seats around the worn walnut table.

"Oh, this smells just like my garden when the tea roses are in full bloom," Fiona sighed with satisfaction after she settled into her chair and wrapped her long, knobby fingers around her porcelain cup.

"Why don't we start at the beginning?" Anne coaxed as she

took a sip of her own tea to steady herself. The memory of their visit with Mr. Crowley still weighed heavily on her mind. This time would need to be different if they wanted to save the shop.

"There's not much to tell," Fiona replied as she set down her cup. "I thought that I'd completed my Task ages ago. You see, when I was a much younger woman, I managed to breed a tulip with a four-leaf clover. The result was the loveliest green flower, and if you plucked it right after it bloomed, you were guaranteed good fortune for a fortnight. The first time I saw the petals unfurl, I experienced such a rush of excitement that I mistook it for my Task. I hadn't given it a thought in years, but a few weeks ago, the scent of burning brush began to follow me everywhere, and I knew I'd been mistaken. It's only a matter of time before the ravens start to come. I've heard that's the natural progression of things."

This, at least, was good news. The smell of burning brush was one of the earliest signs that a witch hadn't completed their Task, so the sisters would have more time to help Fiona. Not much, but every moment counted in situations such as these.

"Have you ever had a reading before?" Anne asked, trying to get a sense of the direction the rest of the evening should take.

"No, this is the first time I've thought to ask for one. Rather funny, isn't it, since there really isn't much of a future left for me," Fiona said, her smile waning a bit at the corners. "Is that going to be a problem?"

"Not at all," Anne reassured her. "It just means that we might have to try a few different methods first, but I have a feeling about what might work best. . . ."

Remembering the cannister that she'd discovered earlier, Anne rose from her chair and walked to the shelves, pretending to hesitate for a few moments before her hands reached for the yellow and orange tin.

"What's that?" Fiona asked curiously as Anne walked back to the table.

"If I'm remembering correctly," Anne began as she stepped back toward her seat and pried open the lid, which had been fixed closed for so long that it took some convincing to loosen, "it's—"

"Marigolds," Fiona gasped with pleasure as orange petals floated out of the tin and began to swirl about the room, dancing in a nonexistent wind to a rhythm of their own making.

Musky but alluring, they infused the fragrance of tea and sweets with an undernote of earth and sunshine. The smell instantly brought the Quigleys back to warm, lazy afternoons spent in the garden during the summer months when their parents had still been with them and life was not yet so full of responsibilities.

As much as Anne would have liked to let them all revel in the memory, she knew it was time to work. Straightening her shoulders, she blew against the petals as one might when making a wish on a dandelion and nudged them in Fiona's direction.

"Oh," Fiona gasped, her mind slipping away from the present and into the past. "This does bring me back."

The sisters gave one another encouraging glances. For when it came to their line of work, reading the past was often essential to understanding a client's future.

"And where, exactly, is it bringing you?" Violet asked.

"To my childhood garden," Fiona replied, her hands now raised above her head as she watched the petals graze against her palms and fingers, clearly enjoying the sensation. "I filled my plot with marigolds to keep the whiteflies from what I was growing."

The tone of her voice hinted that Fiona hadn't been trying to protect turnips or any other kind of commonplace plant.

"And what was that, exactly?" Beatrix asked.

"It was magnificent," Fiona replied. "Or it was *going* to be magnificent. I wanted to crossbreed a Venus flytrap with deadly nightshade. When brought together, I was certain they would create a plant that would bite anyone who passed too close and kill them within moments."

The sisters must have been unable to conceal their alarm, because Fiona felt compelled to add, "It was my intention to train them to attack intruders with ill intentions only."

The sisters nodded, not entirely convinced but wanting to give Fiona the benefit of the doubt.

"And did you ever grow it?" Anne asked.

"No," Fiona replied, her face collapsing into regret. "I was too busy with my tulips. But how I've always wanted to return to the task."

At that, the witch's eyes shot up, darting between the now-smiling faces of the Quigleys.

"My Task. It's been right there this whole time, waiting patiently for me to remember," Fiona said excitedly.

The sisters sighed as they watched the witch's face fill with hope, scattering the petals that had settled across the surface of the table. As Anne glanced down, she saw them fall into the shape of a leaf before shifting once more into the outline of a dog, a symbol of fierce protection. And she knew then that as unusual as Fiona's Task might seem, it would one day help create a safer journey for vulnerable witches trying to wander along the paths of their own destinies.

Without further warning, the witch sprang out of her seat and hurried toward the front room of the shop.

"Miss Pickwix!" the sisters exclaimed as they followed her, wondering where she was going in such a hurry.

"Thank you, girls, but I haven't a moment to spare," Fiona said, flinging on the shawl that she'd left on the wingback chair, dampening her magic before she stepped onto the street. "I've got a garden to plan and only so much time to do it. Though I still have the seeds and think it will be possible in the time I have left. I'll need to clear out the back shed, of course. . . ."

Stopping for only a second in her mumblings to give the sisters a quick wave goodbye, the witch scrambled out of the shop, slamming the door with a loud bang that caused Tabitha to hiss from her resting place underneath one of the tables.

Once the Quigleys took stock of their bearings and realized that they'd managed to succeed in unveiling a Task, a sense of relief sank into the shop, quickly followed by the sisters' gleeful cries.

"We did it!" Violet practically screamed as she clutched both her sisters in a fierce hug.

"There're still two more to go," Anne reminded them, but her tone was hopeful.

"But now at least we know what we've been asked to do is possible," Beatrix said. "Perhaps the key to breaking the curse does rest with saving the shop."

"And we've just taken a leap in the right direction," Violet laughed as she skipped around the room. The house, caught up in all the excitement, changed the colors of the walls from green to bright yellow and began playing the piano that was tucked in one of the spare rooms on the second floor. The sisters could hear the cheerful melody soak through the floorboards from above, and their smiles widened.

"How did you know to use marigold petals?" Beatrix asked Anne once their laughter began to fade. They hadn't even seen that tin in well over two decades, when their mother had tucked it away for safekeeping, and Beatrix wondered how her sister had thought of it so quickly.

"It was just a feeling," Anne replied, trying to appease her sister's curiosity while keeping her own secrets in the shadows. As she spoke the words, she could taste the unfamiliar flavor of a lie on the back of her tongue—a burnt sweetness similar to a singed meringue. "I was searching around in there the other day trying to find something that might help us with Mr. Crowley and stumbled across the cannister."

"Well, lucky that you did," Violet said as she yawned into her palm, clearly spent and ready for a full night's rest. "Shall we finish off the lavender biscuits that I left in the parlor yesterday? I want to settle down a bit before we go to sleep."

"I think that's the best idea we've had all day," Anne said as she looped her arms in her sisters' and led them up the stairs.

But though Violet and Beatrix may not have noticed Anne's lie, as the room sat empty the house began to catch a note of something strange. At first, it thought that the fragrance must have drifted in from the kitchen, but the longer its attention lingered, the more the house realized that the smell of burning marshmallows was coming from the spot where Anne had stood.

The house didn't like secrets. They darkened the hallways and caused dust to settle where it normally didn't, making the hallways smell musky and unwelcoming.

For now, it would watch and wait to see what happened, the house decided as it reassured itself that the sisters had the matter firmly in hand and all would be revealed in good time.

But as it began to close the shutters and stoke the evening fires, the walls couldn't help but wonder if it had made the right choice.

CHAPTER 12

A Rabbit

Represents having enough courage to
overcome fear.

The lilac was in full bloom now, infusing the streets with the scent of early summer, but Beatrix didn't seem to notice the shift in seasons. Though the house kept trying to push her outside for a breath of fresh air in the garden or a stroll around the block, she remained locked in her study, lost in a world beyond the Crescent Moon.

Whenever she wasn't helping in the shop, Beatrix found herself gravitating toward the stack of blank pages that were waiting on her desk. She'd found a deep pleasure in filling them up and seeing her story grow, the characters becoming more and more alive with every passing paragraph. Though she and her sisters still spent a few hours after the shop closed resting in the parlor on the second floor, they weren't lingering over their cups of tea and conversation quite as long as they used to. Violet was like a caged tiger these days, prowling around the room while biting into her biscuits and suddenly shooting out the door whenever she decided which corner of the house would be upturned next. She'd finished with the attic, leaving it in a state of complete and utter disaster that had caused the walls to vibrate with anxiety for almost two days straight. Some of the picture frames were still tilted, a sign that the poor house was having trouble keeping up with Violet's nightly excavations.

Anne, too, seemed preoccupied, though she always remained in her wingback chair well after Beatrix said good night and slipped down to the study. Some evenings, when Beatrix finally realized the time and wandered quietly up the stairs toward her bedroom, she'd see the firelight still glowing in the parlor and peek through the door to find Anne staring intently at the flames. After they'd managed to figure out Fiona's Task, Beatrix thought that Anne might start to relax a bit, but though she seemed lighthearted enough during the day, a change took over her as the night wore on and a glint of something strange flitted across her eyes.

But Beatrix had her own distractions that needed tending to.

She felt a muscle in her wrist tighten, pulling her away from the image she'd been trying to paint with words on the page. Sighing with reluctance, Beatrix set down her pen and stretched upward, working out knots in her back and neck that she hadn't noticed were forming there. Finally permitting herself to slip into the stories that had been brewing in the back of her mind was like wading into a tub of warm, lavender-scented water. Though her body ached, writing was a balm for wounds she hadn't realized were still sore. And sometimes, it seemed as if she might never return to that world of reservations, half-full teacups, and account books, though this sensation quickly faded at the sound of Anne's inquiring voice or Violet's violent footsteps.

The thought of her sisters made Beatrix's chest tighten with guilt. She still hadn't told them that her short story had been accepted or that Donohoe & Company was expecting her to deliver an entire novel by autumn. With the curse hanging over their heads, it hadn't seemed right to share such wonderful news. She was sure they would take it as a sign that greater forces were trying to pull them apart, and though Beatrix didn't think her sisters would forbid her from writing, their reactions might cause an unnecessary tension to overtake the shop.

Beatrix, of course, knew that her recent turn of luck had nothing to do with the curse. In the days following her visit to Donohoe & Company, that possibility had certainly crossed her mind. She'd hesitated at the desk, unable to write a single word for fear it would somehow cause their problems to worsen. But then her mother's diary had opened, and when Beatrix finally worked up the courage to look at what had emerged on the page she read: *She may be the most quiet of my three, but there's a wealth of wonder beneath those brown eyes. And I believe that's the most beautiful part of her yet to be shared.* And whenever a sense of doubt or fear started to creep into Beatrix's thoughts and pull her from writing, the diary would open again with new messages and stories that pushed her forward.

It was like her mother was present in the room, nudging Beatrix away from her tendency to wait until she was satisfied that absolutely nothing could go wrong and moving her toward a stronger certainty in her own choices.

As Beatrix lowered her arms and moved her attention to the tightness in her neck, she wondered when she would have shared the news with Anne and Violet had the curse not been at play. Would she have flung the door of the shop open after returning from Donohoe & Company and told them as they danced around the tables? Or even asked them to come with her to the publishing house and wait on the sidewalk while she went in to meet her fate?

As delightful as these impressions seemed on the surface, when Beatrix looked at them a bit closer she realized they were only daydreams. In reality, things would have unfolded exactly as they had now, and Beatrix would be sitting at her desk late into the night hoping that neither of her sisters would ask why she suddenly seemed so much more invested in her writing.

It wasn't that Beatrix believed they wouldn't take an interest in her work. No, she was quite sure that they would do just the opposite. They would ask about the color of her heroine's hair or why Beatrix had decided on a particularly shocking twist in the plot. And every day, Beatrix would be forced to spread the intricacies of her story out for them to inspect, just as they did with the linen tablecloths while searching for stains and tears at the end of each month. She worried that the story might turn into a kind of crazy quilt then: a dash of Anne's stern attention to detail, a heavy dose of Violet's whims, and very little room left for Beatrix's own imagination to run free. Worse yet, Beatrix knew that she was too accommodating when it came to her sisters to stand her ground, especially when the particularities of the story were still taking shape in her mind.

They'd always been that way, Beatrix supposed, fiercely protective of her and willing to take whatever steps necessary to shield their sister from a world where the silent are often stomped upon. But every coin has two sides, and though Beatrix was grateful for her sisters' care, their attention had only served to make her more doubtful of herself.

Sighing, Beatrix glanced toward the door and wondered if it was time to hide her manuscript in the bottom drawer of the desk and slip between the cool linen sheets of her bed. She didn't want to stop writing, but her thoughts had taken on a darker hue. And now there was an ache in her soul as well as her wrists and neck.

But just as she leaned forward to rise from the chair, the diary flipped open of its own accord, urging Beatrix to sit back down.

Pushing her spectacles into place, Beatrix looked at the page, eager to see what message was waiting to be read:

Today, I taught the girls the recipe for happiness: a strong cup of vanilla tea with two spoonfuls of sugar and enough courage to weave your dreams into the fabric of the everyday.

Beatrix felt her bottom lip tremble, but she managed to wipe away the tears that had quietly slipped from the corners of her eyes, settle back into the chair, and pick up her pen once more.

After all, a story doesn't write itself.

CHAPTER 13

A Fan

Suggests that you are flirting with
temptation.

By the time Violet toppled an entire rack of wine in the cellar, staining the brick floor a deep crimson that the house would spend days trying to remove, she knew it was time to give in.

For weeks, she'd tried to chase that persistent tune from her head by keeping her hands busy pushing aside the tea towels in the linen closet and upturning dusty wooden crates in the pantry. But as time slipped by and she failed to uncover any clues that might help them break the curse, Violet's body had twisted itself tighter than their customers' corset strings. If she didn't leave that instant, Violet was going to explode, likely bringing a good part of the house down with her.

The walls quivered in silent relief as they watched Violet fling a cotton shawl over her shoulders and slam the back door closed. Knowing it would have a few hours before she returned, the house got to work cleaning up pieces of glass and puddles of champagne.

Violet marched down the street, too lost in the whirlwind of her own thoughts to notice where, exactly, she was going.

They had managed to discover the Task of one of the Council's witches, a challenge that had seemed impossible when Violet first learned of it. And though she had been beyond pleased by their success, she was disappointed that they'd only been able to take one small step in the right direction instead of a bold leap. It didn't help matters that she was making a literal mess of her search through the house, her sense of failure growing with every upturned box. As she'd shoved aside clean sheets and dumped tins of buttons and pins onto the floor, Violet had only grown more frustrated, with herself . . . and with her mother.

If Clara Quigley had suspected even the barest possibility of a curse, why hadn't she left them more than her diary? During the first days of her search, Violet had been hopeful that she'd turn the page of a memory book and find something that would point them in the right direction. But as the days turned into weeks and the crisp spring air started to warm, the bitterness that had slept in the shadows began to creep closer and closer to the surface. How could her mother have left them, knowing what might happen, that her daughters could be forced to separate and face an even sharper loss, this time all on their own?

How could she? How could she? How could she?

The question kept beating against Violet's skull, each stomp of her foot falling in line with the rough syllables.

Violet was so caught in the rhythm of her anger that it took her a moment to notice that the sound of the persistent cheerful melody was no longer an undercurrent in her own mind but an actual tune coming from another place entirely.

Looking up with a start, Violet realized that she'd wandered straight to the lakeshore, where the red and white circus tent was glittering like a lightning bug. The hue was dimmer than it had been before, though, and the crowd of curious bystanders was also absent, lending an air of restful emptiness to the scene.

Suddenly, Violet was pulled back to the moment when Emil's hands had gripped her waist, and a warmth that had nothing to do with the change of seasons shot from the center of her stomach to the tips of her toes.

For what seemed like the thousandth time since Emil had swooped her up from the crowd, Violet gave herself a stern lecture for letting her thoughts drift back to him. Facets of that night always seemed to intrude when she needed to stay focused on the task at hand. The sound of his laughter tingling against her neck distracted Violet during her attempts to ransack the house. When she was supposed to take a tray of biscuits out of the oven, she'd get lost in the memory of their feet swinging in unison above the crowd, and she'd linger in the impression until the smell of burnt sugar snapped her back to the kitchen. Worst of all was the sensation of feeling Emil's palm press into her lower back when he had tried to steady her on the bar. That recollection always emerged just as she was about to fall asleep, ruining any hope she had of resting before sunrise.

She hadn't planned on coming back, of course. As spontaneous as Violet could be, even she knew that returning would lead to nothing but trouble. And yet . . .

Out of the corner of her eye, Violet saw an open flap on the side of the tent whip back, which was odd because there wasn't any wind dancing off the lake. Curious, Violet made her way toward the opening, certain that everyone was gone for the night.

But after she'd slipped into the tent and glanced at the center ring, Violet realized that she was mistaken.

Emil was gliding across the top of the tent, jumping from one bar to the next in slow but incredibly controlled movements. As she watched him, Violet suddenly thought that this was what it would probably be like to watch a sphinx fly.

After a few moments, Emil looked to be gaining speed, working his way up to something more impressive. His feet pushed harder against the bar, and after a few swings he launched himself into the air, flipping his body in a full circle before reaching his hands out to grab the purchase that awaited him.

But his fingers landed an inch away from the bar, and Violet screamed as she saw him fall toward the ground.

It wasn't until Violet caught her breath and looked down that she realized a large net had been waiting to catch him at the bottom. She let out a sigh of relief and leaned against the nearest tent post as she watched Emil's black curls emerge and saw a grin flash across his face.

"Wildfire!" he called, swinging himself over the side of the net and making his way across the ring.

"Excuse me?" Violet asked as she straightened her spine, angry with herself for acting like such a fool and drawing attention to herself.

"I told you last time that since you wouldn't tell me your name, I'd need to call you something else, and so I did," Emil said. "With that head of hair and temper of yours, I think it suits you perfectly."

Emil was close enough now that he could reach out and touch one of her curls, which had fallen free of her bun during her walk. But he didn't, which made it worse somehow because Violet found herself *wanting* him to do it and imagining what it would feel like.

She sensed the blood rush to her face, no doubt staining her cheeks a deep scarlet.

"I don't like it," Violet replied. "You'll need to call me by my real name."

"And what's that?" Emil asked as he leaned one shoulder against the tent post. Violet noticed that he'd traded the sequined garment he'd worn during the performance for a simpler black linen outfit that would be easier to practice in. She hated the way it clung to his shoulders and made her remember the spark of excitement that had shot up her spine when he wrapped his arms around her.

"Violet," she answered.

"That's nice," Emil said. "But I prefer Wildfire. Like I said, it suits you."

"It doesn't suit me in the least," Violet hissed. "I don't have a temper!"

Emil said nothing, but his grin wavered at the corners, as if he was trying to keep himself from laughing.

"I don't!" Violet insisted.

"So, you've come back after all," Emil continued, ignoring her protests.

"It was an accident," Violet said. "I didn't mean to come here."

"You didn't mean to walk to the lakeshore well after midnight and straight into a circus tent?" Emil asked, one of his eyebrows arching skeptically.

"Well, yes . . . ," Violet answered, knowing her words sounded false, even to her own ears. "I got a bit lost in my thoughts, and before I knew it, I was here."

"That explains it then," Emil said with a laugh as he wrapped his arm through Violet's and began pulling them toward the ring.

"Explains what?" Violet asked, taken entirely off guard.

"Your head and your heart are in two different places," Emil said as he led them nearer to the ladder that led up to a wooden platform. "If your thoughts are in the clouds, your body needs to fly up and join them. Otherwise, you won't find any peace."

"That's the most ridiculous thing I've ever heard!" Violet exclaimed as she stared up at the platform. "You can't possibly be asking me to climb up that thing."

"No, that's not what I'm asking you at all," Emil answered.

"Thank goodness for that," Violet sighed.

"I'm asking you to jump from it," Emil added.

"You can't be serious," Violet hissed, taking a step away from the ladder as if it had just burst into flames.

"Of course I am," Emil replied. "It's like I told you when we met; our sort aren't meant to stay on the ground. We're only happy in the air."

He let her arm go then and began climbing up the ladder, only stopping when he made it to the very top.

"Are you coming?" Emil asked, his black curls dangling as he poked his head over the side. Though he didn't say it, Violet could tell from his tone that he was daring her to join him.

Violet should have paused, taken just a few seconds to better understand exactly what type of leap she was about to make. But she hadn't made a habit of hesitating, and now certainly wasn't the time to start.

She climbed up the ladder and met Emil at the top of the platform, waving away the hand that he offered to help steady her.

"What, exactly, did you have in mind?" Violet asked as she peered over the side of the platform and tried her best to hide the fact that her heart had just leapt into her throat.

"Nothing too difficult," Emil said as he looked down at Violet, clearly pleased with her reaction. "To start, anyway."

At that, Violet had to fight the impulse to run straight back down the ladder, but she managed to hold her ground.

Without a word of warning, Emil dived from the platform and grabbed onto the closest bar, only to throw himself toward the next and then the next. He was now a good distance away from Violet, dangling upside down with his knees tucked so that his legs were clinging to the bar instead of his hands.

"What now?" Violet asked, trying to sound unimpressed.

"You jump with your arms held high when I say so," Emil said as he began to swing again, moving in wide arches. "And I'll catch you."

"I'm supposed to trust you to catch me?" Violet asked in disbelief.

"I'll always catch you," Emil promised. "I think you know that."

Oddly enough, Violet realized that she did trust him, this man she knew absolutely nothing about and was certain she'd never see again.

"Jump!" Emil called just as he started swinging away from the platform.

Without giving it another thought, Violet threw herself from the wooden boards and flew straight into the open air.

And for the first time, she felt like her thoughts and her heartbeat had finally found the same pacing. She was somehow weightless and solid, moving and still, calm but exhilarated all at once, and a shriek of pure glee escaped her lips just before Emil's hands wrapped around her wrists, stopping her from tumbling feetfirst into the net.

"How did it feel?" Emil asked as he continued to swing them in slow, lazy arches.

Violet glanced upward and saw from his smile that he knew full well how she felt.

"Perfect," she replied with a laugh, not bothering to hide the truth. "It felt perfect."

"Are you ready for a challenge now?" Emil asked, his gaze moving back to the wooden platform, a clear invitation to try again.

"Absolutely," Violet said, realizing that her feet, for once, were completely still.

It was nice, she was shocked to admit. Nice to be above it all and next to this man who smelled of woodsmoke and midnight. Nice to be away from the shop, in both body and mind, and suspended somewhere between dreams and reality without the worry of never falling asleep.

"Then let's get started," Emil said, his smile widening as he dropped them toward the net and their next adventure.

CHAPTER 14

A Ship

*Signals that you will soon go on
a journey.*

As the house started leaving some of the windows open at
night to let in the cool evening air, Anne's dreams took
on a new texture.

The daytime hours moved forward at their proper pace, not
a minute out of sync, but as soon as Anne's head rested on her
lavender-scented pillow, it seemed like the lines between past,
present, and future faded altogether.

She was still catching glimpses of the future when awake. The
signs were everywhere now, from the clouds above the house to
the way the spoons fell across the floor. But these were only hints
of what was to come, and if Anne didn't want to pay them too
much attention, she simply turned her mind elsewhere.

But the land of dreams was another story entirely.

That night, as Anne's breathing slowed and her eyes turned
inward, she stumbled into a scene so visceral that it took her
more than a moment to orient herself. This had already hap-

pened a handful of times before, and Anne had learned by then that the only way for her to distinguish these visions from reality was to pay attention to the contours, which took on a slight hazy hue whenever she was dreaming.

Anne was standing in the corner of a room with four chairs arranged in a circle at its center. One was empty, but in the others sat the members of the Council, engaged in what seemed to be a heated discussion. Though the windows were thrown open, the air was stifling hot, so much so that Nathanial had thrown aside his suit jacket and Hester's brow had taken on a moist sheen. Out of all of them, Isaac was the only one who looked like they weren't bothered by the stuffiness. Anne realized that whenever she was, it must be the height of summer, a good month or two ahead of the present.

Though she knew she couldn't be seen, Anne still took a step back into the shadows that flickered behind the candlelight.

"They've done it again," Nathanial hissed as he pulled at his beard in frustration.

"And with Crowley, nonetheless," Hester said with a shake of her head. "I didn't think it was possible."

"It is what we asked for," Isaac added in a monotone voice.

"But it's not what we wanted, as you well know," Nathanial spat. "We didn't expect them to get this far."

Anne's brow furrowed in confusion. Of course, the thought that the Council members were making the challenge they'd put forth deliberately difficult had crossed her mind, but Anne hadn't seriously suspected that they didn't want them to ultimately succeed. Not when it meant three witches would be forced to suffer in the eternal in-between.

"Their powers must be fiercer than we predicted," Hester said. "The fact that they used hydromancy to discover Crowley's Task proves it."

Pouring dye into a bowl and reading the shapes and ripples that formed across its surface was a notoriously intricate art. Though their mother had shown them the basic steps when they were children, the Quigleys had never attempted it themselves, knowing that the likelihood of deciphering anything useful in the water wasn't promising.

But, if her vision was to be believed, Anne and her sisters had somehow mastered the skill in time to save Mr. Crowley from his uncertain fate.

"They must fail," Nathanial insisted as he pounded a fist against the arm of his chair.

"We still have the third witch," Hester continued. "There's a chance they may not uncover his Task and will be forced to separate after we take the shop."

"The matter is too delicate to depend on chance," Nathanial said forcefully. "There's too much at stake."

"If only Celeste were here," Hester sighed, a genuine expression of loss flashing across her features.

"She's of no help to us anymore," Nathanial said, but his voice softened a bit as his sternness gave way to sorrow. "We have no Diviner to turn to now."

"All we can do is wait and see if they manage to uncover the third witch's Task," Hester continued. "And hope that the other traps we've set push things along."

Anne's heart started to beat faster while she tried to make sense of what she was hearing.

As she reached a hand toward her neck to feel the rapid pulse there, Isaac's eerily gray eyes shot to her from across the room.

Anne jumped but then relaxed as she assured herself that he couldn't possibly see her.

"Someone's here," he whispered.

And suddenly water began rushing into the room through

the doors and windows, as if they were all in a ship that had just plunged bow-first into the sea.

As Anne was swept up in the current, she saw colorful shapes floating next to her in the water: rippling bushes that bespoke secret opportunities, doors opening to different paths, and faces of all shapes and sizes whispering about potential setbacks and changes to come.

When Anne opened her mouth to scream, she breathed in warm lavender-laced air instead of the icy current that she had expected.

She was back in her bed, drenched in sweat from the roots of her hair to her feet.

The house, startled by her rough awakening, poured a glass of water on the bedside table and tried to tug her in its direction with a cotton sheet. But Anne, still lost somewhere between dreams and reality, wasn't paying attention.

Now it was clear as crystal that the Council didn't want the Quigleys to accomplish the challenge put before them so that they would lose the shop. Anne didn't have the foggiest hint about why they were set on the sisters' failure, but she was certain of one thing, at least.

The Council would not succeed. She would not allow it.

CHAPTER 15

An Hourglass

*Reveals that a decision must be made
and a new phase embraced.*

*I*t was a Saturday afternoon in the heat of summer, and the shop had been bursting with customers since the moment the sisters turned the Open sign toward the street. Additional chairs were conjured from the attic to accommodate all the unexpected friends, relatives, and companions who tagged along with the clients whose names were already printed in their reservation book. Peggy and Franny had run out of white cheddar and rosemary scones and resorted to baking an entirely new batch in the kitchen, leaving the Quigleys stranded in the front room, juggling empty tea trays and water glasses as they moved between readings. The Crescent Moon was so full of skirt trains and elaborately decorated hats that people were practically spilling out the door whenever a curious passerby tried to peek in and discover the cause of all this activity.

With that many people packed into the parlor, the house was practically boiling. It tried to freeze ice in the basement and push the cool air through the floorboards, but it was fighting a particularly hot summer day and losing the battle.

The sisters were frantically flitting about the shop like moths who kept hitting themselves against the glass of a gas lamp, distracted to the point where they didn't think to check the mailbox until the very last customer slipped out the front door a quarter of an hour past their normal closing time.

And when they did manage to find a spare moment to pull out the stack of envelopes that had been patiently waiting all afternoon, they discovered that their day hadn't yet come to an end.

A small white card pressed with that now-familiar red seal was mixed between bills and letters. When Anne opened it with shaking fingers, a message greeted them announcing that Mr. Crowley would be stopping by the shop that evening at precisely half past six.

When she shared the news with her sisters, Anne's announcement was met with silence. Turning about the room, she saw Violet standing by the window, absentmindedly looking out toward the twilight-tinted street.

"Violet," Anne said, a note of exhaustion creeping into her voice. "Can you help me carry these teacups into the kitchen? Otherwise, the girls will be here long after Mr. Crowley leaves."

Shaken from her daydream, Violet glanced toward Anne, her purple eyes still hazy with distraction and outlined by dark circles. She was obviously tired as well, and Anne worried that none of them seemed to be getting any sleep.

If Anne had paused long enough to read the margins of Violet's features, she might have found evidence of something else printed there. Enough of a suggestion to inquire further. But as it was, there was hardly time for her to grab another empty saucer on her way to the kitchen, let alone seek out the secrets hidden in the half-moons beneath Violet's eyes.

"Oh, of course," Violet said as she shook herself out of whatever thoughts entangled her and started clearing the nearest table, though certainly not at the speed Anne had hoped for.

Even without the ladies of the Crescent Moon stuffed to the rafters, the front parlor was still too hot, and Anne found herself starting to lose her grip on the tray that held all the cups and saucers. Taking in a deep breath, she carried the dishware into the kitchen, where she found Franny and Peggy adding to the mountain of teacups, saucers, plates, and silverware that had grown across the counters.

"Have either of you seen Beatrix?" Anne asked as she placed her collection of cups on the near-toppling stack. "She slipped out of the parlor before the last table of customers left the shop."

Those clients had lingered well past closing time, pleading with Anne to look at their tea leaves for "just a quick moment" that had extended into nearly half an hour. She'd sat there, trapped as she watched Violet drift between the parlor and the kitchen at the pace of a sleepwalker and lost sight of Beatrix, who'd disappeared from the room entirely.

When no one answered, Anne left the kitchen and marched up the staircase in search of Beatrix.

She found her shuffling down the hallway with a stack of papers in hand, her fingers stained with ink and her spectacles dangling on the very edge of her nose.

"Mr. Crowley will be here any moment," Anne said as she wiped her hands against her apron.

"I see," Beatrix replied, moving the papers out of Anne's view. "What do we need to prepare in the back room? I don't suppose we'll offer any refreshments, considering Mr. Crowley doesn't have a taste for tea."

Anne's temples tightened at this reminder.

"I think it would be best to try hydromancy this time," Anne said as she began to walk back down the steps, hoping that Beatrix would follow her lead. "So, we'll need to take down our largest porcelain bowl and the dyes, of course."

After her vision of the Council, Anne was more determined than ever to keep the shop open. Since then, she'd been slipping into the divination room after midnight to practice, preparing for their next encounter with the witch.

"Hydromancy?" Beatrix asked, not bothering to hide her surprise. "Do you really think that's best? Trying to pull the signs from the water's surface is so tricky and time-consuming, and we haven't been any good at it in the past."

"Hydromancy can be difficult, but so is Mr. Crowley's case," Anne said, trying to tiptoe around her lie. "It's worth our effort to attempt it."

Anne's deception wasn't strong enough to cause that distinct burnt-meringue flavor to settle on the back of Beatrix's tongue, but a slight suggestion of sweetness did start to drift into her nose.

She had stayed up until dawn working on her novel, however, to the horror of the house. And now all Beatrix could think about was how to remain awake long enough to avoid alerting Anne to the fact that she was acting out of the ordinary. So the hint that Anne was also hiding something went completely unnoticed.

Not that Beatrix would have had time to press the issue any further, for the sound of bells clanging against the front door soon drifted up the steps, sending both of the sisters into a panic.

"He's here!" Anne cried, turning toward Beatrix with an odd glint in her eyes. "Can you go to the kitchen and fill a pitcher of water? Then meet us in the back room so we can get started."

Beatrix nodded, but she was troubled by the strange expression on Anne's face. Beneath the dark shadows under her eyes and the hunch of her shoulders, Beatrix could sense that her sister was excited. But she needed to write down a line that had been forming in the back of her mind and hide the pages with her new chapter before joining her sisters in the front parlor, so Beatrix pushed her concern aside and ran down to the study.

Anne trotted in the opposite direction, stopping at the bottom of the steps to take in a deep breath before opening the door and walking into the parlor, where Mr. Crowley stood, slouching his shoulders forward as if trying to shield himself from a biting gust of wind.

"Mr. Crowley," Anne said as she moved forward to take his light summer jacket. "I'm very pleased to see you again."

"Yes, well . . . ," Mr. Crowley replied, evidently at a loss for what to say.

"We're confident that tonight will be much more productive than our last session," Anne continued, hoping to reassure their guest.

This statement did not produce the desired effect, however. Quite the opposite, in fact. Mr. Crowley's eyebrows drew even closer together, and he took a slight step back from Anne, as if about to run.

"We?" he finally asked after recovering a bit of his composure.

Looking about, Anne realized that Beatrix and Violet weren't anywhere to be seen.

"Please make your way to the back room, Mr. Crowley," Anne said, struggling to keep the anxiety out of her voice. "My sisters and I will join you shortly."

Anne waited for the witch to nod and move toward the back room before marching toward the kitchen. As she poked her head through the door, she heard a cry, followed by the sound of porcelain cracking against the floorboards.

"Medusa's curls!" Violet cried from the other side of the door.

When Anne entered the kitchen, she saw her sister sprawled on the floor, surrounded by water and the broken pieces of their favorite pitcher. Tabitha crouched near the hearth, hissing up a storm with eyes still bleary from the nap from which she had been so rudely interrupted.

"What were you doing?" Anne cried. "I asked Beatrix to get the water."

"She found me in the kitchen and asked me to do it," Violet sputtered. "Said she needed to file some paperwork before we spoke with Mr. Crowley."

"File some paperwork?" Anne asked in disbelief. "Violet, get a new pitcher of water and join me in the back room to help find the dyes. Quickly. And if you see Bee, tell her to join us *now*."

Not waiting for a response, Anne turned and walked toward the divination room, where she found Mr. Crowley already waiting at the table.

"I do apologize, Mr. Crowley," Anne said as she pulled a ladder against one of the bookshelves and began climbing toward the top. "We've had a rather hectic day in the shop, though that's no excuse for our tardiness, of course."

Mr. Crowley merely nodded, his eyes flicking toward the door.

"But I think that we've found just the thing to help you identify your Task," Anne continued, pausing as she lifted a white bowl that was a smidge too large for her arms to wrap around securely.

Nearly falling from the rung, Anne steadied herself just in time to keep from taking a tumble. After a moment, she finally made it safely to the floor and set the piece on the table with a thud.

"Here's the water," Violet said as the bowl stopped rattling, a fresh pitcher in hand but her dress still sodden from the accident in the kitchen.

"Thank you, Violet," Anne said.

Violet nodded before pushing past Anne toward one of the dusty cupboards, looking for the dyes among a dizzying number of jars and vials.

"As I was saying, Mr. Crowley, we plan to try and discern your Task using the art of hydromancy. This will involve—"

Anne was once again interrupted, this time by Beatrix, who flew into the room with another pitcher.

"I have the water," she said in a gasp, clearly frazzled.

"Violet's already brought it," Anne sighed, hoping now that the three of them were all in the same space, their natural rhythms would fall in line with one another.

She waited for Beatrix to join them at the table and then turned to Mr. Crowley again.

"My apologies, Mr. Crowley," Anne continued. "Hydromancy, as I was trying to tell you, involves pouring dyes of different colors into the water. Let me show them to you."

Anne turned around, expecting to find Violet waiting by her side with the dyes in hand. But she was still lingering in front of the cupboard, opening drawers at random.

"I can't seem to find them," Violet murmured, her foot tapping against the floor at a rapid pace.

Holding back a sigh, Anne moved toward the cupboard and pulled out a set of vials that had been sitting at the very front of the shelf closest to Violet's face.

"Here they are, Mr. Crowley," Anne said as she brought the vials back to the table and held them up for the witch's inspection, though he was fidgeting with the gold ring on his left hand, obviously distracted. "Now, hydromancy typically involves pouring dyes like these into a bowl of water and reading the shapes that they produce. But the method that we use is slightly different."

Anne waited to see if either Violet or Beatrix would interject to help her explain things to Mr. Crowley. They were both seated at the table now, but after a beat or two of silence Anne realized that they were still lost in their own preoccupations, whatever those might be.

"We'll need something that has special value to you," Anne explained, turning back to the witch. "A trinket of some kind. It doesn't need to be expensive, just meaningful in some way."

"I don't know that I have anything of that nature on my person at the moment," Mr. Crowley said, sitting as far back as his chair would allow.

"Most people do," Anne continued, determined now to get him to cooperate. "A favorite keepsake, a token of love or accomplishment."

"No, no. I don't carry around anything like that," Mr. Crowley insisted.

Anne watched as he covered his left hand, shielding the gold ring that she'd seen him twisting around his finger.

"Your ring," Anne said, holding out her open palm. "That will do."

"This old thing?" Mr. Crowley exclaimed, tucking his hand beneath the table now. "Oh no. It's not valuable at all. Sentimentally or otherwise."

"It will do, nonetheless," Anne said, pushing her palm even closer.

For a moment, it looked as if Mr. Crowley was going to spring up from his chair and flee the shop. But something like defeat sank into his shoulders, and he reluctantly pulled off the ring and placed it with the utmost care in Anne's upturned hand.

Holding the trinket toward the light, Anne noticed that the shape of an hourglass was etched onto its raised flat surface.

"There now," Anne said as she dangled the ring above the water. "I'm going to drop the ring into the center of the bowl, and as it sinks, I'd like you to reflect on how this trinket makes you feel. Does it bring you comfort? Evoke a particular memory, perhaps?"

Mr. Crowley was sweating now, moist rivulets sliding down

from what was once his hairline and into his eyebrows. He opened his mouth as if to ask Anne to reconsider, but she rushed forward, hoping to bring things to a conclusion as quickly as possible.

"Violet, Beatrix, I'll need your help for this part," Anne said as she shifted to make space for them to stand on either side of her in front of the bowl. In the past, they'd always worked together when trying to weave a particularly intricate enchantment, needing to combine their efforts to get a sound impression. Anne suspected that she might be able to cast the spell on her own now that her magic was growing stronger, but she didn't want her sisters to catch on that something was happening. Not yet, anyway.

Beatrix and Violet rose and moved to the places that Anne had opened for them, each resting a hand on either of their sister's shoulders.

They began to whisper a chant in unison, their voices taking on different tones, as if mimicking song through speech. The tenseness that had settled along the back of Anne's neck loosened as she let the words roll through her and mingle with the incantations of her sisters. She took in a breath and smelled the honeysuckle-laced sweetness of Violet's magic tangle with the hint of sandalwood that always appeared when Beatrix was casting a spell.

As the peppermint notes of her own magic began to seep into the mixture, Anne turned her palm and let the ring crash through the water's clear surface. Then each of the sisters took a vial of dye and poured it into the bowl, allowing their voices to become louder and louder.

In the dish, the water began to take on an iridescent hue, and the ripples continued to lap against the porcelain edge despite the fact that the ring had already settled at the bottom.

"It's working," Anne sighed in relief as she gazed into the water to start the reading. "I'm getting the sense of misplaced things. As if something is not quite where it belongs."

To their surprise, Mr. Crowley jumped from his chair and moved to grab the ring out of the bowl.

But before his hand could capture his prize, the ring shot into the air, suspended by a fountain of water.

"This doesn't normally happen," Anne whispered, staring at the ring as it danced before their faces.

Then the band began to spin, turning in circles so quickly that it started to take on the appearance of a sphere. Looking closer, Anne noticed there was something different about the hourglass engraving as well. The small etchings that resembled grains of sand were beginning to flow from one side to the other.

And in that moment, Anne finally understood.

Snatching the ring from the fountain, she stared across the table to face Mr. Crowley.

"Where did you get this ring?" she asked.

"Nowhere," Mr. Crowley answered, his thin frame shaking now. "That is, nowhere of importance. It means *nothing* to me, as I told you before."

"With all due respect, sir, I don't believe that is the case," Anne said, pushing forward. "This ring is not as insignificant as you claim. If what we've just witnessed here is any indication, it is at the very heart of your Task. It doesn't belong to you, and you must return it."

"No!" Mr. Crowley cried as he banged a fist against the table.

The sound reverberated through the room, causing everyone to go still, even the enchanted bowl of water.

"I apologize," Mr. Crowley finally said as he covered his eyes with his hands. "I didn't mean to; that is, I don't think that—"

He stopped trying to carve any order out of his words and sighed.

"Please," he asked weakly, "might I have it back now?"

Anne slowly lifted the ring and dropped it into his waiting

palm. He stared at it for a moment and then carefully slipped it back over the knuckle of his knobby finger.

"Mr. Crowley," Anne said, grasping the back of her chair for support. "You must complete your Task."

"Please don't tell anyone about this," the witch replied, ignoring her completely. "I'd prefer my family not know."

"I'm afraid that isn't possible," Anne said. "The Council cannot be ignored in this matter. You must return the ring, or you will be lost."

Mr. Crowley merely shook his head and chuckled, the sound dry and lacking in humor. It was as if he was laughing at some dark joke only he could hear.

"I apologize for the inconvenience," he said, making his way toward the door. "I wish that no one had made any trouble over this in the first place."

The sisters moved to follow him out, but by the time they reached the threshold of the back room, the bells were already announcing Mr. Crowley's departure from the Crescent Moon.

"He's known what his Task is this whole time," Beatrix said in disbelief. "He just doesn't want to do it. What on earth could he be thinking?"

"At least the Council won't have our heads now that we've figured things out," Anne said triumphantly. "I'll send them a note and let them know what we discovered. That way, we can be through with worrying about Mr. Crowley, at least."

Anne felt pure power washing through her veins now, and it was making her so giddy that she smiled, tickled by the thought of the Council's disappointment and their own victory.

Beatrix and Violet eyed her curiously, confused by her reaction. Anne was normally so controlled and composed that her elation seemed entirely out of place. They'd expected her to be on edge until the moment they knew with absolutely certainty that they'd completed the job laid out for them by the Council, but instead, she looked to be enjoying the challenge.

"Is everything all right?" Beatrix finally managed to ask.

"Of course," Anne replied. "I'm just pleased that we seem to be making progress. I truly think we're weakening the curse with every Task we uncover. As long as we have the shop, we'll be together."

"How can you be so sure that the two things are connected?" Violet asked. "What if we're going down the wrong path here?"

Anne wanted to share what she'd overheard the Council say, but then she'd have to tell them about her visions. She wasn't ready to reveal everything, not when she still didn't understand how the Council and the curse were connected, and when they needed to stay focused on finding the witches' Tasks and ensuring that the rhythm of the shop remained steady. And, if she looked beneath her fears and disillusions, Anne would have been able to admit that, for once, she didn't want to share everything with her sisters. She needed to keep this one thing to herself just a bit longer.

The picture frames began to shake then, their gilded edges tapping so hard against the walls that the paintings nearly fell from their perches. The house was beginning to tire of all the falsehoods floating about the halls and wanted its feelings known.

"Stop that, now!" Violet called out as she tried to soothe the house.

"It's worked itself into a fine temper, hasn't it?" Beatrix murmured.

"All this strain isn't good for it either," Anne said, running her hand along the wainscoting. "I think we all need a bit of rest."

It was on the tip of her tongue to ask them to come sit with her in the parlor and allow the tension of the day to slip away with a few sips of rosehip tea, but she knew without even having to glance at her watch that it was too late in the night to do anything but collapse into their beds.

Violet nodded as she stifled a yawn, though she doubted that the hours to come would be filled with sleep. Fantasies, perhaps, but not sleep. Her body was already itching to sneak out the back door and wander down to the lakeside, where her thoughts had lingered all day.

Beatrix was also already half-lost in the plotline that she'd been pondering while trying to read her customers' fates. She was so very close to drawing one of her chapters to a conclusion, and her mind was racing faster than her pen would be able to keep pace with.

The house, too, would be up until dawn trying to air out the lingering sense of deception that was starting to seep into the very walls. For the best remedy to chase away the trace of secrets is laughter, and that sound was starting to fade from the private quarters of the Quigley home.

Only Anne would find any sleep that evening, though her dreams would refuse her any real rest.

CHAPTER 16

A Barking Dog

Means a friend is trying to warn you.

The house had hoped that uncovering Mr. Crowley's Task would help draw the sisters together, but all it seemed to do was pull them further apart. Toward the unfinished novel. Toward the circus on the lakeside. Toward the future and what it might reveal. The house noticed a tension brewing, nothing that was about to boil over, but a slow simmer that could burn down to a crisp if left unattended.

By the time Katherine's footsteps echoed against the path stones in the garden, the house was wound so tight that it threw open the back door before she even had the chance to knock.

"Is something amiss, old friend?" Katherine asked as she patted the threshold on her way into the kitchen, which stood completely empty.

Dirty cups and saucers were still stacked on the countertops from another busy day in the shop. Exhausted from having to sweep up the cobwebs and dust of the sisters' secrets, the house was working through its daily list of chores at a much slower pace. The thin coat of dirt on the window above the sink and faint smell of mildew did not go unnoticed by Katherine.

"What's been going on here?" she murmured as she stepped into the hallway.

Since her last visit, Katherine had been busy trying to piece together the sisters' puzzle. She'd been hesitant to return to the shop while asking such delicate questions of the witches in her coven for fear that someone might put two and two together and realize that the Quigleys were cursed. Witches often viewed curses as catching, like measles or influenza. If even the suggestion of an enchantment was attached to the Crescent Moon, the girls' business would undoubtedly suffer, and then they'd have an entirely new problem to tackle.

Though Katherine had kept in contact with the Quigleys through notes as she worked on crafting a clearer picture, it was evident now that she should have returned to the shop much sooner.

Instead of calling out into the depths of the house, Katherine preferred a gentler means of getting the sisters' attention. Tossing her lace shawl across a chair and rolling her sleeves up to her elbows, she went to the stovetop and began to boil water for a pot of tea. As it started to roar to life, she reached toward the shelf above and pulled down a familiar tin, taking a moment to relish the fragrance that seeped from the corners of the lid.

And then, when everything was just so, Katherine poured the boiling water over the leaves from the tin, filling the entire house with the scent of peaches and cream. She'd found the blend that Clara had always prepared during the height of summer, and the fruity notes managed to find the Quigley sisters in their separate corners of the house, capturing their senses.

They each became still—Beatrix with her pen poised above the page, Violet with one foot about to walk over the threshold of the front door, and Anne as her eyes gazed into the fire searching for signs that rested in the embers. And then, they rose like sleep-walkers, making their way toward the source of the scent that had crept beyond their childhood memories.

The three sisters reached the threshold of the kitchen and then slowly made their way into the room, unsure of what they might find waiting for them there.

"Katherine," Anne said, her voice tinged with relief and surprise.

But when their guest turned around with the tea in her hand and her eyes met theirs, she froze and then dropped the pot to the floor, the delicate porcelain cracking against the boards.

For a moment, the four of them stood suspended in time, staring at one another with expressions of horror and confusion.

"It's gotten worse," Katherine finally whispered, her hands falling to her sides in shock. "The curse is so much stronger than the last time I was here."

All three sisters reached for their eyes, afraid of what they might have revealed.

"But it shouldn't be," Anne insisted. "We've uncovered two of the witches' Tasks. The shop is safe."

"So I've heard," Katherine said. "It's partly the reason I haven't thought it necessary to visit sooner. You seemed to be keeping the curse at bay, but now I see you've only fueled its fire. What have you three been doing?"

Silence filled the room, but the sisters' thoughts were racing now as they tried their best to push aside the explanation that was both the most obvious and painful.

"Nothing out of the ordinary," Anne replied.

Both Beatrix and Violet were hit with the taste of something sickly sweet, but in their panic, they blamed the sensation on the scent of the tea.

"No, something has changed here," Katherine insisted as she cast her gaze around the room, as if the house would reveal all the secrets it had witnessed. "I told you three to pay attention to your impulses to help decipher what choices were yours and which might come from the curse. Have you been acting in ways that are out of character?"

> *My book.*
> *Emil.*
> *My power.*

These words flitted through the sisters' thoughts like a mantra as they finally came to terms with the dark possibilities that had been lurking behind their hopes.

"We thought things were getting better," Anne said, her voice cracking. "Everything seemed so tied to the Council."

"I know," Katherine murmured softly. "But curses are complex, and we don't know how everything fits together. The two pieces seem to be linked, but I suspect something else it at play as well. And until we discover what it is, you three need to pay attention to your instincts."

All three of the sisters held their breath, unwilling to move forward from one moment into the next.

"I've been doing my best to find out what I can," Katherine continued. "After we last spoke, I started asking about Celeste, the city's Diviner. It seems that she had to step down from her position because she lost her power."

The sisters gasped.

"Lost her power?" Anne asked, shaken to the bone. "How is that possible?"

"It seems that she broke a pledge," Katherine explained. "She swore to keep someone's secret, lacing the bond with enchantments. And when she told the secret that wasn't hers to share, she lost her magic."

"I've never heard of this," Anne murmured.

It seemed like a fate worse than death, being severed from any hint of magic and having to embrace an ordinary existence.

"That's because it's incredibly rare for a witch to consent to such a spell and break their promise," Katherine said. "Celeste must have felt there was a strong enough reason to share the secret."

"Do you know what the secret was or who it belonged to?" Violet asked.

"No," Katherine replied. "But I suspect that she told the secret to the Council. I heard rumors that Celeste might still be hiding in the city. It's my intention to try to find her so that we can get some answers. But it may take some time."

The sisters nodded, disturbed by the former Diviner's fate but hopeful that some light might be shed on their situation after all.

"While I'm gone, I strongly suggest that you try to stay away from anything unusual," Katherine said, her voice becoming stern. "You may claim that things have been normal around here, but I sense that something has changed."

And with that, she wrapped her lace shawl around her shoulders and marched out the door, closing it behind her with a sharp snap.

When the sound of Katherine's footsteps faded into the hot night air, the sisters finally glanced up at one another.

What do you think has changed? was the question waiting to be asked, but none of them could muster the courage to say it.

How could they when each of them thought they knew the answer already?

"What are we going to do?" Beatrix finally whispered as she played with the chain of her spectacles.

"Whatever we have to," Violet replied as she pulled her sisters so close that they felt like one being.

"As long as we're together," Anne added.

The three of them remained like that, an unending circle, each considering what needed to be done.

They knew the night to come would be heavy with difficult decisions.

And that they'd have to make them on their own.

CHAPTER 17

An Umbrella

*Indicates that you will find protection
during troubling times.*

By the time the scent of peaches and cream tea had faded
from the kitchen, Beatrix had yet to drift into a restful sleep.
When she and her sisters had gone to their separate quarters
of the house after Katherine's unexpected visit, Beatrix's bones
had so ached with exhaustion that all she wanted was to fall onto
her pillow and hope to recover from the blow they'd been given.

But just a short while ago, she'd awoken unexpectedly. Startled
by the feeling that she'd forgotten something of great importance,
Beatrix lifted herself from the mattress and knew that she wouldn't
be getting any rest in what little remained of the night. Her hands
itched to wrap themselves around the pen and put words to paper,
no matter how tired the rest of her body was. And her characters
were already stretching themselves inside her head, eager to get
back to the job of helping her weave their journeys together.

Now she was creeping down the stairs toward her study,
where she hoped to fill a few more blank pages before sunrise.

When she settled into her chair and reached for the drawer to pull out her manuscript, though, the house refused to let her open it and rattled the desk so vigorously that her mother's diary fell from its place on a stack of books and landed right in front of Beatrix.

"You don't have to do this," Beatrix grumbled as she tried to pry the drawer open, managing to move it a few inches in the right direction.

In response, the house snapped the drawer closed, nearly pinching Beatrix's fingers, and moved the desk again so that the diary rattled. Now that Beatrix was awake, it was insistent that she get to work shifting through the diary's pages so that she could uncover something useful.

"Very well," Beatrix sighed, coaxed by the house's determination.

She recognized that she had fallen into the habit of waiting for the diary to invite her to open its pages. It seemed rude, somehow, to try to uncover what was hidden beneath the enchantments when the diary had made the voice of their mother come alive again. But as she thought more about Katherine's warning, Beatrix agreed with the house that something had to be done and quickly. She couldn't wait around any longer, hoping that the diary would share something that they could use to break the curse before their life at the Crescent Moon crumbled to pieces.

Leaning over the diary, Beatrix started to lift the front cover, but it snapped closed the instant her finger touched its binding, sending a cloud of dust straight into her face.

"No one's being cooperative tonight, is that it?" Beatrix asked between her sneezes.

The floorboards shook at that comment, angered by the comparison.

"Everyone just settle down, shall we?" Beatrix cooed as she pulled her chair out from under the desk and began to run her hand up the spine of the book.

She whispered endearments and promises so softly that her words barely took enough shape to be understood. They felt like the gentle brush of a spring breeze, and the diary gradually began to loosen its hold, allowing her to peel back the cover and turn the page.

Emboldened, Beatrix shifted her tactics, speaking louder so that her spells had greater force behind them. Her incantations hit the paper like cannonballs, and she could start to see the faded etchings of her mother's handwriting as she peeled back the layers of magic one by one. It took all her strength, but Beatrix was determined to bend the bespelled writing to her will this time and read what lay beneath the disguise.

Finally, she could make out a handful of words, the ink darkening in places just enough for her to see the gentle curves of vowels and consonants:

together

powerful

Fate

disaster
love

hopeless

bargain

Sweat was beginning to ripple down Beatrix's brow now as she tried her best to hold open the diary and uncover how all the words strung together. She needed to push harder so that full sentences emerged, ones that would help save her and her sisters.

But the instant she reached forward to pull back the final layer of magic, the words swirled and shifted, like ladybugs in the cellar that had just been startled by candlelight. They scurried to the center of the diary, where Beatrix had managed to carve a hole in the enchantment, and then the book's magic snapped back, like a band that had been pulled too tight. Startled, Beatrix lost her grip on the spell and dropped the diary on the desk.

She leaned back in her chair and stared at the diary, holding her hands close to her chest for fear that it might bite back if she touched it. The frightening thought that the book might not let her open its pages ever again sent a chill down Beatrix's spine, and tears born of fear and frustration started to course down her cheeks. As so often happened in the shop, she'd been given a task and couldn't manage to complete it, not even when the stakes were so high that they threatened to topple everything she treasured.

Not for the first time, Beatrix wondered why their mother had gone through the trouble of disguising her writing at all. Over the past few months, she'd settled on the idea that Clara Quigley, like many people, wanted to be sure that she had a safe space to give life to her joys and troubles, to make them more tangible so that she felt heard without the risk of asking someone to listen. But now that she was beginning to grasp just how powerful the diary's enchantments were, Beatrix wasn't so certain.

What had their mother been so determined to hide?

As Beatrix wiped at her eyes, though, she caught a flicker of movement from the diary. Curious and concerned, she glanced down and watched as the cover fell open once more and words emerged from the depths of the binding:

Beatrix has found the book of fairy tales that I tried to hide in the attic. As I predicted, she came to me crying about how all the witches seem to meet unhappy fates.

*With some chocolate toffee and soothing words, I coaxed
her to think about what we could do if she didn't like the
ending. And, to my surprise, she dried her tears, looked
me straight in the eyes, and announced that she would
write her own story. I think she will do just that one day.*

As the lines drifted back into the pages, Beatrix felt the tension in her shoulders ease and the ghost of a smile pull at her lips.

When every last syllable had faded away, she pulled out a fresh sheet of paper and turned her attention back to the tale that she'd promised to weave together.

The house was tempted to rattle the desk so that the ink poured across the pages, but when it saw the peaceful expression on Beatrix's tear-stained face it didn't have the heart to disturb her. Instead, it watched as she leaned forward and gradually lost herself in the sentences that were unfurling from the tip of her pen.

But though the floorboards remained still while the gentle sound of words being etched into paper infused the study, it didn't mean the house wasn't worried about how the Quigleys' own story might end.

CHAPTER 18

An Apple

Represents forbidden desires.

As the house fretted over Beatrix, Violet was walking along the lakeside, her footsteps, for once, as slow as molasses dripping from the edge of a spoon. Weighed down by Katherine's warnings and the languid heat of the summer evening, Violet felt like she was wading through a dream where she knew which corner to turn but always somehow missed her cue.

Since she'd returned to the circus, Violet had managed to string together a fragile paper chain of excuses for why she kept letting herself be drawn back to the candy-striped tent. At first, she'd sworn to stop visiting Emil as soon as her curiosity waned and she could direct her full focus back to her search of the house. Violet, more than anyone else, knew that she couldn't divide her attention, and so her plan had been to work the circus out of her system and return to the task at hand once the persistent melody stopped playing in her head.

But the problem was that Emil and the trapeze bars never seemed to lose their luster. And here she was, months later, still determined to master just one last trick before she said goodbye.

With Katherine's words still ringing in her ears, though, Violet had to finally consider the cost of her fascination with flying across the top of the circus tent.

The warnings that had echoed through the kitchen suddenly entangled with Violet's memories of her mother, and she felt her pulse quicken, urging her to pick up her pace. Swearing under her breath, Violet chastised herself for wavering when the path set before her was so clear. She wouldn't be like Clara Quigley, a seer who blinded herself to the consequences that lurked in the shadows of the future.

It was time to say goodbye.

When she finally made it to the edge of the tent, Violet grasped the fabric and braced her shoulders, expecting to find Emil swinging from the bars or standing on the edge of the platform, ready to dive into a new trick as soon as he saw her step into the ring.

But, instead, Violet was instantly ensnared by the flickering flames of candlelight and the voice of a lone violin. It was a slow, whispering melody that cast a net around her soul and pulled it ever so gently forward, like a charmer beckoning a cobra from a basket.

Before she became aware of what she was doing, Violet drifted toward the first row of empty seats, her footsteps slowing to the sensuous rhythm of the music. Another violin had slipped into the song as effortlessly as a lakeside breeze on a blistering day, crafting a duet that started lazily but contained an undercutting heat that threatened to erupt at any moment.

As she drew closer, Violet noticed that though the musicians were hidden in the shadows of the candelabras, pairs of dancers were starting to slip into the ring, so silently that they reminded her of smoke floating upward from a snuffed wick. They'd traded the costumes she'd seen them in during most midnight shows for satin dresses and suits that she suspected were white but reflected the flickering of the flames in a way that stained them a new hue with each twirl. The folds of their skirts shifted subtly from an amber glow to a blueish gray and rosy pink, changing like the stained glass of a kaleidoscope. Crystal headpieces in the shapes of stars caught the light as well, giving the scene the dazzling texture of an overturned trinket box brimming with diamonds and sapphires.

Violet was so transfixed by the violins' duet and the dancers' smooth movements that she didn't realize someone had stepped out of the shadows to join her until a warm, calloused hand brushed along her lower back.

"Hello, Wildfire," Emil's smoky voice whispered against her ear. He was careful to keep an inch or two between them, but Violet could still feel the warmth of his body and had to fight the urge to step backward and see what it would feel like to lean into him.

"What are they doing?" Violet asked, trying to lower her voice as her eyes remained locked on the dancers. She knew with the certainty of someone whose days revolved around deciphering the future that if she turned around to face him in that moment, the plans she'd made on her walk along the lakeside would disintegrate. She could already feel her resolve loosening like the ties of a sail that had been pushed too strongly by the sea winds, but she still had enough will left that she might be able to get the words out before it was too late. As long as she didn't see him smile.

"Practicing a new act," Emil replied as he leaned over her shoulder to watch the dancers glide into position along the rim of the inner ring. They were swaying slowly beside one another, as if using the first steps of the routine to introduce themselves. But something more feverish was resting beneath their carefully controlled steps. The space that the dancers left between their bodies only seemed to accentuate the way the couples were being drawn ever so slowly together by the rhythm of the violins' duet.

"Do you want to join them?" Emil asked, his words startling Violet so much that she took a step back, her shoulders hitting the solid breadth of his chest. As soon as she touched him, Violet felt a blush spread across her cheeks that couldn't be blamed on the heat of the summer night.

"I couldn't," Violet sputtered, thinking that she should shift away. But before she could move, Emil wrapped a hand around her waist and began to sway ever so gently to the music. His hold was a playful invitation, loose enough that she could have easily broken it with the barest flip of her hand. His fingers weren't even touching her, just hovering in the air, waiting for an answer.

"Why not?" Emil asked.

"I don't know the routine," Violet replied, not wanting to admit that she was more concerned that the dance might cause her to make a misstep of an entirely different nature.

"No one's here to see you falter," Emil said as he gestured toward the empty stands.

"Emil—" Violet began, turning around in his grasp so that she could tell him she wouldn't be coming back, that this was the last time they'd see each other.

But the moment she gazed into those dark brown eyes the hue of honey at the very bottom of a jar and saw his lips twitch up into a smile, the bitter words that had been waiting on her tongue crumbled as quickly as ash.

Instead, she didn't say anything at all. Violet just grabbed his hand in her own and pulled him toward the ring, closer to the dancers and the slow, even rhythm that was beginning to shift, like a coal that was starting to catch flame.

Violet may not have known the steps, but Emil certainly did. He kept their fingers entangled but moved his free hand to the side of her hip, guiding her silently through the different movements while the pace of the violins subtly quickened. As she did when they were flying through the air, Violet glided with Emil, trusting that he would keep her from falling.

Though they'd started with quite a bit of space between their bodies, the texture of the song brought them closer and closer together until her face was pressed against the soft curve of his neck and she could smell the scent of embers rising from his skin.

And before the final whispers of the violins drifted into the night, Violet decided that she wasn't ready to say goodbye. Not yet.

CHAPTER 19

A Monster

*Symbolizes fears that brew within you
rising to the surface.*

A sense of exhausted defeat sank itself into Anne's weary hands as she sat in the parlor with only Tabitha's muffled snores for company. The house hadn't even permitted Anne to keep the fire going, afraid that the heat would lull her to sleep before she made a choice. Instead, she rested on the edge of her wingback chair, the fine details of the room obscured by the darkness that the flickering candles couldn't chase away.

But Anne had been grateful that the house refused to let the wood catch in the hearth. The flames were always a source of distraction now, each lick of the light creating a puzzle that Anne had been eager to solve. They danced against one another in the most confusing fashion. Abundance waltzed alongside Loss. Longing intertwined with Fear. Frustration and Fulfillment merged together in the shadows. And it all had to do with their own future somehow.

She'd been enthralled by these hints of what was to come like a child at a lantern show, waiting on bated breath to see what the next trick of the light would reveal. Even Beatrix and Violet had noticed her odd fascination with the fire, confused that she insisted the house strike a piece of kindling when the shop had been so hot earlier in the day.

Now Anne realized that every moment she'd spent gazing into the flames had given the curse more strength. It was *her* fault; of that she was convinced.

She'd been so tempted to explore her powers, stretching them to see how far they might pull her, that Anne hadn't accepted the obvious. It wasn't a coincidence that her new abilities were progressing just as the curse awoke, but she'd pushed that possibility to the side. And for what? To distinguish herself from her sisters and have something, just this once, that was her own?

Tears started to fall then, the waves of guilt pouring out of Anne's body in deep, rough wails that made the house shudder. What had she done? All her life she'd tried to protect her sisters, and a single lapse in judgement now threatened to unravel the delicate threads of their lives. She was the Tower, struck down by hubris and a desire to reach beyond her grasp.

Anne had unleashed something within herself, and now it was changing her. It was changing all of them. Was there any way to stop what she had begun?

The sensation of fur brushing against her palm drew her back to the present. Tabitha had risen from her perch and dropped something on Anne's lap.

"What have you brought me?" Anne asked as she scratched behind the cat's ears and reached toward the unexpected gift.

It looked like a tangled mess, a knot of worn black satin ribbons that had likely been left under a chair or in a corner for decades.

But as Anne raised the curious bundle closer to her face, she froze.

It was full of dust, cobwebs, and magic. Her own magic.

"Where did you get this?" Anne asked, half hoping that the cat would actually give her an explanation.

But Tabitha merely yawned and marched toward the door, pawing at it until the house finally pushed it open for her.

Anne knew what it was. The knotted ribbon was evidence of a binding spell, a kind of enchantment used to keep witches from practicing their craft. This one didn't seem as if it were designed to do away completely with someone's magical abilities, merely damper them. But holding the strange artifact between her palms, Anne was positive that it had been cast by her own two hands. The tattered fabric smelled of peppermint, black tea, and early morning dew, the fragrance that arose whenever she did any spell casting.

But the trouble was that Anne had never dabbled in that kind of magic, which meant that Tabitha had brought the ribbons from the future. She did that from time to time, carry back small trinkets from the moments that she slipped in and out of.

Anne suddenly realized that she was going to cast a binding spell, and all indications suggested that it would be on herself.

The thought horrified her at first. Binding oneself wasn't necessarily a painful act, but it caused a witch to feel somewhat separated from their body, not quite at home in their own skin.

And then a new idea began to take shape.

Perhaps if she bound her magic for a short time, that would give her a better chance of breaking the curse. These visions were certainly not helping matters, only muddling an already complicated situation, as she had learned from her dream vision. And they had grown into a secret that needed to be kept from her sisters, further separating them from one another.

In between two heartbeats, Anne accepted what needed to be done.

She rose from her spot on the floor and followed Tabitha's path out the door, hoping that the house would cooperate and allow her to return to the back room undisturbed.

Sensing that something wasn't quite right, the house watched Anne, curious but uneasy. Once Anne entered the divination room, the jars started rattling slightly on their shelves.

"Shh," Anne whispered as she ran her hand against the mantle, consoling the jittery house. "This is going to help, not hurt. I swear."

Moving carefully toward the shelves, she drew out a book that had been so well used over the centuries that it should be falling apart, but it always managed to hold itself together. Their mother had been fond of telling them that the bonds of tradition and love for the craft were what kept the leaf-thin pages from crumbling, and so, for the longest time, Anne was convinced this meant that any kind of altercation between the sisters would cause the book to disintegrate.

Noticing Anne's distress, her mother had told her that it wasn't so simple, that love doesn't become untethered in an instant and, in any case, the book didn't work that way. But a part of Anne was never persuaded away from her initial assumption.

Resting the giant tome on the table, Anne carefully flipped through the pages until she found what she was searching for.

"'*Ad Tempus Vinculum*,'" Anne read out loud, trying to make the words feel more familiar against her lips.

This was a spell that their mother had never taught them. She believed it was unnatural to try to tie back someone's abilities, that problems of this nature should first be tackled in a less dramatic way.

But Anne didn't have time to dally with possible alternatives. Tabitha's gift was a clear sign of that. Focus was what Anne needed to solve the curse, not distracting glimpses into a future that she feared would show her alone, whittling her life away without the company of her sisters.

The signs were confusing now, but they would become clearer soon enough if her most recent visions were any indication. She didn't like the path they were leading her down. If she allowed herself to stay firmly in the present, that might give her just enough time to change what was to come.

After reading the instructions, Anne rustled through the cabinet drawers until she found what she needed: the stub of a black candle, a small pair of silver scissors, and two black satin ribbons that were the same length and width as the ones that Tabitha had dropped in her lap.

Referencing the book one last time and tweaking the spell for her own needs, Anne sat at the table and began to utter the enchantment.

"Bind and bound what this thread wraps around. To see in others, but for myself, leave the future unfound."

As Anne whispered these words, she worked the ribbons into a sequence of tight tangles and then tied them around her own wrists.

By the time she'd chanted the spell three times and pulled the final knots, the candle had burned itself to a mere puddle of wax and flickered out. But just before the room was shrouded in darkness, she caught a glimpse of thin, smokelike threads creeping from the ribbons and sinking into her skin.

It was done. The enchantment was only temporary, but she hoped it would keep her newfound powers in check for a few months at least. In the meantime, she'd hide the makeshift bracelets under her sleeves. Once the curse had been broken and they were celebrating their birthday, Anne would tell her sisters the truth. And then they would reverse the spell together.

As long as they *were* together.

CHAPTER 20

An Overturned Cup
Signifies criticism and judgement.

In the weeks that followed, the scent of iced vanilla cake laced with strawberries and thyme infused the front parlor, beckoning ladies in from the summer sidewalks and encouraging them to let time slip by while they recovered from the heat. They sipped on crystal glasses of chilled mint lemonade as the Quigley sisters deciphered their fortunes, listening to the rumble of their predictions like a child taking in the murmur of their mother's voice during a nap on the seaside. This desire to rest and move at a slower pace hadn't touched Beatrix, though, who returned to her desk every night to knit together the next section of her characters' story.

On a particularly warm evening just before the summer came to a close, Beatrix sat locked in her study while the house hemmed and hawed, amplifying every squeak of the floorboards in the hopes of distracting her. It was still hurt that she had decided to keep writing and refused to open the nearest window to help release the heat that lingered in the room.

Since her last encounter with her mother's diary, all Beatrix had wanted to do was rush back to her manuscript and write, hunching over the desk until her fingers refused to grip the pen for a single second longer. When lost in a world crafted by her own words, Beatrix found herself over and over again. She might still speak too softly and fret over every choice that needed to be made while working in the shop, but on the page she was decisive and became familiar enough with her own reflections to know that nothing needed to be second-guessed. Between the lines, Beatrix learned that she was someone worth getting acquainted with.

And, when each chapter was finished, she'd taken such pleasure in wrapping the pages up in twine and carrying them to the publishing house, where Jennings pored over them like a pilgrim who'd finally reached a point of worship.

Every time he turned over the pages of a new section, Beatrix would stand by the corner of the desk, trying her best to not look nervous while he assessed her work.

"Wonderful," he'd murmur every so often, as if he simply couldn't help himself. "Just wonderful."

And whenever he reached the final line, Jennings looked up from the page as if in a daze and told Beatrix that the story was perfect. That not a single word needed to be altered and he would fight tooth and nail with any editor who tried to pick and pull the manuscript apart.

Then she'd wander back to the Crescent Moon and start the whole process over again, losing herself in a wealth of words that needed knitting together. Before she even picked up her pen, Beatrix was leaning into the story, her thoughts already entangled in possible plotlines. And the longer she wrote, the more comfortable she felt in her own skin. It seemed like she'd drunk an entire bottle of champagne all on her own and was happy to just float along wherever her story decided to take her.

But though writing felt as natural as breathing, that didn't stop Beatrix from pausing every so often to wonder if the story she was crafting stemmed from her own imagination or the curse.

Had her desire to write been nothing more than a distraction meant to pull her away from Anne and Violet? As Beatrix's eyes rested on her mother's diary, every instinct in her body told her that couldn't be the case. Her stories came from her and her alone, and it was a trick of Fate that everything seemed to be happening at once.

Beatrix knew enough about the way destiny works to understand that nothing was coincidental, but she preferred to shy away from the worst of possibilities.

Perhaps the best thing to do was finish this one chapter and take the next a bit slower, just to be cautious. Beatrix was convinced that she didn't need to give up writing entirely, not when her mother's diary seemed to be offering her such encouragement. But perhaps giving herself a chance to better reflect on the situation wasn't a poor choice.

The thought caused Beatrix to loosen her grip on the pen and set it aside. Reaching forward to snub out the wick of the candle and return to bed, Beatrix promised that she would try to pace herself in the weeks ahead. But as the flickering light hit her outstretched hands, she stilled.

Her skin was covered with words.

Letting out a shriek, Beatrix lost her balance and sent the chair toppling backward, the brisk movement causing the candle to blow out. The sound echoed through the room, waking the house, which had just drifted off into a restful slumber.

As she extended her hands, all Beatrix could see in the rays of light coming from the gas lamps in the hallway was fair skin marked by a few ink stains. Had she gone mad then?

"Shh," Beatrix whispered as the floorboards began to vibrate beneath her knees, a clear sign that the house wanted her to explain what was happening.

Grabbing the box of matches that rested in the drawer, Beatrix quickly moved to light the wick again, her hands shaking so badly that she broke four of the wooden sticks before the flame caught.

At first, she didn't notice anything amiss, but as she tilted her palm just so, she saw them again. The words were so white that she could hardly make them out, like a faint scar that's healed after months of careful tending. But they matched her handwriting, and as Beatrix looked even closer, she realized that she was reading snippets from her story.

In a fit of panic, Beatrix unbuttoned her sleeves and shoved them upward, searching for more words against the flesh of her arms. When she found none, she threw her dress and petticoat off entirely, scanning her legs, stomach, breasts, and even the skin between her toes for the descriptions and plot twists that appeared in her manuscript.

But the strange writing seemed to be restricted to her hands.

How long had it been there? Days? Months?

Since Beatrix had started to write her novel, she'd been so consumed by descriptions and lines of imaginary dialogue that it was entirely possible this phenomenon had gone unnoticed.

And then another question began to take hold, one that caused her skin to grow cold: Did this have anything to do with the curse?

Flinging herself away from the desk, Beatrix began to pace across the room so quickly that the house decided to stretch out the dimensions a bit so that she wouldn't have to turn quite as often.

Writing had become the center of her existence. She'd thought of little else over these past several months, and when she wasn't sitting at her desk trying to weave together a new chapter her mind was lost in possibilities for her characters. Beatrix had thought nothing of that, of course. She was passionate about writing, and so it was expected that she'd want to be working on it whenever she could.

But what if there was something more to it?

Beatrix didn't feel like she was under an enchantment—not one that grew from the workings of another witch, at least. No, it seemed like she was developing some kind of new skill that involved more than being able to string together a solid sentence. Her story felt alive, and maybe it was in some way, and not just in the metaphorical sense.

Consumed with a sudden need to be rid of the manuscript entirely, Beatrix found some brown paper and twine and began to wrap them around the stack of papers. By the time she was finished, it looked as if she was trying to restrain her chapters with all the knots and ties.

After shoving the parcel to the very back of her desk, Beatrix closed the drawer, locked it, and threw the small key on top of the bookshelf for good measure. Whether that was to keep the writing contained or prevent Beatrix from giving in to temptation was unclear.

Beatrix's hands were starting to itch, right where the words were inscribed against her flesh. Her fingertips ached for the feel of the pen, but she knew that this was the right decision . . . for now.

Holding her hands back up to the candlelight, Beatrix saw that the words on her flesh were starting to fade. Distancing herself from the words on the page seemed to be helping, and she hoped that by morning every last vowel and consonant would have disappeared entirely.

After all, what choice did she have but to go back to the person she'd been before hoping for something more?

CHAPTER 21

A Tent

*Suggests restlessness and a desire for a
change of scene.*

Violet had discovered that she loved the sensation of falling.
As she threw herself headfirst from the platform, she
relished living in between—in between the sky and the ground,
the present and the future, dreams and reality. Over the past few
months of training, she'd realized it was the only place where she
was truly free.

Suddenly, she felt Emil's grip on her ankles, and she knew that
he was about to swing her upward again so that she could grab
the closest bar and continue the routine.

But just as he loosened his grip so that she could move forward, Violet slipped from the present into the past, her thoughts
drawing back to Katherine's warning. In that instant, she lost
her sense of place in the air and missed the bar by an inch, panic
shooting down her spine though she knew the net would be there
to catch her at the bottom.

She hit the ropes hard, bouncing upward a few feet before
settling back down again.

"You seem distracted tonight, Wildfire," Emil said once he'd dropped into the net beside her.

Violet turned to face him, struck once again by the flash of his playful smile. She'd expected the effect to fade the more she came to see him, but to her surprise, it hadn't. When she stepped into the tent and his gaze locked onto hers, the beat of her heart started to gallop, just like the horse at the bottom of a teacup.

Their bodies were pulled together like dragonflies caught in a spider's web, and when Violet turned to face him their noses were practically touching. She had thought it would take longer to get used to being this close to Emil, but while she was flying across the bars the reassuring grip of his hands had instantly felt completely natural. They'd yet to venture outside the tent, though, preferring to spend their time swapping sharp remarks as they danced through the air. She knew that one of the caravan wagons along the lakeside must belong to him, but Violet preferred to keep their encounters in the ring, where there was enough space to put distance between them if she felt they were becoming too entangled.

"It's nothing," Violet said, determined to keep her life at the Crescent Moon apart from the circus.

She hadn't told Emil about her sisters, and he hadn't asked. Though he shared little details about his life with her while they dangled their feet off the edge of the platform—that he had been on the trapeze since before he could walk, that he was from New Orleans, that he enjoyed moving from one city to the next— Violet never shared parts of her life outside the tent in return. And Emil didn't try to pry anything from her, knowing that like all other birds, she'd only hop forward when she knew it was safe to do so. He was the kind of person who let others share their secrets at their own pace, happy to enjoy the present rather than reaching for an answer that would reveal itself in good time.

And, as he'd realized the first night that he pulled Violet from the crowd, he did so very much want more time with her.

Emil wrapped his arm around Violet's waist and started to sway the net lazily back and forth, like a hammock on the shoreside. The tent was still warm with the summer heat, and their bodies, too, were hot from practicing on the bars. But Violet liked the sensation because it made her feel like a child again, dozing under the full sun in the garden without a care in the world. Her eyes fluttered closed, and she felt the muscles in her legs and thighs relax for the first time all day.

"I was thinking that it's time to put you in front of a crowd," Emil finally murmured.

Sluggish now, Violet didn't register what he had said at first. But when she did, her eyes flew open, and she found herself staring straight at Emil's lips, which were turned upward in that familiar mischievous grin.

"You can't be serious?" she asked, bewildered.

"Why not?" Emil asked, pulling her closer. "You've learned enough for a full routine, and with that head of hair, you're sure to dazzle everyone."

He reached upward and pushed aside some of the curls of her fringe, which had grown long enough to tickle her cheekbones.

"We could call you Coggia's Comet," Emil continued, and Violet felt a chuckle starting to rumble in his chest.

"Well, that's better than Wildfire, at least," Violet said, not wanting the conversation to go any further.

Refusing to give up, Emil gently covered her eyes with his hands. They were rough and calloused, but Violet enjoyed the feel of them.

"What are you doing?" She smiled, placing her own hands on top of his.

"Imagine it," Emil replied. "You're standing at the top of the platform without the net beneath, ready to take that first push into the air and leap toward the swing."

"Don't be silly," Violet laughed uncertainly.

"The crowd's eyes are fixed on the crimson creature that's drifted down from the ceiling. And as you start to swing, their curiosity shifts to captivation. Will the beautiful woman be able to make the jump? Will she catch the bar in time? Your heart's racing too just before you take that final push and fly. For you don't know the answer either."

Not bothering to interrupt him, Violet allowed herself to sink into the scene. To feel her hands gripping the swing tighter the instant before she needed to take that first leap of faith. To sense the suspense radiating from the crowd and feel the air brush against the sparkles of her costume.

"You take a breath," Emil continued, pausing for a moment to inhale deeply.

Violet found herself doing the same, taking in a long, shaky breath and letting it slip out between her teeth.

"And then you leap, throwing yourself toward the trapeze, and for an instant, you're flying—suspended in the moment. And nothing that came before or will come after seems to matter."

They were quiet then, each lost in the same daydream. Emil kept his hand over her eyes, perhaps to encourage Violet to stay in the realm of imagination. Or perhaps because he was already there himself and had simply forgotten.

How had he known just what to say to make Violet realize what she wanted more than anything else in the world?: to be a falling star shooting through the air without a thought of where she was heading or when the light might burn out.

And before she knew what she was doing, Violet had pushed Emil's hands away and was brushing her lips against his, wrapping her fingers through his inky black curls so that she could pull him even closer.

Emil responded in kind, tightening his hold around her waist and taking in the feel of her like he'd been dreaming of since the moment he swooped her up from the crowd and saw the fire flash in her eyes. They sank into the net, their clothes tangling together until they looked like a butterfly about to emerge from a cocoon.

While Violet drank in the taste of Emil, all fireside smoke and midnight, she thought that there was nowhere else in the world she'd rather be.

And as their kiss deepened, heating to a point where Violet felt they were going to singe the knots of the net and fall straight to the ground, a single thought worked its way to the surface.

I don't want to leave him.

The realization was like diving into Lake Michigan on the coldest of February evenings, and Violet shoved herself away as if distance might help ebb her desire.

What was she doing? Hadn't Katherine said to be wary of their impulses? To resist any temptation that might give the curse more strength? Hadn't she promised herself to bring everything to an end?

She was no better than her mother had been, heading toward sure disaster as fast as her feet could carry her. And her sisters, once again, would be the ones to suffer.

Frantically, Violet began to climb up the net, and before Emil knew what was happening she threw herself over the side and started running in the direction of the tent flap.

"Violet!" she heard Emil call out just before she stepped into the night.

His voice was laced with confusion and longing.

And though her heart was crying out to her in the same way, she didn't turn back.

CHAPTER 22

Spades

*Foreshadow arguments, unrest, and
bad luck.*

ime at the Crescent Moon continued to turn, and before
anyone thought to notice, summer slipped ever so slowly
into autumn. The house took all the light linens that had still
been resting against some of the more comfortable chairs in
the parlors and exchanged them for thick woolen blankets that
customers could use to ward off the brutal Chicago chill. Then it
collected the floral decorations that were lingering in corners of
the shop and replaced them with dried marigolds, crisp red and
brown leaves, and cinnamon sticks.

The customers certainly noted the difference with a surge of
delight. They lingered in the threshold of the shop just a moment
longer to savor the first whiff of cloves and cardamom and then
sank into their chairs in a way that suggested they would order
a second pot of tea and enjoy the present company a tad longer
than originally planned.

The house was pleased by these reactions, but it was disappointed that the Quigley sisters didn't seem to relish the change of seasons as they normally did this time of year. Their troubles wouldn't fade completely with rich fragrances and inviting textures, but the house knew from experience that soft surroundings made tongues less quick to cut. And it had hoped the familiar scents and patterns would help them feel more hopeful.

Since the height of summer, they had withdrawn into themselves, returning to their regular routines with the enthusiasm of sleepwalkers. The house noticed that Beatrix had stopped scribbling in her study and that she was spending less time trying to decipher her mother's diary, flipping over the cover only to close it shut a moment later. Violet, on the other hand, had taken up her destruction of the house again and was prying up floorboards using the back side of a hammer, searching through each nook and cranny with more care and attention than the house thought her capable of. Now more than ever, she seemed desperate for some sort of sign. And then there was Anne. . . .

"But surely, there must be some kind of mistake," Mrs. Wilson, one of their regular customers, said as she stared across the table at Anne, a look of desperation in her eyes.

"There is no mistake, Mrs. Wilson," Anne insisted, her tone stern and laced with exhaustion. The ties of her binding spell held firm during the daytime, but at night when her mind was more vulnerable, magic kept trying to seep in. When Anne felt it trickling through her dreams, she'd shake herself awake just in time to prevent the entire enchantment from unraveling. It had been like that for weeks, and now she was so tired that making it through her daily rotation of readings seemed impossible. Though she normally took pride in remaining patient with her customers, even those like Mrs. Wilson who kept the shop's doors open well past closing time, Anne was finding that her endurance was wearing thinner than a doily.

"I see clear as day at the bottom of the cup that your friend is planning to move to Chicago," Anne continued, her voice firm.

Mrs. Wilson had just received a cryptic letter from an old friend in New York whom she planned to visit while they were both traveling through Cincinnati the following month. The message suggested that she intended to make a serious change but didn't offer any details that would help Mrs. Wilson piece the mystery together.

And she was none too pleased with Anne's prediction.

"But I simply don't understand it," Mrs. Wilson wailed into a lace-trimmed handkerchief. "Henrietta loathes the cold and believes that Chicago is the place where social ambitions go to die. I can't imagine her uprooting herself from New York to come here."

"Mrs. Wilson, I'm rather confused," Anne said, setting the cup onto the saucer with a firm clink of porcelain that drew the attention of the only remaining customers in the shop, a pair of women who were speaking with Beatrix as they buttoned themselves back into their woolen coats. "Henrietta is your closest friend. Shouldn't you be happy that she's moving here?"

"We happen to be friends *because* of the distance between us, not *in spite* of it. A little of Henrietta goes a long way, let me assure you," Mrs. Wilson retorted tightly. "Miss Quigley, perhaps you could try again?"

"We've been through two cups of oolong already, Mrs. Wilson," Anne sighed as she resisted the urge to glance at her watch.

"But there could have been some kind of misunderstanding," Mrs. Wilson pleaded, dancing on the edge of panic now that her friend's migration seemed all but imminent.

"Mrs. Wilson, I really must insist—" Anne began, only to stop when she saw Violet appear at her side.

"Is there something wrong?" Violet asked, confused that Anne wasn't able to bring the reading to a smooth conclusion.

"Oh, Miss Violet," Mrs. Wilson wailed, dabbing the corners of her eyes. "She says that Henrietta is coming to stay . . . *permanently*."

Violet reached for the cup that Anne had abandoned so roughly on its saucer. She turned the rim to the right, and then a bit to the left, her brow furrowing with concern at what she saw there.

"I believe that my sister has misread your leaves on this occasion, Mrs. Wilson," Violet said, trying to keep her tone professional but failing to keep the shock from tingeing her voice.

"Misread?" Anne instantly murmured, reaching for the cup. "Where?"

"Here," Violet said as she pointed her finger toward two curved lines. "See, these indicate interrupted travel, not a trip that will be completed. But I can see how it happened, Mrs. Wilson. The symbol is almost identical to the sign for challenges ahead, which is another sequence of curves."

Anne stared into the cup for a few moments longer, but when her head began to lower a fraction Violet knew that she saw it too.

"An honest mistake," Violet whispered, the taste of the word unfurling a bitter flavor in her mouth. Anne never made mistakes, especially when it came to reading the leaves.

"Please accept my apologies, Mrs. Wilson," Anne said. "It's been a very long day, and I'm afraid my eyes are tiring."

"Does this mean that Henrietta is not coming to live in Chicago?" asked Mrs. Wilson as she rose from the table, hesitant but hopeful.

"She won't be coming here," Violet answered with certainty. "It seems that she currently intends to make the move, but her plans will be derailed."

"Thank the Lord!" Mrs. Wilson exclaimed, clearly too elated

by the news to be angered over Anne's misinterpretation. "But of course, you don't mean derailed in the literal sense. Henrietta is so fond of traveling by train."

"Not at all," Violet said reassuringly. "I highly doubt a tragedy of that kind will be involved in deciding her course."

"Well then," Mrs. Wilson said, releasing a deep breath and moving toward the entrance. "Now I can visit her in Cincinnati without a care in the world."

Violet led her to the front door, where she helped Mrs. Wilson into her woolen cloak and tried her best to push the woman onto the street. But she kept rattling on about her trip to Cincinnati, her ridiculous hat blocking Violet's view of Anne, who was still sitting at the table and staring into the empty cup with a firm expression.

She needed to ask her what was wrong.

Just as Violet finally convinced Mrs. Wilson to step over the threshold and was about to turn the Open sign to Closed, though, another figure appeared at the door and walked inside.

"Good evening, ladies," their guest said in a clear, deep voice that reminded the Quigleys of crisp winters. As he shook off his jacket and hung it on a peg in the entryway, the fragrance of chilly January nights and fresh snowfall filled the shop.

They'd just welcomed a winter witch.

Though the Quigleys had encountered his type before—the Midwest was practically bursting with winter witches who drew their magic from cloudy, sunless days and temperatures that made your breath freeze, after all—this one seemed even more powerful than most. They could practically see icicles forming on the floor as he moved toward them, outlining every single one of his footsteps.

He must have been the final witch sent by the Council.

"Welcome," Beatrix said, her voice wavering as she stepped

forward to take their visitor's hand, startled by the icy blue intensity of his eyes. "I assume you're here to see about your Task."

"I hope to do more than see about it," the man said with a chuckle, his eyes crinkling about the corners.

"Of course," Violet said, unable to keep from smiling. "We'll do our best to help."

She and Beatrix turned to Anne, expecting her to take the reins and lead them forward, as she always did. But to their surprise, she hadn't even risen from the table yet, her eyes still focused on the bottom of Mrs. Wilson's cup.

"Anne?" Violet finally managed to ask.

She slowly looked up at them, her eyes widening in shock as she noticed their guest and realized what she'd missed.

"I apologize," Anne said as she abandoned her chair and moved toward the witch. "I was lost in thought. If you'll just follow us this way, Mr.— I'm sorry, we haven't been told your name."

"Gunderson," the witch replied. "Joseph Gunderson. And I already know you three, so no need for introductions there. I've heard about what you were able to accomplish with the other two witches that the Council sent your way."

It was obvious that he believed his fate rested in three very capable pairs of hands. Normally, Anne would have been flattered, but under the present circumstances, she only felt more rattled by his confidence in them.

"We're honored to help you uncover your Task, Mr. Gunderson," Anne said as she stepped toward the back room with Violet and Beatrix trailing behind her. "If you'll just follow us this way, please."

Once everyone was settled in their chairs and Mr. Gunderson had a chance to take a few sips of tea and a large bite out of a cinnamon bun, he waited for one of the sisters to push the conversation forward.

But none of them spoke, and the only sounds that filled the room were of Violet's feet tapping against the floorboards and the chain of Beatrix's spectacles hitting the side of the table as she twirled it nervously between her fingers.

They were waiting for Anne to chime in and set everything on the proper course, but she seemed too intent on rubbing her wrists beneath the fabric of her dress to pay any attention.

Violet and Beatrix would have to begin the session themselves.

"Mr. Gunderson," Violet finally said. "How long have you known that your Task still needs to be completed?"

"Oh," Mr. Gunderson replied, leaning back on his chair as he pondered the question. "I'd say since the beginning of the year. I started waking up in the middle of the night because it felt just like I was falling. That's never happened to me before. I've always been a sound sleeper, mind you."

"I see," Violet said with a sigh of relief. The signs that Mr. Gunderson was experiencing indicated that he was at a much earlier stage than either Fiona Pickwix or Mr. Crowley had been. Not that they could waste any more time trying to figure out what he needed to accomplish. It could be something that required a great deal of effort, and they weren't willing to risk pushing anything close to the end when the consequences were so dire.

Violet and Beatrix waited for Anne to ask the next question, but she didn't, and so Beatrix was forced to forge ahead. Things were starting to feel out of sync, as if the session were a wobbling top about to tip over to one side.

"And what did you believe your Task to be?" Beatrix inquired.

"Now there's a story that I haven't told anyone in quite a while," Mr. Gunderson said, a smile growing across his face. "How much detail would you like?"

Winter witches were notoriously long-winded storytellers. Months of nestling next to crackling hearths with their fingers wrapped around hot mugs of cocoa loosened their tongues and encouraged them to kindle moments of warmth that cut through winter's chill. They could spend days weaving together a single tale, often starting in one place and ending up somewhere that the listener couldn't have predicted. The fact that Mr. Gunderson had taken the time to ask Beatrix how long he should spend on the story showed that he was taking the situation very seriously indeed.

Beneath his wide smile and boisterous personality, he was deeply frightened.

"Just enough to understand why you mistook it for your Task," Beatrix replied. "It would be better if you focused on how you felt."

"I'll do my best," Mr. Gunderson said before he cleared his throat and continued. "The long and the short of it is that I came into my Task rather late in life, or so I thought. I lived near the lake in Wisconsin next to the most beautiful grove of pines I'd ever set eyes on. You see, these weren't any ordinary trees. They were the home of forest spirits, as old as the land itself."

Beatrix nodded in appreciation. Forest spirits were very rare indeed. Humans, especially in the last several centuries, had driven them to near extinction.

"When the logging company marked the grove for cutting, I felt such a deep compulsion to stop them that I was sure it was my Task. And I stayed up late into the night for several weeks making the wind blow so harshly that the loggers refused to stay and left the site in peace."

"That was very noble of you," Violet said.

"It didn't feel like a choice at the time. The thought of the trees being logged kept plaguing me until I had to do something to put a stop to it. That's why I thought it was my Task. At least I can't say it was all for nothing. I keep a small cabin up that way and visit every so often. Those trees are still there and just as beautiful as ever. I would have saved them even if I hadn't believed it was my life purpose. If I had known, though, perhaps I could have saved myself as well."

"Well, we'll do our best to help you discover what it is you still need to take care of," Violet said, pausing for a moment to see if Anne would join the conversation.

But, once again, she was met with that unfamiliar silence.

"Beatrix," she said, her tone a tad shriller than she intended. "Why don't you explain what our main aim is for this first session?"

"Oh, yes, of course," Beatrix replied. "Mr. Gunderson, today we are simply going to decide what method of divination is best suited to your individual needs. Though we might get lucky and discover your Task in the next few hours, it is more likely that you'll need to return at least once more."

Anne felt a tingle of guilt pricking at the back of her neck. The night before, she'd fallen into a deep sleep, where another vision tried to creep in through the knots of her binding spell. It had chilled the tips of her toes and fingers and, upon reflection, was likely a clue that would have helped her discover Mr. Gunderson's Task. But she'd hastily brushed the premonition aside, frightened of what it might reveal.

"That is more or less what I expected," Mr. Gunderson said with a nod.

Now Violet and Beatrix waited for Anne to start speaking so that they could move on to the next step, but she was lost in her memory of the dream and the sensation of the invisible bonds pressing against the flesh of her wrists. It wasn't until she felt a firm kick against her shin that she realized everyone was waiting for her.

"Oh, where were we?" she asked with a blush.

"We were just about to start finding the method of divination that's best matched to the situation at hand," Violet said, becoming more frustrated now. "Why don't we begin with the cards?"

"Yes, of course," Anne murmured as she tried her best to focus on the present.

Choosing the right means of searching out Mr. Gunderson's future proved to be more difficult than the sisters expected. Over the next three hours, they kept rushing from the table to the cabinets to retrieve various instruments and materials: tarot cards, ruins, dust, and even a jar of spiders. And it wasn't a lack of cooperation on the part of Mr. Gunderson that caused the delay. No, he was more than willing to open himself up to the process, even when it meant letting a horde of insects crawl across his palm. Instead, the problem stemmed from an imbalance that was growing between the sisters. They kept colliding at the table, their hands and elbows knocking together at the most inconvenient moments. They always seemed to be a beat off from one another, the normal sequence of their process becoming riddled with gaps that kept them from reaching any real clarity.

By the end of the session, they were able to determine that the crystal ball was the best tool to use during their next meeting. But it was a result that they should have been able to reach in a matter of minutes, not hours, though Mr. Gunderson didn't seem to realize that was the case.

"I must say that I'm very pleased with how things are progressing," he said as the Quigleys led him toward the front door. "It's reassuring to think that Fate might be bargained with after all."

"Yes," Anne replied, her thoughts straying away from their guest and toward a plan that had been forming in the back of her mind. "Nothing is set in stone if one is only determined enough to change it."

"Indeed," Mr. Gunderson said with a tip of his hat before saying his final goodbye and walking out onto the street.

"Anne," Beatrix murmured as soon as she saw her sister's shoulders tighten. "I'm sorry the session didn't turn out the way we'd hoped. Next time will be different. It's only that there's so much to consider at the moment."

"You're right," Anne said. "We have too many distractions. It's time to do something about it."

"What do you mean?" Violet asked, concerned by the steely tone that was creeping into Anne's voice.

"I mean that the diary obviously isn't going to show us anything useful. And there aren't any clues to be found in the house. We need to start thinking about what we're going to do if the curse doesn't subside by our birthday. There's already a chill in the air, and the first snow will come sooner than last year."

"What are you suggesting?" Beatrix asked, frightened by the glint in Anne's eyes.

"That we bind ourselves to the shop," Anne answered, staring boldly at her sisters.

A chill swept down Beatrix's and Violet's spines.

"Out of the question!" Beatrix cried. "That kind of magic is entirely too unpredictable."

"It would only be for a few months at the most," Anne asserted. "Just enough time to avoid the curse and figure out how to break it for good. We can't be separated from one another if there's no way to leave the house."

"But we can't be sure of that!" Violet exclaimed. "The spell is too temperamental. We could be trapped here for years, decades even."

"At least we would be together," Anne said, thinking of all the nights they had gone their separate ways instead of staying where they were meant to be, together in the warmth of the family parlor. If they couldn't even manage to maintain that ritual, how could they be expected to fight the curse without using a bit of magic to keep them on the right track? "And I'm doubtful that the spell would warp in a way that keeps us here for that long."

The house was also troubled by Anne's proposition. Getting the chance to see more of the Quigleys was always a welcome thought, but a spell of that sort would turn their home into a prison, and it would feel compelled to start acting differently. Where it might have once opened the curtains a tad wider to let in the sun, it would shun the light in favor of shadows. And the stale, musty odor that comes from closed doors and windows would become a familiar fragrance. It might even start neglecting the garden if its interest started to move inward, and all the cheerful mums and elegant rhododendrons would wither in the winter chill.

No, a binding spell wouldn't do at all. Panicked, the house began to clatter the pots and pans that were hanging in the kitchen. There was something it had been hiding from the sisters since closing time, and now seemed like the perfect moment to hand it over.

"What in Hecate's name?" Anne murmured as she walked quickly toward the commotion, annoyed that the house had interrupted such an important conversation.

When the Quigleys stepped into the kitchen, they saw a note held together with that distinctive red seal sitting on the table, daring them to open it. Tabitha sat beside it with a contemplative expression, as if considering whether to bat the envelope with her paw and knock it to the floor.

"What does the Council want now?" Anne asked as she shooed away the cat and reached toward the message.

She peeled open the wax seal and carefully pulled out a note, afraid that it might burst into ash at any moment.

"They're giving us until first frost to uncover Mr. Gunderson's Task," she announced.

"First frost?" Beatrix cried. "They can't possibly expect us to do that. Not when he has so much more time than the other two."

Anne clenched her fists at her sides, trying to control the anger brewing within her. Her bonds were vibrating with pure rage, and she worried they might untangle if she gave in to her instincts to throw the closest teacup across the room.

"Then we can't bind ourselves to the shop," Violet insisted. "Not yet, at least. It will use up too much of our magic."

An enchantment of that sort would drain them, leaving them ill-equipped to uncover another Task.

"Anne?" Beatrix asked, concerned by what seemed to be lurking beneath the surface of her sister's rigid composure.

"We're going to reveal the third Task," Anne finally said as calmly as she was able. "And then if the curse doesn't lift, we'll bind ourselves to the shop."

With her words still echoing through the room, she turned and walked out, leaving her sisters in stunned silence.

As Beatrix and Violet listened to her angry footsteps, the note burst into flames, sprinkling flecks of gray ash against the floorboards once again.

CHAPTER 23

A Sparrow

Represents forgiveness.

The house rattled every time Violet ripped up a new floor-board, shaking all the teacups in the kitchen and knocking more than one gilded picture frame askew.

After Anne's announcement, Violet had gone straight to the third floor with a hammer in hand and attacked the hallway with a vengeance, prying up the nails and pushing the boards aside in the hopes of finding any sort of clue beneath. Distraught, the house was following behind her as quickly as it could, securing the boards back in their rightful places as soon as Violet finished one section and moved on to the next. But she was shifting in a frenzy, chipping the corners of the boards and scratching the varnish. The house would be up all night trying to keep pace with her.

Violet hadn't left the shop since she'd run from Emil, and it felt like the walls were starting to close in. She'd even stopped ventur-ing out to the market, preferring to ask Peggy to go and avoid the risk of wandering toward the lakeside, where the circus beckoned.

When Anne had insisted that they bind themselves to the shop, Violet should have been relieved. The security of knowing that she wouldn't be tempted to walk through the threshold and let her feet lead her nearer to the source of the persistent tune that was still beating through her veins would have made things so much easier.

But as soon as her sister had mentioned the binding spell, Violet's first impulse was to run—run straight out the front door before the shackles of an enchantment could tie her down.

Her next thought had been Emil. He was, after all, what she wanted to run toward.

During her waking hours, Violet managed to keep him pushed to the back of her mind if she focused on the work that needed to be done in the shop and, when the Crescent Moon closed for the evening, ripping up every surface of the house to uncover any secrets that might be hidden beneath the beams and plaster. But everyone has to sleep sometime, and when Violet's body threatened to collapse and she reluctantly crawled into bed her dreams always brought her back to the candy-striped tent on the lakeshore.

Groaning in frustration, Violet picked up the floorboard she was holding and threw it roughly to the side. The wood hit the wall, causing something inside to loosen and fall to the floor with a metallic clink. Before Violet had a chance to even blink, something shiny and round rolled through a small crack in the plaster and landed next to her hand.

Ever so slowly, she reached down and picked up the object, drawing it closer to her face. And when Violet realized what she was holding, her eyes widened in surprise.

Resting in the center of her palm was Clara Quigley's wedding ring.

It was a simple gold band that the sisters hadn't managed to find after her death. They'd assumed their mother had taken it off in her grief and stored it out of sight, but the ring had never reappeared. Until now.

Shocked by how warm the metal felt against her skin, Violet carefully turned the ring over to inspect the inner surface. Before their father died, Clara had never removed the band, not even when her daughters begged to wear it around their thumbs. Violet had always wondered what was inscribed on the inside, but whenever she asked, a knowing look would settle in her mother's eyes before she shook her head and changed the topic.

On one side, Violet could make out the roman numeral VI. Instantly, her mind went to the Lovers in the tarot deck, a card that depicted a couple next to an apple tree with a serpent that peeked out from between the branches. It was a sign linked to love, temptation, and trials that would need to be overcome.

As Violet's gaze settled on the inscription carved along the other side of the ring, her hands started shaking so badly that she almost dropped it into the open recess of the floor.

Forgive me.

Tears were pouring down her face now, hot and unrelenting. She'd kept them bottled up for so long that the sorrowful release was agonizing, tearing at her ribs and chest and refusing to let go.

Violet couldn't stay in the house a moment longer. There were too many memories that had marked the walls, and they were threatening to fall in on her, pulling her deeper into the past. She needed to get out and move toward something new, something fresh that wasn't weighed down with so much pain and grief.

Leaving the ring on the floor, Violet sprang up, sailed down the steps, and ran out the back door toward the one place that she knew she'd feel free.

When Violet walked into the circus tent, the midnight show was in full swing, and she was instantly lost among sparklers and sequins. Turning her face upward, Violet searched for the flash of

Emil's costume as he flew above the crowd, but all she saw were the shadows cast by the candelabras.

Her heart started to beat faster as she pushed through the lion tamers, baton twirlers, and waltzing couples, hoping to catch the scent of cinders or the sound of his laughter. But no sign of him emerged that could point her in the right direction.

Perhaps she wasn't meant to be here after all. Perhaps all she was destined for was a life on the ground. Perhaps—

"Wildfire!" she heard someone cry as a pair of warm, strong arms wrapped around her waist, pulling her into the smell of smoke on a crisp summer night.

Emil.

For a moment, he just held her, as if making sure that she was real and not a trick of the light, and then he pulled her even closer, ensuring that she couldn't run away again.

"I thought you weren't coming back," Emil said, his voice rough with worry. "I waited every night, but you never walked into the ring."

When that final word left Emil's lips, the image of her mother's wedding band flashed through Violet's mind.

And in that moment, she decided to let go of the past and take a chance on the temptations that had been waiting for her.

Violet moved her hands along the sides of Emil's neck and pulled him close, leaning into the softness of his lips and relishing the sensation of being away from everything beyond the tent and letting herself simply fall into the moment.

Not missing a beat, Emil did the same, running his hands through her hair and whispering words that she didn't know but somehow still understood.

And she didn't speak again for quite a while. Not about her past. Not about her future. In the silence, she decided to linger in that strange space between imagination and sensation, where all was possible and nothing grounded.

CHAPTER 24

A Dragon

Heralds sudden and impactful changes.

The study had been getting tighter and tighter ever since Beatrix threw her manuscript in the back drawer of the desk and promised herself that she wouldn't write another word.

At first, she thought the sense of the walls coming closer was an echo of her own imagination, but as Beatrix took stock of the bookshelves and file cabinets, she realized that the house was taking away an inch of the room at a time. Her chair was now so close to the wall that she couldn't pull it back and had to climb on top of it and then tuck her legs under the desk to get settled.

It didn't help matters that her basket of unread correspondence was growing more unruly with every passing day. Large envelopes from Donohoe & Company spilled over the edge and onto the floor, each one heavier than the last. Though she hadn't opened any of them, Beatrix knew what she would find if she tore apart the seals: Jennings' questions, asking her why she hadn't come by the publishing house to share her progress and reminding her of the deadline for the novel that was fast approaching.

It was a shame, really, that she'd stopped so close to the end. There were only a handful of chapters needed now to draw the story to a satisfying conclusion, and she'd had trouble focusing on anything but those final scenes over the past few months. As she poured tea for the ladies in the shop, her mind drifted to her characters and the threads of their stories that were waiting to be strung together. And while putting the accounts in order, she found that her dots and dashes formed odd patterns that looked more like sentences than neatly numbered totals. Then there was the persistent itch on her hand, right where her pen normally rested against her fingers. She'd tried everything from beeswax to chamomile leaves, but nothing could soothe it.

Worst of all, though, was the feeling that she was once again sinking into the background of her own life.

It had been harder than she expected, returning to the version of herself whose thoughts could only be expressed through silences and shy glances. Everything she said felt so incomplete, so void of its true meaning. She'd found herself speaking less, only saying what was absolutely necessary to finish a reading or abate her sisters' suspicions. Anne and Violet seemed distracted enough anyway, each of them lost in her own world as they ate around the kitchen table. They followed the same routine as before, but the movements seemed empty now, as if they were puppets attached to strings. It was like putting on a favorite sweater that suddenly seemed too long in the sleeves and tight around the collar.

Beatrix placed her hands on the top of the desk and could practically feel her manuscript calling to her from the drawer, begging to be brought out again and finished.

But she couldn't, of course. It was unthinkable. Wasn't it?

Beatrix only had a few chapters left, and with the speed at which she wrote, they could be knit together in a few sittings.

Then she could pass it on to Jennings, and by the time he needed anything more from her, she and her sisters would have uncovered the final witch's Task and broken the curse.

With each passing thought, Beatrix felt her hand reach toward a stack of blank pages that rested on the corner of her desk, eager to pull aside a clean sheet and fill it with words. But she paused just as her fingertips were about to touch the paper, willing herself to pull back and avoid temptation.

A rattling noise caught Beatrix's attention, and she turned toward the shelf to see her mother's diary shaking free from its spot between a dictionary and one of their old reservation books. She'd tried to flip through its pages since giving up on the novel, but it remained blank, no matter how much she pleaded for a paragraph to seep through the paper.

It certainly seemed to have something to say now, though.

Beatrix gasped as the book flew off the shelf, just barely missing her head before landing on the desk with a thud. The cover opened, and Beatrix leaned forward to see what awaited her there.

Write.

The single word was nestled in the very center of the page, glaring at Beatrix like a beacon.

"No," she murmured. "I can't."

The page turned, revealing the same message on the next sheet.

Write.

"I can't," Beatrix repeated, but this time, her tone was less insistent.

And she started to wonder if one of the reasons it had been so easy to push away the manuscript in the first place was because of a lurking fear that she wouldn't be able to finish it. As confident as she'd been while flying through the story, Beatrix realized now that there had always been a shadow of self-doubt waiting in the back of her mind like a seed silently taking root. In avoiding the final chapters entirely, she would never have to confront the possibility of failure.

The pages turned faster and faster now, so quick that the single word inscribed over and over again began to look like it was moving.

Write.

Write.

Write.

Then, when the diary ran out of pages and it reached the back cover, the whirlwind stopped, revealing the key to the drawer on the last sheet.

With shaking hands, Beatrix reached forward and grasped it between her fingers, feeling the warmth of the metal against her thumb.

And as she began to think about the very first lines of the next chapter, words started to float across her skin. This time, Beatrix didn't scream. Instead, she stretched her hands toward the light and took in the gracefulness of her own handwriting, admiring the way each curve of a consonant glided gently across the coves of her knuckles. The words seemed more like beauty marks than scars now.

Releasing a shaking breath, Beatrix took the key and unlocked the drawer to the desk. Before she even reached into the darkness, she could feel the story there, vibrating like an anxious dog waiting to be taken out for a walk. After untying the binding knots and turning to the place where she'd left off, Beatrix paused with her pen poised above the page.

But only for a moment. Because, for the very first time, Beatrix was done hesitating.

She launched into the story, eager to hear the sound of her

pen scratching the page and breathe life into the scene that was unfolding with each new sentence.

And somewhere between the first line and the last, Beatrix would find the words that made her feel at home with herself once more.

CHAPTER 25

A Thimble

*Emerges when there are problems at home
that need mending.*

As Anne leaned into the cushion of her wingback chair in the parlor on the second floor, she couldn't help but feel like she was being buried beneath the weight of her own enchantment.

At night, the visions that seeped into her dreams were so forceful she'd wake up to find that the threads of her binding spell had loosened, like a delicate lace shawl that had been handled too roughly. During the day, her focus was split between running the shop and continuously knitting the bonds back into place to keep her power from slipping out. It wanted a greater challenge than deciphering the leaves at the bottom of her customers' cups, and if given free rein, Anne knew she'd start seeing glimpses of her own future in the candle flames and glassy reflections of the mirrors in the parlor.

With the first snow fast approaching, she was afraid to see these hints of what was to come. If she didn't look away quickly enough, she'd catch glimmers of sequins or smell the fragrance of freshly cut paper. These sights and scents were so foreign to the shop that Anne didn't dare ask what they meant. But as the days moved forward and these signs continued to appear whenever Anne brushed against Violet or laid her hand on Beatrix's shoulder, she started to suspect that she wasn't the only one keeping secrets.

The thought had stunned Anne at first. She and her sisters had shared every hope, fear, and passing impression since before they could speak, conveying their shifts in mood without the need for words. She'd tried to push the possibility aside, but the taste of burnt lemon and cream of tartar lingered on the back of her tongue after she spoke with them. And gradually, she came to accept that they might be holding fragments of themselves from view, just like she was.

But every time Anne thought of asking her sisters what they were hiding, the threads of her binding spell would take advantage of her lapse of attention and start to loosen. All her energy seemed to be spent on tying the knots back together.

Worse still was the fear that if the bindings broke completely, she might not have the desire to pull them back together.

She was beginning to understand what a bird who'd had its wings clipped must feel like—stifled and longing to soar.

Running a shaky hand through her hair, Anne wondered if this sense of being pulled back emerged with her new powers or if it had been there all along. As a child, she learned to limit her abilities to match her sisters', the habit growing so strong that Anne had stopped even thinking about what she was doing. Pausing to ensure that the pace between the three of them was even became instinctual, as automatic as the ticking of the tiny hands of her clock.

When their mother had passed on, Anne continued to hold

back for Violet's and Beatrix's sake, but she also began taking on the additional weight they couldn't carry. The grief of losing their parents was a heavy burden, so Anne had been the one to step forward and ensure the next chapter of their lives began on a steady note. She'd let Beatrix linger in her study when they needed another set of hands in the front of the shop and didn't disturb Violet when she got lost in her daydreams.

Anne had slipped into her mother's shoes and found that, though the toes pinched a bit and the leather dug too deeply into the sides of her ankles, she could walk in them just enough to manage.

But things were starting to change somehow. Though Anne couldn't put her finger on the precise moment, she'd begun to wish that Violet and Beatrix would start keeping pace with her and not the other way around. Her tone was more strained than it normally was when she asked Violet to tend to a customer waiting by the door, and she didn't move toward Beatrix's table as quickly as she used to when she saw her struggling to find the right words to soothe a client who'd been frightened by the signs at the bottom of her cup.

And at the end of the day, when she went to the parlor alone to try to tend to her loose threads, Anne was consumed by guilt. When had she lost the strength she needed to hold the three of them together? How could she be so selfish, questioning her responsibilities when she needed to protect what was dearest to her heart?

Leaning into her upturned palms, Anne began to let the tears that had been building within her spill down her cheeks and onto the flesh of her wrists, where they burned against the threads of the binding spell, filling the parlor with the scent of singed satin.

She let herself become lost in the uncertainties and doubts

that had plagued her since the spring, deciding it was safe to give in to her sorrow now that she was alone.

If she'd been paying enough attention, Anne might have noticed that beneath the scent of burning satin, the smell of marigolds was gradually infusing the room. The house noticed it instantly and tried to tug at Anne's quilt to get her attention, but she was so consumed by her own grief that its efforts went unheeded.

It wasn't until Tabitha stood up from her spot near the hearth and started crying that Anne bothered to look up.

"What is it?" Anne asked as she rose from her chair and moved to the center of the room, where Tabitha was gazing fixedly at the corner near the window. When she ran a hand down the cat's spine, she could tell that the creature was alert and excited, as if she'd seen someone familiar.

But no one was there. Anne only saw white curtains dancing in the crisp breeze that filtered in through the open pane.

"Don't be so silly," Anne murmured as she lifted Tabitha in her arms and buried her nose in her black fur.

She continued to chide the cat as she carried her out of the parlor and toward her bedroom, where she planned to settle in for another restless night.

But the house's attention stayed fixed on the spot where Tabitha had been staring.

And after a few moments of silence, it realized that Anne might not have been alone after all.

CHAPTER 26

A Bat

Foreshadows a fruitless endeavor.

Though the scent of cinnamon and nutmeg grew stronger in the shop with every passing day, the house noticed that the warmth was beginning to flicker out of the Quigleys' conversations. Though they still spoke to one another about the business, they were so entangled in their web of worries that they forgot to reach up to tuck a curl that had escaped their sister's bun or hide the last pecan biscuits in the back of the pantry, where they would be left for safekeeping. They shied away from one another for fear that their secrets might unravel when brought closer to the light.

It didn't help matters either that the steady rhythm of the shop seemed to have been disrupted. Pots of Earl Grey were delivered to ladies who'd ordered white peony tea, and the signs seemed to slip from one part of the cup to the next during the Quigleys' readings, forcing them to revise the stories nestled within the leaves. Worst of all, visitors whose names couldn't be found in the reservation book kept appearing at the door, demanding a table and refusing to return to the windy streets until they'd fortified themselves with a piping hot cup of tea and something sweet.

By the time an unexpected visitor slipped into the Crescent Moon on a particularly busy day in late September, Anne's attention had been captured by a group of debutantes who all wanted hints about the slew of holiday balls they were eagerly preparing for. Beatrix was still taking refuge in her study, where she planned to stay until she pressed an ear to the door that led to the front parlor and couldn't catch a whisper of the young ladies' gleeful giggles, which erupted every time Anne pointed to a heart or a fan that fluttered from the rims of their cups. This left Violet, who'd just stepped into the tearoom to replace a batch of scones she hadn't realized were burnt before serving them.

She was so distracted by her mistake that the figure lingering on the threshold nearly went unnoticed. It wasn't until the scent of scorched rosemary and cheddar was overpowered by chrysanthemums that Violet looked up and came face-to-face with Mr. Crowley.

"Oh!" Violet cried as she stumbled back and dropped the entire platter to the floor. "Mr. Crowley, we didn't know you'd be stopping in today."

Mr. Crowley eyed the scattered scones skeptically and then, after some consideration, bent down to help Violet collect them.

"The Council didn't send me this time," he grumbled once the platter was stacked again. "I came of my own accord."

"Well, I'm afraid all our tables are full at the moment," Violet said as she blew a strand of her fringe from her eyes. "But if you can wait, we'd be happy to sit and give you a reading and a pot of tea."

"I'm not here for a reading," Mr. Crowley said. "Or tea."

He said the last word as if Violet had offered him arsenic.

"Then what are you here for, Mr. Crowley?" Violet asked,

allowing some of the impatience she felt for the man slip into her tone.

Mr. Crowley's lips pressed together in a firm line, as if he was battling with himself over whether to say something or not.

"To apologize," he finally spat, giving his cane one quick tap on the floorboards before he leaned more heavily onto it.

"To apologize?" Violet asked, stunned. "Whatever for?"

"For being difficult," Mr. Crowley replied. "I was rude when you discovered my Task, which was uncalled for. It's been bothering me ever since."

Violet didn't know what to say, and so she merely stood there silently as the clicks and chatter of the tearoom continued around them.

"The Council gave you a challenging job," Mr. Crowley continued. "And I was no help. I could have handled everything more fairly."

"Does that mean you're going to complete your Task?" Violet asked hopefully. As gruff as the witch could be, Violet didn't enjoy the thought of him suffering as a ghost.

"No," Mr. Crowley answered, his answer firm and unmoving as a mountain. "I won't be completing my Task."

"But why?" Violet asked, genuine concern and curiosity texturing her voice.

"There are some things worse than death," Mr. Crowley murmured, the expression in his eyes growing distant, as if he was slipping away from the Crescent Moon entirely and toward another time or place.

Surprising herself and Mr. Crowley, Violet reached forward with her free hand and placed it on his forearm.

"If you ever change your mind, don't hesitate to see us again," Violet said. "We'll help any way that we can."

Mr. Crowley glanced down at Violet's hand in shock but didn't shake her away. Instead, he lifted one of his own and gave her fingers a quick but reassuring pat.

"I know that," Mr. Crowley said. "But my mind won't change. I have my reasons, and let that be enough. Pass on my apologies to your sisters. I know you three just wanted the best for me."

And with that, Mr. Crowley turned and walked back into the street, leaving behind him the chill he'd let into the front parlor and more than a few unanswered questions.

CHAPTER 27

A Face

*Appears when you realize what makes
you unique.*

The street front of Donohoe & Company looked oddly cheerful in the lamplight, as if it had finally been able to loosen its suspenders after a long day of work.

Staring up at the bronze sign that hung just above the door, Beatrix couldn't help but wonder why she didn't feel the same way. Grasping her manuscript tighter to her chest, she couldn't believe that she had finally finished it. Somehow, she'd managed to bring the story to a comfortable close, and when Beatrix had settled a period at the end of her very last sentence the oddest sensation of complete and utter satisfaction had poured through her veins.

She'd expected to feel exhausted then, tired to the bone after staying up late into the night to meet her deadline, but that hadn't been the case at all. As soon as Beatrix leaned back in her chair to stretch out her aching wrists, her mind had already wandered to an entirely new plot. Before she knew it, a whole crowd of characters were stepping into her thoughts to introduce themselves and ask Beatrix if she wouldn't mind hurrying up to help them come alive on the page.

Now, instead of sinking into the warm quilts that the house had spread across her bed, all Beatrix wanted to do was hand over her first story so that she could move on to the second.

But she couldn't, of course. Beatrix had promised herself that she'd stop writing after she finished the novel so that she could focus on convincing her mother's diary to share something more. Hopefully, now that she'd brought the story to an end, the diary would be appeased and decide to show her what it had been holding back.

Beatrix slipped her free hand into the bag she'd thrown around one shoulder and ran her fingers over the spine of the diary, reassuring herself that it was still there. She didn't want to leave it behind for fear that she might be absent when it decided to speak again.

All Beatrix needed to do was slip the manuscript through the mail slot, and then she'd finally be able to focus.

But as Beatrix stepped closer to the glass panes of the doors, she saw that the office wasn't as empty as she thought it would be. In the darkness, she could see the light of a single gas lamp flickering, casting the silhouette of a man against the bookshelves.

Suddenly, the shadow looked up, and Beatrix stepped back, feeling like a child who'd been caught peeking through a keyhole.

She moved away from the door on impulse, ready to flee down the block to avoid embarrassment, but before her feet could hit the sidewalk the door opened, revealing a rather disheveled Jennings. His brown hair was poking out in all directions, and the rumpled state of his shirt hinted that he'd spent a long day at the office.

"Miss Quigley?" he asked, clearly torn between delight and confusion. "Is that really you?"

"Why, yes," Beatrix said, unsure of what to do.

The reason she'd come so late to drop off the manuscript was to avoid running into Jennings. She was worried that he might be upset with her for not answering his letters and for keeping him waiting with bated breath about her progress on the book. The thought of Mr. Stuart berating his assistant had caused her no end of guilt, and she'd hoped to meet Jennings face-to-face only after he'd seen that she'd upheld her end of the bargain and finished the story.

As her gaze slowly moved from her shoes to Jennings' face, though, Beatrix was relieved to find that he didn't look annoyed at all. His expression conveyed quite the opposite, in fact. A wide smile stretched across his face, and some of the signs of exhaustion faded from around his eyes as they sparked with delight.

"Come in, come in," Jennings insisted as he opened the door wider. "You'll catch your death in this cold."

Beatrix stepped through the threshold and into the office, which didn't feel much warmer than the street had been.

"I've come to give you this," Beatrix said without further ado, pushing the manuscript into Jennings' arms.

"You've finished it?" Jennings asked as he turned the bundle of pages over. He stared at the manuscript as if deciding whether to relish the moment or rip the twine with his fingers and dive into the story as quickly as possible.

"Yes," Beatrix said, her voice more confident than she had expected. "I did."

"And how do you feel?" Jennings asked, his eyes moving away from the pages and toward her face.

"Wonderful," Beatrix answered, knowing it was the truest word she'd spoken in a very long time.

A smile grew on her own lips then, and the two of them laughed, caught up in the thrill of having turned the page on a very surprising chapter.

"This calls for a celebration!" Jennings declared as he placed his fingers gently against Beatrix's elbow and guided her toward his desk.

"What kind of celebration?" Beatrix asked as she sat on his chair, her tone more curious than hesitant now.

"Nothing too elaborate, of course," Jennings said as he disappeared down the hall and returned with a brown glass bottle. "I want to stay awake long enough to read your book."

"You can't intend to start so soon," Beatrix laughed as he produced two glasses from a cabinet resting along the back wall and placed them in front of her.

"It's all I've been thinking about doing since you agreed to write it," Jennings replied earnestly as he tipped the bottle over the glasses, releasing a sweet and smoky scent into the room. "There's nothing like finishing a story that has you hooked, is there?"

"I don't suppose there is," Beatrix agreed, taking the glass that Jennings offered and indulging in her first sip. The bourbon burned a bit as it traveled down her throat, but it chased away the chill in her toes and loosened the strain that had built up between her shoulders ever since Anne insisted that they bind themselves to the house.

"What's next then?" Jennings asked as he lifted his own glass. "Have you got an idea for a new book?"

"Don't you think you should find out if that one's any good first?" Beatrix asked, pointing to the manuscript, which sat in the center of Jennings' desk.

"I don't need to read it to know that it's pure magic," Jennings replied. "You've got a special gift, you know that?"

Beatrix blushed and, as was her habit, opened her mouth to

brush aside the compliment. But she surprised herself and managed to stop the words before they left her mouth. Instead, she merely smiled and thought, *Perhaps he's right.*

"I can't possibly let myself consider the next book until you and Mr. Stuart tell me what you think of the first," Beatrix replied. "And I have other responsibilities to tend to."

The thought of the troubles she'd left behind at the Crescent Moon made her shiver.

"Your family?" Jennings asked, a bit nervously, as if he worried what the answer might be.

"My sisters," Beatrix replied in a rush, wondering why she cared that this man knew she didn't have a husband waiting for her back home.

"Oh," Jennings said happily, and then glanced away, obviously trying to hide his relief. "They must be delighted about your writing."

"Actually," Beatrix continued. "They don't know anything about this."

"You mean that you've finished the book?" Jennings asked.

"No," Beatrix clarified. "They don't know anything about the book at all. I haven't told them."

"But, surely, they've read your work?" Jennings insisted. "The short story that you sent over? You must have shared it with them?"

"No," Beatrix answered, glancing away from him and toward the darkness. "I haven't."

"But whyever not?" Jennings asked, his voice rising with surprise. "It's marvelous. They'll love it."

"I'm not so sure," Beatrix said. "I don't believe that it's what they want me to do. You see, we run a shop, all three of us together. And if my attention is focused elsewhere . . ."

Beatrix let her words dangle there, not wanting to even contemplate the possibilities.

"But they'll understand once they've read the book," Jennings insisted. "They'll see how wonderful it is."

She thought of what Anne and Violet would think when they found that their meek sister, practically afraid of her own shadow, had stepped beyond the bounds of the shop and shared a secret side of herself with the whole world.

And not with them.

A fresh wave of guilt washed over Beatrix then, the weight of it causing her shoulders to hunch forward. She felt her hand drift toward her spectacles to play nervously with the chain, pulled back once again to the Beatrix of shame and second guesses.

Sensing her anxiety, Jennings reached forward and clasped her hand in his, drawing it away from the chain and toward the top of her manuscript.

"If they love you, they'll understand," Jennings finally said. "And they'll relish every word that you share with them, just as I have."

Beatrix moved her gaze back to his face then and was startled to realize that even if she didn't believe what he was saying, the words were a comfort nonetheless.

"Won't you give me just a hint about the next book?" Jennings asked, somehow recognizing that they could leave that thread of conversation where it rested for now and pick up a new one.

Beatrix smiled, and somewhere between her second and third sips of bourbon she decided it was time to move on to the next story.

They sat there until the sun began to rise through the window with Beatrix telling Jennings all the details of her next plot as they poured into her imagination like a river. By the time she stepped back onto the street, her voice was hoarse from speaking so much, this time without a single hesitation.

CHAPTER 28

A Wagon

Indicates movement toward the unknown.

The caravan looked like the inside of a trinket box that had been rattled about one too many times. Sequined costumes were thrown haphazardly across the floor, patchwork quilts peeked out of the corners of the bed, and sawdust that had been carried in from the big tent on the bottoms of boots covered everything, just as powdered sugar dusted the tops of particularly sweet biscuits.

Most would cringe at all that colorful chaos, overcome with the urge to rush back home and organize their own belongings, but Violet relaxed into it, happy for once to not have to keep anything neat and orderly.

It wasn't like the shop, where things always needed to be accounted for down to the very last teaspoon. Everything had its place, and that's what the customers who came to see them wanted most: structure and predictability.

Violet had always believed that she and her sisters were in the business of ruining surprises. They were the cousins who peeked past the paper wrapping on Yuletide presents and reported their findings to their younger relatives, who were pleased by news of their gifts but paid for that foresight with the loss of wonder.

Ironic, then, that Violet never could seem to find *her* place in the shop. Now more than ever, she seemed to be floating between rooms and tasks like a butterfly caught unexpectedly indoors. It hadn't helped that the house wasn't letting her touch anything other than a wooden spoon or pair of oven mitts. It was done following her around repairing the wreckage that she left in her wake, and whenever she reached to so much as pull a piece of wallpaper back it lurched away. Now she felt more useless around the shop than ever, unable to focus on the readings of their customers during the day and worthless when it came to uncovering another clue after closing. She was starting to think that Anne might be right in believing there was nothing they could do but resist the curse, evading its grasp but never breaking it completely.

But the idea of closing herself indoors always sent a sharp tingle of fear over her collarbones.

Perhaps that was why she'd slipped away from the shop as soon as Anne and Beatrix had turned their backs, as she had nearly every evening since she'd found her mother's wedding band, and run back to the circus tent.

Perhaps that's why she was now in this kaleidoscope of a caravan, drifting between wakefulness and sleep in Emil's bed with her dress tangled among the mess on the floor.

Perhaps that's why she found herself wondering if she should ever leave and return to the Crescent Moon, where everything that mattered was in disorder.

The thought shook Violet from her lazy half slumber, and she shot up in the bed and shook her head, as if willing the words that were still echoing in her mind to fade away.

Awoken by Violet's sudden burst of activity, Emil slowly

opened his eyes and tried to decide if this was a dream, reality, or some mixture of the two. When he was certain that the sheets beneath him were the stuff of cotton threads and not spun from the web of slumber, he turned his head and watched as Violet sat suspended by indecision, one hand caught in her wild red curls as her eyes darted from the bed to the door.

It should have taken him by surprise, how quickly she shifted from being so entirely in the moment to focusing on her troubles. Though he still hadn't learned any details about her life beyond the circus, Emil suspected that Violet was running from something that she wasn't certain she wanted to let go of.

"What's happening behind those violet eyes of yours, Wildfire?" Emil asked as he gently took hold of her arm and pulled her toward him, inviting her to rest against his chest. He could feel her heart beating as fast as a hummingbird's and was afraid that she might fly away again.

Violet was prepared to make an empty excuse to keep him at a distance, but in the nights that she'd returned to the circus she'd felt her resolve loosening bit by bit. And now she was ready to finally share something with him that wasn't tinged in sawdust from the tent.

"I'm thinking about my sisters," Violet said quietly, the words so soft that they were almost lost in the sound of the wind that beat against the sides of the wagon.

Emil blinked, surprised that she had answered his question, and then reached for her palm so that they could clasp their hands together. He remained quiet, waiting for her to continue at her own pace.

"Our parents passed away some years ago, and they're all that I have left," Violet murmured as the thumping in her chest began to ease into the rhythm of Emil's slow, steady breaths. "But something's changing between us."

"What do you mean?" Emil asked, his free hand trailing up and down the soft skin of her back.

"It's difficult to explain," Violet replied, unsure of how to proceed without mentioning the curse. "But for our whole lives, we've been so in sync with one another. Every wish and movement practically sensed well in advance. I knew we weren't the same, but what makes us each unique allowed us to fit together perfectly, like gears in a clock. But now, I fear we want different things, and we're being pulled apart."

"Pulled apart by what?" Emil asked.

"I'm not sure," Violet answered honestly. "By something greater than ourselves, I fear."

"You mean destiny?" Emil asked.

"Exactly," Violet replied. "And I'm afraid that we'll be forced down paths that aren't of our own making. I want a choice."

"Does it matter very much?" Emil inquired.

"What do you mean?" Violet asked, turning her head upward so that she could face him.

"Well," Emil answered. "If what you desire and what's destined for you are the same, does it really matter how everything is sorted out?"

"But it's not the same," Violet insisted, though her words sounded hollow. "At least, it shouldn't be."

They laid there in comfortable silence for a few minutes, more so finding themselves coming together in the steady tempo of their breathing than getting lost in their own thoughts.

"It seems to me that the next step is figuring out what, exactly, you want," Emil finally drawled so slowly that Violet wondered if he'd drifted back to sleep and was speaking to her from a dream. "That way, you'll know if fate is something you need to be afraid of in the first place."

Violet knew that what she wanted was resting right there beside her. But how could she reconcile what she felt for Emil with her desire to keep everything at the Crescent Moon the same, for fear that the whole structure would unravel? Trying to interlace a fourth partner in the tightly woven fabric of the shop seemed impossible, but so did the idea of giving up the thrill that shot through her body whenever her eyes locked with Emil's as they flew across the tent.

As she felt Emil's breathing deepen and knew he'd truly fallen back asleep, Violet pushed aside those questions and decided to let herself be like the Fool in the tarot for just a bit longer. And as she, too, drifted back into her dreams, she pictured herself walking along a path next to a cliffside without a care of where the trail would lead her or whether one misstep might send her into a field of daisies or over a ledge.

For now, she was happy to remain in the between places that didn't quite fit anywhere else.

CHAPTER 29

A Severed Thread

Warns that a bond might break.

As Anne pulled the kettle off the stovetop and moved to pour the water into a teapot, she sensed the ties of her binding spell loosen. It felt just like when the clasp of a bracelet is coming undone and you only have the barest second to catch it before the delicate stones hit the ground. She moved to lace the enchantment tighter, but in her haste, she let go of her grip on the kettle's handle, causing the hot water to splash onto her hands.

Anne lurched away from the stove and clutched her burning skin to her chest. She was making too many mistakes now, and her sisters were going to start to notice, if they hadn't already. The three of them had been so distant from one another that she couldn't remember when they'd spoken about something that wasn't related to the shop or the curse. How long had it been since they'd warmed the parlor on the second floor with their laughter?

Glancing up at the ceiling, Anne wondered what part of the house Violet was tearing apart. She couldn't hear any creaks or curses, but the walls had been kind about muffling the sounds that came from Violet's vigilant efforts. At least Anne knew exactly where to find Beatrix, who was doubtlessly tucked away in the study trying to decipher their mother's diary. Sighing, Anne considered how much longer she should encourage them to try to uncover clues from the past that weren't there to be discovered in the first place. But as Anne thought about the glimpses of the future that she was so desperate to avoid, she started to ask, once again, whether her sisters were more concerned about keeping the secrets of the present from view.

The thought made Anne's chest tighten, and she tried to resist the urge to find her sisters and beg them again to bind themselves to the house. Though they spent every day together working side by side in the shop, Anne could feel something icy and dark growing between them. It had started in earnest during the hottest days of summer and only worsened since the warmth wafting from the lake had settled into a crisp autumn breeze. The sense of things that remained unspoken sat in the house like a cold and silent creature, waiting to bite when tensions and tempers were high.

Before she could chase that thought any further, though, the house started to rattle like it always did when someone was approaching the garden gate. Anne's gaze moved to the back of the kitchen just in time to see the door swing open of its own accord, revealing Katherine, whose hand was held just inches away from the handle.

"I've never quite gotten used to that," Katherine murmured as she stepped through the threshold and turned toward Anne.

The older woman's mouth set in a firm line, and Anne clutched her hands closer to her chest, understanding that she was about to receive yet another blow.

"It's worse, isn't it?" Anne whispered as she took a shaky step toward her guest.

"I'm afraid so," Katherine said, reaching up to frame her chilled hand against the side of Anne's face and look deeper into her eyes. "The essence of the curse is glowing so strongly now that it's almost faded out the color of your eyes."

"Can you show me?" Anne asked.

When she'd first learned of the curse, Anne had avoided glancing at herself in the mirror for fear of what she might discover. But after Katherine's last visit, she had taken to peering at her reflection in the looking glass above her mother's old vanity, willing herself to see what lurked there. Anne had suddenly felt that the curse seemed worse because it was invisible, as if catching a glimpse of it might give her the strength she needed to strip it of power. But all she ever saw were her own pair of light blue eyes, framed by dark circles and worry lines.

"Perhaps," Katherine said with a nod. "I didn't think it was possible earlier, but now that it's so strong, you might be able to see a glimmer. Do you have a mirror?"

Anne moved to retrieve a silver hand mirror from the shelf above the stove. She'd put it there when they first opened the shop so that Violet could make sure she didn't have any flour on her cheeks before she stepped into the parlor. Her hand shook as she thought of its new purpose.

Stepping beside Katherine, Anne raised the mirror so that it reflected both their faces, the vibrant auburn of her hair a shocking contrast to the white locks that framed her friend's temples.

"I don't see anything different," Anne said after a moment.

"That's because you're not looking with your inner eye," Katherine replied. "You're trying too hard. Just let go and you might be able to see the barest hint of the curse there."

She gestured toward her own eyes with one hand and rested the other on Anne's shoulder, pushing her forward.

Anne closed her lids then and took in a deep breath, letting her heart slow and trying to focus on the scents and textures of the kitchen so that she was centered in the moment.

And when she finally felt grounded in her own skin, Anne opened her eyes and considered her reflection once more.

When she saw what was staring back at her, the mirror fell from her hand and cracked against the floorboards.

Her blue irises had transformed to gold, so bright that she could have been a tiger peering at its prey from the shadows.

"Strong indeed," Anne gasped as she grabbed onto the back of a chair for purchase.

"I'm afraid so," Katherine said. "If we don't manage to change things before the frost sets in, it will only become worse."

Once again, Anne's mind returned to the idea of convincing her sisters to tie themselves to the house, and she became so consumed by the plan that her attention began to slip. Taking advantage of the situation, the threads of her binding spell started to untie themselves, eager to slink to the floor and scurry away. And they almost managed to do so.

At the very last moment, Anne realized her spell was unraveling, and in her panic, she shoved the sleeves of her dress upward to ensure they hadn't fallen away entirely.

The instant she felt the cold air of the kitchen on her skin, Anne remembered that she wasn't alone, but it was too late.

"Anne," Katherine gasped, the shock in her voice echoing through the room as she reached forward to grab Anne's wrist. "What did you do?"

Anne pulled herself away before the older woman could touch her, afraid that the contact might break the fragile tethers that she was at that very instant tying back together. She turned her back to Katherine and only answered when she felt the bonds of her enchantment pressing firmly against her flesh once more.

"I had to," she finally murmured.

"What in Hecate's name would convince you to bind your-self?" Katherine continued, lightly touching Anne on the forearm so that she would face her again. "And at a time like this, when you need all the strength you can muster?"

"I'm afraid I've already said too much," Anne replied, her voice textured with genuine regret.

Katherine pinched the bridge of her nose and shook her head, as if trying to shake away a memory.

"What?" Anne asked, confused by her reaction.

"It's like I've drifted into the past and am reliving a moment with your mother. In this very kitchen," Katherine murmured.

Suddenly, the taste of shortbread and sweet dreams touched Anne's tongue, and she, too, was drawn back toward memories that were shaking themselves free of dust. In an instant, Anne was a little girl again, her feet dangling from the kitchen chair as she took in the distant chatter of adult voices. She remembered. Just as her mother knew she would.

The trembling in Anne's hands worsened as she considered just how frightened she had become over what the future might reveal. And how much she was willing to give to have her mother by her side again, ready to chase away all the monsters that lurked toward them from the shadows.

"Is that such a bad thing?" Anne asked. "She would have been able to sort out our troubles."

"I'm beginning to wonder if she's not at the heart of things still," Katherine sighed.

"What do you mean?" Anne asked, startled by the sudden turn in conversation.

"I've been able to track down Celeste," Katherine announced. "She's moved to the edge of the city and is doing her best to stay in the shadows, but I managed to find her."

"And what did she say?" Anne asked, eager for the barest hint of hope.

"She was very reluctant to tell me anything at first," Katherine replied, a shadow overtaking her eyes as she stared directly at Anne. "Stripped of her power, she's a sorrowful creature."

Anne felt a tingle of warning creep up her spine, but she pushed the feeling aside.

"But she did tell you something?" Anne asked.

"Yes," Katherine said as she struggled to find the words to continue. "She did."

"Is it so very bad?" Anne whispered.

"No, my dear," Katherine assured her as she grabbed her hands in hers. "Only confounding. You see, Celeste told me whose secret she shared."

"She did?" Anne asked, grateful that they'd collected at least one piece of the puzzle. "And whose was it?"

Katherine's grip tightened, bracing Anne for what was to come.

"Your mother's," she said.

Anne's first thought was that she must have misheard her. Their mother never kept secrets.

"What could she possibly have had to hide?" Anne finally managed to ask.

"I'm not certain," Katherine answered. "Celeste refused to tell me more, but it must have been something important; otherwise, Clara would have never insisted on such extreme measures to protect it."

"So, Celeste recently told my mother's secret knowing the price was her power," Anne said. "It doesn't make sense."

"No," Katherine agreed. "Nothing about this seems to fit together."

Anne released Katherine's hands and turned around the

room, as if searching for something among the kitchen shelves that would provide an answer.

"You have to release yourself from the binding spell, Anne," Katherine insisted. "That type of magic will tear you apart from the inside out, and you'll be left no better than Celeste."

"At least I'll be with my sisters!" Anne exclaimed, throwing her hands in the air in defeat. "These powers started to emerge at the same time you realized we were cursed. That can't be a coincidence. Resisting them is the only chance I have at keeping us together."

"My dear, you've been resisting your power long before I saw the curse reflected in your eyes," Katherine replied.

Anne scoffed, but the sound lacked conviction.

"Ever since you were a child, I've seen the way you've tended to Violet and Beatrix, more a mother than a sister," Katherine said. "And you've done so at the expense of your own abilities. There's always been the potential for something great waiting within your soul, but you've refused to grow into it."

"It doesn't matter anymore," Anne sighed. "As you said, any instincts that seem unusual are linked to the curse. I can't risk losing this life."

"I didn't say all your impulses were connected to the curse," Katherine clarified. "Only some of them."

"But you can't guarantee this isn't going to drive us apart," Anne said. "As you told us, curses are complex, and there's no sure way to know this isn't going to push us down the wrong path."

"Anne . . . ," Katherine continued, but she stopped when she saw the determined set of Anne's eyebrows.

It was like looking at a mirror image of Clara, and Katherine knew that nothing she could say would change Anne's course.

"I'm going to fix this," Anne declared as she watched Katherine tuck herself deeper into her cloak and move toward the back door.

"But at what cost?" Katherine asked, her voice so quiet that she could have been speaking to herself.

The question lingered in the kitchen as Anne stood there and listened to the patter of her friend's footsteps fade into the night.

And then, as the implications of what Katherine had told her began to sink deeper into her bones, Anne decided that it was time to share her secrets with her sisters. They would help her decide what needed to be done and pull her beyond the nightmares that had consumed her waking thoughts, as they always had before.

The house shook in confusion while it watched Anne fly up the staircase toward the third floor, where she expected to find Violet prying up the boards or pulling apart the plaster.

"Violet!" Anne cried, the name made unfamiliar by the sobs that were pouring from her throat. "Violet!"

But no matter how many rooms and corners she searched, her sister was nowhere to be found.

Her chest burning now, Anne bolted back down the steps so quickly that the railing shifted closer in case it needed to catch her. She flew toward the study and pushed the door open, eager to see the sight of Beatrix glancing up at her with that bemused expression that made her heart melt.

But her chair was empty.

They were gone.

The moment she realized that both her sisters had slipped out of the house, Anne stiffened, the warmth of expectation that had grown in her chest chilling to an icy hardness.

Once again, her sisters had left her to carry the burden she'd been handed alone.

Wiping the tears from her eyes, Anne grabbed ahold of her

binding spell and pulled it even tighter. They could keep their secrets, and she would tend to hers as she saw fit.

And the house knew that no amount of woolen blankets and evening fires in the world was going to chase away the frost that had settled in Anne's heart.

CHAPTER 30

A Tower

Signifies crumbling illusions and
mistruths.

The days passed by in a swirl of cloves, ginger, and cardamon. Talk of butterflies and good fortune seeped into neighboring conversations about clouds that beckoned troubles on the horizon and the sound of crisp cinnamon shortbread being cracked in two by laced fingers.

But no one lingered over their table as the hours crept nearer to closing, begging the sisters to let them stay beyond their allotted time, just long enough to find another sign among the cold remains of their hibiscus tea. Even the bite of mid-October couldn't keep them from leaving the Crescent Moon by closing, though they failed to understand why, burying the sense of strain that they sensed but couldn't name under excuses about dinner menus and overflowing cable cars.

By the time the Quigleys received another calling card from the Council alerting them to Mr. Gunderson's next visit, they didn't even worry about how they would get all their customers out of the shop before he arrived. The last woman in the parlor walked out the front door nearly half an hour before closing time, refusing the extra slice of spice cake that Violet offered her with kind excuses about the difficulty of carrying it on her walk home.

This left plenty of time to clear the porcelain and pastry crumbs and set up the divination room, where Tabitha was resting on the highest shelf, staring down with an air of disinterest at the crystal ball that the sisters had moved from its place in the corner of the room.

Anne was nervous about being so close to the crystal ball again. The bonds of her binding spell pulled against her wrists whenever she stepped near it, and she worried what might happen if she gazed into the shadowy depths beyond the glass surface.

But Violet and Beatrix had insisted, arguing it was the most obvious form of divination that they hadn't tried yet. Not wanting to draw suspicion, Anne had meekly nodded and let them carry it to the table.

Once everything had been set and laid ready for Mr. Gunderson's arrival, the Quigleys were shocked to find that they had absolutely nothing they wanted to say to one another.

After a lifetime of easy chatter and gentle laughter, they couldn't even muster the most cursory of comments to fill the time. Words pieced themselves together in their thoughts, but the feel of them was so formal and tainted with tension that the sisters couldn't bring themselves to let them roam in the open air.

By the time the bells rattled against the front door, the house was so worked up that it was starting to move all the paintings in the parlor upside down. But Mr. Gunderson, who was beginning to lose some of his jovial spirit at the thought of becoming a specter, was so lost in his own worries that he failed to notice the odd decorative scheme or the hint of desperation lingering in the room like a hat that had gone out of season many moons ago.

He saw that the door to the back room was ajar and didn't bother waiting to be welcomed. Instead, he rushed toward where he hoped his turn of fate awaited him and found the three sisters sitting silently around the table.

"I do hope that I haven't kept you waiting," Mr. Gunderson said, misreading their silence as annoyance.

Beatrix and Violet waited for Anne to take charge, but she remained seated in her chair, staring fixedly at her hands, once again not making the slightest indication that she intended to greet their guest.

Rattled but not wanting to appear rude, Beatrix and Violet stood at precisely the same time and managed to knock into each other with a spectacular smack.

"We do apologize, Mr. Gunderson!" Violet cried once she managed to right herself.

But she said this at the exact moment Beatrix exclaimed, "Mr. Gunderson, please sit down!," so both their words became a jumbled mess, leaving their poor guest in quite the state of confusion.

"Please, please," Violet said, gesturing toward the open chair.

Experiencing the same sensation that overtook him whenever he thought he'd left something at home but was too far down the street to turn back and retrieve it, Mr. Gunderson tried to brush away his uneasiness and settle down to business.

"As we mentioned last time, the crystal ball is likely going to be the best tool for discovering your Task," Beatrix said, periodically moving her eyes toward Anne, who had knotted her fingers tightly together, as if she were trying to keep something captured between her palms.

With a flick of her wrist, Violet blew out most of the candles in the room, leaving only the ones on the table burning.

The light from the flames cast shadows on the smooth surface of the crystal ball, where dark figures began twisting against one another with the grace of dancers performing a particularly wild waltz.

"Now, we'd like you to look into the shadows here, Mr. Gunderson, and just try to focus on whatever feelings emerge," Beatrix instructed. "Push your energy toward the crystal ball, and we'll start the reading."

Not needing to be told twice, Mr. Gunderson immediately began harnessing the fear that had grown in his stomach ever since he'd awoken that morning to the screech of the ravens flocking outside his windowsill and pushed it forward.

Interpreting the shadows that started to grow against the crystal ball's surface should have been simple for the sisters. This kind of reading was similar to searching out the signs that rested at the bottom of a teacup, and the figures that were forming out of their guest's deepest worries were both clear and plentiful.

But Violet and Beatrix were straining to make any sense of them, their foreheads furrowing in frustration as they watched the shadows move across the curved surface.

Anne, on the other hand, was trying to distance herself from the signs that were begging her to give them some attention. She could practically hear them whispering in her ears and tugging firmly against her chin, but the threads that had started to unravel throughout the day refused to remain knotted, and she feared what might happen if she tried to gaze away from the present. The binding ties kept loosening and loosening to the point where Anne felt the slightest movement might cause them to untether.

"That image there, perhaps it is a cat?" Violet suggested, her words lacking even the slightest hint of conviction.

"It looks more like a fallen tree to me," Beatrix replied as she ran her fingers across the cool surface of the crystal ball, hoping that the contact would bring her closer to a realization.

Meanwhile, Mr. Gunderson's concern was starting to grow. The fact the Violet and Beatrix were struggling without the direction of their sister was becoming quite apparent, and though usually a polite and patient witch, he wanted the process to move a bit faster.

"What do you see, Miss Anne?" Mr. Gunderson asked, turning his gaze directly toward her.

Anne was prepared to give a vague response, but Mr. Gunderson's tone, so full of dread and faltering hope, wrapped around her heart and caused her to cast her eyes over the crystal ball.

And in that instant of distraction, the threads of her binding spell fell to the floor and crept under a heavy oak wardrobe in the corner, where they hoped to remain hidden for at least another century or so.

Finally free, the powers that had been steadily growing within Anne let out a shudder of relief and then spilled from her fingertips, eager to stretch themselves and ease the ache of their restriction.

They latched onto the crystal ball in a frenzy of excitement, and through them Anne could feel Mr. Gunderson's future dancing in the shadow of the flames in remarkable detail. Reading tea leaves had always felt like putting together a puzzle of impressions. She picked up on the threads of foresight that were printed within the cup and then tried to tie them to the feelings that drifted from a client. The process of weaving everything together was challenging at times, but it always felt like there was an answer to be found if she was patient enough to figure out how everything fit together.

What was happening now felt nothing like that. The future wasn't something that needed to be thought through or sensed out. It was merely there, waiting to be absorbed in all its clarity. Anne felt as if she was breathing in memories of the past rather than glimpses of what was to come, and the sensation was so full of different textures, tastes, smells, and sounds that she could have sworn these moments belonged to her and her alone.

Anne wasn't even staring directly at the crystal ball anymore, just keeping it within the barest corner of her eye. She was too preoccupied with trying to move toward the tangle of emotions that called out from the shadows and pleaded with her to take hold.

And when she did, it became abundantly clear what Mr. Gunderson would need to do to please Fate.

"Have you received an unusual letter recently?" Anne asked, her voice taking on a hue that caused it to seep into the corners and cracks of the room.

"A letter?" Mr. Gunderson asked, bemused by the direction that the conversation had taken but feeling slightly more relaxed, as if he'd glanced in the window of a particularly welcoming bakery during a harsh Chicago winter and warmed at the thought that refuge from the biting wind was only a few steps away.

"Yes, anything out of the ordinary that gave you pause?" Anne insisted, knowing their solution was within reach.

"Well, I'm embarrassed to say that I haven't been sorting through my mail as I should be," Mr. Gunderson replied. "My secretary has taken over my business correspondence, and I've asked him to stack all my personal letters in a basket next to the desk so that I can focus on the matter at hand."

"I would say it's time to go through that stack, Mr. Gunderson," Anne said. "You'll find your Task in one of them."

"Are you certain?" Mr. Gunderson asked, vocalizing the question that was on the tips of Beatrix's and Violet's tongues.

Anne paused for a moment and then released a deep sigh that bespoke of resignation to a force more willful than her own.

Her decision to finally embrace her powers was so potent that the house suddenly stopped all the clocks, which would always run precisely three minutes fast from that moment onward.

"Yes," Anne finally said. "I'm certain."

Haunted by the sound of the ravens' shrieks that were still lurking uncomfortably on the edge of his attention, Mr. Gunderson decided not to waste any time with particulars and began to rise from his chair.

Thanking the sisters in a tone that was both excited and distracted, he rushed out of the shop and onto the street, determined to take advantage of this sudden turn of events and set his destiny to rights.

"Do you think when he figures out his Task, the Council will send word?" Violet asked once she heard the chimes rattle against the front door.

"I would think so," Beatrix replied. "After all the trouble they've put us through, the least they can do is let us know they won't be closing the shop."

"And then, do you think . . . ," Violet continued, wanting to ask if the curse might lift the moment Mr. Gunderson discovered his destiny and they saved the Crescent Moon, but she didn't finish her sentence for fear that Anne might bring up the idea of binding them to the house.

Instead, they sat in strained silence for a few minutes more before Beatrix's brow furrowed, her gaze flitting back and forth between Anne and the crystal ball.

"How did you know where to have him look, Anne?" she finally worked up the courage to ask.

"I saw it in the crystal ball, same as you," Anne replied tersely.

But the sisters felt as if they'd stepped on the moist, pebbled back of a toad, a sign of a half-truth, and knew something was not quite right.

"Anne, what's going on?" Beatrix asked. "We didn't see a letter in the shadows, so how did you?"

"Why are you prying into this?" Anne cried, pushing herself away from the table with such force that the crystal ball fell off its delicate stand and onto the floor, where it rolled itself toward safety beneath the table.

Startled by the force of her reaction, Beatrix and Violet remained rooted in their chairs, staring at Anne as if a stranger had suddenly taken possession of their restrained and ever-optimistic sister.

"Haven't we enough trouble to deal with without begging for more?" Anne continued. "For weeks, you have done nothing to help me, and you aren't interested in binding yourselves to the shop to ward off the curse. In fact, I'm starting to wonder if you're trying to make things more difficult."

"Anne, we wouldn't—" Violet began, only to feel the words that she was about to speak wither in her mouth, turned to ash by her sister's sharp and unyielding stare.

"This house reeks of secrets," Anne continued. "I've ignored it. Made excuses and tried to focus on what needs to be done. But the scent is unmistakable and has gotten so strong that it's impossible to breathe without the reminder that you both have been lying, either to me or yourselves. I haven't figured out which yet. So excuse me if I've decided to hide a few things of my own for once."

And with that, Anne turned and left the room, her anger so potent that the door slammed of its own accord just after she stepped over the threshold, leaving Beatrix and Violet to sort through their miseries without her.

CHAPTER 31

A Kite

Anticipates a lengthy voyage.

The next morning, the sisters awoke to find frost coating the inside of their windows. An unnatural chill saturated the air that would have caused them to shiver if it weren't for the fact that the house had drawn the frigidness from the Quigleys themselves.

Franny and Peggy, who'd left their coats on after discovering that the kitchen was colder than the street, were able to coax the house into warming up a bit with compliments and promises of apple strudel, which always filled the first floor with a yeasty aroma that the walls found particularly pleasing.

But by the time customers began shuffling through the threshold, a slight iciness still lingered in the parlor, where the sisters managed to work side by side without acknowledging one another's presence.

Their clients felt a spiking numbness creep into the tips of their toes and fingers but quickly brushed aside the odd sensation, attributing it to nothing more than the approaching midwestern winter and draftiness of most Chicago homes.

It was a strange afternoon for readings as well. Where the sisters hoped to find hearts, they discovered hourglasses. Signs were just a tad too distant from the rim to tell clients that good fortune was just around the corner. And more often than not, a sip or two was left at the bottom, washing away the residue when tipped over and draining the cup of foresight.

Once again, the customers found their minds drifting away from the tea shop, their thoughts snagging on a memory or errand that kept them from asking for another reading, as was their usual custom. Not even Violet's pumpkin spice cake or the welcoming arrangements of chrysanthemums and sunflowers that sat atop each and every table could keep them there that day.

By the time the last saucer was cleaned and Tabitha had licked every crumb off the floor, it was still daylight, and the house, empty of bustling customers and left to worry about the Quigleys, was starting to chill again.

Distressed by the tension that had wound itself so tightly between its inhabitants, the house tried its best to keep everyone in for the evening. When it sensed Beatrix slip silently from her study wearing her thick woolen cloak, it began to extend the floorboards and switch all the rooms around. The door that once opened out to the hallway led Beatrix into the attic, the steps emptied into the cellar, and the quick walk to the front door stretched on for so long that she felt the muscles in her calves begin to ache.

But Beatrix, who had received a letter from Mr. Stuart just before the shop opened asking her to visit that evening, was determined and knew the house's tricks enough by this point to work around them.

Though she might find her room entirely rearranged when she returned as a sign of the house's dissatisfaction, Beatrix was able to free herself and catch the cable car that would drop her in front of Donohoe & Company precisely four and a half minutes before her appointment.

Nearly out of breath from the exertion of darting around Chicago in such a hurry, Beatrix took a moment to collect herself in the entryway, but she'd hardly had a chance to brush the windblown curls from her face before she heard Jennings' voice.

"Miss Quigley!" he called from his desk, tossing the papers that he'd been holding to the floor and striding over to where she stood. "I'm so glad to see you."

"It's nice to see you as well," Beatrix said, a grin working its way across her lips as the smoky taste of bourbon spilled into her memory.

"We've all finished the book," Jennings whispered, as if sharing a particularly important secret.

"Oh," Beatrix said, surprised that they'd gotten through the story so quickly. "And what did you think?"

A strange expression flickered over Jennings' face, giving the impression that he was about to discuss something reverent.

"It was absolutely—" he began only to be cut short by Mr. Stuart's booming voice.

"Amazing!" Mr. Stuart cried as he barreled forward. "It's quite frankly the best thing I've ever read."

Shocked by this assessment, Beatrix could do nothing but stand there in awed silence.

"Come, come," Mr. Stuart said as he threaded his hand through the crook of her arm. "We have business to discuss!"

Showering Beatrix with compliments and exuberant praise with every step, Mr. Stuart steered her toward his office down the hall, where she settled into the chair on the other side of his desk in a daze.

"Let's get down to it then," Mr. Stuart said as he pulled out Beatrix's manuscript, which, to her surprise, looked like it had fallen off the back of a carriage and been stomped on during the busiest hours of Chicago traffic.

"We haven't been able to put this down," Mr. Stuart said, his fingers tightening possessively around the pages.

"We?" Beatrix asked, confused.

"Yes, well, it seems Jennings here couldn't keep his hands off the story, and it wasn't long before some of the others got hold of it. Though, I assure you, it hasn't left the building!" Mr. Stuart explained, casting a disapproving glance toward Jennings, who appeared uncomfortable but not the least apologetic.

"It's enchanting," Jennings insisted, taking a step closer toward the desk, as if he was about to reach out and grab the manuscript.

"*Jennings*," Mr. Stuart warned as he pulled the pages closer to his chest and sat down in his chair across from Beatrix, clearly unwilling to give the novel up for even a second.

Beatrix tried to absorb everything that had just been said. It didn't seem possible, all this praise, and she was unsure of what to do.

"I'm pleased to hear that you both enjoyed the book," Beatrix said. "But surely you have some criticisms? I know that there's always room for improvement where writing is concerned."

"Not in your case," Mr. Stuart replied. "It's a first for me, but I don't want a single syllable of this book touched. We'll print it just like this, and you're going to be a sensation. An absolute sensation!"

"You can't mean that, Mr. Stuart," Beatrix insisted. "I've never heard of a book being so perfect that it didn't need any revisions."

"Miss Quigley," Mr. Stuart said as he leaned forward and rested one of his hands against the desk. "It's very difficult to describe, but while reading your work, it feels as if the words slip right off the page and thread themselves into your soul. I know that sounds dramatic, but when you write about a scent, it is as if the aroma actually fills my nose. When your characters bite into a particularly delicious meal I, too, experience the flavors and textures of the food. It's unlike anything I've ever encountered, and I'm honestly not sure how you do it. But the important thing is that it works!"

That gave Beatrix pause, but before she could linger too long on the potential meaning of what Mr. Stuart had said, he launched into the next part of his speech.

"We typically don't move this quickly on a piece, but my associates and I believe that it is best to act in haste in your case. We've already printed your short story in this week's issue to drive up interest—"

"You printed my short story?" Beatrix asked. "But I thought it wouldn't appear for a while yet."

"It's all in the marketing, Miss Quigley," Mr. Stuart explained. "We have to publish when it's most advantageous. Next is the book!"

"Wait a moment, Mr. Stuart," Beatrix demanded, holding her hands up as if she were trying to stop a freight train. "When, exactly, do you intend to publish the book?"

"Instantly," he replied.

"Instantly?" Beatrix asked.

"Well, as soon as possible, at least. In the hope that you would agree to my terms, I've already had our team of proofreaders start on your book, though they've found nothing that needs to be fixed on that front so far," Mr. Stuart said.

This was all beginning to feel a bit too much for Beatrix. The room was starting to tilt at an odd angle, which was typical in her own home but not within the walls of Donohoe & Company. Much more concerning, however, was the tingling sensation that was beginning to spread across Beatrix's hands. Beneath the soft leather of her gloves, her skin itched, and the nerve that ran from her wrist to her thumb trembled, as if she had been holding a pen for hours without a moment of respite.

"We're working up the cover design right now, though we'll want your approval, of course. That's usually not the case at all, but your input will likely be invaluable," Mr. Stuart continued, drawing himself further into the fantasy that had started taking shape in his mind the moment he'd finished the final line of Beatrix's book. It featured sale numbers that were sky-high, over-flowing bookshops, and profits—oh, the profits!

"I'm happy to help any way that I can, but I'm sorry to say that I don't know much about—" Beatrix began, only to be interrupted by Mr. Stuart.

"And we'll need to start building the schedule for your tour right away. Last week could not be soon enough!" he exclaimed.

"Tour?" Beatrix managed to ask, her throat going as dry as day-old scones.

"Yes, your book tour!"

"But I've never heard of a first-time author having a tour," Beatrix croaked. "Who would come to hear me speak?"

"Everyone!" Mr. Stuart declared. "Everyone will be clamoring to meet you once they've read your book."

"I imagine you'll have a lecture schedule that will rival Mark Twain's by this time next year," Mr. Stuart said, his eyes gleaming at the thought of the crowds.

As he rattled on about routes and sales numbers, a single image began to creep into Beatrix's thoughts. She saw herself sitting in a private cabin in Central Station, surrounded by piles of luggage and hunched over a small notebook, her hand scribbling furiously over the pages while the sound of whistles and the murmur of hurried travelers hummed in the background. As the train began to lurch forward, Beatrix realized that her imaginary self never even bothered to look out the window, where a pair of silhouettes stood, almost entirely obscured by the mist of gray smoke.

The shock of it pulled her back to reality, where Mr. Stuart was still discussing the details of his plan, unaware that Beatrix hadn't been paying him the least amount of attention.

"We'll book you a ticket to Philadelphia for the week after next," Mr. Stuart was saying, his hands waving over his desk calendar as a captain might over the maps that would lead their crew along a safe passage.

"The week after next?" Beatrix gasped. "You want me to start as soon as that?"

"Of course. What do we possibly have to gain from losing momentum at this point? What we need is to push forward!" Mr. Stuart replied as Jennings nodded vigorously in agreement.

"But—but what about the book? How can we possibly get everything finalized in that amount of time?" Beatrix pleaded.

"You just leave that to us! We'll need you to look over the final copy before we begin the printing process, but I'd prefer if you didn't overwork the story, not when it's in such good shape already," Mr. Stuart said.

"I don't really know if that's the case," Beatrix replied.

"You'll soon learn that if you keep your writing to yourself until it feels perfect, no one will ever read it," Mr. Stuart laughed.

"And it truly is perfect as it is, Miss Quigley," Jennings added softly, clearly worried that Beatrix might decide to alter the text in any way and disrupt the delicate masterpiece that had already become a familiar friend. "I don't think it would do any good at all to change a single word."

"But this isn't nearly enough time for me to prepare for such a journey. How long would I be gone?" Beatrix asked.

"Months, perhaps even a year. We won't want to keep you

away forever, of course. You'll need to have time to write the next book, but I doubt the public will be satisfied with a brief tour once they've read your work," Mr. Stuart said.

"My sisters . . . ," she whispered, the words fading into the breath that she had been holding on to.

"Oh, what fools we've been! Of course you'd want to consult your family on the matter. Feel free to bring them with you," Mr. Stuart said as he leafed through his appointment book and began marking it in a fury.

"I don't believe that will be possible," Beatrix murmured. Trying to picture Anne in the middle of New York City—or anywhere outside of the teashop for that matter—was as difficult as imagining her standing in the middle of Antarctica.

She sighed at the thought, and Mr. Stuart finally seemed to realize that their conversation was taking a toll on her.

"But that's enough for one day, Miss Quigley!" Mr. Stuart cried as he rose from his chair and extended a hand toward Beatrix. "Stop by early next week once we've had a chance to draw up a contract, and we can talk about all ours plans then. In the meantime, just relish your success. It's certainly well deserved, and Donohoe & Company is thrilled to have you among our ranks. You're going to be a sensation! An utter sensation!"

Beatrix stood as well and took his hand, giving it an absentminded shake before Jennings led her out the door and down the hall.

"Are you all right?" Jennings asked once they'd reached the exit to the street, noticing the stern set of Beatrix's shoulders and her sallow complexion.

Beatrix paused to consider the question. There was so much to try to sort through in order to find an answer.

"It all seems so coincidental, doesn't it?" Beatrix asked.

"It seems more like fate to me," Jennings laughed, the sound carrying a genuine note of sincerity. "And to think, I almost didn't find your short story in the stack."

"What do you mean?" Beatrix asked, a chill skittering down her spine.

"We get loads and loads of submissions every week," Jennings explained. "And on the day your story came in, the pile was stacked so high that the whole thing collapsed. Papers flew across the floor, and your envelope slipped right under the cabinet in the back of the room. It would have stayed there, too, if someone hadn't picked it up and returned it to me."

"Who found it?" Beatrix asked, afraid of what he would say without quite knowing why.

"Well, the funny thing is I don't actually know," Jennings replied as he raked a hand through his disheveled hair. "I hadn't seen him before. He was probably an author or businessman who'd come to ask about posting an advertisement. All I really remember is that he had the strangest pair of eyes. They were so gray you could almost see straight through them."

Beatrix's mind leapt back to the night that the Council had first visited the shop, and instantly the face of Isaac, the silent third member, was staring eerily back at her through the veil of the past.

Beatrix felt the blood drain from her face, and her knees were shaking so uncontrollably that she worried she might collapse.

"Miss Quigley?" Jennings asked, his voice filled with concern as he took a step closer to her. "Are you quite all right?"

"Yes, yes," Beatrix replied breathlessly as she pulled her cloak closer and moved toward the door. "It's just all so much to take in. And I need to head back now."

"All right," Jennings said, though he still looked worried. "I'll see you next week then? When you stop by to sign the contract?"

"Of course," Beatrix murmured with a stiff nod, though she could taste the lie on the back of her tongue.

As she walked down the sidewalk toward the closest cable car, Beatrix pondered how all the fantasies that she'd woven together over the years were becoming a reality. She was within arm's reach of success, recognition, and, more than all of that, the knowledge that strangers would welcome her stories into their hearts.

But her victory seemed so artificial now that it was entangled in the possibility that everything she'd worked so hard for might be the result of Fate or the meddlesome Council, rather than her defiance of them.

Was she in control, or were the threads that determined her future so well fitted that she couldn't even sense they were shackling her to a given path?

And when all was said and done, would she even be able to tell the difference?

CHAPTER 32

A Wheel

*Suggests that one chapter is about to turn
into the next.*

As Violet stepped down the avenue, she was pleased to find that the strain that had built up between her shoulder blades was yielding to the soothing melody of the circus, which was always pulsing in a low register beneath her skin but grew louder the nearer she came to that vibrantly colored tent. If she had thought to pause a moment and take note of her own heartbeat, she might have been surprised to find that it matched that unheard but deeply felt rhythm exactly.

But Violet was not one to stand still, and so this strange synchronization went unnoticed.

As she approached the tent, the ticket master, whose smile was just as wide as it had been that first evening despite the lashing winds that swept up from the lake and threatened to knock his top hat clean off his head, ushered her toward the front of the line and through the entrance with a wink. He knew a good love story when he saw it, though from the expression on Violet's face he gathered that the plot might have taken an unexpected turn.

She tried to smile back at him but found the task too difficult. It was as if her dimples were etched in marble, the strain of it causing an ache in muscles that she hadn't even been aware of before.

The ticket master noticed the change and gave Violet a reassuring pat on the shoulder as she slipped within the dim folds of the tent.

It was still too early for the first show of the evening to begin, and she only saw a handful of faces sitting in the crowd, some of them familiar. She was not the only one drawn by the whimsy of the circus, though no one else ever stayed after the final lantern had been extinguished and the magic of the performance tucked itself away from sight.

As soon as Violet took a few more steps, she started to sense that something was not as it had been before. The fabric of the tent was rattling from the harsh winds, causing candy-striped waves to ripple across the ceiling and strain the ropes until they looked as if they might snap. And the people sitting in the crowd, though eagerly awaiting what was to come, were all wearing thicker coats and carried the discomfort that comes with the shift of the seasons, hunching in their seats or rubbing their hands together to try to abate the cold that would linger until the stands started to fill with more warm bodies.

The tent was getting restless, it seemed, disgruntled by the change in weather.

Disturbed by this subtle shift, Violet began to walk toward the back of the tent instead of finding her usual seat in the front row. She slipped out of the flap that led to the performers' makeshift village and made her way to Emil's wagon, where she nearly ran into him just as he was bending over to walk through the threshold.

"Hello, Wildfire," he chuckled, steadying Violet so that neither of them tripped down the wooden steps. "In a bit of a hurry, aren't we?"

Violet tried to think of a witty retort, something that would lighten her spirits and bring her even further away from the troubles she'd left behind in the shop. But her thoughts were clouded with regret, guilt, and—dare she even admit—anger, and instead of laughter, her throat filled with a rough sob.

The grin that had been tugging at Emil's lips immediately hardened. He wrapped one sequined arm around Violet and pulled her inside, where her sadness wouldn't feel like such a self-betrayal.

That trinket box of a wagon was warm from Emil's exercises and the small stove where a few embers still glowed. The costumes, piled high atop the covers and sneaking out from beneath the bed, looked so cheerful and inviting that Violet almost believed if she tucked herself within the explosion of fabric her troubles would be lost among the vibrant textures and patterns.

Sensing that she needed something to warm her from within, Emil poured a bit of whiskey into a chipped cup and nudged her to sit on the only other piece of furniture in the room, a small but serviceable footstool.

Letting his unspoken question rest between them for a moment, Emil waited for Violet to speak, giving her a chance to choose when to let her worries out into the open, where—for better or worse—they would become more tangible.

"Things are cracking between me and my sisters," Violet finally whispered, taking a sip from her cup. The liquid burned her throat and made her declaration feel just as painful as it sounded. "And I don't know how to put them back together."

"Do you want to put them back together?" Emil asked.

Surprised by the question, Violet took a moment to consider.

"I'm honestly not sure. Certainly not in the way they were before. I'd rather them remain broken if that was the case. Oh, what a horrible thing to say!" she cried, her voice shattering as she uttered the words that damned her as a traitor to her sisters.

"It's not terrible. It's merely true," Emil said. "You know, just because you care about someone doesn't mean you have to stay the same person forever. Sometimes, you can love the people in your life so much that you become afraid of what might happen when you start to change. The threat of loss keeps us from taking a risk, and the dreams we have remain just that, fantasies. But love isn't meant to be like that, fixed and unrelenting. It needs room to grow, to make mistakes and turn into something new. It has to account for the living parts of yourself."

"But I do love them," Violet insisted. "With all my soul."

She felt that love running through her veins even now, peeking through the anger and hurt that had kept her from even looking at her sisters for more than a few fleeting moments that day.

"I know," Emil replied, pulling her closer. "But it might be time to consider if you can go on loving them in the same way without losing yourself."

"I don't know if it can be different," Violet whispered. She and her sisters had been locked in their web of affection and dependence for so long now. Their bonds had taken shape during childhood and seemed to be coated in bronze, never to shift as Emil suggested they should.

Emil leaned back slightly so that he could look into Violet's eyes, those purple windows that so clearly reflected whatever emotions were pushing themselves toward the surface.

"The circus is leaving," he finally said.

The tempo that Violet's heart had been following quickened.

So that's why the tent had been acting so strangely. It was agitated, ready to move out of Chicago and toward warmer climates, where it wouldn't shiver against the furious winds that whipped relentlessly from the lake.

"What?" Violet asked.

"We're leaving for the winter," Emil continued, leaning forward so that his words brushed against her cheek. "Come with me."

Violet's first impulse was to pull him close and linger in the thought of remaining in the caravan, where nothing was in need of mending. She was surprised about how easy it was to imagine what it would feel like to wake among the crazy quilts of the bed while the wagon's wheels moved below her. The sensation was so delightful that she almost lost herself to it entirely, but whatever fantasies she'd managed to slip into faded at the memory of the troubles she'd left behind at the Crescent Moon.

"Come with you?" Violet asked in the same tone she would if he had proposed they take a hot-air balloon to the stars.

"Yes, leave Chicago and join the troupe," Emil nodded, touching his forehead to Violet's as if the contact would help his hopes and dreams drift into hers.

"But what would I do?" Violet asked, picturing herself sitting in the stands, an ever-watching shadow to the spectacle. To be so close to magic and never feel as if her own life was fantastical. How would that be any different from the years she'd passed at the shop?

"Perform with me, of course," Emil said. "The crowd always likes to see two trapeze artists, especially when one is as beautiful as you are."

"But I couldn't," Violet insisted. "I'm not good enough."

"You're fantastic," Emil said with genuine respect for how quickly she'd been able to pick up the art. "I've never seen someone take to the bars like you have."

Sensing hesitation in the furrow that began to knit itself more deeply between Violet's brows, Emil sprang up and started digging through the pile of costumes.

"What are you looking for?" Violet asked, confused by his rapid shift in attention.

"Put this on," Emil said as he tossed a velvet bodysuit with gold tassels toward Violet.

"Why?" Violet asked in wonder, her hands clutching the soft folds of the fabric.

"To see if it fits!" Emil explained. "So that you can join the midnight show."

"You mean tonight?" Violet gasped, shocked by his proposal. "I can't possibly perform that soon."

"What are you waiting for?" Emil asked as he touched her softly along her shoulders, his question hitting Violet straight in the heart.

It was on the tip of Violet's tongue to refuse again, but a memory slipped to the front of her thoughts. She remembered the tingle that shot from the top of her scalp all the way to the very tips of her toes whenever she watched him soar against the stripes of the tent, his body casting dancing shadows into the crowd. The tension that was only released when she saw him land safely on his platform. And the overwhelming reverberation of applause that echoed through the tent when the audience shared something that was more than approval—awe.

What *was* she waiting for?

"I need to think about it," Violet said as she pulled the velvet costume closer to her chest and began to turn toward the door. "All of it."

With every step she took, the thought of her sisters and the curse became stronger and stronger, and by the time her hand was wrapped around the handle, she was already consumed by consequences. She couldn't wander down the same path her mother had, one that led to love that bloomed into loss.

"I think we were meant to find each other," Emil said, his voice breaking a bit around the edges as he saw her hand reach for the handle of the door. "I knew it the moment I first saw you outside the tent."

Violet's hand froze in mid-air, and an icy sensation trickled down her spine, as if frozen fingers were skittering along her back.

"What do you mean?" Violet asked as she turned toward Emil, her chest tightening when she saw the look of hope and fear that was etched across his face. "The first time you saw me was during the midnight show, when you pulled me up from the crowd."

"No," Emil said with a shake of his head. "I saw you earlier, when you were trying to get a ticket but didn't have anything to buy it with. Your red hair caught my eye when I was walking around the corner of the tent. I was about to step away, but a man saw me staring and stopped me."

"What man?" Violet asked, her mind shrinking back from the words that she suspected Emil would say next.

"He had a beard and a stern expression," Emil said. "I remember being surprised because he didn't look like a romantic, but he told me that he thought I should try and get you into the show, that it seemed like the place where you needed to be."

Violet's mind flashed to the steely gaze that had stared back at her during their meeting with the Council, and instantly she felt as if a fist were squeezing all the warmth from her soul.

"I know you don't have a high opinion of destiny," Emil said as he took a hesitant step forward. "But won't you take a chance on it just this once?"

Violet didn't reply, unable to find the right words when she needed them the most. She wanted to close the distance between them, wrap a hand around the back of Emil's neck where his curls crept over his collar, and rest her head against his chest, where the beat of his heart might steady the whirlwind of thoughts that threatened to consume her.

But instead, she reached for the handle again and pushed it forward, letting the harsh whip of the wind into the wagon.

"You'll be back, though?" Emil asked, remaining where he stood, knowing that the choice had to be hers and hers alone.

"Of course," Violet said with a nod as she paused to take in the sight of him, perhaps for the last time.

As Emil watched her slip out the door and into the fading twilight, the oddest flavor of burnt meringue began to blossom at the very back of his tongue, from where he could not fathom.

CHAPTER 33

An Eye

Symbolizes realization or awakening.

*B*ack at the shop, Anne was sitting in the private parlor trying her best to avoid reading the signs that were beginning to sliver out of the corners of the room, eager to vie for her attention now that she was free from her bonds.

The house, focused entirely on Anne after failing to keep Beatrix and Violet indoors, had redirected its energies to the task of keeping its remaining occupant calm. It had rattled the teacups that hung from hooks beneath the cabinets in the kitchen, creating a porcelain wind chime that tinkled until Anne relented and prepared herself a cup of chamomile tea. Then, while she was still boiling the water in the small copper kettle, it kindled a fire in the grate of the parlor and pushed her wingback chair just a few inches closer so that the warmth would be sure to sink into her toes. When Anne climbed the stairs to the second floor and settled in her chair, the house even pinched some of the perfume that still clung to her mother's favorite shawl, which had been taken up to the attic and placed in a cedar chest, and pushed the scent through the floorboards until it tickled Anne's nose.

The aroma of marigolds encircled her, and she sighed into it, conflicted by the memories that the scent awoke.

"Thank you, old friend," Anne murmured to the house, giving the arm of her chair a loving pat. "But I need to focus on the present, not the past."

"But what of the future?" a voice called from the fireplace.

"Oh," Anne said in surprise as she looked up to find the faces of the Council staring down at her from above the mantle.

Just as before, they looked as if they were sitting in the middle of the parlor, each resting in one of the sisters' places with expressions that suggested they were eager to talk.

"You haven't said a word, Miss Quigley. Has the shift of seasons given you some kind of a cold?" Hester asked in a tone that implied she was not concerned in the least about the state of Anne's sinuses.

"No, I feel perfectly well," Anne replied as her fingers tightened around the handle of her teacup.

"Hmph," Nathanial scoffed, clearly sensing her annoyance.

"Have you come to discuss the witches who you sent our way?" Anne asked, hoping to move the conversation along so that they would leave her in peace. "I believe it would be best to bring the matter to a close, given that my sisters and I have done all we can for them."

"The Council considers that situation fully accounted for on your part," Hester replied, pausing a moment as if giving careful consideration to what she planned to say next. "Miss Pickwix is well on her way to finishing her Task, and Mr. Gunderson has begun his journey as well. There was a letter that he'd overlooked recently, the one that you instructed him to read, I believe. An old friend from up north informed him that a glen of trees he had some previous attachment to is under threat again. He's convinced saving it is what his final Task is meant to be, and so we, too, are quite satisfied with that result. No, we are here to discuss something else."

"I do apologize that we weren't able to do more for Mr. Crowley, but I don't see how my sisters and I—" Anne began, only to be interrupted by Nathanial, who leaned forward in his chair to glower through the glass.

"Crowley is a lost cause," he spat. "You've identified his Task, but he refuses to complete it. And though this situation is certainly unprecedented, we do not force witches into avoiding eternal unrest, no matter how ridiculous that decision may seem. Crowley is a witch of middling power who has had no interest in developing his abilities, and so we expect that any disruptions that emerge from his choice will be minor and easily dealt with."

"I'm glad to hear you're satisfied with our work," Anne said, permitting herself a small sigh of relief. "If there is any way we can help the Council in the future, the Quigleys are only too willing to serve."

"But it is not the service of the Quigleys that we require," Hester continued, leaning so close to the mirror that her breath fogged up the glass. "It is only you."

Anne remained silent, stiffening as the meaning of the words uncoiled and filled her stomach with the same sensation that erupts when you look over the precipice of a particularly high cliff.

"I don't know what you could possibly want from me," Anne said, tucking the quilt closer to keep from trembling.

"There is no need to pretend any longer," Hester replied. "We know that your power has grown, so much so that you've surpassed the expectations we all held for Clara."

Anne stiffened at the mention of her mother.

"And that you were watching us from the past," Nathanial added. "Quite an unusual ability for a seer, to stand so firmly in the future."

"I still don't understand what you're asking for," Anne said, wanting them to get to the point.

"We want you to join the Council as the city's Diviner," Hester answered, her words simple and blunt.

"You can't be serious?" Anne gasped impulsively.

"Oh, I assure you that we couldn't be more serious about the matter, Miss Quigley," Nathanial grumbled. "The position has gone unfilled for long enough. Without a Diviner, we can't foresee threats to the coven or help put any witches on the right path to completing their Tasks."

"But surely, there must be someone more powerful than me," Anne said in disbelief.

"No," Hester replied, as if the idea had taken her by surprise as well. "There isn't. You are one of the strongest seers we've ever come across, and without you, the witches of Chicago will suffer."

Anne remained silent, drowning in the sea of her own thoughts.

"You may view us as villains, Miss Quigley," Nathanial said with a sigh. "But please let me assure you that the truth is much more complex. Without us, the delicate fabric of our existence would tear into pieces that couldn't be patched back together again, not with all the magic in the world. It's a heavy burden, one that comes with making difficult decisions, but the cost is well worth it."

"You could still keep the shop," Hester added. "Even expand it if you wanted with the resources you'd have at your disposal as a member of the Council. But, to be entirely clear, this is a path that you will need to travel alone. Our work needs to remain a mystery, and you could not share your secrets with Violet or Beatrix."

"How could I consider working with the same people who

tried to separate me from my sisters?" Anne asked bitterly, angry now that their names had been brought into the conversation.

Hester and Nathanial glanced at each other with hesitant expressions.

"Tell her," Isaac's flat voice echoed through the room.

"It would be best if—" Nathanial replied, only to be cut off.

"Tell her," Isaac repeated. "She needs to know."

"What do I need to know?" Anne asked, her pulse beating so wildly that it outpaced the ticking of her clock.

"Your mother's secret," Hester answered, her voice splintered with sorrow.

Anne's spine stiffened, and she hesitated between leaving the room and learning the answer to the question that had lingered in her mind since Katherine's last visit.

What had her mother been hiding?

"Celeste lost her power because she decided that your mother's secret could no longer be kept," Hester continued. "When you three were just young girls, your mother came to a realization about her Task. She was terrified of what she had to do and went to Celeste to inquire if it was possible to change her fate. Your mother was a strong witch, and if she didn't complete her Task, there would be dire consequences, disruptions to the web of destiny that we couldn't even fathom. And so, when Celeste learned that she might purposefully avoid it, but didn't yet know why, she promised your mother that she wouldn't tell her secret to better understand how the situation could be dealt with. And that's when she discovered why your mother was avoiding her Task."

"And why was that?" Anne asked, the hairs on her arms rising in expectation.

"Her Task was to ensure that her three daughters would separate," Nathanial answered softly, knowing the pain his words would cause.

Anne's heart stopped, and for a moment, she hung suspended somewhere between the past, present, and future.

"Celeste couldn't get a clear glimpse into your futures, but she did manage to glean that for you three to complete your own Tasks, you would need to travel down different paths. You couldn't remain together forever," Hester said. "And it was your mother's job to ensure that you would separate and follow your own destinies."

"But she didn't!" Anne exclaimed. "She didn't complete her Task."

Again, Hester and Nathanial cast nervous glances at each other.

"According to Celeste, there's a chance that she might have . . . set things in motion," Nathanial finally said.

"What do you mean?" Anne asked.

"It is our belief that Clara put a curse on you," Hester replied, her words rough as if they left a bitter taste in her mouth.

"No," Anne said instantly. "She couldn't have done that to her own daughters. She couldn't."

"Celeste visited Clara in this very house not long after she came to her for help," Nathanial continued. "She said that your mother no longer seemed concerned, and when she looked into your eyes, she caught a glimmer of a newly cast spell. We believe that Clara knew what needed to be done but couldn't face the consequences. She must have put everything into motion so that you left one another after her death, but not before."

"No," Anne insisted again, refusing to put the pieces together that would so clearly fit. "If that was the case, why did you feel the need to try to separate us yourselves? Why not just wait for the curse to take effect?"

"Because, though your mother was a talented witch, curses were not her specialty," Hester replied. "Earlier this year, Celeste started to notice small suggestions that your mother's decision to delay her Task was already having an influence. Some witches began to notice their clocks were moving backward instead of forward. The leaves on the trees around the lakeside were turning amber in April, and the sidewalks seemed to shrink exactly six inches during the busiest time of the day. These were only the barest hints of what was to come if your mother had indeed failed to complete her Task. She was extremely powerful, and when that kind of energy isn't harnessed in the proper direction, it creates chaos. So, Celeste decided to tell us Clara's secret at the cost of losing her own magic to help save the Chicago coven."

"We couldn't leave the matter to chance," Nathanial added. "And so, we interfered as best we could without disrupting anything your mother might have done."

"What did you do?" Anne asked, horrified by what she was about to hear.

"Beatrix has an interest in the written word," Hester said. "And, so, we ensured that her submission to a local publishing house fell into the right hands. She has quite the talent and managed to write an entire novel. Her editor is arranging the details of her book tour as we speak."

Anne stiffened as she remembered the scent of freshly cut paper that emerged whenever she caught a glimpse of Beatrix's future.

"And I think it's quite obvious to all that Violet isn't the type to stay rooted in one spot," Nathanial continued. "She needs activity. All it took was sending her whispers of music and ensuring she gained entrance to the circus on the lakeshore and she was lost in the possibilities of living a life of movement."

The flash of sequins in Anne's visions suddenly made sense now.

"And me?" she asked. "How did you plan to pull me away?"

"The shop," Hester answered. "It is, after all, what you love the most, aside from your sisters. We didn't intend for you to uncover the witches' Tasks, so that we could close the doors of the Crescent Moon and, perhaps, drive a wedge between you three in the process. But you defied our expectations and succeeded where we needed you to fail."

"So, it was all your doing," Anne muttered, gripping the arms of her chair.

"No, my dear," Hester said. "There is something else at work here. We believe it's the curse, but the texture of the whole situation is off. And, so, we can't be sure."

"But you changed us," Anne insisted.

"All we did was nudge you onto a path," Nathanial replied. "We never change the course of destiny. All we do is give people a slight push in the direction that they've already considered. It is up to them to walk their path, if they choose."

"So, there's still a chance that we'll stay together?" Anne asked, confused by what all this meant.

"The only certainty is that if you do so, there will be unexpected consequences," Hester answered with a sigh. "We hope that you make the right decision."

"You're acting as if we have a choice," Anne scoffed.

"There is always a choice," Hester said. "Otherwise, what need would there be for us to steer people toward their destinies?"

They sat there in silence. Even the house had stilled, trying its best to absorb all the revelations that had echoed through the parlor.

"I'll need some time to consider everything," Anne finally said, her tone hollow, as if all the love had been siphoned from her soul.

"Very well," Hester said. "But don't take too long. The coven needs you, Anne."

Anne nodded while Hester and Nathanial started to shift in their chairs, as if they were about to leave the room.

But Isaac's gaze remained fixed on Anne.

"What?" Anne asked, no longer frightened by the haunted look in his eyes. All her darkest fears and desires had already been brought out into open view anyway.

"It's time to embrace the future," Isaac said. "And stop lingering in the past."

With those parting words, the Council members vanished, leaving Anne to stare at her lone reflection in the mirror.

Sinking deeper into the chair, Anne began to draw her attention to the thoughts she'd swatted away like pestering gnats over the past few months. Perhaps it was indeed time to look toward the future.

And so, she allowed the house to tuck her quilt in a bit tighter and stared down at the leaves that rested against the bottom of her cup.

CHAPTER 34

Swords

Predict quarrels between loved ones;
when crossed, they indicate that you are
coming to a crossroads.

By the time Violet and Beatrix returned home just after sunset, Anne's chamomile tea had long grown cold, the cup abandoned on the side table as she watched the crackling fire, which the house continued to replenish as a means of keeping its mind off the family's troubles.

They arrived at the exact same moment, Violet through the kitchen door around the back and Beatrix through the front. When they tried to creep toward the staircase and sneak into the privacy of their bedrooms, they found the steps missing, replaced by a hallway that led straight to the parlor on the second floor.

Evidently, the house thought it was time for the Quigleys to talk.

When Violet and Beatrix met in the hallway, they avoided looking each other in the eye, though it was difficult for them to understand why. Perhaps it was the discomfort that comes in the moments when you must decide whether or not to tell the truth, to let your hidden confidences become the heart of spoken conversations. Maybe it was from the shame of keeping a secret from a person who truly cares for you. Or it could have been the mutual sense of dread that they were both experiencing, the feeling that their lives were about to change in ways both unprecedented and potentially irreparable.

Whatever the reason, the sisters continued down the hall and opened the door to the parlor, silently wondering what Fate had in store for them.

Anne heard the creak of the door, which the house amplified, but she remained still, continuing to look into the flames with a hard expression that rested uncomfortably across her brow and lips.

Not knowing what else to do, Beatrix and Violet sat on either side of the settee and waited.

"You smell of sawdust and paper," Anne said before adding more quietly, "and lies."

A heavy tension filled the room, uncomfortable and persistent, like a stain that spreads across white linen the more you try to rub it out.

"I think that it's time I told you both something," Beatrix finally said, hoping that if they started talking in earnest, the horrific awkwardness—more befitting strangers than sisters—would fade when the familiar cadence of their conversation deafened this strained silence.

"You've written a book," Anne said flatly, her tone as cool and smooth as the marble cutting stone that rested on the kitchen counter.

Surprised, Beatrix took a moment to collect her thoughts before asking, "How did you know?"

"The Council came while you two were out," Anne replied, her fingers tightening around her cup. "They know everything."

Violet, who had been picking nervously at her hands and tapping her foot against the floorboards, was now sitting still as death.

"They know that you've been writing and have finished a novel. That you'll soon be leaving on a tour across the country," Anne said.

"Leaving?" Violet asked, turning toward Beatrix with wide eyes.

"Nothing's been decided," Beatrix said hastily, though her words sounded weak, even to her own ears.

"They also know about your fascination with the circus," Anne continued, not bothering to look away from the flames and toward Violet, who tucked herself deeper into the crevices of the cushions, where she hoped to disappear.

"It isn't what you think," Violet said, not defensively but in a broken tone that suggested she only wanted to make them better understand.

Oh, how Violet wished that she were in the tent, flying from one platform to the next and feeling as if she were suspended in time, where her worries were forced to stay at bay. That thought instantly flooded her with guilt, however, and caused her cheeks to burn with shame.

"They even knew my secret," Anne murmured.

"What do you mean?" Beatrix asked, stunned.

"I can read my own fortune," Anne declared. "I tried to bind myself so that I couldn't see it, but my powers are taking on a will of their own. The signs appear everywhere now. In the leaves, in petals, in the ripples of my water glass, in the shadows that sneak across the wall, even in silences. And do you know what they keep telling me?"

Anne turned her gaze toward her sisters then, her unblinking blue eyes moving steadily from one mirror image of her face to the other.

"They tell me that we will separate," she said with a note of finality, like she was merely reading aloud the last line in a particularly tragic novel. As if there were no more pages left to turn.

"It isn't true," Violet insisted. "There must be a way."

"We just haven't tried hard enough," Beatrix added. Her mind was still trying to piece together what Anne had just confessed, and because of that, she barely registered the words that slipped from her mouth.

"That is the first true thing you've said in months," Anne said. "We haven't tried hard enough. I would go so far as to say that you both haven't tried at all. Quite the opposite, you seem to *want* the curse to take effect."

"Don't say that!" Violet cried, her voice becoming hoarse with the screams that she was trying to hold back.

"And why not? Isn't it about time we confront it? Do you know what I was thinking of just now? That magic depends on our willingness to make it real. It grows from a place within ourselves where a fervor for the craft burns bright. You both have lost your *will*. That's why you've been so distracted. Not because of fear over the curse but because all your passion for divination has been spent. It is no longer born of love but of obligation, as tedious as sweeping the kitchen floor or clearing up the saucers. Your magic knows the difference between desire and duty, even if you refuse to admit it aloud to me."

"Anne, we won't let this happen," Beatrix insisted.

"Deny it then!" Anne shouted, lurching forward in her chair and stabbing her finger toward her sisters. "Deny that you want to leave! That you love something more than the shop, than the craft—"

She almost added, *Than me*, but found it impossible to say the words.

But her sisters felt what had been left unsaid.

"We do love you, Anne!" Violet cried. "I love you both as my own self."

"It isn't enough, not anymore," Anne sighed, shaking her head. "Not with the curse working against us."

"Of course it's enough," Beatrix said. "Can't we find a way to break it? To pursue our paths and remain close?"

At that, the texture of the room shifted. Though cloaked in care and concern, Beatrix had unwittingly admitted the truth: she wanted to leave her sisters and find her own way. The house sensed it, and all its windows turned black, as if it felt too vulnerable to let in even the finest ray of moonlight.

"Our mother wanted this," Anne murmured. "Why else would she have cursed us?"

The room stilled, as if the three of them had willed time itself to stop.

"That is a wicked thing to say," Violet said, her temper finally rising.

"It's true!" Anne cried. "Celeste told Katherine that the secret she shared was our mother's. And when the Council was here, they said that her Task was to separate us. And that they believed she cast a curse that set everything in motion."

"But she loved us," Beatrix whispered.

"You can still love someone and accept the inevitable. She, of all people, knew that," Anne countered, thinking about how devoted their mother had been to their father despite the fact that she knew he'd pass on too soon. It was something that she'd always seen on the horizon of their future, and the knowledge that she would be separated from her soul mate made her savor him all the more. But perhaps the same attitude that had allowed her to love so fully was the thing that stifled her own daughters.

"I don't believe it," Violet declared. "There must be another explanation, something we haven't considered."

"I think so too," Beatrix agreed. "It doesn't make sense. We can still figure out how everything fits together before it's too late."

"With what time?" Anne cried, throwing herself out of her chair and moving behind it in an attempt to shield herself from her sisters and all the pain that was seeping into the very core of her being. "We have no time! The cold has settled in, and the first frost is nearly here. Snow is coming soon. I can feel it in my bones."

"We're going to fix this," Beatrix insisted, clutching the arm of the settee as a sailor would while trying to steer a boat through a fearsome storm.

But Anne merely gave a short shake of her head, her shoulders sinking in toward themselves, resigned. It was as if she'd used all the words left in her body and it was shrinking as a result.

"Bee's right," Violet added. "There must be a way, and we'll find it in the time we have left."

Anne looked into their eager faces, hard but still creased with a lingering sense of hope, and wanted to conjure up the memories that they shared, so full of warmth and the comfort that grows from stability. There were plenty to choose from, of course. Sunny summer afternoons spent lounging in the garden where the scent of honeysuckle and marigolds mingled with the taste of lavender lemonade. Cozy February evenings in this very parlor, full of the clicking of Violet's knitting needles and the rustling of pages being turned. And crisp autumn mornings, when the three would gather around the kitchen table and take a few moments to simply enjoy one another's company over cups of hot cider and apple scones before the day started in earnest.

But every time a glimmer of these recollections tried to rise to the surface, it was overshadowed by the small but piercing divisions that had slowly torn at their bonds over the past several months. Anne thought of Violet's face, so often turned away from her and out the window, where the entire world waited to be explored. Then there were Beatrix's fabrications that allowed her to craft characters of her own making and shield them from her sisters.

Oftentimes, the sting of a slight lingers longer than the sweetness of a smile. And that was the way of it with Anne as she dangled at a crossroads. She was the woman in the tarot holding two swords who needed to choose which she would relinquish. It was time to let one of them go and commit herself to a path.

So she did.

The corners of her frown sinking just a bit deeper, Anne turned away from the sisters who, as Violet had so earnestly expressed, had been her very own self and left the room.

Beatrix and Violet were still trying to catch their breath when they heard the sound of the kitchen door slamming, announcing that Anne had left the shop.

Not even the house tried to stop her.

CHAPTER 35

A Tunnel

Represents a moment of clarity.

The wind shoved against Violet as she walked down the rainy streets toward nothing in particular. After Anne had marched out of the house, she'd thrown a cloak across her shoulders and run after her, hoping to convince her to come back. But she hadn't known which direction to go, and after making more than a handful of turns to no avail, Violet accepted defeat. Instead of returning to the shop, though, she'd chosen to wander while her thoughts slowed to meet the new pace of her footsteps.

It felt as if the weather was conspiring to push her back home, but that made her even more determined. She hunched into herself and barreled forward, needing to feel like she was making progress, though she hadn't chosen a destination. When faced with inevitable loss, small victories seem more profound, after all.

When she finally began to notice the ache in her feet, Violet looked up from beneath her hood and realized that she had walked all the way down to Grand Central Station. She shivered as the icy rain began to turn into hail and ran under one of the building's swooping arches, where she took a moment to shake off her soaking cloak and take stock of herself.

It would be impossible to walk any longer on the streets, and so Violet decided to take refuge in the white marble lobby, where it would be dry if not warm.

Alert to the wet claps of her heels across the stone floor, Violet entered the cavernous room, packed with rows upon rows of wooden benches, occupied by only a handful of passengers. Most were witches who preferred to travel during the night when they didn't have to be so wary of camouflaging their magic, but there was a human or two, their heads resting against the backs of their seats as they waited, bleary-eyed, for whatever train they were hoping to catch.

Violet had only been in this building once since it opened years earlier, when the marble shone so clean that it was almost blinding to look at and the benches hadn't acquired a single worn spot. And even then, it had been merely to take a quick glance at what their customers were bustling about in the shop, some excited about what they deemed to be progress and others horrified at how much noise and dust it would bring.

To Violet's eyes, the station seemed much less grand in the middle of the night, as if it was absorbing the dulled and exhausted emotions of its travelers. But she, of course, was not in the mood to search out beauty, only the things that most mirrored her own feelings, which were torn and dingy about the corners at the moment.

She no longer felt like the Fool, happily toeing the line between bliss and destruction. Instead, she was trapped in a maze of her own making, wondering if she'd find a way out in time to patch together the broken pieces of her heart.

Violet was so consumed by her own thoughts that the sound of her name almost went unnoticed.

"Miss Quigley?" a scratchy voice asked.

Stopping mid-stride, Violet halted and looked back at the bench that she'd just passed by.

Nestled in a bundle of wool and a boiler hat that had been carried along on one too many outings, a familiar bemused gaze met hers.

"Mr. Crowley?" Violet asked, nearly stumbling as she stared at the last person she'd expected to cross paths with that evening.

They remained silent for a moment, merely taking in the sight of each other, before Violet remembered her manners.

"Are you here to catch a train?" Violet asked hesitantly, wondering if Mr. Crowley had finally had enough of the Council's interference and was planning to run away to parts unknown so that he could spend the remainder of his days however he wished.

"No," Mr. Crowley answered simply. "Are you?"

"No," Violet replied, not wanting to explain why she was in the middle of Grand Central Station at that hour.

"Why don't you take a seat?" Mr. Crowley asked after another few beats of awkward silence, gesturing toward the empty spot beside him.

"If you don't mind," Violet said, wavering. All she wanted at the moment was to be alone, but it seemed rude to ignore Mr. Crowley now that they had spotted each other. The dour expression on his face suggested that he felt the same. Both had sought to escape company but were too well-mannered to extract themselves from the situation.

"Would you care to tell me what you're doing here?" he finally asked, his hand tightening around the cane that was resting atop his knees.

"It's a rather complicated story," Violet said, uncomfortable that, for once, the tables had turned and she was the one who needed to answer delicate questions.

"I don't have anywhere in particular to be," was Mr. Crowley's response. "And neither, I would hazard to guess, do you."

"Right you are," Violet said, resigning herself. "I left the house to find Anne."

Mr. Crowley didn't say a word, merely waiting for her to continue.

"You see," Violet said. "We've had an argument."

"Family troubles," Mr. Crowley sighed, as if the phrase was a familiar one.

"Yes," Violet replied, uncertain if she should say more. "We've been having a disagreement of sorts about our future."

"Humph," Mr. Crowley grumbled.

"You see," Violet said. "I thought that we all wanted the same thing, had the same vision if you will. But I was wrong. I've found that I might wish for another sort of life, one with someone who brings out the parts of me that I had tucked away."

Mr. Crowley nodded, looking entirely unsurprised.

"And if I'm honest, I'm afraid of not knowing where following this new path is going to lead me," Violet continued. "When you fall in love, you have to do so knowing that the loss of it is going to happen eventually, don't you?"

"How ironic," Mr. Crowley murmured after a moment of silence, so quietly that Violet almost didn't hear him.

"Excuse me?" she asked.

"You know, I come here at night to just sit and see what it feels like to be somewhere that isn't here nor there," Mr. Crowley said. "It's not the start, but neither is it the end."

"I'm afraid that I don't understand," Violet admitted, embarrassed that she wasn't catching the underlying significance of what he was trying to express.

"It reminds me of what's ahead," Mr. Crowley explained. "All these people, suspended in time, waiting for what comes next."

Violet realized that he was talking about becoming a ghost, and her brow furrowed in confusion.

"Do you remember when you asked me what I thought my Task was?" Mr. Crowley asked.

"Yes," Violet said, recalling the story that he had told them about continuing the family business.

"Well, I never believed that was it. In fact, when I identified my Task, I became determined to never complete it."

Now it was Violet's turn to remain silent and allow Mr. Crowley to share his story.

"You see, when I was growing up, there was a human who lived just across the street from me," Mr. Crowley began. "We were the same age, almost down to the day. His name was Philip."

Mr. Crowley paused here, as if the act of saying the name out loud was so painful that he needed a moment to recover.

"As we got older, our friendship grew into something more," Mr. Crowley continued. "We had to keep it a secret, of course. My family would have never accepted a relationship with anyone but a witch of our sort, and the humans have their own prejudices."

"That must have been difficult," Violet said.

"It was," Mr. Crowley replied, his eyes clouded from gazing far into the distance of the past. "But whenever we were together, it was like stepping out into the fresh spring air after being shut away all winter."

"What happened to him?" Violet asked, afraid of what the answer would be.

"I began to sense death," Mr. Crowley replied. "I'd go to see him, and the scent of it would cling to my clothes for days afterward. At first, I denied it, but I soon accepted that we didn't have much time left. And, worst of all, I realized that because his life was about to be cut so short, Philip wouldn't have the closure he needed to sever his ties with this world and move on to the next."

"You don't mean . . . ?" Violet asked, not wanting to finish her question.

"He was going to become a ghost, stuck in between for eternity," Mr. Crowley said. "At first, I tried to find a way out of the whole situation, but one morning, we woke up, and I knew that by the next sunrise, I'd be alone."

"But what does this have to do with your Task?" Violet asked, though she already suspected where his tale would lead.

"You see, Philip had a ring," Mr. Crowley continued as he lifted his hand to show Violet the band on his left ring finger, the one with the hourglass whose sands moved back and forth of their own accord. "He wasn't supposed to have it. He'd found it on the street when he was just a child and wore it ever since, first on a string around his neck, and then, when he got big enough, on his hand. The moment I saw it, I knew that it was my Task to figure out who it belonged to and return it."

"And did you discover where it belonged?" Violet asked.

"No," Mr. Crowley answered. "Because the moment I accepted Philip wasn't coming back, I asked him to give it to me and promised that if he did so, we would be together again. Because I had no intention of returning the ring. I wasn't going to complete my Task because what was eternity worth if I couldn't spend it with him?"

Violet felt tears slip from the corners of her eyes and graze the sides of her cheeks.

"Doesn't it frighten you?" Violet finally asked, her voice rough. "Not knowing what it will be like?"

"I've lived a life where every single moment seemed to be accounted for in advance," Mr. Crowley said. "Aside from Philip, nothing has been unexpected. I've not experienced a single moment of spontaneous joy. It's time, I believe, to take a risk."

That must have been how their mother felt when she'd decided to step down the path Fate had outlined for her at the bottom of her cup. And, Violet finally admitted, it was how she felt about Emil. As hard as she had tried to fight it, she did love him, even if it meant taking a risk that she'd lose him one day.

"I don't know that you'll make a very good ghost," Violet finally said, a laugh entangling in her tears.

Mr. Crowley's brows furrowed together at first, but then they relaxed as a small but perceptible smile toyed at the corners of his mouth.

"And why's that, exactly?" he asked.

"You're not very patient," Violet explained. "If our sessions with you are any indication, that is."

"No, that is certainly not one of my virtues," Mr. Crowley conceded with a dry chuckle. "But Philip was, and I suppose we'll have a lot of time for him to teach me."

"I've never been around a ghost anyway, so you shouldn't take my comment to heart," Violet said. "Perhaps you'll do a spectacular job at it."

Mr. Crowley turned to her in confusion.

"But I thought you knew," he said, his brows knitting together again.

"Knew what?" Violet asked.

"That you have one," Mr. Crowley explained. "In the house."

"I'm sure you're mistaken," Violet insisted. "We've never noticed any signs of a spirit."

"It's hiding from view," Mr. Crowley said. "Tucked in the shadows, which is quite unusual. Ghosts aren't normally ones to keep quiet. It's almost as if it doesn't want anyone to know it's there."

"But who could it be?" Violet murmured at the same moment she remembered the wedding ring that had slid so suddenly out of the plaster walls and straight into her hand. As if by magic.

CHAPTER 36

A Lion

*Means that you are about to find
your inner strength.*

Alone in the shop, Beatrix was sitting in the corner of the parlor on the first floor, her mother's diary sitting open on her lap.

After Anne and Violet had rushed out the door, she'd moved downstairs and sat in the same spot that Katherine always did, on the worn velvet chair beneath Clara Quigley's portrait. She'd only intended to catch her bearings there and wait until her sisters returned so that they could tell her what to do, but it didn't take long for her to remember that she was through with hesitating and could trust her own instincts, which were demanding that she open the diary's worn cover once more.

And as she spoke to the pages, coaxing them to reveal what was waiting to be pulled from beneath the book's enchantments, the diary listened. She didn't quite understand why, but it felt more eager than ever to push the words beyond the enchantment and share them with her, the spine practically vibrating in anticipation.

She could see the gentle curves of vowels and consonants start to rise, but like fog in the early morning, the scrawl was so faint that Beatrix couldn't read it yet. It seemed to be waiting for something to happen before it gave the sentences over to her entirely.

Beatrix was still trying to convince the diary to let the words go when she heard a knock that drew her attention to the front door of the shop, where she saw a head of straight brown hair sticking out in all directions peeking through the glass.

"Jennings?" Beatrix murmured as she rose from the chair, wondering what he was doing there so late in the night, or at all, in fact.

Rushing to the door, Beatrix turned the lock and opened it wide, letting in a strong gust of wind that had just swooped in from the lake. The house shuddered, shaking all the picture frames in the room, and Beatrix hoped that Jennings wouldn't notice.

But she needn't have worried, because he was preoccupied with balancing a burlap sack over one shoulder, which looked so heavy that Beatrix wondered how he'd managed to carry it down the street.

"Miss Quigley," Jennings finally said, trying to sound as professional as he could while catching his breath. "I know this might seem unconventional, but may I come in?"

"Of course," Beatrix said as she gestured for him to step inside.

Jennings stumbled into the entryway, threw down the sack, and then braced his hands against his knees, obviously doing his best to recover. Then, he straightened and looked around the room, his eyes filling with surprise and then appreciation.

"It's a tea shop," he remarked, taking in all the polished wood tables and fine linen. "And a very comfortable one at that."

"Yes," Beatrix replied. "It's ours."

But she wasn't quite sure that was the case anymore, and saying the words caused the oddest pain to settle in her chest, like she was showing someone a home that she'd lived in before but hadn't stepped into in quite some time.

"Jennings," she said after a beat. "What are you doing here?"

"Oh," he replied, remembering that now wasn't the time to get distracted. "Well, after the meeting with Mr. Stuart earlier today, you seemed so worried. Like you were reconsidering the book and were a bit daunted by the thought of the tour."

"It was quite a lot to take in," Beatrix said, embarrassed that her concern had been so clearly displayed for all to see.

"Of course it was," Jennings agreed, nodding furiously. "But it's been bothering me that you still might not understand."

"Understand what?" Beatrix asked.

"Just how wonderful your writing is," Jennings replied. "And then, when I was about to stop working for the day, I went to the mailroom and saw something I thought might help."

In one movement, Jennings grabbed the burlap sack, untied the rope at the top, and turned the entire thing upside down.

A sea of letters poured onto the floor, covering the oak boards in envelopes that were all addressed to her.

"What's this?" Beatrix asked as she bent down to pick up the one that had landed closest to her feet.

"They're letters from our readers," Jennings explained. "They've been coming in by the droves, apparently, since we printed your short story."

"You can't be serious," Beatrix said, stunned. "It's been barely any time at all."

"I know!" Jennings exclaimed. "But they absolutely loved it."

In a rush, Beatrix started ripping open envelope after envelope, her eyes dancing across the pages, catching only snippets as she dug through the wealth of words.

I've read it thirteen times already, but I can't seem to stop. It's enchanting. When will you—

It was like talking to an old friend. I normally don't care for fiction, but the moment I—

—such a difficult month, and when I read your story, it reminded me to be happy again. It was the most magical sensation. . . .

Please tell me you are working on something new! I'll be checking the paper every day until—

Beatrix sat back on her heels, let out a deep breath that she hadn't realized she'd been holding on to since she'd first submitted her story, and laughed.

"What is it?" Jennings asked.

"Nothing," Beatrix replied with a smile. "It's only I've realized something that I should have noticed a long time ago."

Her readers' admiration for her work might seem inexplicable to most, but after looking through just a handful of the letters, Beatrix finally understood the reason for it.

She was a word weaver.

On her walk home from Donohoe & Company earlier that evening, she'd started to consider the possibility. Mr. Stuart's exuberant reaction had forced her to confront what she'd unknowingly been pushing to the side for months, that her powers were shifting toward a different kind of craft. The idea that every sentence she wrote was laced with magic was both thrilling and terrifying. Word weavers were made, not born. Witches with this ability were initially gifted with other skills, their new powers emerging gradually as they picked up a pen and slowly began to fall in love with the act of stitching stories together. But magic always requires a sacrifice, and a word weaver's original talents unraveled as their new ones became more tangible.

Because it was fastened from the hands of a word weaver,

Beatrix's writing nestled itself in the very hearts of her readers. Her magic flowed into the sentences of her stories, giving them a depth that made the text impossible to put down. The words hummed, beckoning readers to cling to the pages and not let them loose until they reached the very end. That was why Mr. Stuart and Jennings had been so enthusiastic about her novel and eager to see it printed. Though they might not suspect that the pull of her writing was the result of true magic, they knew her books would be lifelong friends, stories that people would reread every year to feel a sense of welcomed familiarity and satisfaction. They would bring a laugh when it was most needed, companionship on days where winter seemed to reside within someone's very soul, and perhaps even a tear or two whenever a particular turn of phrase brought back memories that had been buried beneath the weight of daily burdens.

She'd never be able to see the future again, not in the way that generations of Quigleys had before her, but as Beatrix looked down at the letters scattered across the floor, she understood that it was a price worth paying. Because Beatrix now knew that it wasn't something that the Council, or perhaps even Fate, had dealt her. No, this new life was one born from her own passion and talent, and she'd been the one to make the choice.

"I can't tell you how much this means to me, Jennings," Beatrix said as she leaned forward and wrapped her arms around his neck, enfolding him in a fierce hug.

Jennings stiffened in surprise but quickly returned her embrace, laughing so deeply that Beatrix could feel the deep rumbling of his chest.

"Does this mean you'll do it?" Jennings asked. "You'll write the next book?"

"Yes," Beatrix said, her voice firm with conviction. "I believe it means exactly that."

"And you'll tell your sisters?" Jennings inquired, his eyes darting toward the doorway that led to the stairs, as if he expected Anne and Violet to appear at any second.

"Yes," Beatrix replied, her tone still steady. "I'm going to tell them everything."

"Well, I'll let you get on with it then," Jennings said as he rose from the floor and brushed off his coat. "I've probably stayed longer than you'd like anyway."

"I always enjoy your company, Jennings," Beatrix said as she walked him to the door.

"Thank you, Miss Quigley," he replied, a faint blush spreading across his nose and cheeks. "Perhaps you might call me John now that we'll be seeing more of each other. Mr. Stuart will tell you the details next week, but he wants me to assist you on the tour."

"I'm very pleased to hear that," Beatrix said. "Good night, John."

It might have been a trick of the wind, but after Beatrix closed the door, she heard the faint noise of someone humming as they walked down the street.

She would have lingered at the threshold to be certain, but before Beatrix could lean closer to the door, a rattling noise near the velvet chair pulled her attention to the other side of the room.

Glancing up, Beatrix saw that her mother's diary was shaking on the side table, beckoning her forward.

"What's this about?" Beatrix murmured as she walked to where the diary sat and saw that the words had solidified on the page.

And when she made sense of what they said, Beatrix's eyes opened wide, and she sank into the chair in utter disbelief, unable to move her gaze from the page until she'd read every word three times over.

CHAPTER 37

A Black Cat

Foretells good luck.

*W*hen Anne reached Katherine's door, she was shivering and soaked to the bone. As soon as she'd marched over the threshold of the Crescent Moon, the memory of her friend's warm apartment, stuffed to the brim with dried herbs and flowers, had slipped into her thoughts, and it hadn't taken long for her to decide that was where she needed to go.

Though she'd managed to catch one of the last cable cars of the night, the walk from the station had been merciless, the icy rain that was winter's calling card beating against the hood of her cloak until it felt as if it was trying to pull her flat against the sidewalk.

She had managed to make it to the building and up six flights of stairs to the very top, but as soon as she knocked on the door and wilted against the frame, Anne felt as if she was going to collapse.

"Katherine?" Anne called through the crack, hoping that she hadn't stepped out to tend to a customer of her own. "It's Anne."

At first, no one responded, and Anne braced herself for another tumultuous walk back to the Crescent Moon, but just as she was about to step away from the threshold and toward the stairwell, a soft, unfamiliar voice echoed from the other side of the door.

"Anne Quigley?" it asked.

"Yes," Anne replied, startled to find someone else in Katherine's home.

The lock clicked open, and a few seconds later a woman appeared in the open doorway. She looked to be around Katherine's age, but her face held a sort of timeless quality that made Anne second-guess her initial assumption. Though the skin around the woman's haunting eyes was smooth, perfect lines of gray streaked her dark hair, and she looked worn, as if all the life had been drained from her, leaving an empty husk in need of support.

"I'm sorry," Anne said as she stood dripping next to the door. "I needed to speak with Katherine, but I see she isn't here."

"She's stepped out," the woman explained as she looked Anne over from head to toe. "On an errand, I believe."

"Well, I suppose I'll need to come back later then," Anne sighed, the words garbled by the chattering of her teeth.

"Why don't you come inside?" the woman asked as she pulled the door wider. "It's cold out there."

Anne wasn't in the mood to talk with anyone, let alone a stranger, but the thought of facing the chill of Chicago's streets was too much to bear. And so, she nodded and moved into the room, leaving a trail of water behind her.

"Please, sit," the woman said as she pointed to one of the wooden rocking chairs next to the small but serviceable fireplace. Katherine's apartment wasn't particularly spacious, especially with all the tools of her trade tucked in every nook and cranny, but no one could say it wasn't welcoming.

Anne did as she was told and slunk into the chair, stretching her freezing fingers as close as she dared to the flames. A few moments later, the woman appeared next to her holding two mugs of steaming tea.

"Thank you," Anne said as she accepted one of the mugs and held it greedily between her hands.

"It's no burden," the woman replied before sitting back in her rocking chair and letting a comfortable silence slip into the room.

It wasn't until she'd emptied half of her cup that Anne realized her mysterious hostess had known her name.

"I'm afraid I haven't introduced myself," Anne finally said, turning to face the woman.

"That isn't necessary, though," she replied. "I already know who you are."

"But I can't say the same," Anne said.

As soon as the words left her lips, though, and she looked directly into the woman's face, Anne was instantly pulled back to the vision she'd had of the Council's summer meeting. She remembered the dark circles under Hester's eyes and the way the firm set of Nathanial's features had softened during their discussion about the Diviner. And then everything clicked into place.

"Celeste," Anne whispered, shocked that the person who'd given up her powers so that she could share Clara Quigley's secret was now sitting within arm's reach. That she could ask her anything she wanted.

But Anne's heart was still heavy from the answers that had already been revealed, so she slumped back into her chair, unsure of how to continue.

"You are as good as I suspected," Celeste said with a slow nod as she continued to gaze into the fire. "Better than me—perhaps even better than your mother."

"But you don't know me at all," Anne said, not unkindly. She was merely exhausted from disappointment and the confusion that comes with realizing that some things just can't be stopped.

"Oh, but I do," Celeste replied. "I've seen so, so much."

"And what have you seen?" Anne asked, wary of what she might hear but curious all the same.

"That you'll make a difference," Celeste answered. "Quite a difference indeed. It was one of the reasons I told your mother that she needed to complete her Task, to ensure that you might step down the path that would lead to your destiny. I'm not sure what it is, but I sense that it will be complicated. You'll need all the power you can muster, and that means embracing who you really are."

"And who is that?" Anne asked in disbelief.

"One of the most powerful seers our people have been gifted with in generations," Celeste said simply. "It's a talent that cannot go to waste, not just for your sake but everyone else's."

"You sound just like them," Anne muttered as she thought of the Council, turning away to gaze into the bottom of her cup, where the leaves were swirling into shapes that she recognized but didn't want to interpret.

"I'm not surprised," Celeste replied, understanding exactly whom Anne was speaking about. "After all, I'm the one who insisted that they ask you to replace me."

Anne's gaze snapped back to her so quickly that she nearly spilled what little tea was left in her mug.

"You asked them to offer me the position?" Anne gasped.

"Not only that," Celeste replied. "I told them that you would accept it. Because I know that you will. You're not the type of person to turn your back on the people who need you."

"My mother did what she thought was best," Anne said, her tone hardening.

"I'm not accusing Clara," Celeste explained with a shake of her head. "In the end, it was clear that she knew her path better than anyone else. But you are not your mother, Anne. Your destiny has taken on a different texture."

"One that isn't tethered to my sisters, evidently," Anne sniffed. She could feel tears pressing in the corners of her eyes but managed to hold them back.

"You are a very distinct set of daughters," Celeste said. "Did you honestly expect that every dream you held would be the same?"

"I had hoped all the ones that mattered would be," Anne murmured.

"Well, you were wrong to think so," Celeste said. "People change, and if you try to hold yourself back to prevent it, all three of you will end up breaking."

For a few minutes, the only sound came from the fire crackling in the hearth, but eventually, Anne worked up the courage to speak again.

"Did she do it?" she asked. "Did our mother curse us?"

"I don't know, child," Celeste said, her voice as soft as a rose petal. "And any power that I might have used to find out has faded away."

Anne slumped forward, pressing her elbow against her knees so that she could rest her chin in the palm of her hand.

"But I do know that Fate isn't as rigid as most might think," Celeste continued. "She can be bargained with when presented a strong case."

"And you believe my mother was able to make a bargain?" Anne asked.

"I believe that Clara Quigley was not the type to accept a Task she didn't feel was correct," Celeste answered. "And that she had enough wit to make a convincing argument."

"So you believe she wanted this to happen for some reason?" Anne asked. "That she planned for us to separate?"

"What she wanted, Anne, was for you three to be happy and follow your own paths," Celeste said. "So that you could grow into the women the world needs you to be."

Anne sighed then and looked back into her cup, opening the inner eye that she'd been keeping carefully averted and taking note of the shapes that rested in the tea.

Open doors faded into candles and cups, signifying new opportunities, help from strangers, and rich rewards. As hard as she looked, Anne couldn't even spot the barest edge of an axe or dagger. When asking whether the path set before her was the right one, there didn't seem to be any dangers or trickery lurking in wait.

"And isn't this what you've always wanted anyway?" Celeste asked, her voice pulling Anne away from her search for a shadow of a doubt. "To embrace your power and see how far it might carry you?"

Away from the Crescent Moon and the memories it held of her sisters, Anne finally admitted that was exactly what she'd wanted—to live a life where she was at the center. To care for herself instead of others. To discover who she really was, even if it meant standing apart.

"It is what I want," Anne said, letting go of all her resistance in a single deep breath.

And in that moment of acceptance, she felt something shift within herself, a bond that she hadn't known was there loosening and twisting as if trying to work itself into a new knot.

She heard the door open then too, and the sound of Katherine greeting Celeste, but Anne had closed her eyes to focus and didn't open them until she could feel her friend standing in front of her chair.

"Anne?" she heard Katherine ask. The scent of frankincense and sage crept closer to Anne's nose, and she knew her friend was kneeling in front of her, waiting patiently as always.

When Anne was ready, she finally opened her eyes, unsure of what she would find.

"Oh, Clara," Katherine murmured when she caught sight of Anne's irises. "You did leave something behind, didn't you?"

"What is it?" Anne asked as she reached toward her face, panicked about what was reflected there.

And then Katherine did the strangest thing. She smiled and touched Anne's shaking hand with her own.

"I was wrong," Katherine said, her words heavy with relief. "It's not a curse at all!"

CHAPTER 38

A Lantern

*Suggests that secrets will soon
come to light.*

As the house sensed that the Quigley sisters were being drawn closer together, it began to brighten all the gas lamps in the hallways, eager to expose the secrets that had been lurking in its corners once and for all. It felt the quick footsteps of Violet and Mr. Crowley along the back alleyway and could hear Anne speaking with Celeste and Katherine even before they turned onto the street. Something was finally about to happen, and though the house didn't know precisely what, it could tell that by sunrise everything would be different.

Beatrix was waiting in the parlor on the second floor, drawn there by the warm fire that the house had kindled while she continued to read her mother's diary and wait. She knew exactly when her sisters had entered the house because the sage green walls flashed a vibrant purple that deepened into the richest brown before settling into the lightest shade of blue just as everyone filtered up the stairs and into the room.

"I need to tell you—"

"We have to talk about—"

"You wouldn't believe what I just—"

Anne, Beatrix, and Violet spoke all at once, their words entangling together in a rush of excitement. And then, before they bothered to try to sort out who would go first, they collapsed into one another, their arms linking and foreheads touching as they tried to steady themselves.

"It's not a curse," Anne finally said. "It's a blessing."

"What do you mean?" Violet asked, her head poking up in surprise.

"Curses and blessings can be almost impossible to distinguish," Katherine said, taking a step forward. "Especially since they are often different sides of the same coin. This one must have been cast by a powerful witch, because the blessing only emerged when you accepted it. That's why I mistook it for a curse. The only thing reflected in your eyes was hurt and pain, but they were masking something else entirely."

"But what did we accept, exactly?" Violet asked, more confused than ever.

"We're not sure," Anne said. "But the moment I knew we should walk down different paths, something inside me loosened, and the blessing was revealed."

"I think that I can help explain," Beatrix said, running back to her spot on the settee and grabbing the diary from where she'd left it resting on the side table. "It's all in here!"

"Has the diary revealed something more?" Anne asked.

"It has," Beatrix said as she turned the pages until she found a particular paragraph. She'd read it so many times that evening that she could have recited it by heart. But the words resting there were crucial to their story, and it seemed important to get every syllable just right.

My Dearest Ones,

If you're reading this, you have finally accepted that
your paths are starting to diverge. Forgive me for keeping
secrets from you, but everything needed to be set just so
for the wheels of Fate to turn in the right direction.

I don't have time to explain every detail. You three
are waiting in the next room, still young enough to enjoy
playing with that enchanted cloak you've found in the
attic, and the spell the word witch has given me to write
in the diary is wearing thin. But I will do my best to share
what secrets I have left.

As I watched you three grow older and your powers
began to take on a shape of their own, I realized that
my Task was to separate you. The gifts you possess are
rare, and though your destinies intersect, they aren't
meant to be braided together in a single strand. But I
couldn't push you apart knowing that you'd be alone
when your father and I passed on, and if I used magic
to ensure the deed was done later, you wouldn't be able
to see one another ever again. The enchantment would
have twisted into something ugly, the love you have for
one another buried under petty grievances and hurts that
can't be healed. No, you needed to stay together long
enough to move forward but, when the time was right,
have the opportunity to make a choice to go your separate
ways yourselves. In order to ensure you could come back
together, the decision needed to come from within.

And, so, I had to make a bargain with Fate. I know
some might believe she's as cold and rigid as stone, but I
know a different side of her. It took some convincing, but
once I explained that the threads of destiny would remain

*where they needed to be, she was open to discussion. She
let me give you a blessing and delay the completion of my
Task to give you a choice.*

*I'm running out of time, and so, I'll use my remaining
words to tell you that I love you, to the very depths of my
soul.*

*Embrace who you are because I've seen what you
become, and the vision is breathtaking.*

*With All My Love,
Your mother*

By the time Beatrix had said the final word, the parlor was
heavy with memories of the past. And, slowly, the house felt
something it hadn't sensed for a long time seep through the
empty cracks and crannies of the plaster: acceptance and hope
for the future.

"She did want us to stay together," Anne murmured as she
touched her sisters' hands. "Just not in the way we expected."

"Yes," Beatrix said. "She wanted us to make the choice. Otherwise, it wouldn't have worked out the way it needed to."

A thought suddenly dawned on Anne then, and the feeling of
cold needles ran down her spine.

"But if she didn't complete her Task, doesn't that mean . . . ,"
Anne began, shying away from the shocking thought that drifted
to the forefront of her mind.

"Yes," Violet replied, her voice rough from tears. "She's been
here this whole time, watching over us as a spirit and waiting for
us to finish the Task for her."

She took a step toward Mr. Crowley then and put her hand
through the crook of his arm, pulling him forward.

"He's sensed her," Violet continued. "Sitting in the shadows out of sight, nudging us along whenever we stumbled from our paths."

"Is she here right now?" Anne asked, turning about the room, searching for the barest hint of a sign that their mother was still with them.

Mr. Crowley opened his mouth to answer, but before he could say anything, the lamplights flickered, and the overpowering scent of dried marigolds filled the parlor, wrapping each of the sisters in a soft floral embrace. And then, the window flew open, and the scent disappeared through the pane and into the night.

Their mother had said goodbye, and she was off now to finally reunite with their father, who'd been waiting patiently to have her in his arms once again.

"She's gone now," Mr. Crowley said once the wind had died down. "She's free."

"And so are we," Anne added as she turned toward Beatrix and Violet. "I'm sorry that I've tried to keep you both here when you're meant to go out on your own. I love you so much that I smothered you, afraid that if we changed, we'd lose what we had before."

"It's not your fault alone, Anne," Violet whispered. "All of us have been hiding bits of ourselves for too long."

"Well," Anne said with a smile. "I can't wait to see them."

The clock on the mantle struck half past eleven then, and Mr. Crowley stepped forward, thumping the floor with his cane to get everyone's attention.

"I gather there's plenty of time for that later," he said before pointing at Violet. "This one has an appointment that she shouldn't miss."

Violet blushed a deep scarlet and stared at him with her mouth agape. On their walk over from the station, she'd told Mr. Crowley the entire story that had unfolded in the circus ring. He'd hardly said a single word the entire time, and so Violet thought he hadn't really been listening.

As it turns out, that wasn't the case at all.

"What kind of appointment?" Anne asked as she stared at Violet, her eyes wide with curiosity.

"A date with destiny, you might say," Mr. Crowley explained. "She's due to perform at the circus's midnight show with a handsome young man who's asked her to leave the city with him."

"Is that true, Violet?" Beatrix asked. "Are you going to leave with him?"

Violet bit her bottom lip and started tapping her foot against the floor, unsure of what her answer would be.

She'd been gnawing at her choice all evening, darting so quickly back and forth from one answer to the next that she was dizzy with indecision.

But before she could reply, Anne grabbed her sister by both shoulders and turned her chin upward so that the electric purple of Violet's eyes bled into her own blue irises.

"I'd say it's time to stop being afraid of the possibilities, wouldn't you?" Anne whispered.

Violet's foot stopped tapping as she allowed herself to dream of what her future held with Emil, the outlines of the fantasies she'd woven when trying to drift into sleep taking a starker shape.

And then, she felt something click into place.

"Yes," Violet finally said, a feeling of deep satisfaction and excitement starting to course through her veins. "I believe it is."

CHAPTER 39

A Star

Appears just before things that are
meant to be.

Violet waited nervously next to the ladder at the back of the tent where she knew Emil would appear to begin the midnight show. With only the velvet costume that he'd given her beneath her coat, she should have been freezing, but the adrenaline and constant stream of questions from her sisters kept Violet from noticing the chill.

"What's he like?" Anne was asking as she blew a warm breath into her palms.

"Is he handsome?" Beatrix followed up with a question of her own, stomping her boots against the ground to wake her aching toes.

Violet had already told them about Emil on their way to the lakeshore, but her sisters obviously weren't satisfied yet.

"He's . . . ," Violet began as her eyes darted across the crowd, hoping to catch sight of Emil's inky black curls, but before she could say anything more, she saw him approaching the ladder, dressed from head to toe in black sequins. As he got closer, Violet noticed that the playful glint in his eyes had been dimmed by something else, sadness perhaps, or disappointment. And his shoulders, normally thrown back in a way that suggested he was ready to take on the entire world, were hunched forward, as if he was carrying a heavy weight.

But when Emil's eyes moved toward the ladder and he caught sight of Violet, he froze, his expression shifting to confusion for just a second before that wide grin appeared once more.

"Wildfire!" he cried, stepping forward so fast that he looked like a flash of lightning in the night sky. He wrapped both hands around her waist, swung her in a circle, and then leaned forward to press his lips to hers.

They stood wrapped in each other, a tangle of spangles and tassels, until Anne's voice brought them back to reality.

"I guess you have your answer, Bee," she said with a laugh. "He certainly is handsome."

Only then did Emil realize that they weren't alone and he was surrounded by not one but two women who looked eerily similar to Violet. Though there was certainly no mistaking them for one another. In his eyes, Violet shone the brightest of all.

"We'll leave you here and take our seats," Anne said as she gave Violet's arm a reassuring squeeze and pushed Beatrix, who was still staring with her mouth agape at Emil, toward the tent flap.

Emil didn't let go of Violet's waist, but he put more space between them so that he could stare at her costume, which made her look just as he'd predicted: like a comet ready to launch through the stars.

"I've made my choice," Violet said slowly, wanting to be sure that he heard every word.

"And what is it?" Emil asked, leaning forward so that a few of his dark locks fell into his face.

Violet reached her hand up to push them back and then let her hand rest on the side of his neck, where his pulse was beating fast.

"You," Violet replied. "I'm choosing you and the life we'll have together."

Emil smiled and reached for her again, pressing her body against the ladder in an embrace that became so heated they nearly didn't hear the first strain of the melody that signaled the show was about to begin.

"We need to go," Violet declared, breaking away from him to catch her breath. "Or they'll start without us."

"So, you're really going to do it?" Emil asked. "You're going to perform?"

"Of course," Violet replied with a smirk as she grabbed hold of a rung on the ladder and began to climb to the top. "Did you think I'd be too afraid?"

"No," Emil answered with a laugh. "I don't believe you're afraid of anything."

✦

Back in the tent, Anne and Beatrix had settled into their spots in the front row next to Katherine, Celeste, and Mr. Crowley, where they were all waiting for a sign of Violet and Emil.

"You do think she's had enough training, don't you?" Beatrix asked as they stared up at the small, moon-shaped hole at the top of the tent. "There's no chance of her . . . falling?"

"As many times as she's slipped out of the house, I'd say she must be an expert by now," Anne said, but her own voice was laced with worry.

Suddenly, the lights in the tent faded into complete darkness, and the crowd's attention was drawn to a pair of trapeze artists who were being lowered, ever so slowly, from the top of the tent.

Emil was sitting on the bar with Violet draped across his knees, as if she were asleep, the moonlight causing the gold tassels on her costume to twinkle. He looked like the night sky, and she a star whose light was just barely peeking over twilight.

And then Emil began to sing, the deep timbre of his voice filling the tent, lulling everyone into the slow and steady rhythm of the performance until Anne and Beatrix forgot that they were spectators and felt entirely immersed in the scene.

That is, until the final line of the score faded away, and Violet slipped from the bar and through the darkness, a gold flame against the shadows that seemed as if it was about to be extinguished.

Anne's and Beatrix's screams mixed with the cries of the other people in the crowd as she continued to cut through the air.

And then, Violet suddenly stopped, her hands having caught a barely perceptible bar that someone had thrown at just the right second, and she swung her body upward so that she had enough momentum to fly into the second move of their routine.

"I don't know if I can watch any more of this!" Beatrix cried, but her eyes never left the sight of Violet and Emil dancing through the air, not even when the candelabras came to life and the other performers emptied into the ring, their hands full of fire and sparklers.

It was like watching the moon trying to chase a falling star, and neither she nor Anne could look away.

✦

Much later, when the ballet dancers and jugglers started to leave the ring, signaling to the crowd that the show was coming to an end, Anne and Beatrix shuffled to where Violet and Emil were stepping onto the sawdust for the very first time that night.

But before they could approach them with the list of compliments that had been growing in their minds since they'd slipped through the top of the tent, a little girl with tousled blond hair and an impish smile beat them to it, wrapping her arms around one of Violet's legs and staring up at her with open adoration.

"Hello there," Violet said with a laugh as she placed a hand on top of the child's head.

"You were amazing!" the girl cried, practically vibrating with excitement. "One day, I'm going to fly just like you."

"That's wonderful," Violet replied. "Just be sure that you have a strong set of wings first."

"I will," the girl reassured her before a woman's voice cut through the crowd.

"Amelia!" she cried. "We have to go."

As the child gave Violet one last hug and darted into the crowd, the strangest thing began to happen. Violet stumbled back as she experienced the sensation of warm oil pouring down her scalp and into her bones. It was as if she were trying to get up after lying in the summer sun for an entire afternoon.

"What's wrong?" Anne whispered just as Katherine and Celeste joined them.

"I don't know," Violet replied. "I feel odd. Like my bones have turned soft in the most satisfying way."

Katherine and Celeste gasped and then turned to each other with a knowing smile.

"What?" Violet asked, alarmed.

"You've done it," Katherine said as she wrapped Violet in a fierce embrace. "You've completed your Task."

Violet's gaze flitted back to the crowd, where she saw the girl riding on the top of her father's shoulders, waving goodbye as they marched out of the tent.

"You must have put that little one on her own path," Celeste said. "I have a feeling she's going to do something extraordinary."

"Then this is really what I'm meant for," Violet whispered as she reached out to clasp Emil's hand in her own. He wasn't quite sure what they were talking about, but he was patient enough to know that Violet would explain everything once she had the chance. And that the answers were going to be well worth the wait.

"Of course it is," Anne said as she took in the sight of Violet beaming under the twinkling lights of the ring.

Her sister, it seemed, was finally home.

CHAPTER 40

A Crescent Moon
Signifies prosperity.

*W*hat's this sign about?" Mrs. Stephenson asked as she slipped through the front door and allowed Anne to remove her winter coat. "Closing early today? I don't believe I've ever seen you shut the doors before afternoon tea."

"My sisters and I have a personal matter to attend to," Anne explained as she hung Mrs. Stephenson's heavy woolen garment on one of the crowded pegs and tried to make herself heard over the chatter and sounds of spoons clinking against porcelain.

The front room was positively crowded that day, as if their customers had somehow awoken with the knowledge that the shop was trimming down its normal hours that afternoon and knew to arrive well in advance to get a reading before the weekend. Laden with gaily colored boxes and bags, the spoils of their Friday shopping, the women of Chicago were eager to take a moment's refuge from the frigid streets and enjoy the warmth of the Crescent Moon, which, though packed to the brim with customers, somehow seemed lighter and more welcoming than ever.

Nestling deep into their chairs and allowing their posture to falter just a fraction, the Quigleys' customers focused on enjoying themselves before having to make the inevitable trudge toward the cable car that would deliver them to their homes. They quickly pushed aside the worries that awaited them and allowed themselves to relish the scent of freshly risen raisin bread and comfortable conversation that infused the room.

"Well, I'd better claim my seat, then," Mrs. Stephenson said with a smile as Peggy stepped forward to guide her toward one of their few open tables. "I have a few questions to ask and could use a pot of warm tea."

Mrs. Stephenson pulled off her gloves then, and that's when Anne noticed a sparkling engagement ring glimmering from her left hand.

"I'm looking forward to getting a few answers of my own," Anne said with a grin before watching Mrs. Stephenson disappear into the crowd.

The decision to push the ladies out early had been spontaneous, though not entirely unexpected. As Anne had predicted, the sisters could feel a change stirring in the air. It was an odd combination of the chill that creeps gently across the skin as the weather begins to shift and the sense of anticipation that arises just before life itself takes a dramatic turn.

That morning, as the sisters gathered around the table and Violet cracked open a window to let out some of the heat that was brewing in the kitchen, they smelled it: the aroma of the season's first true snowfall. The clouds, like a delicate web of lace doilies, still had a bit of sunshine slipping through here and there, but the sisters knew that by twilight the sidewalks would be blanketed with a sheet of white snow and the time would come to say their goodbyes.

The occasion, of course, called for an early closing, no matter how busy the shop had been over the past few weeks.

"The Crescent Moon is brimming over this afternoon," a

familiar voice murmured, and Anne turned to find Katherine standing near the front door.

"It is," Anne said with a soft smile as she let her gaze drift over the scene that warmed the shop to its rafters. "But we'll be shutting the door a bit ahead of schedule."

"So I've heard," Katherine replied, reaching forward to wrap Anne in an embrace that smelled of sage and second chances. Her bones ached in the way they only did when autumn had decided to give way to winter, and she knew what that meant for the Quigley sisters.

"But there's still enough time for tea and a plate of Violet's brown butter madeleines if you'd like," Anne said. "The woman who's been sitting in your chair is about to take her last bite, I believe."

"That sounds lovely, dear," Katherine answered. "But I think I'll need a table this time."

Confused, Anne looked over her friend's shoulder to see Celeste and Mr. Crowley, both wrapped in tight woolen coats and scarves, shuffle into the shop. Though they still looked a bit worn around the edges, a glint of hope that wasn't there before seemed to shine in their eyes.

"Of course!" Anne cried as she pointed toward a round oak table that sat just near enough to the crackling fire that the chill of the afternoon wind would melt from her guests' toes before they took their second sip of tea.

"One last thing," Katherine said as Mr. Crowley and Celeste went about the task of shedding their winter layers. She reached into her pocket and pulled out a small velvet bag the color of amber, handing it over to Anne as if it were a star freshly fallen from the night sky.

"What's this?" Anne asked as she tugged at the delicate rope that held the bundle closed.

"A birthday present," Katherine replied.

Upturning the bag, Anne watched as three delicate pendants poured into her waiting palm. They were carved into the shape of marigolds, a nosegay of gold flowers that winked back at her when the light hit them just so.

"There's one for each of you," Katherine said. "A reminder that you're forever together, no matter where you find yourselves."

Fighting back the tears that threatened to trail down her cheeks, Anne pulled Katherine close and whispered, "Thank you. For everything."

Wiping at her own eyes, Katherine nodded and returned her embrace before walking toward the table by the hearth with Celeste and Mr. Crowley, who gave Anne reassuring pats of their own as they passed by.

Turning back toward the parlor, Anne searched for her sisters in the sea of satin and scones. She found Beatrix at one of the smaller tables tucked closest to the fire talking with a petite young woman whose face was etched with excitement. Beatrix's ability to read the signs was dwindling every day as her word-weaving abilities grew stronger, but what she lacked in foresight she made up for as a storyteller, and the girl was transfixed by whatever tale Beatrix was crafting.

The day after the sisters had accepted their mother's blessing, the three had wandered back up to the family parlor for the evening, where Beatrix presented Violet and Anne with a copy of her book. Just as Beatrix had hoped, Anne and Violet had dived into the manuscript with gusto. And contrary to what she had feared, they didn't offer a single word of criticism. In fact, they hardly uttered a word at all, not even bothering to turn their attention away from the text for a few seconds to stretch or refill their teacups.

For though they were sisters, Anne and Violet were certainly not immune to Beatrix's word-weaving magic. Unable to stop, they read through the evening and into the early morning hours, their backs pleasantly sore from sitting for so long in one position. By the time the house opened the curtains to let in sunrise, all three sisters were still sitting in their spots across the family parlor. Anne and Violet had fallen asleep the moment after they'd finished the final line of the novel, but Beatrix was still awake, tucked into her corner of the settee with a fresh stack of paper and her new story shifting through her mind. It was a moment so infused with happiness and acceptance that once Beatrix finally broke away from the page, she knew this was a memory that she'd be bottling up for the future, a recollection to turn back to while traveling on her own in unfamiliar but intriguing new cities.

After reading Beatrix's story, Anne couldn't help but be thankful that she was leaving the shop, at least for now. Her stories would be a soothing balm to so many people who needed the steady comfort of a good book to distract them from their troubles. Anne would miss her desperately, but Beatrix needed to step outside of the Crescent Moon and start sharing her new magic with the rest of the world. And if the reviews of the critics who had received early copies of Beatrix's book were any indication, she'd be welcomed with eager and open arms. Anne had already decided to start clipping them out of the daily papers and pasting them into a scrapbook that she could open whenever she needed to remind herself why her sister had said farewell to the Crescent Moon.

A rattling noise drew her attention to a larger table near the kitchen entrance, and Anne saw Violet gesturing wildly at a group of elderly women, who looked slightly taken aback by her showmanship. Tired of trying to keep her hair back, she'd cut the loose strands that had been hanging over her eyes into a proper fringe. The short but wild curls fell just above her brows now and bounced up and down whenever Violet moved, as if they were extensions of her vibrant energy.

Anne also caught sight of Emil, who had offered to help in the shop that afternoon so that the sisters would be able to close on time. With a tray of cheddar and rosemary biscuits balanced expertly atop his shoulder, he had stopped for a moment to watch Violet, a broad smile stretched across his handsome face. He certainly was attractive—as many of their customers were discussing from behind their gloved hands—and, to Anne's great relief, extraordinarily kind.

Violet had brought him back to the shop after their first performance together, and since then Emil had folded himself into the sisters' lives as easily as Franny had slipped the raisins into the bread dough the day before. Anne, who had expected to feel like she was trying to stuff her foot into a shoe that was too small, was shocked by how comfortable they all were with one another already. And, though she hadn't dared tell Violet, she saw the shape of a swan appear in the fire as the two reached for each other's hands. Her sister had managed to find a true and loyal partner, and their love would be lasting.

"Are you all right, Miss Anne?" Peggy asked, pulling Anne from her thoughts.

"I'm perfectly fine, Peggy," Anne said with a slight smile. "Just taking it all in."

"The shop won't be the same without them," the girl sighed, knowing exactly what memory Anne was in the process of capturing: the last time all three sisters worked in the shop.

"No, but all things must change," Anne said, feeling the truth of her words. "And we are heading in a prosperous direction."

Peggy's smile widened at that. Anne had told the girls about the renovations that they'd be making to the shop over the next several months and promoted them both to co-managers, which had sent them into fits of joyous squeals. Together, they'd be working to hire additional staff and move the Crescent Moon into the next phase of its cycle. She'd be the only reader left, but they all knew that the exclusivity of the service would only serve to draw in customers who were eager to pay more for a slot on the schedule. And with the continued development of the downtown department stores, the crowd of ladies looking for a hot cup of tea laced with a hint of magic would likely grow as well. Not that Anne needed to guess at these things anymore. All the signs were pointing toward a definite and assured success, especially when Anne went searching for hints about her new position as the city's Diviner. She'd gone to see the Council with Celeste after accepting her path, ready to let her power grow without constraint and discover what destiny had in store.

Reluctantly acknowledging that the moment she'd been trying to etch into her mind was already passing away, Anne nodded at Peggy and began the process of walking between the tables and gently reminding their customers about the early closing.

The ladies uttered playful disappointments but were otherwise cooperative, resisting the urge to request that their cups be refilled or ask for just one last biscuit. They said their goodbyes, requested that the bills be added to their accounts, and braced themselves for the windswept streets, which were beginning to take on a sharp crispness that hinted snow would soon be falling. Only a single table needed to be convinced to leave, the one where Katherine, Celeste, and Mr. Crowley were laughing over mugs of warm cider and fresh cinnamon buns. The three of them even lingered in the entryway as they slipped back into their coats and agreed upon their next visit to the shop.

When Anne managed to shuffle everyone out and shut the door behind them, she heard Beatrix's voice echoing down the stairs from the second floor.

"What's the matter?" Anne called up from the landing.

"The house!" Beatrix cried. "It's locked me out of the room, so I can't bring my trunk downstairs."

Anne sighed at the thought of seeing her sister's luggage near the front door and understood what had driven the house to such behavior. Beatrix was leaving for Philadelphia on the last train of the evening, and it didn't want her to say goodbye either. But go she must, and her bags needed to be at the door for the carriage to pick up and drop at the station.

Leaning her forehead against the threshold, Anne murmured, "It's time to let them go, my friend."

When she broke the bitter news of Beatrix's and Violet's departures to the house, she'd tried to soothe it by explaining that the three sisters would be reunited next autumn, when they'd promised to return to the shop well in time for their next birthday. The circus' run in Chicago had been so successful that it didn't take much for Emil to convince the manager to have the troupe return, though they'd leave as soon as the snow started to settle in. And Mr. Stuart, eager to keep Beatrix pleased, had already booked a series of talks in the Midwest throughout October. By that time, she'd have seen enough of the world to have plenty of stories to share with her sisters. In the meantime, Anne told the house that she would climb up to the family parlor every evening and read aloud whatever news the two had shared in their letters, which they swore would arrive often enough to cause the postman complaint.

This hadn't been enough to content the house, however, and it kept emptying the trunks that her sisters were desperately attempting to pack.

The walls radiated under Anne's temple, as if trying to hold back a shuddering sob.

"They'll be back," Anne said softly, believing with her whole heart in what she was saying. "I promise."

At that, the floorboards quaked, and Anne heard a door upstairs being thrown open.

"That's more like it!" Beatrix declared.

"I suppose you'll want to carry your things down now too?" Anne asked Violet, who was helping Emil clear the tables of used plates and crumbs.

"We've already moved everything to the kitchen," Violet said. "I thought it might be best to do it when the house was distracted with all the customers."

Anne nodded, thinking that it was odd but not entirely disconcerting to hear how Violet referred to herself as part of another unit, a pair. They were already moving on, their thoughts wrapped up in each other and some town down south that Violet had never heard of but where she knew winter's frigid grasp couldn't reach.

The sound of Beatrix dragging her trunk down the steps drew Anne's attention back to the current moment, and she reminded herself to savor what was happening now.

"I think that it's time," she said, her face turned toward the window, which she knew would soon be full of thick, white snowflakes.

Hearing this, Beatrix and Violet lost their excited expressions and assumed a worrisome air. Though they normally were eager to catch a glimpse of their own futures, the definitiveness of what might be revealed frightened them a bit now. Worse yet, what if they could no longer sense their futures at all, even on this special day, when the memory of their heritage was at its strongest? They were about to forge their own paths, but the uncertainty of the destinies they were about to embrace was still too much to contemplate.

"Come on," Anne said as she looped a hand around each of her sisters' and led them toward the coatrack, where the house had already hung their thick winter coats and knit scarves after dusting them off from the attic. "Let's keep to tradition one last time."

Beatrix nodded stiffly while Violet turned and allowed Emil to give her a soft kiss on the temple before they walked toward Anne and quietly slipped into their coats.

Stepping onto the sidewalk, the sisters linked arms and looked up toward the gray clouds, where they saw the very first snowflakes of the season starting to make their way toward the street.

"What if our visions show that we won't be together again?" Violet asked quickly, her voice cracking along the corners.

"If the last few weeks have taught us anything, it's that fate isn't always what it first appears to be," Anne said as she gripped her sisters' hands just a dash harder, her touch soft but firm.

"Whatever happens," Beatrix said as she returned the gesture. "I love you both, more than is possible to express in words."

At that, Anne, Beatrix, and Violet turned their faces toward the sky and watched as the snowflakes came closer and closer, until the very first one moved a hair's breadth from Anne's cheek and landed on the cold pavement.

Instantly, the sisters were swept into a vision, one that wasn't based in sight or touch or even smell, but sound.

Laughter rang in their ears, worn and rather haggard but full of contentment.

It was the sound of three old women, enjoying one another's company as they neared the end of a journey that had brimmed over with adventure and adoration.

Acknowledgments

I should start by confessing that I am not a word witch.

This novel didn't spring from my pen ready to be shared with the world without a single alteration. Instead, something much more magical happened . . . a group of people believed in my story enough to help me make it what it is today.

I want to extend my deepest gratitude to my agent and literary fairy godmother, Adria Goetz. She was the very first person to meet the Quigley sisters, and she saw something special enough in them to tell me that they should be introduced to readers and not remain within the confines of my own imagination.

The book that you are holding is also the result of the painstaking work of my editor, Elizabeth Hitti. I could not have asked for a more talented individual to help me take that initial manuscript and turn it into something truly magical. I will be forever grateful for the enthusiasm that she has shown for my writing and her ability to help me grow as an author.

I'd also like to thank the other members of the Atria team, who have all supported the book from the start and worked tirelessly to get it into the hands of readers. In particular, I want to extend my gratitude to Dayna Johnson, Holly Rice, Morgan Pager, Jimmy Iacobelli, Jim Tierney, Annette Sweeney, Kyoko Watanabe, Barbara Wild, and Lacee Burr. It's their dedication to storytelling that's helped craft my dreams into reality. I also want to express my appreciation for the Simon & Schuster sales force, who shared so much love for the book and made the publication process feel like an author's fantasy come alive.

Of course, I wouldn't have thought to write a novel in the first place without the support of my family, born and found. My parents and siblings have encouraged me to write since I could pick up a pencil, and I hope that I've managed to reflect the barest twinkle of the love I feel for them in the pages of this book. Then there have been the sisters I've had the good fortune to find along the way, after I stepped over the threshold of home to start my own journey. Their laughter and steady support will always be what causes clovers and crescent moons to settle at the bottom of my own cup.

Finally, I'd like to thank my husband, who's always ready to fly with me toward the stars and into our next adventure.

About the Author

Stacy Sivinski was raised in the Appalachian mountains of Virginia and now is a writing and literature professor in the Midwest. She holds a PhD in English from the University of Notre Dame with a specialty in sensory studies and nineteenth-century women's writing. In her fiction, Stacy focuses on themes of sisterhood, self-discovery, and magic. *The Crescent Moon Tearoom* is her debut novel.

ATRIA BOOKS, an imprint of Simon & Schuster, fosters an open environment where ideas flourish, bestselling authors soar to new heights, and tomorrow's finest voices are discovered and nurtured. Since its launch in 2002, Atria has published hundreds of bestsellers and extraordinary books, which would not have been possible without the invaluable support and expertise of its team and publishing partners. Thank you to the Atria Books colleagues who collaborated on *The Crescent Moon Tearoom*, as well as to the hundreds of professionals in the Simon & Schuster advertising, audio, communications, design, ebook, finance, human resources, legal, marketing, operations, production, sales, supply chain, subsidiary rights, and warehouse departments who help Atria bring great books to light.

Editorial
Elizabeth Hitti

Jacket Design
James Iacobelli
Jim Tierney

Marketing
Dayna Johnson

Managing Editorial
Lacee Burr
Paige Lytle
Shelby Pumphrey

Production
Vanessa Silverio
Annette Pagliaro Sweeney
Kyoko Watanabe
Barbara Wild

Publicity
Holly Rice-Baturin

Publishing Office
Suzanne Donahue
Abby Velasco

Subsidiary Rights
Nicole Bond
Sara Bowne
Rebecca Justiniano